MOSCOW
WINTER

Images courtesy of Shutterstock.

"Moscow Winter," by Douglas Clark. ISBN 978-1-63868-091-8 (softcover); 978-1-63868-092-5 (hardcover); 978-1-63868-093-2 (electronic).

Published 2022 by Virtualbookworm.com Publishing Inc., P.O. Box 9949, College Station, TX 77842, US. ©2022, Douglas Clark.

To Josie for all that she is and what she means to me.

MOSCOW WINTER

A NOVEL

DOUGLAS CLARK

PART ONE

Paris, France

Chapter 1

Nazi occupied Paris | July 1943

Viktor Neiman's legs felt stiff cramped in the rear cockpit of an RAF Lysander single engine aircraft. The cockpit's original design was for one passenger in addition to the pilot. Modifications made for the Lysander aircraft of Squadron 161 of the British Royal Airforce allowed for two passengers seated uncomfortably facing each other. RAF Squadron 161 was a highly secret special duties unit. The lumbering Lysander was perfectly suited to infiltrating British Special Operations Executive agents into Nazi occupied France and exfiltrating French Resistance operatives. Designed for reconnaissance, it had moveable slats that allowed it to reduce air speed to close to an aerodynamic stall speed of only 65 miles per hour. Ideal for short landings and takeoffs.

Neiman was a lieutenant in the U.S. Army but working as part of the newly created Office of Strategic Services. Spies and saboteurs patterned after the British SOE. With a head start in covert operations against the Nazis, the SOE mentored the OSS as part of the American-Anglo alliance fighting Nazi Germany.

Crossing the northern coast of France at low altitude to avoid German radar, Neiman could see the English Channel surf lit by the full moon on this summer night. The fortified coastline blacked out to prevent nighttime British bombing raids against

1

German defensive positions. An hour later, the pilot told them to look for lights indicating the landing site. Flashlights directed skyward once French Resistance fighters on the ground heard the engine of the Lysander. A risky maneuver for those on the ground and the occupants of the Lysander.

Neiman understood the difficulty of even finding the landing site at night with only moonlight and no navigational aids in the aircraft other than a compass. His last such mission was aborted forcing rescheduling to a month later to coincide with the next full moon. This mission looked to be on target as the pilot excitedly said, "There they are! Look about twenty degrees to the left of our heading."

As they approached closer, faint lights defined an L-shaped pattern. The pilot responded in Morse code with the acknowledgement recognition signal using a light mounted in the undercarriage. A couple of minutes later Neiman felt the Lysander lose speed rapidly and almost float down into a field surrounded by hedgerows.

Once on the ground, the Lysander rolled to the end of the long side of the L then turned left to line up for immediate take-off. The maneuver provided barely sufficient distance to take off and clear the trees as tall as a two-story house along the hedgerow.

Neiman popped the canopy and along with his SOE colleague climbed to the ground using the fixed ladder mounted to the side of the aircraft. Disembarked, they shook hands with two men who immediately climbed into the aircraft. Within a minute, the Lysander was again airborne.

The members of this resistance group known as *Alliance* quickly hustled Neiman and the SOE agent to an awaiting truck stacked with crates of produce. Neiman and the Brit hid amongst the crates out of site next to the cab. The driver explained he had papers allowing the produce truck as a civilian vehicle to move about at night. If stopped by German or French police, his presence explained as taking produce to arrive early for the open market in nearby Reims. The plan called for spending the night in Reims at a safe house then traveling by train to

Paris. Their forged cover documents as railroad employees explaining their exempt status from forced labor service in Germany.

Neiman and the SOE agent left Reims Maison Blanche train station in the early morning without incident. Two hours later, they arrived in Paris at Gare de l'Est in the 10th Arrondissement district. Neiman knew Paris well having lived there for twenty years. They were to make their way on foot walking south to a rendezvous at the Fontaine Saint-Michel on the south side of the River Seine at noon. Missing that window, again at five o'clock. Their contact a street vendor selling used wrist watches.

A middle-aged man in a shabby suit stood to one side of the iconic fountain. A folding cart displayed his offering of watches on a felt tray. Behind him was a crutch propped against the pedestal supporting one of the winged lion statues.

Approaching the vendor, Neiman gave the recognition code. "My current watch does not keep accurate time. Do you have a reliable one for sale?"

"All these are fine instruments, Monsieur. Perhaps this Swiss military watch with a rugged stainless steel case?" the vendor said providing the appropriate counter response. "You are to go to 28 Rue Jean de Beauvais. Apartment 204. Announce yourself as Mr. Jones."

Although not required, Neiman bought the watch. Times were difficult for every Frenchman in occupied Paris especially those doing dangerous work with the Resistance.

No sooner had Neiman concluded the purchase than the shrill sound of a police whistle pierced the tranquility. Four French police began converging from two directions. The situation deteriorated rapidly.

The French police brandished revolvers coming straight toward the street vendor. A targeted arrest meaning the police had the vendor under surveillance. That meant waiting for the vendor to make a suspicious contact. Carrying two million francs hidden under a change of clothes and a shaving kit made bluffing their way out impossible if detained and searched. Suspected of spying meant handing them over to the Gestapo and a very unpleasant ordeal.

The vendor however had no intention of submitting quietly. Producing his own handgun, he fired several shots striking one of the French police officers. The other three officers unleashed returning fire hitting the vendor with several rounds.

Having turned and walked several steps away from the vendor, Neiman and the SOE agent chose to appear as bystanders rather than react. Unarmed, there was little else they could do.

Two of the police officers approached them pointing weapons while the third looked to his wounded colleague. Blood begin pooling on the sidewalk around the body of the street vendor.

One officer shouted, "Papers!"

Neiman and the SOE agent extracted their false French passports and travel authorizations as railroad employees handing them over while the other police officer covered them with his revolver.

"What is your business in Paris?" the officer said.

Neiman answered, "Transferred temporarily to work on new renovations to the main line to Lyon. We just arrived from Reims. Walking to Gare Lyon to report for work."

"Open your valises."

Both Neiman and the SOE agent set down their bags. The money was underneath their clothing in a false bottom. It would not withstand a thorough inspection.

The officer began pulling out the clothing from the SOE agent's bag and scattering the contents on the pavement. Neiman anticipated the uncovering of the bundles of French francs concealed in the bottom at any moment. Discovery would seal their fate. His training taught to remain focused looking for any opportunity no matter how desperate. Shot dead a better death than unrelenting torture to end with a worse death.

The police officer rummaging in his colleagues bag suddenly pulled out the false bottom. Seeing the money he exclaimed, "Mon dieu!"

4

In that instant, the officer holding his pistol on Neiman looked toward his colleague. Neiman reacted without hesitation by moving into the man deflecting his gun arm while smashing his knee into his groin. The SOE agent immediately kicked the officer under the chin while still bent down going through his bag. Neiman disarmed the injured officer clutching his groin in agony.

The SOE agent was not as fortunate. While disabling the officer with his kick, the third officer shot him twice. Falling to his knees, the SOE agent returned fire but missed. The police officer shot him a third time.

With no way to save his colleague, Neiman grabbed his bag and the police officer's revolver then began running south down Boulevard Saint-Michel. The remaining uninjured officer took pursuit blowing his whistle.

Neiman then spotted two other police running north toward him forcing him to turn left onto the Rue de la Bucherie. The short street ended in two blocks to an open square and park next to ancient church of Saint-Julien-le-Pauvre. The two additional police close behind him began firing. Suddenly he felt a sharp pain in his left hip causing him almost to fall.

He continued running into the park with trees and bushes but losing ground to the pursuing officers. Coming to a stone wall, he ducked behind it. He could not go on, the pain already sapping him of strength. He must make a stand here. Checking the police officer's revolver, he had six rounds. His only chance was to ambush his pursuers as they came around the corner of the wall only ten feet away. Kill or be captured. That meant reserving the last round for putting a bullet in his head. No assurance he could reach his cyanide tablet in time.

Seconds later, both police officers came running around the corner of the wall together fixed on closing the gap of their suspect. He shot both as they turned in surprise to find him kneeling only feet away against the wall.

While necessary for his survival, shooting French police nevertheless was profoundly disturbing. He was French. The German occupation forcing cooperation from the French civil servants. Impossible to understand the undoubtedly conflicted sense of duty these police officers experienced. Might they have instead chosen to be *résistants*?

The original officer that gave chase never appeared. Yet by no means safe. Neiman was in a bad way evidenced by just the effort of standing up proving difficult. A quarter of a mile to walk to the appointed rendezvous address. At least he knew the area intimately from his years attending the Sorbonne. The entire sector soon to be swarming with French police and perhaps the German Wehrmacht. Time was critical. Each step radiated intense pain. His left pant leg darkened with soaked blood.

The wailing of police sirens urged him to hurry. He held tight to the revolver in his pocket. A bullet better than days of torture by the Gestapo then death by guillotine, the French method of execution.

Ready to collapse, he came to the outer door of 28 Rue Jean de Beauvais. He rang number 204. A female voice answered. "Who is it?"

"Mr. Jones."

The door lock clicked open and he entered. Facing the staircase, he grabbed the handrail for support. Putting weight on his left leg was now impossible. It took a couple of minutes to hobble up four stairs. A pretty woman appeared at the top of the landing.

"Are you Jones?"

His face bathed in sweat he struggled in reply, "Yes. Wounded. Need help."

The woman rapidly descended the stairs. Seeing the blood, she took his valise and grabbed his left arm offering support.

"You are alone?"

"Yes. My colleague and the street vendor are dead. Shot by police."

Breathing heavily, they made slow progress but the woman pulled on his arm urgently.

"Please, we must move quickly before you are seen."

Once inside the apartment, Neiman collapsed on the floor. Not knowing what to do, the woman grabbed a cushion from the sofa and placed it under his head.

Weakly he said, "What is your name?"

"Best we use code names. Mine is Sparrow. You must remain Mr. Jones."

He nodded imperceptibly.

"I must make a telephone call," she said.

An hour later, the woman opened the door for three men. Neiman was still lying on the floor. She did what she could to make him comfortable. After removing his suit jacket, she gave him water, and tried to stem the bleeding with a sheet bound around his waist to compress the wound.

Moved to a bed, now barely conscious, the last thing he remembered was a large gauze pad placed over his nose. An hour later he woke. Still drowsy from the ether anesthetic, the pain in his hip was intense enough to make him gasp.

A man said, "A doctor just removed a bullet from your hip. You will survive but it will be some time before you can walk. My code name is Raven. For covert agents you and your colleague created an almighty disaster. French police and German Gestapo are conducting a widespread search. You must stay here to recover and take your chances. Tell me what happened."

Finished with recounting events, Raven said, "I understand. The street vendor was a good man. Wounded in the Great War. A jeweler by trade. Hard economic times then the German occupation forced him to sell used watches. Hated the *Boche*. Active in the *Résistance* since the German invasion. Died the death of a French patriot. Sorry about your colleague."

"I still have a mission to accomplish," Neiman said.

Raven raised his eyebrows. "Well the immediate concern is hiding you so you do not comprise our Paris network. Unfortunately, you are a liability."

Neiman's mission was to interview the source of extraordinary high-grade intelligence on the German rocket program for their V-1 and V-2 weapons threatening Britain. He knew only she was a young woman with the code name Amniarix. She was part of a subnetwork called the *Druids* of the larger resistance organization Alliance. The face-to-face was to ascertain the credibility of the intelligence and determine the potential for expanding on the information.

"For that I am truly sorry. Fortunes of war for both of us. How is it this woman is able to consistently gather such highly secret information?"

"Not sure myself. You be the judge of that if we can arrange a meeting. She works as a translator for a French syndicate of industrialists. They often meet with German military staff in Paris to discuss commercial issues. That often involves arranging contracts with French firms supporting various German military programs. Including their rocket program."

By the strain and perspiration evident on Neiman's face, Raven said, "The doctor left morphine for the pain. I suggest Sparrow give you an injection and you rest. We can talk again tomorrow. Sparrow is one of my best agents. She will see to your needs since it is impossible to move you."

* * *

The search for the killer of the French police in the Latin Quarter tapered off after a few days when no informers offering information. Staying put proved the best security. The first days under the care of Sparrow were awkward. Getting to the toilet using a crutch still required Sparrow's help. Wearing only pajamas provided little decency when she needed to pull them down to change the dressing on the wound each day. Stepping into the bathtub to bathe required her assistance.

During one such moment, Neiman said, "repeatedly seeing me naked, isn't it about time we called each other by our real names?"

She smiled and blushed. "My name is Inga Jansons."

Both could feel the sexual attraction.

"I am Viktor Neiman. Glad to meet the woman risking her life for my sake."

"We all risk our lives fighting the Germans."

Neiman nodded. "Where are you from?"

"I was born in Latvia. My parents left Riga in 1920 during the post-WWI chaos. The newly created Latvian republic descended into economic depression with runaway inflation. My father was a jeweler. Our wealth was in jewels and gold affording the means of setting up a new life in Paris."

"Past tense? Is your father deceased?"

Her eyes downturned. "I do not know. You see I am Jewish. French police arrested both my parents from their jewelry shop last July. They were among the thousands of Jews in the great Vélodrome d'Hiver Roundup. Sent first to Drancy then onto the German concentration camps in the East. I do not know where or if they are still alive."

"How did you escape arrest?"

"I was living on my own at the time. Working for the Resistance since 1940. Using a false identity. Never identified as a Jew."

"What do you do in the Resistance?"

She gave him a mischievous smile. "I am a forger."

He laughed. "And how did you learn such a trade?"

"Taught by an expert. A brilliant young man. Only nineteen years old, he can forge anything. I work with him not far from here in an underground lab."

"Is that where you go most of the day?"

"No. Not since I have you as a houseguest. I have a legitimate day job. I am a still photographer at a film studio in Joinville-le-Pont near the Bois de Vincennes.

"That's quite a distance to commute. How do you get there?"

"By bicycle."

"We also have something else in common other than fighting the Nazis, Inga. Like you, I am French because I grew up in Paris. Born in Moscow to Jewish parents. Also like you, they became victims to a tyrant. In my case Joseph Stalin rather than Adolf Hitler. Been escaping from both these monsters all my life.

She nodded. "My mother was Russian. She spoke to me in both Russian and Latvian as a child. Do you speak Russian?"

Smiling, he replied, "Да."

"Wonderful. Raven also speaks Russian."

So began something of a domestic relationship. They talked about their pasts in Russian. Difficulties living in occupied Paris. German confiscation of all manner of goods for use in the war effort. Food shortages and rationing made survival increasingly a challenge. The black market became essential. Although the situation was better in the rural areas and the Vichy French State in the south, local demand for agricultural products prevented enough consumables reaching the occupied larger cities. Chronic fuel shortages created bleak winters.

Stuck inside the apartment they developed a bond. For Neiman, nighttime became a time of reflection and wrestling with his emotions. He slept in the only bed forcing her to sleep on the sofa. Attracted to this beautiful interesting woman perhaps sleeping naked during the hot nights just outside the bedroom made sleep difficult.

* * *

By the third week, Neiman sufficiently recovered to resume his mission. Jansons announced that Raven was bringing Amniarix to the apartment tomorrow morning. With a look of disappointment, she said, "Raven also said you are leaving the following day."

"Where am I going?"

"Back to London of course."

"How is that to happen?"

"You will take a train south to the unoccupied Vichy zone."

"How do I manage that?"

"You will travel under false papers as an injured railroad worker returning to your family home in a village outside Clermont-Ferrand for convalescence. Someone will meet your train when you disembark. They will identify you by description and the man walking with a limp and a cane giving the recognition signal *Sparrow sent me*. You are to fly back to London the same way you arrived. From another secret landing site."

Neiman sighed offering her a broad smile, "Such is war. I was beginning to like it here."

Jansons looked at him then averted her gaze to mask her emotions. "Raven provided a second-hand suit for the journey and that shabby suitcase on the floor. The clothes suitably showing wear befitting your identity."

* * *

Raven showed up at Jansons' apartment early the next morning. When Neiman came out of the bedroom, both men looked at each other with expressions of surprise.

Raven said, "I thought you looked familiar. Now I am certain we have met."

"I thought the same but was a little foggy from the anesthesia. Once recovered, I recalled. You are Professor Rozovsky. I attended two semesters of your economics class in my first year at the Sorbonne long before the war."

"But I was told to expect an American. The student I remember was French-Russian."

Neiman replied in fluent Russian, 'That would be me. I fled Russia during the civil war. Fled France to the United States after Germany invaded. Pearl Harbor left no alternative but to go to war as an American. My name is Viktor Neiman."

Professor Yuri Rozovsky said, "Yes, of course, Neiman." He enveloped Neiman in an embrace kissing both cheeks. "Did you further your education in economics?"

"Afraid not, Professor. I graduated with a degree in art history. Worked at the Louvre then in New York until the war. Right now like you, my profession is spying against the Nazis,"

Rozovsky turned to Jansons, "Inga, here is a tin of real coffee. Black market with a foreign label. How about making us a pot. Amniarix should arrive soon."

All three began making small talk in Russian. Neiman learned that the Russian expatriate community he knew growing up in Paris remained largely intact. Amazing since two-thirds of the population evacuated Paris to the unoccupied Vichy French

State puppet state or to foreign countries for the few with financial means. However, leaving Paris held the possibility of resuming some type of normal life. While many of the Russian community were educated professionals and other White Russians fleeing the Bolsheviks in the early 1920s and late 1930s, they did not represent a particularly affluent class.

An hour later, Amniarix arrived. A petite pretty brunette Jansons' age although she looked younger. Everyone reverted to his or her code names.

Once seated, Rozovsky launched into the interview. "Mr. Jones is with American intelligence working closely with the British SOE. The astounding information you provide is of the highest value to the Allied effort. Mr. Jones, I will let him explain the reasons for this face to face visit."

"Raven is correct, Mademoiselle. The coded transmissions of your material receive the highest priority and distributed to those making military and political decisions. My unusual visit to interview the source is to understand how these senior German military officers and officials can be so free with such secret information."

Amniarix smiled, "What you mean is why would they reveal such information to someone as insignificant as me." Neiman began to protest but Amniarix raised her hand demurely. "My apologies, Mr. Jones. I did not put that very well. The simple truth is I am only part of these conversations as an interpreter. After a time, I become part of the surroundings. Like speaking into a recording device. These men become caught up in the discussion complicated by the language barrier for those on both sides. I find by listening carefully I find opportunities to insert questions under the guise of clarification."

"Well you are certainly effective. Are you expected to take any notes?"

"Oh, no. I am only the interrupter. I just listen and repeat the conversation in the other language."

"How did you become so fluent in German?"

"My mother is a gifted linguist with a degree in languages."

"I have seen the coded transcripts. They include a staggering degree of detail. How do you manage remembering all that information?"

"Do you speak German, Mr. Jones?"

"Yes."

"If you recite a long passage in German I will attempt to translate it verbatim when you are done."

Surprised, Neiman thought for several moments. "Very well. I recall a letter written by Ludwig von Beethoven to his brothers reflecting on his despair because of his progressing deafness. It is called the Heiligenstadt Testament."

Neiman recalled much of the German text from memory since he wrote a paper on Beethoven's extraordinary feat in overcoming his disability. Amniarix listened and after he finished she began repeating the words verbatim in French.

Everyone listened transfixed as she repeated what he said.

Not fluent in German, Rozovsky and Jansons looked at Neiman who smiled shaking his head. "Amazing. Just amazing. How are you able to accomplish that?"

"I don't really know. Born with the ability. Something like photographic memory but with spoken words. Realized I had the gift from my earliest years at school."

"Some of your material is in technical jargon. Do you understand what you are translating?"

"Very little. I ask for an explanation in order to translate. Other than that I do not understand the subject matter."

"If you do not understand the subject, how can you ask questions to expand on the information?"

"Doing this often enough, I can sense when there is controversy or misunderstanding so I can interject a question for clarification which sometimes yields further information."

"You are possessed with remarkable talents, Amniarix," Neiman said. 'That certainly explains the quality of your intelligence."

* * *

After making their farewells to Amniarix and Yuri Rozovsky, Neiman looked at Jansons. Both felt a sadness. He must leave early in the morning to catch a seven o'clock train from Gare Lyon. Averting her gaze, she turned and went to the kitchen. "I will prepare us something to eat. You have a long day ahead of you tomorrow. We shall share a bottle of wine I have saved for a special occasion. Now is such a time although a very sad occasion."

"Inga, please come here."

She turned toward him but remained in the kitchen. "There is nothing to say that will make the pain go away. You must leave. We may never see each other again. By the time the war ends who knows how we will feel about our short time together."

What she said was true. Trying to argue otherwise would be disingenuous.

"Let's enjoy what time we have left tonight. I have great affection for you, Inga. I cannot forget our time together. While you prepare dinner. I will take a bath. Might be days before I get to London. Everything depends on the moonlight and the pilot locating the site."

Careful to use a minimum of the hot water given the fuel shortage, he filled the tub with only a few inches of water and began washing while standing as usual because of his injured hip.

Minutes later, the bathroom door opened. Turning, he took in the sight of Inga standing there naked. She put her index finger to her lips. "Please do not say anything. Let us just enjoy our few remaining hours in intimacy. We both want to make love. I see how you look at me. I could never live with myself if I did not follow my heart before you left me."

Chapter 2

Washington D.C. | December 1947

***

Neiman successfully escaped occupied France in 1943 following his ill-fated mission and serious wounding. Although only a general practitioner, the French doctor did an adequate job in repairing the wound to his hip. Able to walk almost normally, the only residual effect was a slight limp. Not enough to inhibit his eventual return to fencing as his means of exercise. However, the six months of rehabilitation ended his wartime service in the field.

Soon after returning to London, he moved to the Research and Analysis branch of the OSS. By 1945, he held the rank of major. His intellectual skills in interrupting seemingly disparate pieces of intelligence into a broader picture proved more satisfying than adventures in the field.

From the moment he lifted off into the night cramped in the rear cockpit of the small RAF Lysander aircraft almost four years earlier, Inga Jansons never left his thoughts. Not for lack of trying to reconnect. Although liberated in August 1944, Paris remained in chaos and WWII raged on. He was stuck in London working day and night as the Allies pushed eastward across France toward Germany. Then came the last-ditch German offensive in December stopping the Allied advance. What became known as the Battle of the Bulge continued to the end of January

1945. Unable to establish contact with Inga Jansons or Yuri Rozovsky, he did not know if they survived the German occupation.

It was not until Germany surrendered in May 1945 that Neiman was able to track down Yuri Rozovsky now returned to his faculty position at the Sorbonne. After repeated attempts, he managed to reach Rozovsky by telephone. Expressing his joy for his old acquaintance surviving the war, he asked about Jansons. The expectation evident in his voice.

After a pause, Rozovsky said, "Inga is well, Viktor. She is married."

Neiman's turn for a long pause. "Ah, I see. Happy for her that she is resuming a normal life."

Rozovsky sensed that Jansons became attracted to Neiman after caring for him during his recovery. Perhaps more than mere attraction. Yet only together for a few weeks then separated with no expectations when they might again see each other, life naturally moved forward. Brief encounters usually recede into nothing more than memory.

"She is working in a photography studio along with her husband a noted photographer from before the war. I will tell her you asked about her."

Shattered, Neiman turned the conversation to talk of what each was currently doing and their respective prospects with the war now over. After exchanging addresses and vowing to remain in touch, Neiman sat silently at his London desk absorbing the reality of never reuniting with Inga Jansons.

* * *

Although the war in the Pacific still continued, Allied victory in Europe in May 1945 shifted U.S. intelligence efforts toward the Soviet Union. Yet a time of anything but peace in Europe except for cessation of armed hostilities with the Nazi Germany. Joseph Stalin's ambitions soon established a new world order centered on the United States and the Soviet Union emerging as surviving superpowers. If not yet clearly enemies, at least hostile political competitors. For those in the U.S. intelligence community an unsettling time requiring an abrupt shifting of objectives demanding different capabilities. Established at the start of WWII, the wartime OSS had no peacetime organizational history. Operating under the direct command of the military Joints Chiefs of Staff, the OSS was essentially a hybrid special operations force and intelligence organization.

While Neiman proved particularly skilled in intelligence analysis, what did that mean in terms of pursuing a career? Plans for returning to Paris now shelved. The shattered fantasy of reuniting with Inga Jansons changed everything. The chaos of rebuilding France after four years of German occupation adding a further depressing dimension.

In October, Neiman's professional situation became even more uncertain. President Truman abruptly disbanded the OSS. That decision precipitated by listening to isolationists counseling against the need for a peacetime intelligence service.

Truman soon realized that immediate post-war circumstances demanded the United States establish a civilian intelligence organization for the first time in its history. Difficult to understand U.S. resistance to such a course since most major world powers historically possessed foreign intelligence gathering organizations. Directing efforts not only toward enemy countries but also against allies. International politics turned on confidential information.

While dramatically downsizing, OSS functions transfer to other established government departments. Former operational functions and staff moved to the War Department. OSS research and analysis staff moved to the State Department. Neiman was among those offered a position with the newly created Bureau of Intelligence & Research branch of the U.S. State Department, known by the acronym INR. His former OSS boss in London, Paul Kline, was now the Assistant Secretary in charge of the INR.

With no other immediate professional prospects, Neiman accepted the position and relocated to Washington D.C. in the winter of 1945. His work continued much the same except with his assignment now shifted to the Soviet Union given his fluency in Russian.

President Truman soon reversed direction again after disbanding the OSS. Despite wide opposition from all the various governments departments involved with U.S. intelligence, he established the National Intelligence Authority. A separate civilian cabinet-level intelligence agency to oversee the newly created Central Intelligence Group comprised largely of former OSS officers. With the passage of the National Security Act of 1947, the NIA and CIG evolved again into the National Security Council and the Central Intelligence Agency. This continual reorganization did little to contribute to the CIA's transformative central mission of providing intelligence on the Soviet Union.

Not only did the CIA lack a history of conducting peacetime espionage, other factors created substantial obstacles. The majority of its officers came from field operations in the OSS during WWII. Essentially a clandestine special operations force. Their missions rarely included developing intelligence sources in enemy territory. That function fell to local resistance groups. Yet the greatest obstacle was the closed society of the Soviet Union with a pervasive secret police infiltrated into every sector of civilian and governmental affairs. Ruled by a single autocratic leader feared by everyone for his brutal past and bent on an aggressive posture toward the West.

Neiman understood full well the inadequacies of the CIA. His analytical role in the State Department's INR gave him the widest possible security access to all U.S. intelligence products. He soon realized that the British Secret Service, MI6, possessed the best intelligence on the Soviet Union. That however still represented few effective penetrations yielding high-grade political or technological information.

Threatening moves characterized this battle of nerves between intractable opponents. A sustained hostility with no end. Both sides interplaying short-term objectives to achieve longer range strategies in a zero-sum contest. The American financier Bernard Baruch used the term *Cold War* in a recent speech. International politics played as a never ending chess match on a global scale. Like WWII, the Cold War affected the entire world by the necessity of aligning with a particular side in the contest between the superpowers.

While his work provided a challenge, Neiman hated the environment of Washington D.C. Politics crowded out everything else. A cultural wasteland compared with his eighteen months living in New York before WWII. The social fabric centered on the semi-transient elected officials or those careerists in the civil service bureaucracy. For someone from cosmopolitan Paris and New York, living in Washington offered nothing but his work. He seriously began considering leaving government service and returning to his interrupted pre-war career in the art world.

Neiman's malaise feeding his professional uncertainties abruptly ended when returning to his apartment one day in the spring of 1947. Among the few pieces of mail was an airmail envelope. The return address read Inga Jansons, 20 Rue Cassette, Paris. The shock caused him to drop his keys.

Once inside he sat in his comfortable chair by the window, a mix of emotions fueling anxiety bred of the unknown. Expecting the letter to contain some explanation, that would only serve to open the emotional wound believed relegated to the past.

My dearest Viktor,

How can I ever apologize for remaining distant? Yuri told me you inquired about me over a year ago. I felt that might be awkward. Painful for both of us. Yuri also told you I was married. At the time, I was going through a rough patch. The marriage was a mistake.

I became involved with a successful photographer. The foolish attraction probably bred of loneliness. The affair led to collaboration professionally with me sharing his studio. Mistakenly thinking I was in love, the opportunity to be working professionally doing my own photography blinded me. It was not long before our relationship began falling apart. That started when I began getting noticed and independently landing commissions. His work already enjoyed a reputation. He is gift-

ed, but as I discovered, so am I. Our work was different in style but that did not seem to matter. That we were together provoked comparisons by critics. Andre's artistic jealousy ruined any possibility for a future.

As awful a mistake of marrying Andre was, once we divorced I realized the larger more dreadful mistake I made earlier. The mistake of not understanding the depth of our connection experienced those few weeks years ago, Viktor. My rational mind ignored the chemistry that connected us in so profound a way.

I do not know your personal circumstances. Are you in love with someone? Married? I hope not. Terribly unfair to ask that, but I dare not make the same mistake again if there is to be a second chance for us. Unfair to assume you still feel the same way after these years. The same way I knew you felt about me that last night when we made love. Probably no right to ask forgiveness for never explaining my situation long ago. Regardless of everything that happened, you are constantly on my mind. I was in love with you in 1943 but never understood it was love rather than infatuation given the circumstances. It devastated me when you left. I never knew if you successfully escaped France and made it back to London until Yuri contacted me.

I am still in love with you, Viktor. Please tell me if there is a chance for us to be together again.

Your beloved,
Inga

* * *

It took several readings followed by a long silence to digest the meaning of Inga's letter. His reaction was immense joy. Her expression of love a wonderful shock. That is what his emotions declared. Yet after four years would his feelings for her stand up to reality? Was she a fantasy perpetuated over time in his mind? Worse to reunite and for either or both of them to realize they were making another mistake.

Regardless, he must pursue his feelings and proceed with haste. That meant getting to Paris as soon as possible. Perhaps he could fulfil multiple objectives by selling his boss on sending him to Europe rather than working in Washington. Something on his mind for some time now made imperative by Inga's expression of love. The first order of business was to respond with a telegram.

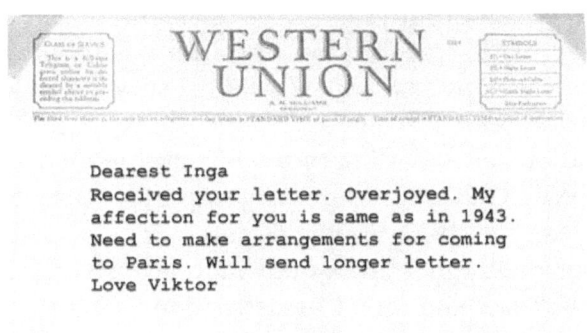

```
Dearest Inga
Received your letter. Overjoyed. My
affection for you is same as in 1943.
Need to make arrangements for coming
to Paris. Will send longer letter.
Love Viktor
```

Well before receiving Inga's letter, Neiman's plan for returning to Paris and getting out of Washington began taking shape months earlier. His idea had a professional foundation. His analytical work on the Soviet Union rested on the quality of the intelligence product gathered by the newly created Central intelligence Agency and to some extent on the British Secret Service.

The CIA had no intelligence resources directed at the Soviet Union and their Eastern Bloc countries acquired by occupation during WWII. Nor did the former OSS officers compromising the majority of CIA intelligence professionals possess any background in developing espionage sources or running counterintelligence operations. The older British MI6 was only slightly more successful infiltrating the closed Soviet Union police state. Their wartime efforts almost exclusively directed toward Nazi Germany. The CIA struggled under reorganization as a separate civilian agency evolving from their OSS wartime past as part of the War Department. Their military mindset found them inadequately equipped to function under the different circumstances of the Cold War.

In 1947, the CIA inherited what constituted the United States' subcontracted organization for intelligence against the Soviet Union and Eastern Bloc. Called the Gehlen Organization after its head, former German Wehrmacht Major General Reinhard Gehlen.

Neiman knew Gehlen's biography from classified Army Counterintelligence Corps files. During his time as a prisoner of war by American occupying forces, Gehlen audaciously talked his way not just to freedom but also into a new intelligence career. Another exceptional feat of political survival in his remarkable military career.

As head of German military intelligence on the Eastern Front during WWII, Gehlen incautiously reported German military failures as early as 1942. Strategies and tactical maneuvers often dictated personally by Hitler. Personally aware of the details of *Operation Valkyrie*, the failed assassination attempt of Hitler in July 1944, Gehlen managed to escape the subsequent purge against anyone even remotely associated with the plot. His consistent independence resulted in Hitler personally dismissing him from his command in the final weeks before Hitler committed suicide and Germany surrendered.

Gehlen prepared for the future. His future as well as promoting a future for Germany. As early as 1942, he anticipated Germany's defeat. Ideologically opposed, the Western Allies must break with the Soviet Union once Germany ceased to be a common enemy. A resurrected Germany becoming essential as a natural buffer between Western Europe and occupied Soviet territory. Territory Gehlen knew Joseph Stalin would never relinquish.

Just days before the war ended, Gehlen and a select group of devoted officers buried 52 steel drums packed with microfilm containing six years of espionage work against the Soviets. Useful now as bargaining capital while held in a POW camp in the American occupation zone. Gehlen found a way to engage the U.S. Army in negotiations. A remarkable achievement since U.S. policy forbade Army officers from listening to anti-Soviet statements from former Nazis.

Independent-thinking U.S. Brigadier General Edwin Sibert, Chief of Intelligence for the 12th Army group took the initiative to interview Gehlen in depth. Sibert ignored the standing policy order and arranged for Gehlen to turn over the hidden information. Going further, Sibert began searching POW camps to assemble selected Gehlen subordinates from his wartime intelligence command. Sibert then relocated Gehlen's reconstructed core group to a secret location, before advising his superiors of the extraordinary intelligence potential. Reinhard Gehlen asserted that the United States now possessed broad intelligence on Soviet post-war intentions and inherited a readymade espionage organization with assets in the Soviet Union and Eastern Bloc. U.S. Army Intelligence had no way of verifying Gehlen's claim.

Gehlen negotiated a deal through Sibert preventing his possible prosecution for war crimes as a senior Nazi military officer in exchange for gathering intelligence for the United States. By the end of 1946, Gehlen employed an organization of 350 former Nazi intelligence officers secretly funded by the United States.

Although Gehlen's wartime material appeared impressive, Neiman's extensive review of post-war reports from the reassembled Gehlen Organization cast doubts on the quality of the intelligence. The recurring lack of corroboration was a vexing problem. Corroboration among Gehlen's own multiple sources was chronically lacking. Neither the U.S. Army Counterintelligence Corps, nor the CIA had independent means for verification. As an analyst expected to render an informed opinion, he needed to understand the Gehlen Organization firsthand. What the CIA took as high-grade intelligence raised too many questions for Neiman's analytical process. With the Gehlen Org's reports, it was often impossible to separate fact from hearsay, or even deliberate misinformation. The CIA was top heavy with operational cowboys rather than pragmatic intellectuals.

Yet it was not possible to ignore Gehlen's Soviet intelligence value entirely. Neiman needed to understand the intelligence gathering process in greater depth to contribute in framing his analytical summary reports. Reports read by the Secretary of State and the President. Everyday brought new contentious issues between the West and the Soviet Union. Stalin was doing everything possible to incite hostility with the United States. With Europe as the principal theater of the Cold War, Neiman could be more useful positioned in Europe. He would argue for Paris becoming the logical base because of its position on the continent rather than London. A perfect solution professionally as well as personally.

Chapter 3

Washington D.C. | December 1947

Sitting in the office of his boss Assistant Secretary Paul Kline, Neiman presented his argument for relocating to Europe. The office was overheated and permeated with cigarette smoke. The skinny chain-smoking Kline was always cold and the air thick with smoke. Yet Neiman respected and personally liked Kline. They thought alike in their approach to interpreting intelligence. Analysis at best was an imperfect process.

"Okay. Looks like you did a thorough job of researching Gehlen. What's your read on him?"

Neiman responded, "He was of course a Nazi but so was every German officer in the Wehrmacht. Going against Hitler's delusional sense of prosecuting the war was bold but more telling as to Gehlen's motivations. Gehlen new Germany could not win the war even at the onset of the Battle of Stalingrad in 1942. Of no strategic value, Hitler squandered his chance to strike a decisive blow against the Soviet Union before winter closed in. Gehlen realized then that Hitler would continue to make irrational decisions. In 1942, the Western allies successfully invaded North Africa. The Soviet Red Army went on the offensive following German failures on the Eastern Front. By 1943, facing American material resources and Soviet human military resources, Gehlen understood Germany could not even play out the war to an armistice."

Kline was a great listener. More than once he listened to Neiman lecturing on some subject. He lit another cigarette and leaned back in his chair letting Neiman continue.

"Gehlen came from a family of Prussian militarists. A career army officer and old school German nationalist. He saw Hitler bringing Germany to ruin. He shared in the sympathies with the July 1944 plot to assassinate Hitler. Gehlen knew the plotters yet chose to remain outside the effort. Something must have caused him to back away. Clever enough to avoid hanging in connection with the plot during Hitler's unrestrained retaliation. He may be a German nationalist and obviously anti-communist, but his foremost concern is for Reinhard Gehlen. "

"So you do not trust him?" Kline said.

"I don't know. He is smart. A brilliant survivor. Although he disagreed with Hitler, he was still a Nazi prosecuting the war. Not only surviving denazification, he persuaded the United States to employ him in a privileged secret position. Gehlen runs his operation with no oversight. The CIA has no intelligence-gathering capabilities. They also lack the capacity to evaluate the quality of the Gehlen information. CIA reports indicate that only Gehlen's staff knows the identities of the sources.

"If Gehlen manipulates intelligence for some ulterior purpose, it becomes impossible to detect. If he goes as far as manufacturing information as a means of staying in business then we are in very deep shit."

Kline said, "And how do you propose to make that assessment by going to Europe?"

"First of all, by the time information arrives on my desk it has gone through multiple levels within the CIA or Army Counterintelligence. Rarely do I see the raw intelligence product from Gehlen's organization. Closer to the source, I avoid Washington bureaucratic filtering.

"Then we must factor in the pressure exerted on the CIA to produce intelligence on the Soviets. I have no proof, but that pressure undoubtedly looks at Gehlen's intelligence with a believability bias. In general terms, my presence will constitute an independent evaluation using audit techniques."

"Wonderful. Not likely the CIA will welcome that from an outside agency," Kline said sarcastically.

Neiman shrugged. "If my situation becomes awkward, Secretary Marshall outranks CIA Director Hillenkoetter. Both in terms of clout and former military rank."

"Don't be a smartass. I don't relish being caught in an internecine government shit storm blowing my way," Kline responded. "You are the best intelligence analyst in the U.S. intelligence community, Viktor. You can also be a pain in the ass when contending with those you deem of lesser abilities. You think clearly and produce exceptional work. You can also leave a lot of debris along the way. I remember skirmishes you fought with the Army when you were in London during the war. Now you are critical of the performance of our former OSS colleagues in the CIA."

"I hear you. Paul. But this is too important. We have a formidable new enemy in Stalin. A threat that may turn out equal to that of Hitler. We need to get on top of this quickly."

Kline let out a long sigh and lit another cigarette. "Okay. If I send you to Europe, what is your plan? You cannot just bull your way into CIA operations."

"I gave that some thought. The CIA is a new agency. Considering how Truman disbanded the wartime OSS, he initially felt little need for a peacetime intelligence service. Fortunately, he listened to wiser counsel. Yet Truman intended to create an independent agency of his own making. Despite opposition from the military establishment, the State Department, and the FBI, he instead created the Central Intelligence Group, which became the CIA just months ago.

"Within that reorganizational chaos the State Department created the Bureau of Intelligence and Research. That was George Marshall's doing. He understood the need for the State Department to have its own intelligence branch, albeit smaller in scope by restricting it to analysis. Our stated mission is *to harness intelligence to serve U.S. diplomacy.*"

"I appreciate the civics lecture. Now get to the fucking point."

"My point being we need to exercise our mission prerogative *to serve U.S. diplomacy*. That mission becomes more critical with confrontation by the Soviet threat. A confrontation fought through foreign policy maneuver. If I go to Europe and start sticking my nose into CIA operations, I need some high-level authority."

"What the hell are you suggesting?"

"I go there as Secretary of State Marshall's intelligence advisor on the Soviet Union."

"What the hell?" Kline sat up and crushed his cigarette out in the overflowing ashtray. "You expect me to go to the boss with your screwball idea to spy on the CIA?"

"No. I am simply asking to get us a meeting with the General. I will make the case. Using of course more polite terms like auditing, inspecting, or collaborating rather than spying."

Kline shook his head and rolled his eyes. "Why should Marshall agree to this?"

"Look at his many comments after we brief him. Asking the same questions I raise about the quality of the intelligence on the Soviets that almost exclusively comes from the Gehlen Organization. General Marshall has President Truman's ear on foreign policy. Any CIA pushback will not intimidate him.

"U.S. foreign policy is dominated by continual reaction to Soviet hostile confrontation. Marshall sees world stability resting on economic recovery from the war. His speech at Harvard in June of this year laid out a proposed path for a U.S. led recovery. Stalin publicly rejected the proposal immediately because it obviously threatened his strategic ambitions in Europe.

"The Soviets instead began a systematic rape of conquered territories under their control to pay reparations for economic recovery of the Soviet Union. General Marshall will keenly appreciate the need for high-grade intelligence on the Soviets. I am the one that writes most of the Soviet-related intelligence summaries and critiques those of the CIA. I speak German, Russian, and French so I am self-sufficient."

With his hands clasped together and elbows on his desk, Kline sat starring at Neiman for several moments. "Very well. You make a compelling argument. Not sure the General will see it that way, but I will arrange a meeting and add my support for your proposal. Keep your comments brief and to the point. Don't try to oversell the General. He is the smartest guy I ever met. Not afraid of making bold moves. If he agrees with your proposal, he will support you. If he doesn't he will tell why. I will let you know how I make out."

* * *

A week later, Neiman and Kline sat across the desk from Secretary of State George Marshall, the former five-star army general and U.S. Army Chief of Staff during WWII. Widely respected by other general staff officers and elected officials. Marshall was responsible for the selection or recommendation of many of the most senior commanding army officers serving in WWII. These included Dwight Eisenhower, George Patton, Mark Clark, and Omar Bradley.

Marshall was noted for his extraordinary problem solving skills. Not only in choosing the right people for challenging responsibilities, but the ability to analyze complex circumstances and create successful solutions. It fell to Marshall to supervise the increase in size of the U.S. Army from 200,000 in 1939 to over eight million within three years.

Although confident in his argument, Neiman still found selling his proposal to someone of Marshall's intellectual stature intimidating.

He stuck to Kline's admonition to be brief and present his proposal clearly using fact-based arguments where possible. Marshall understood the basic premise as presented by Kline prior to this face-to-face and listened for ten minutes letting Neiman state his proposal. For the next twenty minutes, Marshall asked pointed questions for clarification. Kline let Neiman respond, commenting only when Marshall directed a question to him.

As the back and forth concluded, Marshall said, "This is more about evaluating the German Gehlen Organization than the CIA. Is that correct, Mr. Neiman?"

"That is essentially correct, Sir. However, I harbor concerns about the CIA's vetting process. Since I speak German and Russian fluently, I can deal directly without an interrupter getting in my way."

"If I send you over to Europe, the CIA will rightfully raise a complaint for interference with their official prerogatives."

"I appreciate the realities of the delineation of responsibilities, Sir. However, this is an unusual situation in that our intelligence is coming from a third party. An organization entirely comprised of a recent enemy of the United States. The only common purpose between the Gehlen Org and us is the shared recognition of the Soviet Union as the new common enemy of Germany and the United States. Our common interests end there. The circumstances are not unlike our forced partnering with Stalin to defeat Hitler. On its face, trusting an organization of former Nazis for information of vital importance to the United States is fundamentally troubling."

Marshall responded after a moment. "I share your concerns, Mr. Neiman. Soviet opposition affects everything we do to rebuild the European economy. Accurate intelligence is paramount to navigating our path forward.

"I wish to move forward with sending you to Europe. Realizing your intrusion into CIA affairs will not be well received, what do you need to make this work?" Marshall asked.

"A letter from you, Sir. Briefly outlining my mission as one of evaluating intelligence acquisition as your special intelligence advisor for European-Soviet affairs. I also propose to get close to our British friends in MI6. The Labor Party does not like the idea of us working with ex-Nazis. I will use that as a basis for probing their independent intelligence on the Soviets and getting their read on the Gehlen Organization's capabilities.

"I also plan to operate from our Paris embassy. Provides a European continental base and affords easy access to occupied Germany, London, Vienna, Scandinavia, and Ankara. All harbor concerns about Soviet aggression. The French are part of this although with the prominence of the French Communist Party, there are concerns of possible Soviet infiltration of the SDECE."

"My point is not to entirely focus on the Gehlen Organization. Principally it is to look at the raw intelligence product before it goes through layers of editing in Washington."

Marshall nodded. "Very well. Paul, will you draft the appropriate document for Mr. Neiman?"

"Yes, Sir," Kline answered.

Turning back to Neiman, Marshall said, "I believe you need to go armed with something more substantial than a letter from the Secretary of State. The CIA will find ways of stonewalling your unwanted intrusion. You need a safe conduct pass to navigate the CIA layers. I know CIA Director Admiral Hillenkoetter. I will try to get him to issue you a letter ordering full cooperation by CIA staff. Paul, set up a meeting in the next couple of days. Just Admiral Hillenkoetter and me. No staff. Easier to do this off the books so to speak."

***

Mid-morning several days later, Kline walked into Neiman's office and handed him two envelopes.

"Well you got what you wanted. One is from General Marshall the other from Admiral Hillenkoetter," Kline said and sat down. "Hope you know what you are doing. Not likely you will make many friends barging your way into CIA affairs carrying these letters as weapons.

Neiman opened Marshall's letter first.

OFFICE of the SECRETARY
UNITED STATES of AMERICA DEPARTMENT of STATE

December 12, 1947

To: Personnel of the U.S. Department of State and the U.S. Intelligence Community

Subject: Senior Foreign Service Officer Viktor Neiman

United States senior foreign service office Viktor Neiman shall act as the Secretary of State's special advisor for European intelligence matters. Mr. Neiman's function is to evaluate the sources and methods for gathering intelligence vital to U.S. foreign affairs in order to establish the quality of the information. By agreement with the Director of Central Intelligence, Rear Admiral Roscoe H. Hillenkoetter, you are hereby directed to provide Mr. Neiman access to all related information regardless of classified status.

George C. Marshall
United States Secretary of State

The second letter from Admiral Hillenkoetter mirrored that of Marshall's. An unusual document granting such access for someone outside Central Intelligence. Undoubtedly the product of George Marshall's stature and persuasive skills.

OFFICE of the DIRECTOR
UNITED STATES of AMERICA
CENTRAL INTELLIGENCE AGENCY

December 15, 1947

To: Personnel of the Central Intelligence Agency

Subject: State Department Senior Foreign Service Officer Viktor Neiman

United States senior foreign service officer
Viktor Neiman shall act as the Secretary of
State's special advisor for European intelligence matters. Mr. Neiman's function is to
evaluate the sources and methods for gathering
intelligence vital to U.S. foreign affairs in
order to establish the quality of the information. Mr. Neiman possesses the highest-level
security clearance. You are hereby directed to
provide Mr. Neiman access to all related information and render all necessary support to
facilitate his mission.

RH Hillenkoetter

Rear Admiral Roscoe H. Hillenkoetter
Director Central Intelligence Agency

"So when do you intend to leave?" Kline asked.

"Probably in a week. Need to pay a visit to CIA headquarters in Langley. You can help pave the way by arranging a meeting with someone that can give me the lay of the land of key CIA personnel assigned to Europe. Be sure to invoke my new status. I need to hit the ground running once in Europe and do not want them to allow those in the field to delay compliance by saying they need clearance from Washington."

Kline nodded. "We also need to discuss maintenance arrangements, especially communications, right away. I suspect much of your communication might be particularly sensitive. Best I get it directly without it passing through other hands. And since you are going into the field, what about a code name for you?"

"Okay. Let me think of something appropriate. "Neiman reflected for several moments before saying, "Since I am committed to going after the Soviet Caesar, how about Brutus."

"That will do. You are now Brutus in your dispatches. Let's discuss other matters over lunch."

His audacious plan was a product of months of thought. It made sense in light of growing Soviet confrontation toward Western Europe and CIA intelligence gathering inadequacies. Yet he could not deny the letter from Inga acted as the catalyst to take action. Whatever his personal motivations it was still professionally the right move.

That afternoon, in a euphoric mood, Neiman drafted a telegram to Inga Jansons.

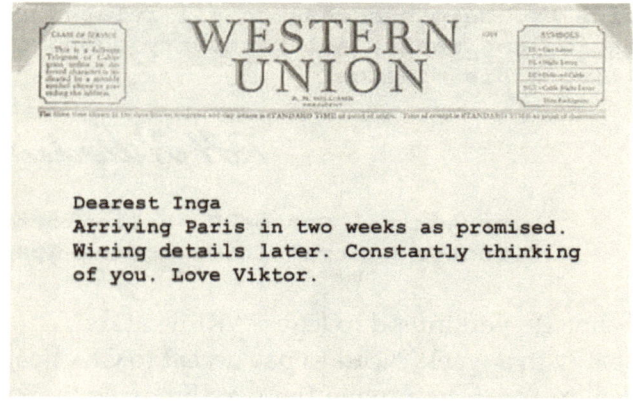

WESTERN UNION

Dearest Inga
Arriving Paris in two weeks as promised.
Wiring details later. Constantly thinking
of you. Love Viktor.

Chapter 4

Paris | December 1947

Viktor Neiman departed Washington by train to New York. After spending a couple of days with his aunt and uncle, he departed New York on TWA's transatlantic flight to Paris on Friday December 19. With stops in Gander, Newfoundland and Shannon, Ireland, the Lockheed Constellation flight took 17 travel hours. Arriving at five o'clock PM local time the following day at Paris Orly Airport, he looked out the window seeing light snow accumulation on the tarmac. No matter, he was back in Paris.

As he stepped into the warmth of the terminal, he instantly recognized Inga Jansons. His first reaction was delight. She looked fabulous. Paris casual elegance. Holding a fur-collared wool coat, she wore a form-fitting turtleneck white sweater with jeans and calf-length black leather boots. The latest in avant-garde Parisian fashion casual statement with an edgy tone. Auburn hair falling to her shoulders. Her distinctive dark blue eyes gave a striking look to her face, evident even from a distance.

She rushed to him as he dropped his briefcase to the floor catching her embrace. As they kissed, tears streamed down her cheeks.

"Oh my God! I am so happy, Viktor." As she attempted to wipe away her tears, he kissed her wet cheeks saying, "And I could not be happier. These past years you never left my thoughts. Spending the rest of the war in London I fantasized about us reuniting. Learning you married devastated me but did not diminish my continual thoughts of you."

"I am so sorry, Viktor. Once I realized my marriage was a mistake it became much worse knowing I also probably lost you."

He kissed her again. "Together again is what is important. I recognized soon after our weeks together that I was in love with you. That never changed, Inga."

He said that without reservation. Once he saw her, the same attraction he felt four years ago returned instantly. His instincts involving life events usually proved correct.

"Let's get home and start making up for all the lost time," she said grabbing his arm and pulling him toward the baggage claim area."

They sat with hands entwined as the taxi made its way north into the center of Paris toward the left bank of the River Seine. As they crossed into the 14th Arrondissement then into the Montparnasse district, Neiman felt his return home. This is where he grew up after leaving Russia at the age of nine.

Even in winter with a blanket of snow on the ground and the trees barren of leaves, this was still his Paris. As the taxi progressed up Boulevard Raspail crossing into the 6th Arrondissement just west of the Jardin du Luxembourg he recognized specific buildings. A turn onto Rue de Vaugirard then another turn onto Rue Cassette brought them to number 20. A particularly inviting apartment building built around a courtyard in classic Parisian style.

The rear windows faced out on an area with large trees. By spring, it would add a view of green to this quiet Parisian neighborhood. It really felt like home located less than a half mile west of the Sorbonne where he earned his undergraduate degree.

They ascended the stairs to Inga's apartment. As she extracted the key, she turned to him embracing him saying, "Welcome to our new home." After giving him a long kiss, they entered.

"What do you think?" she said with pride.

Tastefully decorated, it was the framed photographic enlargements on the wall that drew his attention. He examined them slowly moving from one to another. He shed his coat then moved to look more closely.

"These are your work?"

She nodded. "You like them?"

"Not only do I like them, they are exceptional. Your use of light creates distinctive moods. This one draws the viewer into what otherwise would be just a mundane subject. This is remarkably artistic work, Inga. This is art that captivates."

She moved toward him and embraced him tightly with her arms about his waist. She made sure he could feel her breasts pushing against his chest. "We can discuss art later. Right now, I want you. Since receiving your letter I have thought of little else than making love to you."

In the bedroom, they began helping each other off with their clothing. Moving hands over bare skin as they pulled off undergarments, both gasped at the touch of breasts and genitals. The delight of intense sexual arousal generated by two people in love.

Their lovemaking was both tender and charged with passion. Each devoted great attention to pleasuring the other. Both became lost in exploring what most aroused the other.

Resuming normal breathing after their extended exertions, Jansons laid on her side with Neiman's right arm around her. Rising on one elbow, she rolled over his abdomen to look at the scar on his left hip from the surgery to repair the bullet wound in 1943. She touched the ridges of the four-inch long incision. "Does this still bother you?"

"Not much, except for a slight limp. Hardly noticeable unless you look closely as I walk.

As her breasts rubbed over his midsection, she reached down and held his growing erection. "This feels inviting but I am famished," she said giving him a lengthy kiss.

Swinging out of bed, she stood facing him letting him stare at her body. "I already have a cold dinner planned with a good bottle of wine.

She put on her robe and he pulled on his pants and shirt.

The dinner prepared ahead of time earlier that day. Charcuterie, cheeses, baguette, and salad accompanied by a bottle of Bordeaux. In the kitchen, she turned on the radio finding a music station. A befitting live performance by Edith Piaf.

Before preparing the food, she said, "Would you like a whisky before we eat? I bought a bottle of Scotch."

"Wonderful," he responded and turned her around to face him. "I could not be happier, Inga. After constantly thinking about you, our lovemaking feels as intense as that first time years ago. The intervening years apart meant nothing. This is right. I love you, Inga."

She kissed him and tears came to her eyes. Embracing him, "It is right for me too. I love you, Viktor. Never leave me."

After the meal and wine, the long emotion-filled day began taking its toll.

She said, "Let's take a bath. We both must be a little sticky."

Taking a bath together, they could not avoid the opportunity for foreplay. Quickly toweling off, they returned to the bed sufficiently aroused to resume slow protracted lovemaking before falling asleep. Perhaps that was Jansons intention. Cleanly bathed afforded the pleasure of kissing one another in all their intimate areas.

* * *

The next day they slept late waking to the comforting feeling of being next to the person you love. Jansons explained she rarely schedule studio work on Sunday so they can spend the day just being together.

Looking at the photographs on the walls, he said, "Speaking of your work, do you work at your own studio?"

"Yes. Before the divorce, I started my own business. Tough go at first, but I took a couple of clients with me that gave me a start."

"How did you get into photography?"

"I loved art but did not have the talent to paint. After receiving my first camera as a teenager, photography captivated me. I went on to study and earn a degree in 1938 from L'École Estienne, the traditional name of the l'École Supérieure des Arts et Industries Graphiques. Not far from here in the 13th."

Neiman waved his hand gesturing toward the photographs on the wall. "But where did you learn to do this kind of art?"

"I was fortunate to get a job with the noted Rapho photographic agency after graduating. It provided the opportunity to work with several important photographers. Hungarian refugees, so I fit in. They influenced my work as I started my career. They worked largely with humanistic subjects. Yet I learned how to use light and shadow from their expressive work. My subject matter is now more eclectic. Paris architecture provides endless photographic opportunity. The agency relocated to New York after the German occupation so I had to find other work.

"I found a position as a still photographer for Joinville Film Studio. Not much of a job. Nothing artistic. Mostly publicity photographs of film actors."

"Yes, I recall. You travelled a long way by bicycle each day to work. It was lonely without you during the day while recovering from my wound. How did you become involved with the Resistance?"

"A friend of mine worked as a courier for the Druids network. That's how I came to know Yuri. She knew how much I hated the Boche and recruited me. They had a need for a photographer. Taking photos of documents and photos for false identification papers. I worked with a group of three others in a makeshift lab on the top floor of 17 Rue des Saints-Pères.

"Our leader was a young man only nineteen named Adolfo Kaminsky. Like you, a Russian Jew whose family fled Russia. Brilliant forger. Knew chemistry. He understood what paper to use and how to make it appear properly worn. The right ink. He duplicated the small perforations on documents using a sewing machine. Adolfo even learned printing techniques using photographic plates to reproduce quantities of original blank documents. Impossible to distinguish our false documents from originals."

"And you were the photographer?"

"Initially. However, as the demand for false papers for Jews trying to escape France increased, Adolfo taught us many skills. He set up an assembly line. I was his best student."

"Even when you showed up on my doorstep, I was spending my evenings and days off from the studio producing false documents."

"From forger to an accomplished photographic artist. A remarkable journey, Inga.

"What about your career in the art world?" she said. "You told me after graduating from the Sorbonne you worked at the Louvre and then the Metropolitan Museum of Art in New York when you fled Paris. Yet your letter said you still work for the American government. In the foreign service."

"I have not abandoned my interest in the art world. WWII and now this Cold War changed my priorities. As much as I love art, I am not an artist like you, Inga. My government work is important. It also commands my interest."

"What exactly do you do?"

"Still working in intelligence. For the state department not the newly created American central intelligence agency. I analyze intelligence from all American intelligence sources. My work attempts to explain what various pieces of information means. So American diplomats and the President can make informed decisions. That is what I did for the rest of the war after I returned to London and recovered from my wound."

Thinking that meant he needed to return to Washington soon, her face registered concern. "Does that mean you must return to your work in America?"

He clasped her hand as they sat at the small kitchen table. "No. At least not for some time. Since relocating to Washington after the war ended, I wanted to return to Paris. France is more my home than America. Then your letter arrived. A whole new future I never dared image opened.

"I had this idea how to do my work better from Europe. Closer to what Winston Churchill called the Iron Curtain. What I do is important in the battle to preserve democracy in Europe from Stalin's aggression."

"What exactly do you do?"

"I am not allowed to discuss any details. Everything I do involves highly secret material."

"I understand. Why is working from Europe important if others gather the intelligence?"

"Well those are details I also cannot discuss. But I can tell this much, Inga, it involves the Soviet Union. That is my specialty. My background and language fluency in Russian, German, and French make me perfectly suited for my duties. The Soviet Union replaced Nazi Germany as the enemy of western democracies."

"For you and me, Joseph Stalin is a personal enemy," she said.

"That too. Makes my work that much more meaningful. Better that I work closer to the Soviet Union and the communist Eastern Bloc satellite states. My boss in Washington agreed. Working out of Paris allows me to travel easily about Europe."

"Then you are posted here indefinitely?"

"He held her hand. All I can promise is that you and I will be together indefinitely. And I have no plans of leaving Paris again."

He kissed her then said, "I should call Yuri. Tell him I have returned to Paris. We owe him for being the link that brought us back together."

"Of course. Yuri and his wife Yalena are good friends," she said. Standing up from the table, she kissed him passionately holding his cheeks in her hands. Leaning forward her robe opened providing him a look at her breasts. "Don't be too long on the telephone call."

Neiman telephoned Yuri Rozovsky an hour later. Overjoyed, Rozovsky insisted they have dinner that evening at his home. "My wife Yalena is a wonderful cook."

***

When they arrived at the Rozovsky's home, Yuri opened the door giving Inga a hug and the traditional kiss on each cheek. As she stepped into the apartment, he embraced Neiman. "Viktor Mikhailovich! So glad you survived the war to reunite with our beloved Inga." Rozovsky gave him a kiss on each cheek. "She has been her old self once you wrote of your return to Paris. Please, let me introduce you to my wife Yalena."

As they removed their coats and moved to the living room, Yalena Rozovsky entered. The adjectives elegant and stylish came to mind. Embracing Inga, they could be sisters. French women never lose their sense of fashion.

As if an old friend, Yalena also embraced Neiman. "Inga speaks of nothing else preparing for your return to Paris. Having grown up in Paris, welcome home, Viktor."

Yuri interjected, "Yes. Therefore, a true celebration is in order. Since we are all Russian, Inga is half-Russian, we shall celebrate as Russians. Yalena prepared a wonderful dinner. *Solyanka*, *pelmeni*, and some dessert of which I forgot the name served with *smetana*. I will serve us chilled vodka."

The names of the dishes sounded vaguely familiar from Neiman's youth. Growing up in Paris with his aunt and uncle they only ate Russian cuisine at weddings and funerals. The thought struck him that he had no idea what happened to friends he knew before the German occupation. While Paris was his true home, the only people he now knew in France were Inga and Yuri. Even those from only a brief encounter four years earlier. Having fled Russia at a young age never to see his parents again left an emotional void. His aunt and uncle in New York remained his only family. Finding Inga and returning to France seemed a rebirth of life.

Yuri and Yalena welcomed Neiman as if a close friend. Without family, Inga treated them as her aunt and uncle. Their warmth instantly made Neiman feel part of Inga's adopted family.

Although preferring Scotch, Neiman got into the celebratory spirit with repeated toasts of vodka. After recounting the details of his escape from France following recovery from his wound, the conversation turned to international political tensions in Europe. Everyone joined in the conversation. All four shared the same disgust toward communism, the Soviet Union, and particularly Joseph Stalin. Each of them bore emotional scars inflicted by Stalin.

A lively conversation ensued as they discussed developments this year reflecting the escalating tensions between the West and the Soviet Union. The principal Cold War battleground of interest being Europe. With good reason, the United States and the countries of Western Europe feared Stalin had ambitions to extend Soviet occupation beyond those territories captured from Nazi control during WWII.

In May, the United States extended 400 million dollars of military aid to Greece and Turkey to contain communist encroachment in the Mediterranean. The following month Secretary of State George Marshall outlined a comprehensive program of economic assistance to rebuild war-ravaged infrastructure and restore economic stability to Western Europe. What became known as the Marshall Plan appeared the best counter to encroaching communism. Both France and Italy having large communist parties closely aligned with Moscow, presented further challenges.

With much of Germany and Austria now under Western allied military occupation rule, the American Joint Chiefs of Staff immediately announced the first steps in implementing Marshall's plan. Issuing directive JCS 1779, this new occupation policy declared, *An orderly, prosperous Europe requires the contributions of a stable and productive Germany.* This completely reversed prior operative JCS directive 1067 that prohibited economic rehabilitation of Germany.

On the opposing side, the Soviet Union announced formation of the Communist Information Bureau, identified by the acronym COMINFORM. This innocuous label poorly disguised its true nature as the Kremlin's means to dictate directives to satellite Eastern Bloc aligned nations and communist parties in the West.

"Since you are involved with American intelligence, I understand you must be careful with what you say, Viktor. But can you give us your personal opinion about Stalin's intentions?" Rozovsky asked.

"Fact is no one knows Stalin's intentions with any certainty. Obvious he is trying to expand his sphere of control beyond what the Soviet acquired from the war," Neiman said.

Yalena said, "Some fear a possible attack on allied occupation forces in Germany. Is that possible?"

"Possible but very unlikely. Such action would bring military action from the United States. We have long-range strategic bombers and nuclear weapons. The Soviets do not. Stalin understands his military limitations. Therefore he pursues a strategy of intimidation and subterfuge."

"What about the French Communist Party? How much aid do they provide to the Soviets?" Inga asked.

"Hard to say," Viktor replied. "Probably depends if the PCF can expand its political base. De Gaulle did a good job in denying the communists positions of power in the post-war provincial government. President Auriol is a socialist but no communist. He even served in De Gaulle's cabinet. Although politically to the left of Gaullism, he sees the PCF as foreign threat."

Neiman avoided making the comment that Paris was awash in Soviet espionage agents and individuals in the French Communist Party undoubtedly provided material support to Moscow. The PCF served as a formidable cadre of fifth columnists. Nor could he reveal that the U.S. and Britain harbored concern over Soviet infiltration of the French intelligence service the SDECE.

Rozovsky said, "While you must remain guarded in your opinions, I do not. Those of us in the Russian expatriate community are greatly concerned about Soviet subversive influence in France. Communist members of the Resistance exaggerate their contribution. Many prominent artists and intellectuals like Picasso and Sartre openly speak of their attraction to communism.

Even some White Russian émigrés supported the Soviets during the war.

"Don't be too hard on them, Yuri," Neiman said. "Most of those on the Allied side welcomed Soviet military assistance against the Nazis. Hitler made that choice for all of us. A necessary cooperative alignment with one evil to combat a more immediate threat. Since Stalin came down on the right side of history, he is now in a position to pursue larger ambitions."

"Enough talk of politics," Yalena said. "You said this is a celebration, Yuri. Time for dinner and pleasant talk around Viktor and Inga's newfound happiness."

A joyous evening for everyone. Neiman enjoyed the Russian cuisine. Perhaps helped by the copious quantity of vodka, it brought back memories from his early years.

As they left, Yalena embraced Inga then turned to Viktor. She put her hands on his shoulders and planted actual kisses on his cheeks rather than typical European brush-kisses. "I can see why Inga is in love with you, Viktor. A delight for Yuri and me to have found an interesting new friend. We hope to see you and Inga often."

Tomorrow Neiman's brief vacation ended. He must report in at the U.S. Embassy and begin shaping exactly how he intended to discharge his new mission. One constructed of his own making so he felt the added pressure to deliver.

Before going to the embassy, he insisted on accompanying Inga to her studio. Spending the morning together allowed her to show off what she does. They enjoyed a typically late Parisian lunch before he separated to go off to the American Embassy. The Cold War could do without him for a few more hours.

Chapter 5

Paris | January 1948

Neiman checked into the American Embassy in the early afternoon after a long lunch with Inga. Located at 2 Avenue Gabriel, the four-story building overlooked the 17th century Jardins des Champs-Élysées formal royal gardens. On the corner of the Place de la Concorde next to the five-star Hôtel Crillon, the embassy occupied a prestigious place in central Paris just a short walk to the Presidential Élysée Palace. Built in 1931 with a façade that conformed to other buildings surrounding the Place de la Concorde following the demolition of an existing building, its style fit into the elegant right bank architecture not far from the Louvre.

Escorted to the palatial fourth-floor office of Ambassador Jefferson Cafferty, Neiman presented his credentials. The sixty-year old Cafferty was a career foreign service professional already with nineteen years of service as a U.S. ambassador in several countries. Unlike most ambassadorial appointments, Cafferty professed no definable political ideology. He instead pursued the interests of the United States pragmatically with an aggressive style augmented by his tall imposing presence.

After shaking hands with Neiman, Cafferty said, "Please be seated, Mr. Neiman. Washington informed me of your special assignment. General Marshall must think highly of you. You are with the INR branch I believe?"

"Yes, Sir. Intelligence and Research."

"Without getting into sensitive classified areas, may I ask what you hope to accomplish coming to Paris?"

"Certainly, Sir. As General Marshall's letter stated, my job is to evaluate the sources and methods employed in gathering foreign intelligence. Specifically, intelligence gathered from individuals."

"You mean spies?" Cafferty said.

Neiman smiled. "Certainly spies, but also refugees, prisoners of war, international travelers. Human intelligence as distinguished from signals intelligence which is breaking of codes and so forth."

Cafferty nodded. "Washington also provided a brief summary of your background. You are certainly qualified to operate here in Europe with your fluency in the pertinent languages and growing up in Paris. Seems you must also know something of intelligence operations in the field. You were wounded on a mission to Paris during the war. How did you get out of France?"

"With the help of some very courageous resistance fighters and a daring RAF pilot."

"Well, I wish you success, Mr. Neiman with your mission over here. Those in Central Intelligence and Army Counterintelligence will not welcome interference from an outsider. Interdepartmental prerogatives will be a factor irrespective of General Marshall's letter. For that matter, even Admiral Hillenkoetter's letter to his own spy agency people."

"I certainly understand there will be resistance but this is too important. Stalin's repeated aggressive moves threaten all of Europe. My role is to interrupt various pieces of intelligence on the Soviets. Sometimes just fragmented or seemingly unimportant information. Attempting to frame all this into a meaningful picture with a high degree of reliability is always imprecise. Much like assembling a jigsaw puzzle missing pieces with the emerging picture always uncertain. Difficult to evaluate the quality of intelligence sources far removed in Washington. It is the critical aspect missing between information acquisition and analysis.

"The State Department INR is the smallest U.S. intelligence service yet one of the most highly regarded. Our summaries receive close attention at the President's daily intelligence briefings. When I was in the OSS, I experienced field operations before by wounds forced reassignment to research and analysis. So I know what field work is like."

"Well, I wish you luck. You have your work cut out for you. If you need anything, please don't hesitate to seek my assistance. We have an office already assigned to you. After I introduce you around to the senior staff, I will turn you over to Michael Pierce our regional security officer. He can get you squared away with communications procedures and other necessities. Shall we start introductions with the Paris head of station for Central Intelligence?"

"That sounds appropriate given my mission. I appreciate your support, Mr. Ambassador."

Ambassador Cafferty knocked on a door then entered without waiting for an invitation." Got a minute, Frank. Let me introduce Viktor Neiman, secretary Marshall's special intelligence advisor."

Landers stood up to shake hands. "Frank Landers. Central Intelligence station chief here in Paris. Since we will be working together according to instructions from Washington, swing back in here after the Ambassador has made introductions to other embassy staff."

"Be happy to, Mr. Landers."

Among those introduced by Ambassador Cafferty, Neiman spent a productive hour with Michael Pierce the regional security officer of the Bureau of Diplomatic Security Service. The DSS was a branch of U.S. law enforcement. Among their responsibilities was a close working relationship with the FBI on counterintelligence matters. Pierce therefore maintained a working relationship with the CIA, the U.S. Army Counterintelligence Corps, British MI5, and the French SDECE. Those connections provided Pierce a degree of understanding how each of these organizations functioned. After Neiman explained his mission, Pierce readily shared his views to Neiman's questions. He viewed Neiman more as a colleague compared to other foreign service diplomatic staff.

"As to your question about Army CIC staff, they should not see you as a threat stepping onto their turf. Especially given your high-level orders from General Marshall. The American military occupation government makes its headquarters in the former IG Farben Building in Frankfurt am Main. I can provide you a list of senior officers and their functions."

"What is your take on the British relative to Soviet espionage?" Neiman asked.

"I work closely with MI5, the British Security Service. Their job is counterintelligence along the same lines as the DSS and the FBI. I have little direct contact with MI6, the British Foreign Intelligence Service involved with espionage. Can't offer any insights on MI6 activities but from the perspective of counterespionage, Paris is full of Soviet spies."

"What about the PCF?" Neiman asked.

"Perhaps more of a problem. Thousands of potential *fellow travelers* make for a fertile recruiting environment. The PCF is foremost among those communist parties comprising the Cominform. Stalin's creation to coordinate European communist parties under the direction of Moscow."

"What about the SDECE?"

The French *Service de Documentation Extérieure et de Contre-Espionnage* provided the combined functions of foreign intelligence and counterintelligence.

Pierce shook his head. "Since you have the highest clearance level and the need to know, we have reason to believe the SDECE is compromised. How deeply, how high up is unknown. If you must interact with them, be careful."

By late afternoon, Neiman returned to the office of Paris CIA chief Frank Landers. After dispensing with minimal sociable small talk, the aggressive Landers launched into questions about Neiman's interests in coming to Europe.

After Neiman did little more than restate what was included in the Marshall and Hillenkoetter letters, Landers asked more directly, "Sounds like you do not trust the Gehlen Organization."

"I don't have a preconceived bias. Simply a concern. The CIA seems to place complete trust in Gehlen's intelligence product. Carefully worded classified reports suggest Gehlen runs things as he sees fit. Funded by the United States. Wasn't that long ago he was an enemy. Placing that level of trust in a Nazi should raise concerns among everyone. Do we know Gehlen's motivations?"

Neiman's assertive pushback caused Lander a moment of pause. "Somewhat outside my need to know," Landers replied evasively. "Got my hands full with all the Commies in Paris. Best you get closer to the source and make your own assessment of General Gehlen and his intelligence operation."

"I intend to. Gehlen's headquarters is in Pullach outside of Munich. Your counterpart there is Charles Ferguson, senior liaison to Gehlen's operation. Correct?"

"That's correct. Since you are making Paris your base, let me know if I can be of any assistance. Let's have a drink when you are free."

* * *

After Neiman left, Landers placed a call on a secured scrambled line. "I just met this State Department guy Neiman, Charlie. Tried to get his explanation of what the hell he is doing fucking around in our backyard. Like us, former OSS. Not a bureaucrat. Bit of a sonofabitch if you ask me."

"So what's your read, Frank?"

"Says he needs to understand the reliability of our German associates. I sense he doesn't like former Nazis. Found out he's also Russian."

"Russian? What the hell?"

"Don't get the wrong idea, Charlie. He hates the Soviets and Stalin. They killed his parents."

"So he hates Nazis and the Soviets. What is he after?"

"To evaluate Gehlen's organization like he says. The problem I see is what concerns all of us. Gehlen runs his own show. We don't know shit operationally about how he produces his intelligence product. Anyway, my guess is he'll be coming to see you soon, Charlie."

Charles Ferguson was the CIA liaison officer to the Gehlen Organization based in the small town of Pullach a few miles south of Munich in the American occupation sector. The Gehlen Org represented the only functional intelligence penetration of the Soviet Union and the Eastern Bloc countries under Soviet domination. The CIA had no Soviet spies and British MI6 appeared to have no sources of any elevated importance.

From the beginning, funding a self-directed intelligence organization employing hundreds of former Nazis was kept a closely guarded secret. Enterprising Brigadier General Erwin Sibert sold the idea to General Bedell Smith soon after Germany surrendered in 1945. Serving as chief of staff to Eisenhower as supreme commander of the Allied Forces at the time, Smith chose not to inform Eisenhower of Sibert going against orders prohibiting fraternization with former Nazis. General Smith felt the opportunity for intelligence penetration against the Soviets was too important. He also wanted to avoid placing Eisenhower in an awkward position when interacting with the Soviets by affording his boss plausible deniability.

In 1946, Smith accepted a position as ambassador to Moscow where he served for three years. His purpose-driven tenacity combined with his assertive style only added to Soviet concerns about American strategic intentions. Soviet intransigence hardened Smith into a committed Cold War warrior. Two years after returning to the United States, President Truman nominated him for Director of Central Intelligence.

* * *

Before Neiman ventured into Germany to examine the effectiveness of the contracted Gehlen intelligence organization at the source, preparation background work was necessary. Escaping the insular confines of Washington will allow him now to interact directly with counterparts in in the European allied intelligence agencies. The opportunity to obtain direct opinions rather than bland edited reports.

He also needed a couple of weeks in Paris for personal reasons. Beyond the professional requirement to understand circumstances better on the ground in Europe, he needed the opportunity to settle into his new life with Inga Jansons. He could not remember the last time he had taken a leave from work. He expected this mission to prove challenging, definitely stressful. Likely spending periods away from Paris.

That first week of their reunion left no doubt for either of them that they found their life partner. Combined with returning to his beloved Paris with the prospect of spring just months away, life appeared satisfying.

Neiman readily adapted to his newfound domestic life with Jansons. The apartment was superb and ideally located. One evening after dinner while finishing a bottle of wine, she asked, "Where did you grow up in Paris after leaving Russia as a boy?"

"We lived in a fine apartment on Rue de Varenne. My uncle was a physician and my aunt worked at the Louvre when we came to Paris in 1920. Fleeing the Russian Civil War. Later she taught art history at the famous Beaux-Arts de Paris, just walking distance from our apartment.

"A comfortable life. Uncle Stefan and Aunt Lada became second parents. They had no children so I received a lot of attention. Both were socially active. Intellectuals with a strong appreciation of the arts. They met in Saint Petersburg University. They greatly influenced me but I gravitated more to my aunt's world of art rather than medicine. Once I graduated from the Sorbonne with a degree in art history, like my aunt I took a position at the Louvre."

"What year was that?"

"1932. After completing a graduate degree in art restoration, I received a promotion to the acquisitions department. Travelled a good deal throughout Europe. "

"So you had a career in the art world before you left France with the German invasion?"

"Yes. Sadly once again forced to flee my home. As Jews, Uncle Stefan closely followed the news of Hitler's persecution of German Jews. Fortunately we had the financial means to leave France when Germany invaded."

Jansons reflected in silence for several moments before saying, "I remember that terrible time in 1940. My parents probably had the financial means too. My father's jewelry business was quite successful. However, they could not bear the thought of again starting over in another country. Forced to learn a new language and fit within a different culture. Treated not only as outsiders but also as reviled Jews. Unwelcome everywhere. Why is that, Viktor?"

He shook his head. "I do not know. Likely for many different reasons. Prejudice is emotional not rational. It does not come from actual experience. Irrational beliefs usually handed down through generations. People that view Jews as somehow alien find sufficient cause for them to invent reasons. Even extends to non-practicing Jews like my family. There is no generalized reason that explains anti-Semitism."

Jansons said, "Hitler took anti-Semitism far beyond prejudice. Father and Mother could not imagine that Hitler would attempt to kill all the Jews in Europe. So they stayed in France. Two years after the Nazi occupation, arrested and sent to die probably in Auschwitz with thousands of other Jews."

She brushed away a tear. "I remember all the people leaving Paris as the French Army collapsed. I read somewhere as many as two million left the city in just a few days. The chaos. The terrible fear. Cars piled with luggage tied to the roof clogged the main boulevards. Train stations overwhelmed with only limited space on trains leaving the city. How did you and your family manage?"

He let out a sigh. "Far worse than when I left Russia as a boy of nine. As an adult leaving not only all your possessions behind but going into the unknown as a refugee is a life-changing experience. For my aunt and uncle a second time after twenty years.

Well established professionally and socially, I felt guilty for convincing them they could not remain. I can appreciate why your parents convinced themselves that staying was preferable."

"But you knew staying was the wrong choice. Your aunt and uncle are strong people."

"Yes they are. Prospering again in New York. Fortunately, they both spoke English when they left France. Yet for any refugee, the journey becomes traumatic. Physically and emotionally.

"It took us six weeks to reach Marseille. Roads choked with traffic. Abandoned vehicles. People on foot carrying luggage. The biggest problem proved securing enough petrol. Frequent delays until we could locate the nearest black market source. After reaching Marseille, it was another week to arrange passage on a freighter bound for Dublin. That was possible only with a large bribe. Safe in a comfortable Dublin hotel, it took two more weeks to secure an American visa and passage on a passenger liner bound for New York.

"However, your circumstances were far worse, Inga. I know how it feels to lose your parents, but you then had to survive in Paris occupied by Nazis. More than surviving, you risked your life fighting the Germans. Tell me more about how you managed during the occupation."

"You would not have liked Paris during the occupation, my love. Fewer people. Paris had no life. The Boche took everything. Our food, our fuel, our art. Our identity. I survived because Father sensed the end might be near so he had me hide a good deal of money, gold, and diamonds."

"Because you lived in your own apartment you avoided arrest?"

"Yes. I also had papers that did not identify me as Jewish. I forged my own birth certificate and Catholic baptismal record. My papers said I was Inga Jacquet. Father died in the last year of the Great War. Mother died the same year in the influenza pandemic. Forged papers proved I was raised in a Catholic orphanage."

"You were a good enough forger to do all that?"

She smiled with pride. "Very good. One of the best according to Yuri. Let me show you."

She went to her prized 19th century belle epoch mahogany desk and removed a worn folder.

"You be the judge how good these are. Everything produced from scratch. The correct typeface, official seals, watermarks, perforations, correct inks. Adolfo Kaminsky taught me well."

Neiman looked at each document carefully. Feeling them and holding them up to the light. Although no expert, nothing would give them away as forgeries to anyone other than a documents specialist studying them under magnification.

He shook his head and smiled. "I am no expert at documents, but I know something about looking for telling details to identify forgeries from my experience in art acquisitions. I can see nothing about your forgeries that would raise any questions. This is remarkable work, Inga."

* * *

Neiman spent his first week on the job assembling the names of those essential for executing his mission. The list to be a work in process as he pursued field evaluations. Germany and the Gehlen Organization were paramount because they were the only intelligence body with assets inside the Soviet Union and the Eastern Bloc. However, sources within the wider U.S. intelligence community provided useful information from other countries affected by Soviet foreign policies. Italy and Greece being examples.

Additionally other nations such as Belgium, the Netherlands, Denmark, Sweden, and Finland all had good reason to feel threatened by an emboldened Soviet Union. With Eastern European countries already under the yoke of Soviet domination, every Western European country shared a vested concern for Stalin's brand of Moscow-control international communism.

That meant he must travel to the capitals of these countries to assess their respective intelligence-gathering capabilities by talking to their senior intelligence professionals. Then he must determine their willingness to share information with the United States. This in turn raised the question which U.S. agency they chose to channel sensitive information.

Like other countries, the United States suffered problems of inter-agency competition and turf disputes. It existed between Britain's MI5 and MI6. In the United States, not only between the CIA and FBI, but also between the various military intelligence branches. The State Department's small Bureau of Intelligence and Research was treated as some academic institution. Yet in 1948, it was the vital link to shaping U.S. foreign policy in these early years of the Cold War. Neiman's mission was to enhance the quality of INR analysis of intelligence on the Soviet Union by integrating a qualitative assessment of the information-gathering process.

With virtually no reliable Western assets behind the Iron Curtain, that made the Gehlen Organization unique. Germany was the front line in containing Soviet ambitions in Europe. General Gehlen and his band of reconstituted former Nazi intelligence personnel must be Neiman's first stop.

Chapter 6

Paris | February 1948

Neiman began the substance of his mission by briefings from the U.S. Army Counterintelligence Corps. As an integral component of the American occupational forces in Germany and Austria, the CIC was on the front lines of combating Soviet espionage efforts in Western Europe. It was the leading intelligence agency operating in the American occupation zones during the immediate years following WWII. They possessed far more comprehensive information on former Wehrmacht and SS personnel than the civilian Central Intelligence Agency.

It was the CIC that played the operational role in locating and secretly relocating German scientists to the United States in *Operation Paper Clip*. German scientific expertise was vital in continuing the technological struggle of the Cold War. The Soviets attempted to acquire German scientists by seizure. German scientists afforded the opportunity to relocate, overwhelmingly chose the United States over the Soviet Union.

Knowing all this, Neiman therefore wanted the CIC's assessment on the capabilities of the Gehlen Organization. While the Gehlen Organization's owed its post-war resurrection to the U.S. Army, Gehlen resented the tight working controls. With the formal establishment of the U.S. Central Intelligence Agency, Gehlen skillfully negotiated a transfer to become subordinate to the CIA instead of the U.S. Army. He calculated that working for the newly formed CIA would allow greater independence. With his background in the German Wehrmacht, the U.S. Army looked on General Gehlen from a critical perspective.

Neiman utilized his boss Paul Kline and his Washington staff to make the necessary arrangements and introductions to appropriate senior officers in the American Army's occupation headquarters in Frankfurt. After briefings from the Army, he would visit Pullach to meet General Reinhard Gehlen.

Arriving in Frankfurt on an U.S. Army C-47 Dakota, an army jeep met him on the tarmac. A sergeant held a hand-lettered cardboard sign reading *Mr. Neiman.*

The sergeant said, "General Miller sends his compliments, Sir. Let me take your gear."

Brigadier General Miller turned out to be deputy G-2 chief of staff for American occupation forces. G-2 being the broader intelligence branch of the Army with the CIC being a subset section dealing with counterintelligence. Ushered into Miller's office by a junior officer, Miller came from behind his desk to shake Neiman's hand.

"Welcome to Germany, Mr. Neiman. Let me introduce Colonel Bauer my counterpart in the Counterintelligence Corps."

After shaking hands and taking their seats, Miller said, "Mr. Kline briefed us on your mission. Told us something of your background. You are certainly not a typical Washington bureaucrat. Then these unusual letters from General Marshall and Admiral Hillenkoetter. General Marshall carries the highest respect from every officer in the U.S. Army.

"Mr. Kline was somewhat vague about details of how we can assist in your mission. Can you be more specific?"

"Certainly, General. Let me first say, I appreciate you and Colonel Bauer making time for me. Don't need to tell you gentlemen about inter-agency turf disagreements. My role in the State Department's Bureau of Intelligence & Research is to collect Soviet-related intelligence from all U.S. intelligence sources and draft summaries. Suggesting possible broader meanings from collective information fragments is what I do. The INR is

America's smallest intelligence agency but the administration places great stock in our work. I personally draft the INR's Soviet summary for the President's daily intelligence briefing."

By the expressions on the faces of the two officers, that carried weight.

"I read all U.S. intelligence with the understanding that it is not the raw product. I get mostly summaries with an unknown degree of editing, or perhaps taken out of context. Goes through a lot of hands. I came to Europe to understand the reliability and quality of human intelligence gathering on the Soviets by auditing the raw intelligence gathering process. Germany is the frontline battleground in this new Cold War."

"Therefore you have concerns over the Gehlen Organization," Miller said.

Neiman nodded. "My next stop is Pullach. I am here specifically to get an understanding of the Army's G-2 and CIC assessment on Gehlen. The Army found Gehlen and set him up doing the same thing he did as chief of the Wehrmacht's FHO eastern front intelligence during the war."

Turning to Colonel Bauer, Neiman said, "The CIC is the most knowledgeable about former German personnel connected with every part of the Nazi war effort."

"Am I hearing that you have reservations about the Gehlen Org, Mr. Neiman?" Miller asked.

Neiman made a gesture with his hand implying uncertainty. "Yes, I have reservations. Gehlen was our enemy just a couple of years ago. A former Nazi general. He is not our friend. We have in common only Stalin as an enemy. We must assume Gehlen holds his own agenda foremost. My concern is how much independence he enjoys. Not clear to me how he negotiated becoming subordinate to the newly created CIA instead of Army Intelligence."

Miller said, "Because Gehlen is a smart devious bastard. I know that from first-hand experience. That is how he how he did it. The reason was because he did not like our intrusion into what he considered his personal intelligence operation. His staff owes allegiance to the *Organization*. Everyone uses code names.

They even refer to Gehlen as Dr. Schneider or just Doctor. Gehlen is a mercenary serving his own interests as priority."

Colonel Bauer added, "I don't have the interactive personal experience of General Miller, however I know Gehlen second hand through requests from our brethren at CIA. As you pointed out, Mr. Neiman, the CIC has the best files on Nazis. The Germans and especially the SS kept meticulous records.

"Gehlen's name pops up frequently with requests for identity papers for certain former Nazis. People Gehlen claims are vital to his intelligence organization. Among the names are many former SS. Even the occasional name of someone on the U.S. wanted war criminal list appears. The names receive approval at some unknown higher level in Washington. Points to how much they feel the need to give in to Gehlen's demands. The CIA uses their independent civilian status to keep the Army at a distance."

Without commenting on the hypocrisy, Neiman could say the same about those former Nazi scientists the CIC was secretly relocating to the United States under Operation Paper Clip. Instead, he said, "Are you saying that the CIA is being manipulated by Gehlen?"

Bauer just shrugged.

Miller responded, "Do not quote me, but G-2 feels Gehlen has far too much independence. Our information indicates that Gehlen directs all operations unilaterally. The CIA has no capability to corroborate information since they have no assets within the Soviet Bloc. They just fund Gehlen and let him run the show."

Neiman responded, "Others in Washington express the same view. The question always returns to what choice does U.S. intelligence have?"

"There is no good alternative in the short run," Miller said. "We still should take charge of Gehlen's operation. How is he going to resist? What else can an ex-Nazi general do? Just call his bluff if he baulks. He cannot very well switch sides. Eventually we learn enough to take over and replace Gehlen if he doesn't fall into line."

Neiman replied, "I understand your perspective, General. If the sources of Gehlen's intelligence are obscured from U.S. scrutiny that degrades the reliability of the information. I came to Europe to make my own assessment."

Colonel Bauer said, "The CIA will certainly view you as the enemy stepping on their turf. Your letter from CIA Director Hillenkoetter won't carry much weight for those field agents working with Gehlen's staff."

"I expect heavy pushback. I am sure my reputation precedes me. They will view me as a troublesome outsider from a small rival intelligence service. The CIA has an operational focus. They are short on rigorous analytical process."

General Miller said, "What exactly is your reputation, Mr. Neiman?"

"I try to look at the information with no preconceived bias. I avoid the temptation of looking for intel to support my theory. I avoid theories unless grounded in facts. I prefer to suggest possible alternative scenarios qualitatively valued as to probability. Analysis is a work in process attempting to figure out continually changing circumstances.

"To CIA analysts in Washington, I am undoubtedly viewed as a pain in the ass. My summaries frequently differ from their assessments. The CIA tends to ignore intelligence from other U.S. sources. In my case, the CIA resents the fact that I interrupt intelligence they and other agencies gather as interfering with their prerogative. Not surprisingly, my conclusions are often different with theirs."

Miller said, "I wish you luck going into the lair of the spooks. Mr. Neiman."

"What do you know about the senior CIA liaison officer to Gehlen's headquarters, Charles Ferguson?"

Bauer responded, "Ferguson is a piece of work. We call him Gehlen's valet. Ferguson provides whatever Gehlen asks for. Not sure whether he buys into the Gehlen mystique or just enjoys the prestige. Ferguson acts as if the Gehlen Organization is America's white knight saving us from Soviet communism. What if Gehlen feeds us fiction to keep funding flowing?"

Neiman said, "That's what I mean to find out. One last thing. What is the situation in Berlin?"

"Worse by the day," Miller said. "Stalin sees the joint agreement between the U.S., Britain, and France combining our occupation zones economically as evidence of Western resolve to contain Soviet expansion. Stalin will see the expected introduction for a new German currency to replace Reichsmarks as another direct confrontation. The early stages of implementation of the Marshall Plan become a long-term threat. Stalin fears a rebuilt West Germany.

"Berlin's location as a divided city so far inside the Soviet occupation zone has been a source of Soviet irritation since the end of the war. It naturally represents the front line of the Cold War. The Soviets have started stopping trains to check identifications and other means of harassment. They will continue to escalate to more serious measures to test our resolve."

* * *

Perhaps to piss off the CIA, General Miller provided Neiman with an army sedan and driver for the duration of his visit to Pullach. At any rate, it provided a measure of independence. He arranged a seat on a military aircraft to get him to Munich and accommodations at the Hotel Vier Jahreszeiten located in the center of Munich only 12 kilometers from Pullach.

As with most of Munich, the Vier Jahreszeiten suffered substantial damage from allied bombing over the course of WWII. Rebuilding Munich began immediately following a meticulous plan for reconstruction to duplicate the origin architecture. In the two and one-half years since the war ended, the 19th century hotel was well on its way to restoration of its former grandeur. A favored accommodation for American senior personnel ensured a well-stocked restaurant and bar in spite of lingering general food shortages in the city.

Neiman settled in by spending the afternoon reading Reinhard Gehlen's biography again. The reasons behind his reputation as brilliant, devious, scheming, and self-serving well deserved.

During the last two years of the war, Hitler personally assumed supreme command of the military. Not only did Hitler dictate unrealistic strategies, he often interfered by directing tactical operations. Since initiating the disastrous Operation Barbarossa invasion of the Soviet Union, Hitler's military mismanagement ensured Germany's defeat. While the German military high command largely succumbed to Hitler's delusional prosecution of the war, Gehlen continued to furnish realistic military intelligence assessments directly at odds with Hitler's irrational pronouncements.

Gehlen's ability to get away with exercising independence as the chief of the Wehrmacht's Foreign Armies East intelligence organization for the Eastern Front represented a remarkable feat. Surviving as a dissident general officer until the very end of the war attested to his extraordinary abilities of skillful maneuver.

Neiman relaxed that evening with a couple of Scotches and a dinner of German sausages and potatoes. Promptly at eight o'clock the following morning, his military driver was waiting in the lobby.

The short drive through Munich still revealed wartime destruction yet with rebuilding evident everywhere. With 90% of the old city destroyed, rebuilding was a lengthy process for a city of 800,000 inhabitants. A new currency and the infusion of funding under the Marshall Plan would accelerate recovery. Munich exemplified Stalin's foreboding of a reconstituted democratic Germany. George Marshall was correct. Economic stability was the most effective approach to containing Soviet Union ambitions in Western Europe.

Neiman reflected on his personal feelings. He hated the Nazis as much as Stalin and his Soviet regime. Yet Adolf Hitler was dead. The Nazis as a movement destroyed. Whatever their tacit complicity, it was unrealistic and counterproductive to punish the German people at large. He must remember that in his dealings with Gehlen. Whatever his feelings and suspicions, Gehlen's Organization represented the only source of intelligence source from inside the Iron Curtain.

He must also moderate his angst toward the CIC and CIA for employing former Nazis in efforts to bolster U.S. defenses against the Soviet Union. Joseph Stalin clearly represented a direct threat to the United States and its democratic allies. International realpolitik made for uncomfortable choices.

With his thoughts rebalanced to objective mode, Neiman entered the Pullach headquarters compound of the Gehlen Organization after showing his credentials at the entrance gate. The guard informed him that CIA officer in charge Charles Ferguson was expecting him in building number 4.

In autumn of last year, the former U.S. Army liaison officer to the Gehlen Org discovered the site in Pullach. Near the Isar River, the complex consisted of twenty single and two-story houses with a collection of bunkers, surrounded by a wall a mile long. Originally constructed to house the staff of the Führer's deputy Rudolf Hess, it later became the headquarters of Field Marshall Kesselring. Following German surrender, Postal Censorship authorities of the U.S. Army occupied the facility.

Gehlen's staff moved in December 1947 giving the location its name *Camp Nicholas*, the German equivalent for Santa Claus.

Neiman entered the WWII-era bunker housing Ferguson's office and his small CIA staff. His impression was of a claustrophobic work environment. No windows. Crammed with file cabinets and much-used army-issue metal desks. Still winter, the internal heat was set too high and the air clouded with cigarette smoke. The staff wore white shirts with sleeves rolled up and ties removed.

A dower middle-aged woman sat at a desk behind a typewriter just inside the outer door. Looking up at Neiman, she simply said in German, "*Ja?*"

Neiman replied in German, "Viktor Neiman. I am here to see Mr. Ferguson."

Before she responded, a man came up from behind and around the desk extending his hand. "Mr. Neiman. I'm Charles Ferguson. Been expecting you. Let's go to my office."

Ferguson shut the door. "Have a seat. You may want to take off your suit jacket. Hotter than hell in here. Heating system is a disaster. At the other end of this former bunker, it's cold enough to hang meat. So much for German engineering. Can I get you a coffee?"

"Thanks but I had my morning ration at the hotel."

Ferguson sat down behind his desk cluttered with folders. "I understand you came here to evaluate our intelligence gathering capabilities."

"That is not exactly my mission. I am not here to critique your methods. I am here to assess the reliability of the intelligence gathered. My function is to analyze and draw possible conclusions of a vast mix of human and signals information from various intelligence sources. That also includes the military, allies, and the diplomatic foreign service.

"The CIA is America's foremost source of human intelligence on the Soviets. Of course that is only because of the subcontracted services of General Gehlen and his wartime staff of the Wehrmacht's Foreign Armies East intelligence branch."

"So you are here to evaluate Gehlen's Organization?"

"Partly. From everything I've read that might be impossible. I understand Gehlen operationally runs his organization in absolute secrecy. Even his headquarters' staff uses code names. The CIA does not know the exact composition of his staff. Obviously that means the CIA does not know any of his sources. No way to determine the reliability of information. No way to corroborate. The problem seems obvious."

"All that is correct," Ferguson said surprised by Neiman's assertive approach. "Unfortunately that's the cards we are dealt. However, Gehlen is the real article. Wehrmacht files support Gehlen's contention that FHO had a thorough understanding of Soviet military capabilities. He accurately predicted Soviet battlefield intentions and objectively assessed German military weaknesses. All this due to a superb network of sources and brilliant organizational methods. The fact that Hitler overruled the German General Staff from acting on FHO intel does not alter the quality of Gehlen's work."

Neiman responded, "I agree with that assessment of Gehlen's wartime performance. I've spent considerable time schooling myself in Gehlen's background. His brilliance is not in question. However, that was wartime military related intelligence. We are now dealing with political factors."

"Sounds as if you don't trust him though," Ferguson said.

"It doesn't matter if I trust Gehlen or not. My point is there is little to base an opinion on the matter of trust when considering he runs his operation in secret. The CIA has no way of exercising oversight. That casts a cloud over Gehlen's work product. How the CIA handles Gehlen's information also weighs into its reliability. It seems you trust Gehlen without reservation."

Ferguson continued attempting to defend the CIA's acceptance of the Gehlen Org at face value. "What choice does the U.S. have? Ignore Gehlen's material? I tell you the guy pathologically hates communism and the Soviet Union. He's old-line Prussian military."

"Only a couple of years ago, Gehlen was our enemy. A Nazi. A general staff officer. That alone is enough reason to question his motives."

Ferguson said, "I know Gehlen's background. He avoided politics. A committed soldier. Pushed back on Hitler. One of the good Nazis."

Neiman could not contain his anger. "Good Nazi? Exactly what does that mean? Because he is anti-Soviet doesn't excuse him from being part of the Nazi regime. They started WWII. Gave the world the greatest genocide in modern history. Gehlen may be useful but he is still a fucking Nazi."

Ferguson scowled, "Christ, I hope you don't communicate that attitude when you meet Gehlen. Whatever the shortcomings of our arrangement, Gehlen's network is our best source of intelligence on the Soviets."

Neiman raised his hand in a gesture to placate Ferguson. "I understand all that, Mr. Ferguson. I am here to make objective assessments. Regardless of Gehlen's background, if his Soviet penetrations yield reliable information that is all that matters."

Ferguson nodded while remained unsmiling. Stuck with Neiman, he could not avoid introducing him to Gehlen.

From Neiman's perspective, if Gehlen took offense at his questions, so what? What alternative did he have? Since the United States generously funds Gehlen's operation, he has no alternative but to accept oversight. Army G-2 discovered Gehlen thinking he was an intelligence gold mine. Gehlen disliked their intrusion and managed to negotiate moving from U.S. Army control to the newly formed CIA. By all appearances, Gehlen successfully accomplished his objective of freedom to operate unilaterally. About time someone confronted the arrogant Nazi.

* * *

Walking from the CIA bunker to a large two-story house, Neiman asked Ferguson, "How do you address Gehlen?"

"I address him as General."

Inside the house, a young man dressed in civilian clothing sat behind a reception desk. Standing up, he extended his hand. "Herr Neiman?" Continuing in German, "General Gehlen is expecting you and Herr Ferguson."

Upstairs, the young man knocked and opened the door to Gehlen's office. A large but modest office lit by two large windows behind Gehlen's desk. One wall included floor to ceiling bookshelves. Behind a desk, sat Reinhard Gehlen with an oversized map of Eastern Europe framing the opposite wall.

Dressed in a civilian suit Gehlen stood to greet his visitors. A slight man of five-feet seven with thinning hair.

"*Guten Morgen meine herren.*"

"Ferguson replied, "This is Mr. Viktor Neiman. Senior intelligence officer for the United States State Department. Special assistant for Soviet affairs to Secretary of State General George Marshall."

After shaking hands, Gehlen said, "Please be seated," then returned to his chair behind his desk.

There were several comfortable chairs grouped around a low table as you entered the room. Neiman took Gehlen's signal that this was to be a formal meeting. Gehlen maintaining his independence. Attempting to win over Neiman not Gehlen's objective.

Gehlen's countenance suggested restrained hostility. Then again, photographs Neiman reviewed, including Gehlen's POW photograph, reflected a self-contained personality not given to revealing much by expression.

Not surprisingly, Gehlen launched directly into the reason for Neiman's visit. "Mr. Ferguson explains your mission as one to establish the credibility of the intelligence produced by my organization. May I ask what leads you to have reservations?"

"For no other reason than your entire operation is run in total secrecy without any participation by American intelligence personnel. You must admit that is highly unusual since the United States is your client so to speak."

"You mean because the United States funds my organization you should be allowed to see our methods and procedures? Using a business analogy, the client could not expect contracted outside experts to share with them their trade secrets. My core staff consists not only of experienced intelligence professionals, but those experienced against the very enemy we and the United States now face."

"I appreciate your prospective, General. I would not expect you to identify sources or methods you employ in penetrating the Soviet Bloc. As an intelligence professional of considerable reputation, you understand the importance of placing information in the larger context. I believe it possible for you to share with us a deeper understanding of the origin of your information without compromising proprietary integrity."

"I do not agree with that view, Mr. Neiman. The exceptional secrecy exercised by the Organization became standard operating practice during the war. As chief of the 12th Department of the German Army General Staff known as Foreign Armies East, or FHO, I developed the ultra-secret protocol. Are you perhaps aware of the unusual circumstances we in German military intelligence labored under?"

Gehlen was of course referring to the competition with Heinrich Himmler's SS and their intelligence branch the Sicherheitsdienst des Reichsführers-SS or SD. Adding to that was the outrageous military incompetence of Adolf Hitler. Both factors increasingly became problematic for prosecuting the war on the Eastern Front. The Wehrmacht required actionable intelligence not Hitler's delusional strategies to confront the Soviets in the last two years of the war.

"I believe I understand your meaning," Neiman said.

"Then you will understand the need to preserve operational integrity even from internal interference."

Casting a glance at Ferguson, Neiman could almost sense his thoughts. The case for the good Nazi. Neiman concluded something different from Gehlen's past. A gusty clever sonofabitch that now sought to frame his past as a German nationalist rather than a Nazi. Planned for his post-war survival. Beyond all expectations, Gehlen not only escaped prison, but found new employment subcontracting his intelligence services to the Americans. As much as any German business, Gehlen benefitted by the rebuilding ideal of the Marshall Plan.

Neiman persisted. "Preserving tight control of sources on a need to know basis we understand. However, it is essential to have an understanding of the source. Intelligence acquired from active asset penetration is vastly different from the same information acquired through indirect means. I have audited a large cross section of your raw intelligence product. There is a remarkable lack of even the general origin of a piece of information. Does it have a factual basis or is informed opinion? Without framing the information in the context of the source, allows for no credibility determination."

Gehlen's eyes betrayed his irritation. "Unfortunately, the secrecy of the Organization must remain unchanged. Security reduces exponentially with the addition of people. The Soviet GRU and MGB are aggressive. Western intelligence agencies are not immune to infiltration. Any relaxation of access to our procedures by sharing source details with the CIA risks unacceptably compromises security."

"We are not expecting details revealing the precise source. At the least, we must receive sufficient information to establish the provenance of the information or it diminishes in value."

Gehlen leaned forward placing his elbows on his desk and putting his hands together. Letting out a sigh, "Mr. Neiman, I will speak to my staff and determine if we can find some middle ground. Perhaps if we added a qualitative value to each piece of information, would this be helpful?"

Neiman was not about to take this condescending shit from an arrogant Nazi. Although employed by the U.S. State Department, he was no diplomat. Exhibiting his best sarcastic expression, "Hardly adequate, General. As an intelligence analyst, the opinion of another unknown analyst without knowing how they arrive at their conclusion becomes meaningless. Just like security, the more people sequentially interpreting a piece of information distort that information from the essence of the raw product. I like reading the raw product in the original language. Even that depends on understanding something of the source's circumstances."

Gehlen did not intend to debate the matter further. "Mr. Ferguson, does the CIA share the same concerns expressed by Mr. Neiman?"

Drawn into the uncomfortable exchange between Neiman and Gehlen, Ferguson's countenance exhibited distress. "I understand Mr. Neiman's preference for more expansive background. However, the CIA appreciates the unusual relationship we have with your organization, General. A readymade intelligence operation targeting the Soviets provides the United States with an unusual intelligence advantage."

Fucking waffle language. Neiman could add the caveat of the United States benefitting only if the intelligence is viable. Without accountability, Gehlen could manufacture material. His self-interest rested with retaining the United States as a well-paying client.

Gehlen said as a means of concluding the unpleasant exchange, "I appreciate your position with the American foreign service, Mr. Neiman. However, my organization works directly through American Central Intelligence. I believe Mr. Ferguson is diplomatically saying they are satisfied with how I conduct my intelligence apparatus. I will consider your suggestions but cannot commit to making procedural changes to our proven methods."

Anxious to conclude the meeting, Ferguson said, "Is there anything else, Mr. Neiman."

"No. I think not." He stood up and looked at Gehlen, "Thank you for your time General Gehlen. I will direct any further communications through CIA headquarters."

As Neiman and Ferguson stepped out into the cold, Ferguson could not contain his anger. "What the fuck was that about? Gehlen is our only source of intelligence on the Soviets. Did you have to piss him off?"

Neiman stopped. "How do you know Gehlen's information is genuine? What if his staff manufactures information? The CIA exercises no oversight. Nor does it have an interest in achieving a better understanding of the quality of Gehlen's information we pay for handsomely. That is my next area of evaluation. You can enlighten me if I am wrong. As for pissing off Gehlen, so what? Where else can he go to get generous funding with no strings attached?"

Neiman's questioning of Ferguson yielded an even more loosely managed arrangement. At the source level here in Pullach, the CIA did little more than pass on Gehlen Org intelligence as provided without comment. Any attempt at further evaluation came out of Washington. With no means of assessing the credibility of the sources, it forced the CIA to accept the Gehlen's information at face value.

* * *

From Munich, Neiman flew to Frankfurt to catch a flight to Berlin. Air access over Soviet occupied Germany was limited to only three routes. His trip intended only to experience the border tensions existing with the Soviet Union.

Taking a taxi to his hotel, wartime scars remained visible in Western Allied occupied West Berlin. Yet there was progress. Rubble from Allied bombing was no longer apparent. Rebuilding proceeded everywhere providing needed new employment opportunities. Shops conducted business. Factories once again produced goods. A viable German currency stabilized the beginnings of economic recovery. Infusion of capital from the Marshall Plan making a visible difference.

If he needed evidence of Cold War tensions, Berlin was the place. Leaving his hotel, he walked to the border separating Soviet occupied East Berlin by a wire fence. Looking eastward revealed limited reconstruction activity. There were few civilians visible contrasted with many curious spectators on the western side. This was the front line of the Cold War.

German police, the Volkspolizei, patrolled the border separating the two Berlins. Soviet troops maintained a presence with tanks stationed at points where people crossed back and forth. Neiman stood at one such point observing a line of people crossing into West Berlin carrying suitcases holding the hands of their children. Leaving East Berlin with only possessions they could carry made the clearest statement about Soviet oppression.

The impression gave physical form to Churchill's metaphorical Iron Curtain. The lack of reconstruction progress was stark evidence of the growing divide between western democracy and Soviet-styled communism. Occupied East Germany suffered under a command economy directed from Moscow. With the ending of the war, the Soviet Union began extracting reparations from defeated Germany. Dismantling of Germany factories for relocation eastward continued.

East Germany was now a Soviet satellite. Food and consumer goods were in constantly short supply. Individual shops replaced by state-operated outlets. No civilian automobiles travelled East Berlin streets. Cleared of rubble of wartime-destroyed buildings, government-related construction constituted the only rebuilding in evidence.

For Neiman, witnessing Berlin manifested the struggle with the Soviet Union that was only just beginning. The contest not only one of conflicting social-political-economic ideologies but driven by the aggressive ambitions of the absolute dictator Joseph Stalin. His blood soaked reign of successive spasms of terror spanned over twenty-five years. For Viktor Neiman, Joseph Stalin was a focal point of his personal hatred. As the architect of the Soviet Union, it was Stalin that destroyed Russian culture. It was Stalin that forced him to flee Russia as boy then murdered his parents.

As the hotel clerk commented to Neiman, "We live in constant fear of the Russians overwhelming Berlin for a second time. Life in East Berlin is no better than a prison."

The clerk's comments proved prescient. Months later in June the Soviets made the first overt move against the vexing presence of West Berlin. The first international crisis of the Cold War. A siege by blockade. The Soviets suspended all rail and road access into West Berlin. They offered to suspend the blockade if the Western Allies suspended introduction of the newly introduced Deutschmark currency. The obvious economic success of 2.5 million West Berliners was becoming an intolerable example of democratic market capitalism success. Magnified by existing as an island within economically distressed Soviet-controlled East Germany.

The United States and Great Britain responded by beginning a massive airlift to supply the needs of food and fuel for besieged West Berlin. President Truman called Stalin's bluff by supplying Berlin's needs for food and coal for winter heating fuel by sustained daily transport aircraft flights. The Berlin Airlift reached an average of 1500 flights daily, continuing around the clock for over ten months without any incidents of the Soviets interfering with the flights. The implicit threat of war forced Soviet interference with the airlift. Stalin was not ready to engage the West in a shooting war.

Viktor Neiman would later see this as possibly the first evidence of nuclear weapons diplomacy. The Americans possessed a growing stockpile of nuclear bombs in 1948. The Soviet Union did not. However, that imbalance would change.

Chapter 7

Moscow | October 1948

Dimitri Galyorkin and Nicolai Baranovsky were born in the same year in Moscow during a time of monumental turmoil in Russia. Russian participation in World War One against Germany and Austria was going badly. With the largest army in the world, Russian troops suffered disproportional casualties by incompetent military leadership. Not unlike the French and British on the Western Front, senior officers came from the ranks of the aristocracy, holding commands based on social stature rather than military expertise.

The mounting casualty rate fed a growing resentment of the Russian population toward the most absolute monarchy in the world at that time. The unsuccessful revolution of 1905-1907 did not quiet the social unrest. The losses of young men dying on the Eastern Front exacerbated dire domestic circumstances and moved the populace closer to another revolt.

A radical new order replaced the near feudal reign of Tsar Nicholas II, the last monarch of three centuries of rule by the Romanoff dynasty. The Russian Revolution of 1917 brought to power the Bolsheviks, a communist political-economic ideology movement based on the writings of 19th century German philosopher Karl Marx.

The Bolshevik leader Vladimir Lenin set out to consolidate power resulting in brutal civil war lasting five years. Estimated casualties of civilians and combatants throughout the former

Russian Empire ranged from seven to twelve million. Death coming from combat, disease, exposure, and execution. The horrific conflict fought between the Bolshevik Red Army and Russian republicans, known as White Russians, also involved other nationalistic movements in former Russian Empire areas, particularly Poland.

The Bolsheviks prevailed following the inability of the Whites to organize effectively in unified opposition. The Bolsheviks pursued the conflict with the fervor of a religious war. Adding to the horrors for the civilian populations was the *Red Terror*. This amounted to an insidious campaign with the creation of a secret police immediately following the toppling of the monarchy. The Cheka became the blueprint for subsequent Soviet secret police organizations as the central means of repression. The Cheka largely acted independently without oversight or constraint. During the civil war, arrest by the Cheka meant almost certain execution.

The formative early years in the lives of Dimitri Galyorkin and Nicolai Baranovsky continued to be a difficult time for Russia. Vladimir Lenin died in 1924. The Georgian Joseph Vissarionovich Stalin succeeded him as the preeminent figure in the Soviet government. Stalin was treacherous and ambitious. Russia would experience continual conflict during his reign of power.

Growing up, Galyorkin and Baranovsky had much in common. Their parents were well educated and typically bourgeoisie. In the parlance of communism, the bourgeoisie were the middle class that owned most of the wealth and controlled the economic social structure. The enemy class of common people, or proletariat. Both sets of parents stayed in Moscow during the civil war rather than fleeing eastward with many White Russians. Remaining non-political, they occupied useful functions in the new Bolshevik order thereby avoiding persecution from the Cheka secret police.

Galyorkin's father was a chemical engineer and plant manager, his mother taught mathematics in the Russian equivalent to high school. Baranovsky's father was an economic planning official for the City of Moscow under the tsarist regime. A necessary technical expert vital to city administration, he made the transition to the new Soviet government. Baranovsky's mother was a pharmaceutical researcher. All four individuals therefore represented different technical expertise essential for Russian economic recovery following the steep decline in GDP during the years of war.

Dimitri Galyorkin and Nicolai Baranovsky were mathematical prodigies essential to the technological future of a new Russia. Both entered Moscow State University pursuing degrees in mathematics. The two met in their first year sharing several classes. A strong friendship ensued.

Other than their prodigious abilities in mathematics and shared interest in chess, their personalities differed. Galyorkin was reserved and introverted in contrast to Baranovsky's gregarious nature. Intuitively, both embraced the differences forming a deep bonding.

Their interaction enriched their lives. Baranovsky benefited from Galyorkin's reflective thought process contrasted to his tendency to jump to conclusions. Galyorkin benefited socially by Baranovsky's natural tendency to engage and draw people out. Neither having brothers, their relationship grew into one of unreserved trust.

In the oppressive secret police atmosphere of the latter 1930s, trust was a rare commodity, and could prove dangerous. People learned to avoid making any comments possibly construed as reactionary to even close associates. In the context of Soviet-styled communism, that meant any expression critical of circumstances or the leadership. Denunciations could lead to loss of employment position or investigation by the current secret police incarnation of the Cheka now called the NKVD.

Since the turbulent war years of the early 1920s, Soviet-styled secret police repression continued to rely on intimidation by sudden arrest and interrogation. Interrogation possibly turning to various forms of psychological and physical torture. Summary executions without trial became frequent, but now with an insidious alternative worse than the quick death by a bullet to the base of the skull.

The Gulag, the Russian acronym for Гла́вное управле́ние лагере́й, *Glávnoje upravlénije lageréj*, was a system of forced labor camps distributed east of Ural Mountains throughout Siberia. Stalin enlarged the scope of the penal system for the dual purpose of ridding political opposition while providing a renewable source of unlimited forced labor. The system provided Stalin the ability to embark on a wide range of ambitious plans without regard to loss of life. During the great famine of 1932-33, prisoners attempted to survive on 300 calories of food a day.

Galyorkin and Baranovsky knew the risks of speaking your mind. Their special friendship affording frank interchanges became their cherished outlet to survive this new norm of oppression by terror. After receiving their undergraduate degrees both remained at Moscow State University to pursue graduate studies. They continued rooming together but their respective career trajectories diverged. Galyorkin entered the physics department while Baranovsky chose economics.

Galyorkin gravitated to theoretical physics. Perhaps the most abstract field of science applying mathematics in attempting to explain and predict natural phenomena. Baranovsky's choice to pursue economics applied advanced mathematics to explain manmade phenomena. Economics attempts to explain the manmade consequences of the production of goods and services, consumption of resources, and movement of wealth influenced by social behavior and governmental policy. Their different career paths mirrored their different personalities yet held much in common with exploring intractable problems using mathematical means.

Galyorkin was able to immerse into the mental exercise of exploring the abstractions of theoretical physics while ignoring Soviet social oppression. Baranovsky's range of intellectual interest was more eclectic. While they both privately criticized the unreasonable life-altering constraints of Soviet communism, Baranovsky found it more difficult to reconcile. Pursuing a career in economics exposed him to the workings of democratic market-driven economic structure. In spite of the Soviet government's attempt at censorship, Baranovsky understood that western market economic systems provided an overall better quality of life. Sacrificing yourself for the good of the state was nothing more than self-serving propaganda by the Communist Party leadership.

Galyorkin felt the same way but did not share the activist temperament of his friend. Since they roomed together at the university, they could freely exchange frank criticisms of the government. That abruptly changed when Nazi Germany invaded the Soviet Union in June 1941. Operation Barbarossa with an invasion force over 3.8 million-strong attacked along an 1800 mile-long front. Russian forces put up stiff resistance at a staggering cost in casualties. The carnage was so great that the Soviet government passed a military service law making all males between 16 and 28 years of age liable for conscription into the Red Army.

Galyorkin and Baranovsky's skills earned them exemptions from military service. Yet that meant being pressed into other wartime services and putting their graduate studies on hold. It also meant separating to different locations. Baranovsky was to remain in Moscow assigned a position in the Ministry of Armaments procurement logistics section. Because of his studies in chemistry, Galyorkin was posted as an engineer to a munitions laboratory in Ulyanovsk on the Volga River 600 miles to the east of Moscow. Both had sixty days before reporting to their new assignments.

They reveled in having the freedom to discuss any subject and express their feelings without fear of denunciation. Now forced to separate, there was no way to communicate safely as before.

After meeting Galyorkin as undergraduates, Baranovsky introduced his new friend to shorthand for taking notes more efficiently. Baranovsky discovered shorthand while studying English. Developed by a German in the 19th century, it was an early stenography system using simplified features of cursive Latin letters. Enjoying immediate success, translations soon spread throughout Europe and Russia. As a phonetic writing system, the characters document sounds rather than written spelling. As a mental exercise, Baranovsky memorized the characters and began applying them in actual notetaking. Used in stenography, it disciplined the user to listen to the speaker using a means of condensing the material that allowed verbatim transcription keeping pace with speaker. After mastering this for English, he discovered the system was available in Russian. Galyorkin quickly acquired proficiency.

Baranovsky had a natural rebellious streak. The repressive restrictions imposed on society by Soviet government institutions was an affront to independent thinking. Soon after learning of their impending separation, Baranovsky said to Galyorkin, "We need a way that we can communicate candidly in secret, Dimitri."

Sitting in their small dormitory room, the cramped quarters took on a feeling of home now that they must leave the insular security of the university.

Galyorkin nodded. "Yes. Unfortunately, that means communicating by letter. We know nothing of encryption. Even if we develop an encryption method, it will be obvious we are communicating in code. The censors will immediately declare we are engaging in subversive activity. This is wartime. We cannot risk that."

"Of course not. The more difficult problem is finding a means of communicating by a method of encryption that appears otherwise innocuous and entirely normal."

Galyorkin removed his glasses and began cleaning them with a handkerchief. "Really? Sounds like an insurmountable problem to resolve in a short amount of time, my friend."

"Maybe not. I started to think about the problem when we first learned of our reassignments to war-related work. We could be sent anywhere. The real problem is not devising a method of encryption. I did some research on encryption. Cipher techniques using various forms of substitution or transposition for the alphabet have the inherent problem of character frequency of a given language. Therefore, such ciphers are subject to decryption no matter how sophisticated. Basing the encryption method on a changeable key that only the sender and receiver know avoids this."

Galyorkin replied, "So what is the solution for disguising our communications?"

"Chess. We are avid chess enthusiasts. We devise a method of using historical chess games as the key. Each communication uses a different game selected. An algorithm uses the moves and positions of the pieces to convert to text. We use our knowledge of shorthand to memorize a table assigning numbers to each character. That further obscures letter frequency association. I have not worked out the details but I can envision a solution if we both work on the problem."

"Even if we construct the methodology of the encryption, how do we disguise the communication?"

"That should become easier with practice. Our letters will include normal personal material but will always include a discussion of a particular chess game. Our commentary will include chess-related terms to act as code to enable deciphering."

Galyorkin sat back in his desk chair and sighed as he removed his glasses. "Here we are discussing how to secretly communicate while everything is turning dark, Nicolai. The Red Army is suffering horrific losses and the Germans continue to advance. Moscow may fall. Russia may become a vassal state like France."

"Russia is too vast for Germany to occupy," Baranovsky said.

Galyorkin responded, "They will not occupy all of Russia. Just the European portion. East of the Jurals, they will leave to Russians. The vast grasslands of the steppes and the agricultural wasteland of the tundra to the north. Siberia with only its mineral resources and Stalin's penal labor camps."

"Come, my friend. We must focus on our good fortune. Neither of us will become cannon fodder. We shall serve behind the lines exercising our skills for Mother Russia. The Germans have taken on more than they realize. They do not have the military manpower to control both Europe and Russia. Staying connected will be essential for maintaining our morale, Dimitri. Will you help me?"

Galyorkin smiled and nodded. "Of course, Nicolai."

It took a couple of weeks working together to develop their unique method of disguised encrypted communication. The solution was to take the moves of a documented game and using the resulting square position on the board of the moved piece as a basis for mathematically manipulating that position number into any desired number. That number then corresponded to the desired shorthand character identified by an assigned numerical value. To accomplish this, they devised a code disguised in the context of discussing the moves in strategic chess parlance to generate a number from a memorized matrix. This number then multiplies the square position number of the moved part to arrive at a value for the appropriate shorthand character.

The multistep process avoids the inherent vulnerability of identifying letter frequency for a given language, or even to a shorthand character. The approach allows converting the moves of any game into any desired encrypted message with the security of a one time-use cipher.

It took practice to gain proficiency to express a written commentary in short phrases consistent with the chess moves to make the content appear believable as a detailed discussion of a chess game. Offsetting phrases for creating a code key number by commas allowed for creating any desired word. Already possessing proficiency in shorthand notation and exceptional memory skills, memorizing the conversion table numerical value for the shorthand characters became easy.

Their practice soon became a competition for drafting the most believable text content to express a message in code. Deciphering based on defining the position value of each moved piece for a specific game gained speed with repetition. The entire process was similar to learning a new language.

They possessed a book of collected great chess games published in 1933 that they used to study and debate chess strategy. The book was a gift by Baranovsky's father when he went off to the university. Separation from Galyorkin meant they needed another copy for use in their cipher correspondence. Baranovsky resolved the problem by stealing a second copy from the university library.

Galyorkin took Baranovsky's encryption process concept further. As mathematicians, adding another hundred mathematical operation characters to the shorthand character list allowed expressing encrypted equations as well as text.

Both realized no secret cipher was absolutely immune from unwanted discovery. Yet they felt secure that if their chess discussions correspondence appeared genuine, they could avoid raising suspicion. If for some reason they fell under scrutiny, the layering of their encryption method process should obstruct attempts at deciphering. They never committed any details of their encryption process to writing.

* * *

From the outbreak of war with Germany, Galyorkin and Baranovsky began a regular correspondence. Sharing secret information from their assigned work gave them a more informed picture of the war than otherwise possible under Soviet censorship.

Remaining in Moscow with the devastation inflicted by the advancing Germans was terrifying for Nicolai Baranovsky. Beyond the casualties of the outclassed Red Army, reports of wholesale murder of Soviet POWs and civilians became daily news. Baranovsky and everyone remaining in Moscow found a brief period of relief by the end of August 1941. While Red Army losses were horrific, German forces also sustained heavy casualties against Soviet numerical advantage and unexpected resistance of troops defending their homeland.

With advance German panzer units within 220 miles of Moscow, Adolf Hitler intervened and ordered the drive on Moscow by Army Group Center delayed. Over the collective protests of his generals, Hitler redirected lines of supply to support Army Group South's attack on Ukraine.

Involved in the Armaments Ministry, Baranovsky witnessed the frantic efforts to increase Moscow's defenses during the German offensive delay. One million additional Red Army troops and 1,000 new T-34 tanks strengthened Moscow by the time Hitler resumed the offensive against Moscow in early October.

By mid-November, forward panzer formations attempted a final encirclement of Moscow. Getting within 12 miles of the city, Soviet forces repulsed the attack. With the German offensive stalled, brutal winter weather closed off any further opportunity to advance on the city. In early December, the Red Army mounted a counteroffensive forcing German forces into retreat.

Apart from twelve-hour working days in a hectic atmosphere of dealing with continual supply crises, Baranovsky attained rapid promotion to the immediate circle of Boris Vannikov. For someone studying the economics of supply and demand, his wartime work provided a valued education in graduate-level application of large-scale resource organization.

Vannikov proved exceptionally capable in his role as Deputy People's Commissar of Armaments. An unlikely elevation to this post to supplying munitions to the vast Soviet military. Unlikely because at the start of the war with Germany, Vannikov held the post of People's Commissar of Armaments. Two weeks before Germany's attack on the Soviet Union, the NKVD arrested him for failing to carry out his duties. Held in the notorious Lubyanka secret police prison, the NKVD interrogated him under torture.

Under sentence of death, Stalin intervened, ordering Vannikov to document his recommendations for relocating Soviet arms production eastward. Stalin personally reviewed Vannikov's proposals. Impressed and searching for solutions, Stalin lifted the death sentence, releasing Vannikov and appointing him as Deputy People's Commissar for Armaments. Such were the precarious circumstances of everyone in the Soviet Union regardless of rank.

Baranovsky recognized Vannikov's brilliant organizational skills as did Stalin. An excellent teacher and leader to his subordinates, Vannikov became a mentor to Baranovsky. That professional association fueled in him yet another element of resentment for the Soviet system. Everyone was expendable. Justice had no place in Soviet governance predominately dictated by the caprices of Stalin and his lieutenants using the power of a vast secret police.

* * *

Dimitri Galyorkin found his wartime experience rewarding. It also narrowed his career path in theoretical physics to nuclear energy. Much of that was due to a friendship with a younger physics student he first casually met in the physics department at Moscow State University. When Andrei Sakharov joined Galyorkin six months later in the engineering department of the munitions plant in Ulyanovsk, Galyorkin was overjoyed to see a friendly face.

Sakharov was five years younger than Galyorkin. Having shared classes, Galyorkin struck up a close friendship. The outgoing Sakharov replaced the emotional role that Nicolai Baranovsky occupied during their years in Moscow. It was Sakharov's intellectual passion for nuclear physics that began long discussions with Galyorkin occupying much of their off duty time.

As a new field of study, WWII elevated the importance of nuclear research as a possible source for a military weapon of extraordinary destructive power. Nuclear physics engaged scientists throughout Europe and the United States. With the outbreak of war, the science turned from a possible source of energy to the more immediate application as a super weapon. Research in the field everywhere went underground into secret government installations.

* * *

When the war ended in 1945, Baranovsky and Galyorkin returned to Moscow to resume their doctoral studies. Baranovsky returned to Moscow State University, but Galyorkin transferred to the Lebedev Physical Institute of the Russian Academy of Sciences along with Andrei Sakharov. Often referred to as FIAN, its acronym in Russian, acceptance to the prestigious scientific research institute specializing in physics constituted serious professional recognition. Intensive research in the field of nuclear physics directed toward creating an atomic bomb dominated the Institute.

Since the United States success with the first detonation of a nuclear bomb in the New Mexico Trinity test, Stalin understood the strategic imperative for the Soviet Union achieving technological parody. Stalin selected former NKVD chief Lavrenti Beria to head the Soviet effort. Despite his Jewish ethnicity, Stalin placed Boris Vannikov in charge of operations. Unlimited funding attracted Russia's top scientific minds. Lebedev Physical Institute became a key scientific center in the program. An extraordinary professional opportunity for Galyorkin and Sakharov.

Moscow State University and the Lebedev Physical Institute were both located in central Moscow and not that far apart. Baranovsky met Sakharov and soon they became a group of three exceptionally brilliant mathematicians and thinkers that enjoyed spending time together. Although Baranovsky knew nothing of nuclear physics, his gregarious nature and insightful questions made him sufficiently knowledgeable to participate in many of Galyorkin and Sakharov's discussions.

All three received their PhDs in the fall of 1947.

Baranovsky's PhD thesis on western market economics sensitivity to circumstances beyond any central control received substantial attention in both the West and the Soviet Union. The myopic communist economic experts praised his work as a condemnation of market economic failures. Baranovsky did not see the thrust of his thesis in that sense whatsoever. The idiots missed the point looking for material to justify what obviously pointed to the utter failure of communist economic ideology. Instead, he intended the premise of his thesis as a mathematical-based analytical method for explaining broad economic dynamics whether market-based or command-based activities. Quoting from his thesis summary, *The method attempts to explain how fac-*

tors interact with quantitatively variability, and how the effectivity of various mitigating practices to ameliorate negative trend lines requires careful monitoring to avoid counterproductive results from the application of countervailing measures.

Baranovsky's personal views never voiced to anyone but Dimitri Galyorkin remained decidedly reactionary toward every aspect of communist ideology. His studies of western economic systems caused him to see a vastly more successful life for Russians if not suffering under the yoke of Soviet communism. A system designed to benefit those in power within the government. An arbitrary system of single-party rigid political thought with purposely-vague laws and no judicial regulation. A government by decree of a single autocratic leader. Joseph Stalin's decades of leadership were a history of repeated catastrophes of gigantic proportions. Catastrophes causing the loss of millions of lives and lasting suffering to millions more.

Under the veneer of being a successful and engaging Russian intellectual technocrat, Nicolai Baranovsky was deeply unhappy living under the constraints of the Soviet Union.

Although influenced by his close friend Baranovsky, Dimitri Galyorkin was not the same activist anti-Soviet thinker. He viewed his circumstances more fatalistically. Immersion into his scientific work allowed for a certain mental distancing from politics. Even Baranovsky understood that no resistance to Soviet Communistic rule was possible. His personal circumstances of seemingly intellectual freedom were unusual.

The influence of Galyorkin's new friendship with Andrei Sakharov based on their shared scientific work provided Galyorkin some piece of mind. In the summer of 1948, he and Sakharov officially joined the Soviet atomic bomb project headed by two renowned physicists, Igor Kurchatov and Igor Tamm. Henceforth, Galyorkin's life would become increasingly isolated. Work would dominate his entire existence. Challenging work that stretched his intellectual abilities to the fullest. He became closer to Sakharov through working together but missed Baranovsky.

Igor Kurchatov personally recruited Sakharov and Galyorkin to join his All-Union Scientific Research Institute of Experimental

Physics. It was a nuclear weapons design facility. Located near the city of Sarov, the entire area became a closed city given the official name of Arzamas-16. The scientific staff lived in comfortable accommodations and enjoyed excellent food. On the downside, the Ministry of State Security maintained a high presence. Travel outside the exclusion zone was restricted to only that required by their work. Even for senior scientific staff.

Although working with the best Russian scientific minds in physics was stimulating, the intensely restrictive atmosphere otherwise felt like a prison to Galyorkin. Time away from his scientific work became depressing. Chess provided his only outlet where the game consumed his thoughts so completely that it held at bay his pervasive malaise. He missed the counterbalance of hearing Baranovsky's anti-Soviet views. Philosophical exchanges that reinforced the humanity of individual thought. He quickly turned to his secretly disguised correspondence with Baranovsky as a means of coping.

PART TWO

Soviet Union's first atomic bomb test August 1949

Chapter 8

Paris | April 1952

It had been four years since Viktor Neiman's return to Paris. Those years rebalanced his life. Having found Inga Jansons, their affection for each other only deepened. They were happy in every sense of their relationship. Their intellectual and sexual bonding allowed them emotionally to weather the political turbulence of these early post-WWII years as East-West tensions escalated into a new world reality.

With the ending of World War Two in 1945, the combatants all reduced their armed forces. The surviving superpowers of the United States and the Soviet Union however did not demobilize equally. Both countries had military forces strength of close to 12 million each when the war ended in 1945. By 1946, the United States reduced its active military to 550,000 whereas the Soviets only demobilized down to 2.4 million.

The United States began shaping their principal defensive posture centered on nuclear weapons rather than a large standing armed force. Work accelerated on delivery systems of intercontinental ballistic missiles and long-range bomber aircraft. The U.S. initiated *Operation Paperclip* to relocate Nazi German scientists and engineers to America to advance rocketry work already started by the Nazis during WWII.

The Soviet Union did not as yet possess a nuclear arsenal equivalent to the United States. They required a larger standing army to fulfill occupation needs by their enlarged geographic sphere of control which they had no intention of relinquishing. A burden that further restrained economic recovery and improved living conditions for Soviet citizens. Stalin's imperialistic ambitions overshadowed domestic considerations.

Under Soviet occupation, Poland, Hungary, Romania, Bulgaria, Czechoslovakia, and Yugoslavia all became one-party states ruled by puppet communist party governments installed by Stalin. With the Baltic States of Estonia, Latvia, and Lithuania under direct Soviet rule, all of Eastern Europe fell under Soviet control. Yet not everything ran smoothly for international communism.

In 1948, the Soviet Union expelled Yugoslavia from the Communist International because of President Tito's conflicting position with Moscow concerning the Greek civil war. The same day, the Italian Communist Party suffered defeat in the 1948 Italian general election with significant covert help by the United States CIA.

After implementing the Berlin Airlift to supply Soviet blockaded land access to West Berlin starting in 1948, Stalin capitulated by reopening land access a year later. Nuclear diplomacy obviously playing a central role as the unavoidable factor lurking in the shadows causing Stalin to back down a second time.

With the success of the Berlin Airlift, the Western allies merged their occupation zones to form the Federal Republic of Germany, commonly called West Germany in 1949. West Berlin became part of West Germany. Situated inside the Soviet puppet state of the German Democratic Republic, commonly called East Germany, it remained a thriving example of Western democracy in contrast to the visible communist blight of East Berlin.

In 1950, North Korea invaded South Korea. The United Nations Security Council immediately voted to intervene militarily to defend South Korea. Although the Soviet Union was a permanent member of the UN Security Council with veto power, at the time they were boycotting participation in the Security

Council over the dispute of Chinese representation at the UN. Communist forces led by Mao Zedong established the People's Republic of China in 1949 after forcing Chinese national forces from the mainland to the island of Taiwan. The Soviet miscalculated absence from the UN would eventually involve Soviet pilots and communist Chinese ground troops in direct combat on the Korean Peninsula against military forces of a United Nations coalition of western democracies.

Just months before the onset of the Korean War, President Truman announced beginning development of a thermonuclear atomic bomb of unprecedented power. A move designed to keep the United States continually ahead of Soviet capabilities to achieve parity with American nuclear weapons.

Replacing George Marshall resigning for health reasons, incoming Secretary of State Dean Acheson continued implementation of the Marshall Plan. As Marshall envisioned, financing the rebuilding of European shattered economies bore visible immediate results. The North Atlantic Treaty Organization formed in 1949 demonstrated the resolve of Western democracies to contain European expansion of the Soviet Union. It also held the promise of curtailing nationalistic threats such as those arising from fascist regimes like those of Benito Mussolini and Adolf Hitler.

While the Marshall Plan provided the economic means of forging a new Europe, security was equally essential. The original founding twelve member states of NATO included not only the Allied European countries of Belgium, Denmark, France, Iceland, Italy, Luxembourg, Netherlands, Norway, Portugal, United Kingdom, but also the United States, Iceland, and Canada making it a transatlantic military organization. A collective dagger pointed at the Soviet Union for the protection of Western Europe.

Events following the unsuccessful Soviet blockade of Berlin escalated Cold War tensions. The Soviet Union successfully detonation their first atomic bomb in 1949. The same year Mao Zedong proclaimed the communist People's Republic of China. A year later, North Korea invaded South Korea with the encouragement Stalin and Mao Zedong. These events shocked NATO into taking action to establish a central military command center.

A consolidated command headquarters opened in the Paris suburb of Rocquencourt, near Versailles. This now put structure behind the Treaty's fundamentally significant Article 5 obligating the signatories to recognize, *an armed attack against one or more of them shall be considered an attack against them all, and that following such an attack, each member country would take such action as it deems necessary, including the use of armed force in response.*

Occupied West Germany and Austria became the front lines of the Cold War. With western aid rebuilding their shattered social and physical infrastructure, they sided firmly with western anti-Soviet nations of NATO.

Secretary of State Acheson recognized the benefit of Neiman's analytical work independent from the CIA as the State Department's foremost analyst regarding the Soviet Union. Acheson was undersecretary of state in 1947 when the National Security Act created the CIA. Acheson voiced his grave concerns to President Truman. Neither the President nor the newly created National Security Council would be in a position to know what the CIA was doing, or be able to control it if allowed to engage in covert operations. Acheson also considered CIA reliance on outsourced espionage activities against the Soviet Union by Reinhard Gehlen's former Nazis lacked oversight. Acheson wanted his own man close to the European front as his means of a reality check.

Acheson elevated Neiman in civil service rank and permanently assigned him to Europe. He agreed with Neiman about the benefits of readily meeting with foreign intelligence services and directly interacting with European-based U.S. diplomatic staff as providing another dimension to analytical work. Material went through too many filters before reaching Washington.

Neiman's critical views of CIA espionage efforts against the Soviets became more antagonistic with newly appointed CIA Director General Walter Bedell Smith. Smith moved immediately to rescind Neiman's unprecedented access by the State Department into CIA affairs granted by his predecessor Admiral

Hillenkoetter. It mattered little to Neiman. He had no ability to influence the CIA regarding the inadequacy of the Gehlen Organization producing important strategic intelligence on the Soviet Union.

The CIA had little choice since they did not possess any assets within the Soviet Union. Yet their failure was in mismanaging Gehlen. Gehlen did not possess any sensitively positioned sources in the Soviet Union evidenced by the intelligence his organization produced. Neiman suspected Gehlen's network consisted of lower level sources on the fringes. Predominately from Soviet dominated Eastern Bloc countries. Nothing suggesting sources in Moscow. Neiman long ago degraded the reliability of the Gehlen produced material unless corroborated by information from other sources. To a large degree, the Gehlen Org was a welfare refuge for former Nazi military intelligence officers. Perhaps not above manufacturing unverifiable information to maintain their funding.

For that matter, the British could not boast of well-placed penetrations inside the Soviet Union. Since the British Secret Service had been in the espionage business from before WWI, that attested to the difficulties of penetrating such a closed environment. In many ways, the Soviet NKVD was a much a more pervasive secret police state than the Nazi SS Gestapo. With the capricious mass purging of Stalin's Great Terror of the late 1930's, fear became widespread, affecting everyone no matter his or her position in Soviet society. Anticipating Joseph Stalin's intentions therefore came largely from piecing together information from diplomatic, public, and signals intelligence. Defectors, spies, and double agents might deliver windfall information, but that was exceedingly rare in the repressive, paranoid, secret police-controlled Soviet environment where everyone might be an informant.

***

Inga Jansons was the perfect partner for Viktor Neiman. They shared a common background of fleeing their country of birth during war. Both loved Paris. They discovered each other doing dangerous undercover work during WWII. Both had experience as spies and the tradecraft of intelligence work. They both appreciated art from a professional perspective. They spoke multiple languages that invited an appreciation of the culture subtleties.

Jansons became a successful photographer with the eye of an artist. Her work capturing interesting shots of Paris using effects of lighting earned her recognition. With his professional training in art, Neiman could appreciate the emotional impact generated by her black and white atmospheric compositions. She also possessed the varied skills required of a master forger. From his experience, an artistic talent comparable to the talents of an art restorer.

They were good to each other and good for each other in every important way. They married in a civil ceremony in 1949. With Inga's growing reputation as a photographer, Neiman insisted she keep her name as Jansons. He explained that adopting the name of your husband was an anachronism from a time when women did not enjoy the same rights as men. Her professional reputation identified by her name.

Jansons artistic career prompted Neiman to revisit his own interests in art. Intelligence analysis was challenging. Dealing with the most closely guarded secrets was addicting. Yet where would this eventually lead? He would never return to Washington. Paris was his true home. What more perfect place to return to his former career in the art world. The thought spurred him to use his spare time to pursue something useful toward that end. Having earned a graduate degree in art restoration, why not explore more deeply the underlying chemistry of materials and the techniques used by the great painters? Acquiring a growing collection of books allowed him to indulge his interest in art even when traveling for his work.

Both he and Inga maintained a good physical exercise regimen. They enjoyed walking together even in less than ideal weather. Inga retained her war-era habit of bicycling to and from her studio. After a ten-year absence, he returned to competitive fencing as his means of maintaining physical fitness. Rejoining the 19th century fencing school of Salle d'Armes Coudurier at 6 Rue Gît-le-Cœur, he was delighted to find that Master Maurice Coudurier remembered him. During his years at the Sorbonne and before the war, Viktor Neiman placed well in many sabre competitions. After a few weeks resuming repetition of the basics under Maurice's guidance, he was confident about eventually recapturing much of his former competitive abilities. Coudurier was seventeen years older and few at the school could match his skills. The discipline returned quickly. The yoga-style attention to technique and grace provided a range of mental benefits along with physical conditioning.

Paris was now as it was before the German invasion of 1940. It was always Inga's home and for Viktor, his home for twenty years. Although Neiman's position in intelligence placed him outside the diplomatic corps, they occasionally attended embassy functions. Neiman delighted when asked if his attractive wife Inga Jansons would join him. Apart from her beauty, Inga was intelligent and opinionated. A favorite among women as much as men. Along with Viktor, she could knowledgeably discuss art. With their multi-language fluency, Neiman and Jansons became a favorite couple among the international diplomatic community in Paris.

Their social lives included their close friends Yuri and Yalena Rozovsky. The Rozovsky's provided a social environment detached from Neiman and Jansons professional lives. Yet the international implications of the Cold War deeply concerned them.

Stalin was more than a malevolent political figure. He was leading the Soviet Union into repeated confrontations with the West. Everything in this polarized geopolitical world now functioned in the context of the United States and the Soviet Union as superpowers. With the Soviets now in possession of a nuclear weapon capability, apprehension about the immediate future escalated. To Neiman, Jansons, and the Rozovskys, the Soviet threat carried deeper meaning. The sheer depth of Stalin's pathological indifference to human life since coming to power rivalled that of Adolf Hitler's Nazi-era.

As Neiman and Jansons enjoyed an evening together at the Rozovskys following dinner, Yuri said, "Tell me something, Viktor if you can without violating official confidentiality since you are part of the American intelligence community. Do we have any sense of Stalin's objectives? I mean, he is 73 years old. Speculation suggests he spends little time in the Kremlin preferring the seclusion of his various dachas. Now he has atomic weapons. Is he mentally stable?"

"I do not believe any western intelligence agency knows the answer to that, Yuri. You do not have to be a psychiatrist to see that Stalin is a sociopath. History already confirms that. Yet when considering the question might he do something apocalyptic becomes anyone's guess. Penetrating inside the tight circle of power surrounding Stalin has not been possible. I have the same concerns as all of you."

"I have a reason for bringing up the subject. Since before the war I have maintained a close relationship with others of the Russian expatriate community here in Paris. My parents were very much activists with a burning hatred for the Bolsheviks. Like other White Russians including your aunt and uncle, all driven from their places of birth. Yalena and Inga's families suffered the same fate. Many of us have extended family and friends still in Russia. What information seeps out paints the reality of facing constant fear of arrest and destruction of one's family."

Neiman looked at Yuri wondering where he was going with this.

Yuri continued, "My Russian associates not only hear the terrible tales of life in Russia but occasionally receive information of a useful nature to the right people."

"The right people?" Neiman said. "Are you saying sensitive information?"

Yuri nodded. As an old hand running the Druids French resistance network in Paris, Yuri Rozovsky understood the world of intelligence gathering. "It could be. Perhaps you can be a better judge of that. You say your role in intelligence for the American foreign service involves analysis. How do you come by the intelligence used to make your evaluations?"

"The State Department does not directly gather intelligence, either from espionage or signals intercepts. I access foreign intelligence from many sources. Espionage in the form of human intelligence comes under the function of the Central Intelligence Agency. Signals intelligence comes from the American military. Of course, our foreign service diplomats and military attachés also gather information. Then there is a sharing of sensitive information between our allies."

"Would you be willing to look at some of the material my associates have discovered over the last several months?"

Neiman paused for a moment before responding, "Certainly. If it is important, what do you expect me to do with it, Yuri?"

"Pass it on to the right people."

Neiman shook his head. "That might have unintended consequences. I would have to reveal you and your friends as the source. Regardless of its security classification, the CIA would then know of your group. Since they are the designated American agency to run foreign espionage assets, they would demand taking control. You do not want that, Yuri."

"Why is that?"

Neiman must be cautious in revealing too much about his controversies with the CIA.

"I am not allowed to go into detail, but the CIA is not experienced in running espionage sources. They have an operational focus. I am highly critical of the CIA.

"American intelligence also shares with allied intelligence agencies. Too many people will learn of what I will call your network. That also means the possibility of the Soviet GRU or MGB learning of you and your associates. The Soviets have been engaging in foreign espionage since the 1930s. That could place your sources in Russia at greater risk of discovery."

Yuri said, "What do you suggest, Viktor?"

"Let me first determine the value of this information. How do your associates receive the material? Do you have regular means of communicating?"

"The information comes through various methods of secreting it out Russia. Random and highly dangerous for the sources in Russia. I know of one consistent means of communicating between Moscow and Paris."

"Why are these people inside Russia risking their lives to do this, Yuri?" Inga asked.

Yuri looked at Yalena to let her try to explain. She said, "Our friends speak of that often. Their friends and extended family in Russia have lived their whole lives under Soviet repression. Most are educated. They know conditions in the West are much different. Soviet propaganda is unrefined unbelievable nonsense. They are trapped in this environment. I believe this rebellion is a way of coping. A way of declaring their independence, their identity."

"Well said, Dear," Yuri said.

Neiman said, "Very well. Let's examine what your network is producing, Yuri. How about tomorrow? Dinner at our apartment? You can show me some examples."

* * *

The following afternoon, all four were at Neiman and Jansons' apartment. Seated around the dining room table, Yuri Rozovsky laid down a folder containing dozens of typewritten sheets.

"These represent some of the more interesting pieces of information coming out of Moscow. The sources went to elaborate lengths to smuggle out the material. As acts of rebellion, they want to convey information where the subject matter is highly sensitive in nature. The associated risk is otherwise prohibitive. Judge for yourself, Viktor. You too, Inga."

Each sheet contained a message with the date of receipt and the source in Russia identified by a code name. Although fragmented, Rozovsky's information examples all suggested sources with access to sensitive information. People with ordinary jobs administering the bureaucratic machinery. Typists, clerks, translators, cipher specialists, technical staff required to run any organization.

The majority of high-grade intelligence comes from such lower-level sources having access to sensitive information. Highly placed spies were a rare commodity. The CIA had neither. The Gehlen Organization had few sources placed in sensitive positions of any level within the Soviet Union. They harvested information from the fringes in great volume but with little continuity to shape into a cohesive picture.

Neiman remarked, "I see you are running your network as you did during the war. Everyone using code names. What is your code name, Yuri?"

"Raven."

Neiman smiled recalling Rozovsky's code name used during the war.

"I obviously know everyone involved in our Paris group. That is how we started. We all have code names used in any documentation. However, none of us knows the relationship for each individual's Russian sources. From the beginning, I insisted they create and always use code names. We do not share the relationship or the nature of access of sensitive information of any Russian source within the group.

Neiman and Jansons read the transcripts in absorbed silence without commenting. The information formed a disturbing picture of the intrigues among the highest Soviet leaders. Terrifying considering the implications of Joseph Stalin's state of mind.

The selection of information Yuri Rozovsky assembled for Neiman's review lacked continuity but pointed to sources with surprisingly sensitive access. For an amateur espionage network, what Neiman read was impressive. Decidedly different from the nature of Gehlen's output passed to the CIA. The Gehlen Org produced voluminous quantities of information dominated by military-related information. Troop movements, Command changes. Soviet security services operations in occupied territories. Wartime-type military intelligence. Decidedly lacking in political intelligence from credible sources.

Neiman finally said, "Do you have separately acquired information to corroborate any of this?"

Rozovsky replied, "Not really. Some vaguely related material perhaps."

"Meaning no offense toward your associates, how do they know this is not largely manufactured material intended to express their hatred for the subjects?" Neiman asked.

"A possibility. I repeatedly play devil's advocate. My friends can only answer that they know their sources from trusted past personal associations. Some undoubtedly are relatives. All claim their sources have no reason to risk their very lives by creating false information. Think about it another way. None of them has reason to believe their information is even finding its way to western anti-Soviet intelligence services. It is simply a means of explaining the oppressive circumstances they endure to those they trust outside Russia."

"As Yalena said earlier, they derive satisfaction from the act of rebellion itself?" Inga commented.

Yuri said, "Yes. A psychologist might explain it better, but something like that. If you look at some of detail in the communications, it supports the belief that these sources are people with unusual access into the corridors of power. That does not exactly make the material believable, but it adds a measure of credibility."

"How long has this been going on, Yuri?"

"Since last year. Grown large enough that I feel compelled to see the efforts of these courageous people given larger meaning. What do you think, Viktor? Does this have value to western intelligence?"

"The short answer is most definitely. As you pointed out, there is enough substance in the detail to suggest the authors of this information have unusual access. Probably low or mid-level functionaries. Perhaps going through other hands before reaching the trusted people known to your associates here in Paris. The true sources in Russia are possibly others connected to those assigned code names.

"These are people disgusted by those in power in the Soviet state. Stalin's megalomania and paranoia reflected in his propensity for violence. The palace intrigues of those closest to Stalin. Beria's brutal history and his sexually degeneracy. If this were some third-rate country, it would have little meaning. Yet the Soviet Union has already proven itself a totalitarian threat to world democracy. They now possess atomic weapons. They effectively control all of Eastern Europe.

"A couple of these dispatches illustrate the importance of your Moscow network access, Yuri."

October 1951
Subject: Stalin's Kuntsevo Dacha
Source: Blackbird

Report consists of following attachments:
Hand drawn floor plan of Stalin's favored dacha near Kuntsevo
15km from central Moscow.

Hand drawn map showing perimeter fence, guard locations, and barracks of 300-strong MGB special forces security deployment unit.

Report of typical routine when Stalin is in residence.

Neiman commented, "The source is likely someone connected with security or facility maintenance staff. That puts them in position to monitor the comings and goings of high-ranking soviet officials. The report includes insights into Stalin's behavior. Although the dacha outside central Moscow, Stalin apparently orders the attendance of leadership figures frequently to all night affairs of dining, drinking, and watching movies. Is Stalin just lonely or is this a means of controlling his lieutenants?

"Valuable intelligence for piecing together the shifting authority that characterizes Stalin's paranoia by shuffling those that may become a threat to his power. If transmitting the information could become timely, it might provide insights into Stalin's immediate state of mind."

Neiman continued his commentary. "This one is particularly ugly. I have seen classified reports of Beria's sexual deviations from past years. British intelligence reports from during the war. As chief of the secret police, Beria would cruise Moscow by limousine on warm nights pointing out young women. His NKVD bodyguards then abducted the women and brought them to Beria's residence. Following a lavish dinner and wine, Beria then took the women to a soundproof room and raped them. Those denying the sex was consensual faced arrest and imprisonment in a Siberian labor camp. His authority lacked any constraint.

"Although no longer directly in charge of the MGB, the successor to the NKVD, this new material accuses Beria of reverting to his former criminal behavior. Beria may arguably be the most powerful person among Stalin's closest subordinates."

May 1952
Subject: Lavrentiy Beria
Source: Hummingbird

Sister to wife of Beria's bodyguard/driver reports Beria ordering the arrest of young women he points out during evening drives about Moscow now that spring is bringing warmer weather. The women are brought to a specially prepared room in Beria's office complex then raped by Beria. Source states this practice is common knowledge among his security detail however never discussed out of fear of Beria. Source does not know of the ultimate fate of the female victims.

"This information points to Beria's current feeling of power as sufficiently secure to engage in such behavior. Stalin must know what is going on. Undoubtedly, others in power know. Could be used to remove Beria should the political winds change in Moscow."

"Any other communications stand out?" Yuri asked.

"A couple. Several point to anti-Jewish undertones. Those in power using Jews in positions of influence as a political football. Again, it suggests well-placed sources in positions to provide useful intelligence provided the means of continuing communication both back and forth exists."

Rozovsky said, "Well, that confirms my thoughts. We have something here that has real value in combatting Stalin and his gang of criminals. Sounds little different from battling the Nazis."

Neiman replied. "At least your Paris group is doing this by running agents inside the Soviet Union. As with any intelligence service, the problem is how to protect the identity of those covet agents."

"So far, we have done well on that account. No reports from any of my people of sources disappearing," Yuri said.

"That risk elevates once you team up with an established western intelligence agency."

"Any ideas, Viktor?"

"Not at the moment. This represents a significant intelligence penetration. Important enough that American intelligence should not miss the opportunity to make use of your material."

Chapter 9

Paris | May 1952

Since General Walter Smith became CIA director, Neiman's relationship with the CIA deteriorated. Looking at the intelligence product produced by the Gehlen Organization, Neiman saw no quality improvement over the last couple of years. The majority of sources remained from within East Germany with scattered information from Poland and Czechoslovakia. Low-grade material from sources seemingly peripherally connected. The large manpower increase in the Gehlen Organization produced greater volume of material but with no qualitative improvement. Neiman suspected the increase in U.S. funding might be encouraging the manufacture of intelligence.

Gehlen produced nothing directly from Moscow or other major cities within Russia. Rozovsky's adhoc network was better placed for acquiring information from within the Soviet center of power. Neiman's official assessments became increasingly more critical of CIA conclusions. His critiques infuriated the CIA that had no means of defending their positions based largely on uncorroborated Gehlen Org produced material. Neiman turned to relying more on signals intelligence from the U.S. military and human intelligence from allied intelligence services. This included British MI6, French SDECE, Belgian SDRH, Netherlands BID,

Danish DDIS, Norwegian NIS, and the Swedish secret foreign intelligence agency T-kontoret, simply the *T-office* in English.

The friendly intelligence services cooperated with the United States to differing degrees. National interests usually superseded dealing with the collective enemy the Soviet Union. Rivalry also played a part. Even intelligence and security services within a country often withheld information from a sister agency. Britain's MI5 and MI6 and the U.S. FBI and CIA serving as examples.

Further complicating Neiman's stature was that of working within the small intelligence branch of the state department viewed with less importance than the CIA. Not all intelligence services were equal in scope of responsibilities. Counterintelligence often became more important than engaging in the more difficult task of foreign espionage.

The most advanced human intelligence operations were those of the Soviet Union. Both the MGB and the military GRU ran foreign espionage agents. With decades of experience, this raised the specter of Soviet penetrations into western intelligence agencies. Although withheld from the public, British diplomats Guy Burgess and Donald Maclean went missing last year. Under suspicion, Britain's MI5 believed they defected to the Soviet Union. Their close association with high-ranking MI6 official Kim Philby now placed Philby under suspicion.

Neiman began thinking about a way to convey Rozovsky's material indirectly to American intelligence. One approach was to use a friendly nation as a conduit.

Although Sweden remained officially neutral, their secret military intelligence service T-kontoret might offer unique circumstances. Created at the outbreak of WWII in 1939, their focus was exclusively foreign intelligence gathering. Historical relations between Sweden and Russia have taken many turns. Sweden's tendency to go their independent way by avoiding entanglements associated with foreign political alignment was inconsistent. During WWII and the following years, relations with the Soviet Union turned exceptionally cool. Like all of Western Europe, Sweden is mistrustful of Joseph Stalin's intentions. Sharing the Baltic Sea with Soviet puppet states and neutral but vulnerable Finland added to their concern.

Since returning to Europe in his new role in 1948, most of these friendly intelligence services knew him. Generally well received, it took some explaining of the analytical function of the little-known U.S. State Department's Bureau of Intelligence & Research.

Foreign attitudes toward the broader U.S. intelligence community were mixed. Proven capabilities in signals intelligence and code breaking were regarded the best in the world. However, each foreign intelligence service had a different opinion toward the comparatively inexperienced American CIA. The Cold War nonetheless provided common ground for cooperation given the collective concern over the Soviet Union.

Neiman was well aware that Sweden exercised its neutrality situationally. Neiman therefore confined his efforts to establishing relationships with other intelligence agencies to those of NATO countries. The origin of NATO was largely due to the perceived threat of aggression by the Soviet Union toward Western Europe. Since Sweden remained a non-aligned military country, they like Finland did not become NATO member states. Both countries had good reason to distrust Soviet intensions with a history of conflict because of their geographic proximity. Soviet occupation of portions of Finland in the last year of WWII forced Finland to adopt a nonalignment stance for survival. Although officially neutral, Sweden clearly aligned with Western Europe in the distinct polarization of the Cold War.

Neiman saw the Swedish military intelligence agency now as a possible conduit to route information coming out of Moscow from the Rozovsky Network to the Western Allies. They focused entirely on intelligence gathering. They appeared to have no relationship with the CIA. He would explore the possibility of enticing the Swedes to collaborate by passing along Rozovsky's information as if originating with Swedish sources. Although with a strongly socialistic government, Sweden was decidedly anti-communist, making Neiman's idea a plausible scenario.

Such a move was well beyond his authority. It would require authorization from Secretary of State Acheson. He would cross that hurdle later if he first made receptive inroads toward a co-operative arrangement with someone senior within T-kontoret.

An unexpected opportunity arrived to take the first step to approaching Swedish intelligence. Well-practiced in making useful relationships, Neiman understood the necessity of learning all be could about the character and motivations of those involved in his professional work. He needed to reconnoiter how best to approach the Swedes. That opportunity arrived at an embassy reception in Paris for the new U.S. Ambassador James Dunn. Among those attending was the U.S. ambassador to Sweden, William Butterworth. Neiman learned that Butterworth was also the U.S. representative to the European Coal and Steel Community headquartered in Paris.

Enjoying a close relationship with George Marshall and Dean Acheson, Butterworth knew of Neiman. Introduced to Butterworth, Neiman asked if he might have a few minutes to discuss a matter privately before departing the reception. Somewhat surprised why a senior intelligence officer should request a private conversation, Butterworth said, "Of course. What about right now? Perhaps down the hallway over there? I am curious as to how I can be of service to your special field of work."

Once out of earshot, Neiman said, "Thank you, Mr. Ambassador. As you know, my specific area of concern is the Soviet Union. In that capacity, I interact not only with other U.S. branches of our intelligence community, but other NATO allies. The thought occurred to me that although unaligned militarily, Sweden may have intelligence on the Soviets they might be willing to share."

"Wouldn't that possibly compromise their position of neutrality?" Butterworth replied.

Neiman smiled. "Not necessarily. Although neutral, relations between Sweden and the Soviet Union are not cordial. Stalin's blockade of Berlin, their testing of an atomic bomb, now their assistance to the North Koreans must trouble Sweden. Dominating the Baltic Sea puts them in the Cold War frontline equivalent to occupied Germany, Stalin's continued aggressive posture toward the West threatens them as much as any Western European nation."

Butterworth nodded. "You are correct, Mr. Neiman. Like the rest of Europe, Sweden definitely harbors concern over current international political turmoil."

Butterworth's diplomatic response nothing more than waiting for Neiman to get to the point.

"I wish to make contact with Swedish military intelligence, the T-kontoret."

Butterworth shook his head. "That will probably not lead to the type of cooperation you are seeking. Do not quote me, but my contacts in the foreign ministry have stated their position of nonalignment as reason to decline cooperation with prior overtures from the CIA."

"Nonetheless, I believe I should make an attempt. Like you, I am State Department. I have no idea why the Swedes rebuffed the CIA. However, to be candid, the CIA lacks diplomacy. Swedish intelligence may view what I have to discuss differently."

Butterworth smiled. "It is common knowledge that you and Central Intelligence are not on the best of terms. You think Swedish intelligence might be more receptive to whatever you are trying to accomplish?"

"I have no idea what the CIA was seeking. I can only open new talks from a different intelligence perspective."

Neiman could also use obtuse diplomatic jargon that said little.

"Well I will see what I can do to arrange a meeting with someone from T-kontoret."

"Thank you, Mr. Ambassador. I can be reached here at the embassy."

It was a week later when Butterworth called him. "Took some doing and the efforts of the Swedish Foreign Minister to get you a meeting. T-kontoret maintains pretty tight security. I exaggerated a bit by saying that Secretary Acheson deemed it important for you to meet with a high-ranking official of Swedish intelligence. Emphasized your function was analysis vital to

U.S. foreign policy, not intelligence gathering. This Friday at 2:00 pm, you are to meet Deputy Director Konstantin Lindström at his headquarters. Contact my secretary with your travel details and she will arrange a car to pick you up at the airport and get you to the meeting. Good luck, Mr. Neiman."

* * *

Neiman knew he was in for a difficult negotiation. The western intelligence community assumed Swedish intelligence likely had assets operating in the Soviet Union. Yet they did not share information with the CIA or British MI6 according to Neiman's information. Considered of lesser importance because of their neutrality stance, little was known about Sweden's T-office capabilities. However, they could not turn down benefiting by what Neiman had to offer in exchange for playing along as if it was their Soviet penetration.

This first meeting however was just exploratory to test the possibly. Could Neiman trust the Swedes to preserve the secrecy of the Rozovsky network as the source? Before even presenting the scheme to the Swedes, he must establish a relationship. Should circumstances progress favorably, he must then sell it to Secretary of State Acheson. Pursuing this independent route of intelligence gathering was outside the scope of the State Department's portfolio. Circumventing the Central Intelligence Agency represented a daring move. Neiman could find himself playing a high-stakes game of interdepartmental intrigue. Secretary Acheson might baulk at becoming embroiled in a political battle.

Neiman arrived in Stockholm for the meeting with Swedish intelligence after first conferring with U.S. Ambassador Butterworth. After lunching with Butterworth at the Stockholm U.S. Embassy, an embassy driver delivered him to a nondescript office building. No sign signified this as even a government office. As instructed, he entered glass doors into an enclosed small lobby. A desk with a uniformed security guard sat behind a desk with only a telephone. Told that someone would come to escort him to Colonel Lindström's office, the security guard gave him a visitor's badge and a curious look when Neiman gave his name in English. Not a place used to receiving visitors.

Konstantin Lindström entered the lobby from a side door minutes later. A tall distinguished looking middle-aged man dressed in a civilian suit gave Neiman a smile and extended his hand. "Welcome to Stockholm, Mr. Neiman. Your first time here?"

"Yes it is. I appreciate you making the time to see me, Colonel."

Once inside Lindström's office and offered to take a seat at a small round table, Lindström said, "I am having a coffee. Care to join me? I take it strong."

"Yes, thank you. I grew up in Paris and also prefer it strong."

"According to our files, you lived most your life there but you are also American?"

"Dual American and French citizenship. Fled France with the German invasion in 1940. Joined the American army and wound up in the OSS."

"Of course. Obviously, I inquired into your background before agreeing to this meeting. Our organization is small and we pride ourselves on maintaining rigorous security. As you know, we maintain only limited interaction with other foreign intelligence agencies. A byproduct of our national policy of neutrality."

Neiman replied. "Understandable. However diplomatic neutrality does not preclude Sweden from aligning their foreign policy according to its national interests."

This was to be a cordial meeting of establishing a relationship therefore Neiman avoided mentioning Sweden's profession of neutrality allowed them to trade with both opposing sides during World War Two. Not unlike Switzerland. The result for both countries was a strong post-war economy with continued economic gains by participating in the reconstruction of war-ravaged Europe.

"Certainly. Neutrality is only a broad diplomatic definition," Lindström said waiting for Neiman to get to the purpose of the meeting."

Neiman also did not like diplomatic foreplay. The substance of an exchange often becoming lost in unclear language designed to be vague. Neiman's direct style avoided ambiguity.

"My mission in coming here is to seek common ground whereby both the United States and Sweden can benefit by shared intelligence related to the Soviet Union. I am not here to play the diplomat. I am an intelligence professional like you, Colonel. The difference is I am an analyst where T-kontoret gathers intelligence. My function is to prepare summaries on the Soviet Union for use in directing American foreign policy."

"Why does the United States need the services of our comparatively small intelligence service? You have the CIA. As the world's most powerful nation, you also have the full cooperation of the intelligence services of Western Europe."

Neiman nodded. "And none of those intelligence services have substantive penetrations inside the Soviet Union. The United States and Western Europe have exceptionally poor human intelligence sources inside the Soviet Union.

"And you believe Sweden does?"

Neiman smiled shaking his head. "Truth is, I do not know. However, your proximity to the Soviet Union with a shared interest in the Baltic region means your principal focus must be the Soviet Union. The threat to Sweden is no different from any other European nation."

Instead of responding to Neiman's comment Lindström took a different tack. "My sources report rumors there is a personal feud between you and the U.S. Central Intelligence Agency. Is that true and does that play into your search for alternative intelligence producing sources?"

"A fair question. My disagreements are not interdepartmental. I belong to our State Department's Bureau of Intelligence and Research. A small intelligence service like T-kontoret but we do not gather either human or signals intelligence. We just try to make sense of what information we receive from other U.S. intelligence organizations. Our analytical summaries are highly valued by American decision makers. Perhaps I am biased, but CIA intelligence projections regarding the Soviet Union are heavily flawed. "

Lindström also spoke directly. "Those rumors I spoke of are more specific. Your dissatisfaction apparently stems from your CIA's use of Reinhard Gehlen's former German Army's eastern intelligence unit. Is that correct?"

"Yes. The problem is Gehlen runs his operation in absolute secrecy. Although the United States funds his organization, the CIA exercises no oversight. Gehlen's information chronically lacks corroboration. For an analyst, that diminishes the quality of the intelligence product. Furthermore, Gehlen's Org is overrated."

"So you are casting about hoping for something better?"

"I prefer to say exploring all avenues. The Soviet threat is all too real. Stalin is unpredictable. Becoming increasingly aggressive. You can only anticipate what he might do by carefully assessing his past actions. Even a psychopath develops patterns of behavior."

"Well said. Stalin is certainly a threat to all of Europe. I will convey your overtures to share any substantive Soviet-related information with my superiors."

"I appreciate that, Colonel. Yet I came here not asking to share in your intelligence gathering without reciprocating. Does our CIA share useful information with you?"

Lindström appeared surprised by Neiman's question. He answered with a tinge of irritation. "Only when it suits their interest. Usually something related to the Baltic."

"I cannot speak for the CIA however I see all U.S. intelligence products as part of my job. I possess the highest clearance classification. I would have to be tactful and get authorization from Secretary of State Acheson, but I believe an *arrangement* might be possible. A backdoor conduit so to speak."

Lindström smiled at Neiman's unexpected overture. It bore serious consideration. Closer ties with U.S. intelligence could be important. Regardless of U.S. lack of penetration of the Soviet

Union, U.S. naval intelligence with their vast navy and advanced signals intelligence was the foremost in the world. A closer relationship with U.S. intelligence might also engender cooperation among other Western European services.

This meeting also suggested Lindström look more closely into Viktor Neiman before taking the matter to the director. Eventually any decision to expand interaction required further authorization by the foreign minister and prime minister. The responsibility rested with Lindström to vet Neiman thoroughly. What kind of clout did he have? To what extent did the different branches of the U.S. intelligence community compete?

Lindström said, "Are you aware of a meeting that took place in 1948 in Washington between us and the CIA? I accompanied T-kontoret Director Thede Palm. The CIA requested the meeting. Citing a vital confidential matter related to intelligence gathering, they applied diplomatic pressure to our prime minister. "

"No I am not aware of that meeting," Neiman replied.

"The meeting took place at the Swedish Embassy. U.S. Army Brigadier General Edwin Wright, Deputy CIA director chaired the meeting. This was several months into the Soviet blockade of Berlin. International tensions running high with the overt threat of possible Soviet military action against West Berlin."

Neiman interjected, "Yes, I was in Berlin just before the blockade."

"That meeting went badly," Lindström said. "Could not have been worse. Director Palm is a former academician but a brilliant intelligence tactician. General Wright is a former tank commander and army intelligence officer. Different backgrounds and different personalities. They interacted like oil and water. In hindsight, the outcome was predictable. The substance of the American request for the meeting was to pressure Sweden to place the function of T-kontoret directly under CIA command. Although a difficult task to coerce Sweden into cooperation, the CIA could not have selected a worse representative to present their case than General Wright.

"Wright took the arrogant position that just like during WWII, the American's took command of all joint military opera-

tions. Therefore, it should be the same in the Cold War by bringing intelligence under a unified command. The meeting ended
with Director Palm leaving no ambiguity after flatly refusing the
American proposal. Since that time, relations with the CIA have
been almost nonexistent. Any exchange of intelligence occurs
only at the foreign ministry level."

Neiman knew nothing of this but it came as no surprise. "A
regrettable occurrence in view of the real Soviet threat. The CIA
often thinks narrowly while lacking subtlety. A WWII mentality
inclined toward covert operations rather than intelligence gathering. They believe their own preconceived views as fact."

"I cite this past incident only to illustrate Swedish concerns. I
can understand those rumors about your relationship with the
CIA. While you are suggesting something that appears entirely
different, Sweden must be careful. Embroiling ourselves in
American government interdepartmental conflicts might not be
in our best interest."

Neiman responded, "I appreciate your caution. Should we
come to an understanding I would suggest an arrangement
channeled the information exclusively through the U.S. State
Department's INR branch. Arguably, that keeps it within the
realm of foreign relations. Therefore also shielded from any
American internal disagreements. In my role, I have access to the
intelligence product generated by all American branches and can
obtain authorization to share vital information of interest with
Sweden."

Lindström understood the benefits of acquiring intelligence
from the CIA also meant becoming a silent partner in the collective Western European intelligence community. With Norway
and Denmark NATO member nations, this could provide greater
access to regional Baltic-related information related to Soviet intentions. Remaining diplomatically neutral while clandestinely
aligned with western intelligence could prove vital given Stalin's
continuing threatening actions.

Unlike the contentious 1948 meeting, Neiman's overture
seemingly offered a more than equal exchange of benefits with
little risk. While the CIA's reliance on subcontracted human in-

telligence from Gehlen's Organization might lack substantive Soviet penetration, Swedish attempts fell far short of anything approaching important Soviet penetration. Therefore, there appeared little risk into entering into an exchange arrangement with the Americans. The Soviets might eventually suspect but that would alter nothing in already chilly Swedish-Soviet relations.

Lindström's recommendations rested largely on determining the depth of Neiman's proposal. What sort of power did the U.S. State Department exercise with respect to their Central Intelligence Agency? President Truman was not running for reelection in November. How would a new American administration affect the internal balance of American governmental power?

Neiman was unlike General Wright in both his proposal and personal demeanor.

Neiman's proposal appeared a cooperative arrangement with as much or more benefit to Sweden. Neiman was also personable. Someone Lindström could work with.

After another hour's discussion, Lindström said, "When are you retuning to Paris, Mr. Neiman?"

"Tomorrow morning."

"Excellent. I have another commitment I must attend to here shortly, but I would welcome you joining me for dinner this evening if that is convenient."

"Of course, Colonel. It would be my pleasure."

Lindström did not have another commitment. What he wanted to do was to immediately brief Director Palm on Neiman's surprising proposal. His initial apprehension replaced with a cautious optimism about the benefits for Sweden.

* * *

Upon returning to Paris, Neiman planned to lay the groundwork for bringing Swedish military intelligence into the Western Allies' orbit. The addition of the Swedish intelligence service made sense as confirmed by the CIA's clumsy approach years earlier. If he could pull that off, then the possibility opened up of using them to disguise material acquired by Rozovsky's network as coming from the CIA.

Since he clearly overstepped his authority by making the pitch to Konstantin Lindström, he needed Secretary Acheson's authorization before moving forward. Neiman needed to lay the groundwork before making his proposal to Acheson. Although Neiman's title was special assistant to the Secretary of State, he remained officially part of the Bureau of Intelligence & Research. His old mentor Paul Kline a career diplomat and chief the INR. The best approach to Acheson was to sell Kline on the concept. Lay out the benefits of exchanging information with the Swedes while giving them the same material the U.S. gave to the British, French, Belgians, etc. The difference being the INR would be the conduit rather than the CIA. Too premature though to discuss his discovery of the Rozovsky adhoc intelligence network.

On a secure telephone line, Neiman recounted the meeting with Konstantin Lindström to Paul Kline.

"For an intelligence analyst you are one devious sonofabitch, Viktor."

Neiman chuckled. "I take my job seriously. What do think? Will the boss go along with this?"

"He might. He's not a fan of the CIA. I wonder if he knew of this prior meeting Lindström told you about? I will look into that. Certainly validates the importance of acquiring Swedish intelligence cooperation on the Soviets. Acheson and CIA Director Smith are not on great terms. Any repercussions should the CIA find out will not faze him. Besides, he is a lame duck. With a new administration coming into office, undoubtedly Republican, he is out of a job come January."

"What about you, Paul? Will you lend your support? You have influence with the boss when it comes to intelligence matters."

"I support your scheme wholeheartedly, Viktor. About time Sweden got on board. Should Stalin have further designs in the Baltic, neutrality will not protect them. He occupied and annexed Estonia, Latvia, and Lithuania turning them into Soviet socialist republics controlled by Moscow. Now we have East

118

Germany and Poland on the southern Baltic within the Eastern Bloc.

"Sweden and Denmark are the only countries preventing Soviet control of the Baltic region with Finland coerced into neutrality under direct Soviet threat. I support any plan to bring Sweden to the right side of history. They didn't distinguish themselves by selling steel and coal to the Nazis during WWII."

"Thank you for the history lesson," Neiman replied with sarcasm.

"Don't be insubordinate. Now that you have my support, are you ready to sell the boss?"

"Yep. I will present a rough brief without going into detail. A telephone conference with just the three of us. Sometime over the next few days. I will rely on you to catch him in a receptive mood with all the shit going on in the world. The military stalemate in Korea while negotiations go nowhere must be a daily drain on Washington morale."

The conference call between Neiman in Paris with Secretary Acheson and Paul Kline in Acheson's Washington office lasted almost two hours. Secretary Acheson asked Neiman questions enthusiastically warming to the intrigue. Acheson reveled in the intelligence process accounting for his strong support of the State Department's small Bureau of Intelligence & Research.

"Do you have reason to believe Swedish intelligence has important sources within the Soviet Union, Mr. Neiman?"

"I don't know, Sir. They run a tight security operation. Neither U.S. intelligence nor British MI6 knows much about their capabilities. However, if they agree to this arrangement we will find out."

"How's that?" Acheson asked.

"Once we began sharing our intelligence they will feel compelled to reciprocate. Perhaps not with everything they have, but enough to assess their importance as part of the fraternity."

"Quite a coup if you can convince them to participate in your scheme. How do you propose to go about sharing intelligence with them? For many reasons this arrangement must be concealed. How do you accomplish that? The CIA will raise a stink.

The Swedes will not want the Soviets to suspect they are actively aligning with us."

"We run this like an espionage operation, Sir. I act as the control officer and the Swedes become the source. All back and forth communications go through me. Only you and Mr. Kline know what I am doing. So I am not suspected of being a double agent, I get prior authorization from Mr. Kline of anything I share with them. What they provide to us I also route through Mr. Kline. He distributes that to the CIA and appropriate allied foreign intelligence services without attribution of Sweden as the source. Let the CIA take the credit."

"How do I cover that, Viktor? Kline asked. "The State Department is not in the business of intelligence gathering."

"My suggestion is to claim the material comes from an unnamed walk-in source to our embassy. For security reasons, the Secretary of State decided the INR should manage this source. The only people to question this are the CIA. While we see their intelligence product, they never identify sources. Cite the same protocol as the rationale for this case. Give the Swedes a code name as if they are a single source. The implication obviously is a source with extraordinary access. Leave the implication the source serves a wider network operating in Moscow. The Secretary of State refuses to relinquish control to the CIA to preserve the security of the source."

"An amazing piece of subterfuge if you pull it off, Mr. Neiman. Please proceed and keep me informed as to progress through Mr. Kline," Acheson said then turning to Kline, "Paul, document this and label top secret, compartmentalized only for the Office of the Secretary of State. Come next January when you gentlemen have a new boss, I do not want either of you to suffer any repercussions from the inspector general should this unusual arrangement with Swedish intelligence become a contentious issue."

"Yes, Sir," Kline answered. "We will work out a method of transmitting the information directly to me to keep security tight. I will find the suitable informal means for releasing anything coming our way from the Swedes using the old boy intelligence community network."

"And I will likewise find the means of interacting with Swedish intelligence that appears entirely normal," Neiman added.

Acheson concluded the call with, "Excellent work, Neiman. Good luck, Gentlemen."

In constructing this elaborate hall of mirrors, Neiman realized he could isolate the existence of Rozovsky's network from the entire western intelligence community. He launders Rozovsky's intelligence through Swedish intelligence then portrays it as their product. To the Swedes, he also portrayed the source as a walk-in representing a dissident group in Moscow. The sources requiring protection by layers of cutouts. With little known about T-kontoret, it made the perfect conduit for distribution to the necessary western intelligence services, including the CIA. Given Swedish distrust of the CIA and the rivalry with the INR makes this backdoor scheme understandable and acceptable to them. The key will be Sweden's appetite for increasing access to Soviet intelligence by joining the western intelligence community.

Chapter 10

Moscow | May 1952

Vladimir Mishnyov was a close friend of Nikolai Baranovsky. Their friendship began with his marriage to the sister of Baranovsky's wife. Educated at Moscow State University, his undergraduate degree was in history followed by a master's in political science. Like Baranovsky, he found an aptitude for foreign languages. Fluency in English, French, and German in addition to his native Russian provided the ability to read material in the original language. Even under Soviet censorship, limited available Western literature portrayed a far more attractive way of life than Soviet-styled communism.

His father held a mid-level position within the Soviet foreign ministry and his mother taught history in secondary school, the western equivalent to high school. The influence of his parents gave him a worldview beyond the restricted Soviet education system.

Mishnyov's parents actively discouraged their son to avoid any political discussion. If asked, best to reply with a safe pronouncement supporting the Soviet system. Never divulge your true political feelings. As he got older, he could see for himself the dangers befalling people making the mistake of speaking their minds. Candor even to those you might trust could prove dangerous. Denouncement at the very least caused someone to come under scrutiny by the secret police. Both parents cited examples of those around them losing their positions for real or fabricated infractions. Even within the confines of their apartment, they allowed no discussion of politics to reinforce the habit with their children.

The young Mishnyov learned to feed his growing disillusionment in silence. His dissent festered over the years. Not only did he learn to conceal his thoughts, he became adroit at making bland pronouncements citing Soviet accomplishments. Those skills combined with proficiency in several Western languages and proven intellectual abilities earned him a posting to the foreign ministry aided by his father's connections.

His growing dissent found voice when he married. Meeting Dasha in graduate school, he became attracted partly for their shared reactionary views. It apparently ran in her family. His wife sister's was married to Nikolai Baranovsky. Mishnyov's dissent became more strident as he moved closer to his brother-in-law and his wife. The foursome enjoyed unrestrained freedom of expression.

Mishnyov and Baranovsky's professions afforded them a view of life outside the repressive confines of the Soviet Union. Along with their wives, they understood better than most Russians the stark differences in the quality of life outside the Soviet Union.

Dasha Mishnyov proved to be the boldest. She also worked in the foreign ministry. That is where she met Vladimir. She supervised a team of women in the American sector translating documents. In her years of Soviet government service, she was struck by the permitted criticism of the American government by the press. The ability for American political factions to voice opposing views. Living in a single party police state with only government-controlled information exemplified the difference of life in western societies. It was Dasha that advocated to her husband the need to do something more than talk about dissent.

Vladimir Mishnyov's position involved delivering diplomatic materials to Western European Soviet embassies. More than a mere courier, his role required conveying verbal instructions to

Soviet diplomatic staff and answering questions in depth. He was therefore familiar with the content of the diplomatic material he carried making his function highly sensitive. Sufficiently sensitive to warrant close observation when travelling abroad.

One evening alone with her husband discussing their work, Dasha said, "We complain about serving a government we despise, yet we continue to be part of it."

Vladimir raised an eyebrow. "Like everyone, we have little choice."

"That is what I mean. The Soviet State dictates everything in our lives. All controlled by the whims of a murderous madman. Both of us know of people sent to the Gulag. Not for any crimes, but only because they did not tow the party line. We live like galley slaves."

Vladimir sighed, "Galley slaves sounds a little extreme, Darling. We have a pleasant apartment and preferential access to food and goods."

"But we have no more freedom than anyone. Except perhaps you."

"What does that mean?"

"Your trips outside the country. You get to experience life in the West even if only briefly. I would give anything to experience that. You visit London, Paris, Rome."

"I see much but experience very little. I am not permitted time to sightsee or relax. I go from airplane to embassy then back to the airport to travel to another destination. Picked up by a driver undoubtedly MGB. Someone always waiting in the hotel lobby each morning during overnight stays."

"That is what I mean, Vladimir. If not a galley slave then a mid-level overseer."

"Dasha, I share your feelings yet short of fleeing Russia, what can we do?"

"Leaving Russia sounds appealing but unrealistic. Leaving family and friends with uncertain career prospects makes such a thought painful. How could we even manage defecting with Mara?"

"I agree, Darling. Neither of us is ready to become a refugee."

"Instead of becoming refugees, what about dissident?"

A look of concern came over his expression. "Not something to even joke about. No one openly dissents in the Soviet Union."

"Of course not. I am suggesting clandestinely."

"Doing what?"

"Passing information to the West."

His expression turned to genuine concern. "Dasha, that is crazy. What would that accomplish?"

"It accomplishes some salvation of our souls, Vladimir. The galley slave that mutinies becomes a human being again. He may die in the attempt or succeed in taking over the ship. Either outcome preferable to life as a slave. We are slaves, Vladimir."

They hugged each other and fell into silence for several moments.

Dasha Mishnyov was not however done. "Perhaps Uncle Oleg could help?"

"Help? With what?"

"Passing information to the West."

Vladimir shook his head vigorously. "Get that idea out of your head. That is not dissent. That is spying. If caught, it means a bullet to the head."

"Listen, Vladimir. You have access to the highly secret information you transport in your diplomatic briefcase to foreign embassies. You travel to Paris. You could mail sensitive material to Uncle Oleg once outside the country."

"No. That is far too risky," he said. Yet the idea of taking direct action in dissent touched a responsive chord.

Dasha touched his face. "Just think about it." As he started to say something, she placed a finger to his lips. "No more talk. I want to make love right now. A desire the State cannot regulate."

***

Following Dasha's urging for embarking on active clandestine dissent, Vladimir turned to the serious planning of how to go about such a dangerous undertaking. Perhaps just an intellectual exercise but conspiring even by thought against the Soviet State felt satisfying.

The first question concerned his wife's Uncle Oleg. He corresponded with Dasha occasionally. Never anything political although Vladimir knew him to be strongly anti-communist. Probably an understatement given Oleg Leonov's history. He was a legend in Dasha's family.

Leonov's younger sister was Dasha's mother. She recounted the terrible times of WWI that triggered two revolutions in 1917. The first in March toppled Tsar Nicholas II. The ending of three hundred years of Romanoff Dynasty rule wrought unprecedented convulsions to Russia. The March Revolution brought a provisional government into power. Widely unpopular for remaining involved in WWI, it survived only until the October Revolution swept the Bolsheviks into power.

The Leonov family was bourgeoisie. Middleclass with the family patriarch a regimental commander in the Royal Imperial Army of the deposed Tsar. Oleg Leonov was a young officer. Father and son saw combat against the Germans starting with the Battle of Tannenberg in WWI. They continued fighting until Russian copulation in 1917.

Civil war broke out between supporters of the communist Bolsheviks and remnants of the pre-revolution monarchy social order. Oleg Leonov followed his father in siding with the counter-revolutionary White Army comprised largely of former soldiers of the Imperial Russian Army confronting the Bolshevik Red Army. The lack of a unified command by the White Army eventually led the Bolsheviks to push disorganized White Army units far from the major population centers and unable to regroup for effective counteroffensive operations.

Both father and son continued serving in the Caucasus region to the south under the command of Peter Wrangle a distinguished WWI cavalry general. Yet by 1920, the counter-Bolshevik White Movement was losing support domestically and abroad. The elder Leonov died in battle commanding a rear guard action against the Bolsheviks. Outnumbered and facing certain defeat, Wrangle organized a mass evacuation on the shores of the Black Sea. With 127 others from his division, Oleg Leonov escaped eventually making his way to France.

Finding a home in the French Foreign Legion, Oleg Leonov embarked on a distinguished thirty-year career. As an instructor of unconventional warfare, by 1952 he held the rank of colonel in the French Army.

There was no question about Oleg Leonov's anti-Soviet credentials. What concerned Mishnyov was Leonov's ability to pass information to the Americans without compromising him as the source. To determine that required a face-to-face meeting. Difficult and dangerous for Mishnyov to slip away from Soviet security during his trips.

Giving the problem much thought he believed there might be a way. When next scheduled for Paris, arrange his arrival such that he must spend a night in a modest hotel on Rue Benjamin Franklin used previously by arrangement of embassy security. That provided the only opportunity when he was out of immediate sight from the MGB. The plan was to instruct Leonov to dine in the hotel restaurant at the same time. It was not far from the École Militaire. In the restaurant toilet under the sink, Mishnyov would place a matchbook with his room number inside under a spare roll of toilet tissue.

Still a dangerous undertaking. MGB security selected the hotel because they probably had informants among the staff. There was no public telephone. Having stayed there twice, Mishnyov knew of a separate service elevator at the rear of the hotel used by housekeeping. Leonov could take that to join him in his room bypassing the desk clerk. These arrangements to be included in the letter he and Dasha would draft explaining their intentions, then mailed once outside the Soviet Union.

Whether Uncle Oleg would participate remained uncertain with the inability to correspond freely between Moscow and Paris. At least if he declined, Mishnyov could trust his confidentiality. Taking action by talking to someone outside the Soviet Union sent a thrill of expectation mixed with fear through Mishnyov. It signaled no turning back.

Vladimir and Dasha each wrote a letter to Uncle Oleg. Dasha's spelled out their idea of actively resisting Soviet oppression by passing sensitive material to the West. She acknowledged it as her idea. Both she and Vladimir understood the risks. One line of her letter read, *Mother relives the exploits of you and grandfather fighting the Bolsheviks. The terrible history of Joseph Stalin's subsequent rule proved you right. Vladimir and I must now do our part. Many of our friends feel the same way. The repression is so complete it stifles life. The world must fight to contain the Soviet threat ruled by a dangerous dictator.*

Vladimir's letter explained his position within the foreign ministry. Brief and somewhat vague, he emphasized the elaborate need for security. *Soviet secret police keep watch over me while I travel abroad. Therefore, for our safety I must go to exaggerated lengths to conceal all contact with foreigners. Especially someone with your background. We realize we are asking much considering your position with the French Army. When I make contact by telephone from a safe phone once outside Russia, should you decline to participate we will understand.*

He went on to explain the plan. Mailing the letter outside the Soviet Union meant that a face-to-face meeting in Paris must wait for his next trip. Once he knew his precise schedule putting him in Paris, he would telephone using a public telephone speaking in French. Their conversation should remain brief. Does Leonov agree to meet? Is he available on the only evening Mishnyov was staying in Paris? The terse exchange explained by his need to make any telephone calls quickly without observation by Soviet security. That meant from a European airport before passing through passport control. Using a hotel phone was out of the question.

Although having never met Vladimir or Dasha, Leonov had photographs. The letter spelled out the protocol. Make no indication of recognition in the restaurant. Retrieve Mishnyov's room number from the men's toilet. Take the service elevator near the toilet to avoid passing by the desk clerk. His room door will be unlocked. enter without knocking.

This trip took Mishnyov to the Scandinavian capitals of Copenhagen, Oslo, Stockholm, and Helsinki. The timing proved advantageous. It meant that a trip putting him in Paris was likely required soon after. Paris and London were the most important Soviet Union diplomatic missions in Western Europe. Once he landed in Copenhagen, he deposited the letter to Oleg Leonov in a post box before passing through passport control. Having made the decision, he harbored no second thoughts.

As usual, once clearing Danish entry checks with his diplomatic passport, a driver was waiting holding a sign with his name.

* * *

Three weeks later after arriving at London Airport, Mishnyov made the telephone call to Leonov. He arranged for a late flight arriving in the evening for a better chance of catching Leonov at home. He knew Leonov's telephone number but neither he nor Dasha ever dared call. Because of his sensitive position, he assumed the MGB monitored their telephone calls and all international calls regardless of origin. He could never explain a call to a senior French Army officer and former White Russian. Although undoubtedly buried in both his and Dasha's official dossiers, Oleg Leonov must remain a distant relative from before they were born.

"Monsieur Leonov?"

"Who is calling?" Leonov replied with a hint of Russian accent.

"Dasha's husband. Vladimir. You received our letters?"

A pause before Leonov answered. "Yes. You are serious about this undertaking?"

"Yes. I must keep this call brief. Can we meet? Thursday at eight o'clock?"

"Yes."

"You read the instructions?"

"Of course."

"I apologize about the precautions but I do not exaggerate the danger. I look forward to meeting you, Uncle Oleg." He disconnected. No turning back now.

Mishnyov arrived at the hotel restaurant early. He ordered a pastis aperitif, not so much to stimulate his appetite as to calm his nerves. Casually surveying the small restaurant, confirmed Oleg Leonov was not there. Sipping his drink, he picked up the dinner menu for something to concentrate on. The hotel arranged by the MGB meant someone on staff, probably more than one, were paid informers. What he felt was not paranoia. Better to remain fearful than make a blunder. What he was doing was spying. Arrest meant certain death. Possibly also for Dasha. Thinking about the fate of his young daughter forced him to get a grip on his imagination. If he was to be a spy, he must find the means of holding his fear in check.

Promptly at eight o'clock, the maître d' seated a tall well-built man in his sixties with grey hair at a table on the other side of the dining room. Dressed in a civilian suit, Mishnyov recognized from photos the unmistakable strong-jawed face of Oleg Leonov.

Twenty minutes later after ordering dinner, Mishnyov got up from his chair and walked past Leonov's table without making eye contact. Entering the toilet, he placed a matchbook with his room number written inside under the spare toilet tissue roll under the sink.

After finishing his meal, Mishnyov left the restaurant. Leonov followed a short time after going first to the toilet then taking the service elevator. He opened the unlocked door to Mishnyov's room.

Looking at each other, they said nothing for a moment. After Leonov closed the door, they awkwardly embraced under these surreal circumstances.

As Leonov took a seat in one of the chairs in the small room, Mishnyov turned on the radio. Perhaps unnecessary, but circumstances warranted excessive caution.

Leonov said, "How are Pauline and Dasha." Pauline was Leonov's younger sister and Dasha's mother.

"Both are fine. Enjoying our little Mara. She is seven. We have never met but Dasha and I feel we know you. My mother-in-law worships her older brother. Dasha grew up hearing of your military exploits."

Leonov let out a long sigh. "Are you sure you want to go through with this, Vladimir?"

Mishnyov nodded. "Dasha too. As she told you, it was her idea. However, I have fantasized for some time about living in the West. No way for both all of us to defect. Dasha and Mara could never acquire passports. Both of us work in the foreign ministry with access to highly sensitive material. I could never abandon Dasha and Mara by defecting alone. My only alternative to resist our oppression is to become a spy."

"I understand. I think fondly of my early memories of Mother Russia. Even during those violent times as a young army officer. It is not about the place but about our souls as Russians."

They spoke for some time of personal matters before reverting to the purpose of the meeting.

"You asked if I had a way of passing information to American intelligence. That is a complicated question. Like you, for reasons of security I cannot be more specific. I have friends. Russian friends. Part of the large expatriate Russian community in Paris. Many of us came to Paris because of the civil war. The Paris Russian community of which I speak are predominately White Russians.

"France has one of the largest communist parties in Europe but the Russian expatriate community is anti-communist. They hate Joseph Stalin. Many of us have family in Russia. Those that arrived thirty years ago now have grown children just as anti-communist. We learn things from those still in Russia. People like you that live under the thumb of a brutal dictator. A mass murderer. The constant fear of the secret police must make life seem unbearable."

Mishnyov interjected, "Yes. That is why Dasha and I feel compelled to resist. To do nothing diminishes our souls as Russians as you say."

Leonov nodded. "I understand. Back to your question about the Americans, I have a close associate that might help. We often discuss how information secretly coming out of Russia might be used against the Soviet regime. He is no amateur at this. A former French Resistance leader during the war, he understands the world of intelligence. What is at stake are the lives of so many people in Russia willing to risk passing information to those in Paris they trust. Should we pass information to western intelligence we risk leaks that could endanger those sources in Russia. Too many people become involved outside of our control. Security becomes compromised."

"You are saying it is too risky?"

"No. Only that we need to be careful and make sure we do not become expendable to American bureaucracy. What you are offering elevates our efforts well beyond the random access to information our current sources sneak out. You and Dasha work in the foreign ministry. What kind of information do you have access to, Vladimir?"

"Some with the highest secrecy. Information between the Kremlin and Soviet diplomats in Europe. My job goes further than acting as a diplomatic courier. I am expected to explain what are often vaguely written instructions. I answer questions to clarify the sometimes hidden intent and to expand on Kremlin policy."

"You are therefore briefed about the substance of the material you carry to Soviet embassies?"

"Thoroughly."

"Trusted enough to travel unescorted?"

"Not exactly. Once my plane lands, an MGB escort is waiting once I pass through passport control. That is why I went to extraordinary lengths to meet you. Even this hotel probably has informants. I am not allowed to go anywhere other than the embassy and hotel. Always driven about by an MGB agent. Not allowed to take meals at any place not authorized by Soviet security. The MGB fears people like me becoming double agents for the West or possible defectors."

Leonov came here wondering if this might be some Soviet espionage operation. After talking to Mishnyov, he became convinced this was genuine. "What is next, Vladimir?"

"None of this means anything unless these secrets get to Stalin's enemies. That is why I suggested the Americans. They are the other superpower. Britain and France are still recovering from the WWII. It is the Americans that are carrying the conflict against the communists in Korea."

"I agree. I must consult with my friend. I need his help. To convince him this is not a Soviet intelligence trick, he will want to know more. Then approaching the Americans will require convincing them you are not a Soviet plant. Even keeping your identity to just a very few increases the danger to you and Dasha. Are you willing to take that risk?"

"Yes. I told Dasha that others must learn of our identity. I only ask that you do everything possible to limit that to only those you can personally trust.

Leonov nodded. "You have my word, Vladimir. We will need to meet again. There are many details to work out. Tell me this, how do you propose to deliver these Soviet secrets?"

"I will need a camera. A miniaturized spy camera for photographing documents. I read MGB material so I know about such things. We then must work out some method of transferring the undeveloped film."

The prospect of what this could mean overwhelmed Leonov. He was never involved in intelligence. That was Rozovsky's area of expertise.

Talk turned to how to meet again with Mishnyov so closely watched.

"Do you always use this hotel?" Leonov asked.

"Yes. Arranged by the MGB so I have no choice."

"At least it has a service lift and rear entrance close to the toilets unseen from the front desk."

"I wish we could talk further, Uncle Oleg. However, best that we do not press our luck. If you are seen leaving by the rear entrance it could invite unwanted attention. Before we part, I wish to give you something. Something to convince American intelligence of the value of the material I can offer."

Mishnyov withdrew an envelope from his suitcase. "Communications to Soviet ambassadors in London and Paris concerning Egypt. The instability of King Farouk's monarchy is raising concerns. Instructions for exploiting the differences of the Americans, French, and British regarding the Middle East. These are my copied summaries from the origin documents."

Leonov took the envelope and concealed it inside his suit jacket. He then stood. 'Best I be leaving, Vladimir. Telephone me when you can arrange another meeting. I promise to have some answers for you."

They embraced. After checking the hallway, Oleg Leonov made his way downstairs in the service elevator and exited the rear of the hotel.

Chapter 11

Paris | May 1952

Yuri Rozovsky called Neiman one evening. Excitement evident in his voice. "Viktor, something extraordinary just fell into our lap. I have someone you need to meet. Tomorrow is Sunday. Might the afternoon be convenient?"

"Certainly."

"Can we meet at your apartment? Include Inga. She might be of help when you hear what we have to discuss. This involves our foreign enterprise. I will bring my closest associate in our adhoc espionage network. His name is Oleg Leonov. A colonel in the French Army. A White Russian. He fought the Bolsheviks in the Russian Civil War. You can speak freely about anything you would say to me. "

Rozovsky arrived accompanied by a tall muscular older man. When Neiman answered the door, they shook hands. "Viktor, this Colonel Oleg Leonov of the French Army. More precisely, a colonel of the French Foreign Legion."

Leonov smiled and offered his hand. "An honor to meet you Monsieur Neiman."

"And this beautiful woman is Inga Jansons," Rozovsky said as she came up to join Viktor.

"Madame," Leonov said taking her hand. "Yuri has told me about your work together in the Resistance during the war."

After moving to the living room, Rozovsky said, "Oleg is a personal friend and trusted associate in our work collecting information coming out of Russia. A remarkable military career going back to the Great War and the Russian Civil War. A hero to those identifying as White Russians for fighting the Bolsheviks. Like many, he has family in Mother Russia.

"As I explained to you and Inga previously, we keep the identity of those sending out information critical of the Soviet regime a closely guarded secret. Only known to their contact here in Paris. Referred to by a code name. Oleg has come across something so important he and I feel we must modify that rule in this case. I will let him explain."

"Yuri tells me you work for American intelligence, Monsieur Neiman. That becomes vitally important in our efforts. I understand the value of intelligence having served in so many wars. My current duties involve instructing French Army officers in unconventional warfare. Information on the enemy is the lifeblood of insurgency. In a manner of speaking, our group is engaged in insurgency against the Soviet Union. However, unlike you and Yuri, I am not an intelligence professional.

"Like others in the Russian expatriate community, I still have relatives in Russia. In my case, a sister and her two adult daughters. We exchange letters occasionally. Always cautious what we say. Nothing political. They never complain about Soviet restrictions. Both my nieces are married. My niece Dasha holds an administrative position in the Soviet Foreign Ministry. She is married to an official in the Ministry. They understand their correspondence comes under scrutiny by the secret police.

"Her husband comes under more intense observation. You see, his position requires frequent travel to Soviet embassies in Western Europe. I never knew that because my niece could never include such detail in her letters.

"You can imagine my surprise when I received an envelope post marked from Copenhagen. Inside were these letters. One from my niece, the other from her husband."

Leonov handed the letters to Neiman. Both written in French.

Neiman read the one from Dasha Mishnyov first then handed it to Inga.

The letter from the wife poured out a candid recital of Soviet repressed life even for those in their privileged status. She ended with the lines, *'What Vladimir is embarking upon was my idea. We understand the risks but must find a way to actively rebel against Stalin's tyranny. Every citizen is an inmate in the Soviet system. Unjustly imprisoned, rebellion is necessary to preserve your souls.'*

With Dasha Mishnyov's closing words setting the tone, Neiman began reading the letter from her husband. His letter did not dwell further on the reasons expressed in his wife's letter, stating only that he shared her deep sense of disgust living under Soviet oppression. Instead, he stated in direct language what he was prepared to do.

'My position involves delivering sensitive diplomatic materials to Soviet embassies in Western Europe. Briefed on these materials in Moscow, I further explain the intent of the written instructions to Soviet diplomats, answer questions, and convey any responses back to the Kremlin.

I am prepared to deliver the contents of my diplomatic pouch to American intelligence. Possessing only original documents, I need the means of photographing documents and transferring the undeveloped film. Since I am under constant surveillance when travelling abroad, a clandestine secure means of transferring these materials must be arranged.'

Neiman looked at Leonov then Rozovsky as he handed the letter to Inga.

Neiman remarked, "In the jargon of espionage, Vladimir Mishnyov is a walk-in source. Someone offering to become a spy. It is rare. Always questioned as a possible ploy by the enemy to infiltrate a double agent. How can you be sure this not an operation being run by the Soviet MGB or their military intelligence the GRU?"

Leonov replied, "I cannot be sure. I know my niece only through her prior correspondence. Obviously, it never contained anything critical of the government. I have never met my niece Dasha. I only met Vladimir a couple of days ago. I recognized him from pictures when they married years ago."

"Do they have children?" Neiman asked.

"Yes. A daughter. Seven years old."

"It is always possible they are doing this under duress to protect their daughter. None of that we can determine. We should proceed as if Vladimir Mishnyov is genuine, but try to find the means to independently validate his material as we go along. He cannot be a true double agent in the sense that he cannot carry secrets back to Moscow. He can however transmit disinformation."

Leonov extracted another envelope from inside his suit jacket. "Vladimir also gave me this. Said it might prove his intensions to the Americans."

Neiman began reading two handwritten pages.

TOP SECRET AMBASSADOR EYES ONLY

From: Andréy Vyshinskiy, Foreign Minister USSR

To: Soviet Union ambassadors to the United Kingdom and France

Subject: Egyptian political situation & Soviet position with respect to Great Britain and France

Background:

Eighty percent of Egyptians suffer from bilharzia and ophthalmia, diseases easily preventable and treatable with clean water supplies. In 1947, 80,000 died of cholera. Nothing has changed since that disaster to remedy the Egyptian potable water crisis. Farouk makes a public display of his personal excesses. A known glutton, his obesity attests to his excesses. Newspapers report his obsessive gambling at European casinos. Among the world's wealthiest men, the

Egyptian populace suffers in widespread poverty. Everything about Farouk's lifestyle advertises his disregard for the welfare of his people. Farouk therefore becomes symbolic of what is wrong with Egypt governance. His continued rule brings the possibility of a populace revolution instigated by the Muslim Brotherhood. While the West fears a communist-backed revolt, the USSR supports Farouk's removal to avoid the more likely possibility of a populace theocracy taking hold in Egypt.

Farouk's government appears unstable with his continual changes of prime ministers. He is looking for a strong hand to manage insurmountable problems of his own making. Farouk will not find any such solution.

Farouk also embraces Fascism as evidenced by his close relationship with the Grand Mufti of Palestine al-Hussenini. Accepting him into exile in Egypt reflects the Egyptian government's conflict with Britain's dominance in the region by siding with competing French interests in the Middle East. Continually cite that as reason to condemn Farouk pursuing an anti-Semitic gesture directed at the new State of Israel.

Although our position also supports removal of Farouk, as do the imperialists, we see a long-range opportunity. Egypt is useful as a wedge between the

British and French. Your respective missions should find opportunities to exploit differences in their Middle East imperialistic aspirations.

Regardless who replaces Farouk, Egyptian problems are so pervasive that the country will continue to suffer unrest. Our longer-range challenge will be the consolidating power of Islam in the Middle East.

Recently acquired intelligence:

Internal political tensions continue to rise against the unpopular role of King Farouk. King Farouk refuses to make changes to his incompetent rule and the corruption of the traditional political establishment. The Americans fear a populace uprising might encourage a communist takeover. They see installing a strong military government as necessary to stabilize the region given Egypt's importance.

Recently acquired intelligence indicates the United States is planning to support a coup d'état by dissident Egyptian military officers of the Free Officers Movement.

Our intelligence is specific. The United States Central Intelligence Agency has initiated covert contact with the leading figure in the Egyptian Free Officers Movement, Lieutenant Colonel Gamal Abdel Nasser. Labelled Project Fat Fucker, an English expletive characterizing King Farouk's obesity, the operation is directed in the field by CIA operative Kermit Roosevelt and CIA Cairo station chief Miles Copeland. The operation has the highest level of backing by CIA Deputy Director Allen Dulles and Secretary of State Dean Acheson.

This information regarding espionage penetration into American intelligence is not authorized for sharing with any staff. Use this knowledge only to assist in directing diplomatic maneuvering with your respective interactions with the British and French foreign ministries. Once the military junta removes Farouk, we shall vigorously condemn this as a blatant imperialistic move by the United States in conspiracy with the British and French. Position your diplomacy such that the USSR can exploit the situation by seeking influence in the successor Egyptian government. With the destabilization of the Middle East following the Second World War, opportunities abound for increasing Soviet influence in the region.

The sensitivity applies not to the knowledge of this American plot but rather to our obvious penetration into American intelligence. I share this information in order for you to make preparations for our diplomatic response once events unfold.

Neiman looked up and said, "Extraordinary. Mishnyov copied this by hand?"

Leonov replied, "Yes. He asked that we supply him with a miniature camera allowing for photographing documents in his possession."

"What do you think, Viktor? Is this genuine?" Yuri asked.

Whether Mishnyov was genuine or part of a Soviet intelligence operation might still not be absolutely certain. What was genuine was the existence of the CIA's *Operation Fat Fucker*. Neiman read the CIA briefing material a couple of months ago since he saw all CIA distributed intelligence product. He paid little attention since it did not bear on Soviet intentions affecting Europe. If Mishnyov was a Soviet plant, he was sufficiently important to warrant exposing a high-level penetration into Western intelligence. Neiman held concerns about possible Soviet moles in British MI6 but this direct assertion of penetrating American intelligence was disturbing. Both countries exchanged intelligence freely. Constrained by his own security restrictions, Neiman could not however reveal to Rozovsky or Leonov his knowledge of CIA clandestine operations.

"Mishnyov certainly picked something convincing. My security status does not allow me to share anything I learn as a result of my work so I cannot comment on this CIA operation. However, it suggests a Soviet penetration inside American intelligence. For Soviet intelligence giving up such information to establish Mishnyov as legitimate seems unlikely. Regardless what we think, if the Egyptian military deposes Farouk, then we should conditionally conclude that Vladimir Mishnyov is legitimate."

Both Rozovsky and Leonov nodded.

"What comes next?" Leonov asked.

Neiman said, "The problem will be devising a method of exchanging information considering the security restrictions imposed on Mishnyov. Another meeting is necessary between Monsieur Leonov and Mishnyov but we should try to make that the last direct contact except for some emergency.

"What about the camera Mishnyov requested?" Leonov asked.

Neiman said, "The OSS used a miniature camera designed for photographing documents during the war." He looked at Inga. "Can you purchase a Minox and film, Inga?"

"Certainly. My photographic equipment supplier should be able to get me one."

To all, Neiman explained, "The Minox camera is very small. A little over three inches long, one-inch wide, and five-eighths of an inch thick. Weighs about five ounces. Exceptional for taking photographs of documents."

"What about a way for him to transfer exposed film during his visits to Europe?" Neiman said to Inga. To Leonov he added, "Inga has experience in such tradecraft from her work in the Resistance."

"That will take some thought. From Monsieur Leonov's description of security around Mishnyov, using a conventional dead-drop might be difficult and too dangerous," Inga said. "Yuri and I will work on it. How long before Mishnyov arranges another meeting?"

"I cannot be sure. He said it might be a few weeks before returning to Paris," Leonov replied then turned to Neiman. "Yuri explained the dangers of involving our group with an official intelligence service. What are the concerns if we simply start handing over secret material on the Soviets to the Americans?"

"Let me first explain what I do. I hold a senior position in the American State Department's Bureau of Intelligence and Research. My job is to evaluate foreign intelligence involving the Soviet Union gathered by different American intelligence services. The United States has several. The principal service is the Central Intelligence Agency, the CIA. Signals intelligence comes from the military. I have access to all material in order to prepare interpretations and summaries. The State Department is America's foreign ministry."

Leonov said, "Then your work helps shape American foreign policy. I see why Yuri values your advice. Are you not the best person to receive the material produced by our network?"

"Unfortunately, it is not that simple. The State Department does not involve intelligence gathering. The CIA is the agency given authority to engage in human intelligence gathering. Running spies. If I deliver your material, protocol requires the CIA to take over control. That potentially exposes your sources to greater risk."

"Why is that?" Leonov asked.

"Because the CIA has little experience in running spies. They even use a subcontracted spy agency comprised of former WWII German Nazis intelligence operatives to spy on the Soviets. However, the CIA will see your group of Russian expatriates as an amateur organization unlike the German organization. The CIA will take over your group demanding to know the sources. The CIA may also share your material with other allied intelligence services. Too many people will become involved. Soviet intelligence might learn of your group. Look at the document presented by Mishnyov revealing a high-level Soviet penetration into American intelligence. Your group needs a means of concealing its workings to remain independent."

"Do you have a suggestion? Unless this material gets to the Americans it is meaningless," Leonov said.

"As a matter of fact, I may have a solution. Nothing yet final but I should know soon. Using this information about the CIA running an operation in Egypt to dispose Farouk might convince the people I approach to act as a conduit to American intelligence."

"Who are you talking about, Viktor?" Rozovsky asked.

"Swedish military intelligence."

Rozovsky and Leonov both showed surprise.

"How does that insulate us?" Rozovsky asked.

"I pass the information to the Swedes. More specifically Swedish military intelligence known as *T-kontoret*. Translates as the T-office. They pass it on to the CIA as originating from them. I already laid the groundwork."

"I thought Sweden remained politically neutral," Rozovsky said. Neiman shrugged. "Officially they are. However, they also see the Soviet Union as a threat. We know little about their intelligence capabilities yet the CIA tried to pressure them to come under American control several years ago. You can imagine that did not sit well with Sweden."

"Why should they act as a conduit for our information?" Rozovsky asked.

"Because it will force the American intelligence to reciprocate in order to continue the flow of intelligence from the Swedes. Everyone wins. Your information finds its way to American intelligence. Your network remains disguised as a Swedish espionage penetration while remaining hidden from Soviet intelligence. I act as the cutout between your intelligence gathering and the Swedes who believe it comes through U.S. State Department sources."

"Are you sticking your neck out by doing this, Viktor?"

"Not really, Yuri. I am hiding nothing from American intelligence except the source. My superiors know what I am doing. The precautions certainly excusable since either the Soviets have a highly placed mole within the CIA or our cousins in London. American diplomats do not see intelligence traffic. Within the State Department, only my INR branch has access. Our analytical product is annotated with the underlying source detail having a very limited distribution."

Neiman added a caveat. "Knowledge of Swedish involvement must remain only among us. Mishnyov need only know his material reaches American intelligence. I leave that to you to construct a plausible explanation, Colonel."

"Yes, of course. I will give him the camera and film at our next meeting. The same hotel. That only leaves telling him how he can pass the material in the future."

"Other than your meeting in the hotel, the only time Mishnyov is not under direct surveillance is in the airport before passing through passport control," Inga said as if thinking out loud. "That seems the only secure opportunity for him to pass the undeveloped film. If we can create a place of concealment at Orly's international terminal arrivals section, then he simply calls you with a prearranged signal. Where to hide the small package and how to retrieve it requires some inventive work."

"Do his trips always take him to Paris, Colonel?" Neiman said.

"Usually. Almost always Paris and London," Leonov replied.

"Do you have anyone within your group that works at Orly, Yuri?" Neiman asked.

"No."

Yuri said, "So the problem is inserting someone into the airport on a permanent basis. A regular employee with access to the international terminal. Housekeeping staff, maintenance, or security. Must be readily available on short notice to retrieve Mishnyov's package. Mishnyov's arrival could be any time of day with no advance warning."

Neiman said. "What if we send someone with an outbound flight to retrieve Mishnyov's delivery the next day?"

Inga said, "Either way that means the box must be well-concealed to survive for a long period before recovering the contents."

"How big is a roll of film?" Leonov said.

"Two small spools bridged together in cassette, perhaps the size of your thumb to the first joint," Neiman replied.

Leonov said, "The idea of a maintenance employee gives me another idea. What if the drop box is a fake electrical outlet box? Located near other functioning outlets. To the casual observer just a normal appearing part of the environment."

"Yes," Inga said embracing the idea. "We construct the box with a hidden release to open the cover. Screwed into place it appears unremarkable as just part of the environment."

Neiman nodded. "Very good. You were born to this work, Colonel. Sounds like a sound plan unless we think of something better. We can possibly duplicate some variation of this in London or anywhere Mishnyov travels regularly. Now we need to figure out how to implement this at Orly Airport. Time is urgent. Mishnyov's face-to-face meeting with Colonel Leonov needs to be the last."

Rozovsky said, "Oleg and I will get working on it right away. Constructing a fake electrical outlet box should be possible. A member of our network group owns a machine tool business. Installing our own person inside the airport will take some doing."

Leonov said. "It must be someone we trust without qualification. He or she will know this involves spying. Vladimir Mishnyov's life is at stake. Also the lives of what remains of my family in Russia."

Chapter 12

Moscow | May 1952

Nicolai Baranovsky was among several speakers at the International Economic Conference held in Moscow the first week of April. A full professor of economics at Moscow State University at the age of thirty-two, Baranovsky already enjoyed an international reputation. His expertise was market economic principles. An unusual area of academic study for someone in a communist economy. His popularity in Soviet academic and government circles seemed inexplicable.

Baranovsky navigated this apparent incompatible subject with Soviet communist command economic policy by specializing in the field of simultaneously occurring factors impacting market-based economies. As a mathematician, the subject of his PhD thesis mathematically explored how continually changing individual factors acted to affect economic conditions. He created complex models illustrating how unintended consequences and varying rates of change of different factors created dynamic systems beyond the ability for governmental intervention to control.

While explained in the context of democratic market economies, his models applied equally to totalitarian regimes. Baranovsky however focused exclusively on western democratic economic histories as the basis for explaining negative economic swings using his models. To the Soviet leadership he therefore appeared as a critic of western market economic policy. Economists in the West viewed him not as a critic but as a brilliant technocrat with useful insights into universal economic activity.

When pressured for comment about his views on decades of economic struggle by the Soviet Union, Baranovsky became adept at obfuscation. He developed arguments found acceptable to the Soviet leadership. The extraordinary factors of the 20th century fell outside the ability to study Soviet economic policy using his mathematical models. Russia missed the industrial revolution after suffering under an archaic absolute monarchy for hundreds of years. WWI caused a devastating loss of Russian life resulting in revolution followed by years of civil war. Within twenty years, the newly created Soviet Union experienced economic damage caused by a staggering 24 million military and civilian deaths from WWII. Given these historical extremes compressed into the first half of the 20th century, makes it impossible to evaluate Soviet economic policy in comparative terms.

Such well-crafted evasions allowed Baranovsky to hide his disdain for Soviet society while working in plain sight. His academic standing in the international economic community made him a favorite speaker abroad. Carefully evading political comments, he crafted a technical reputation the Soviet leadership chose to view as criticism for failures of western economic policy. The inability to meet the needs of the proletariat. Policies designed to enrich the bourgeoisie at the expense of the proletariat according to Marxist doctrine.

Baranovsky's stature allowed him to travel internationally, without his wife of course. Soviet fear of defection did not extend trust that far.

The tone of the economic conference appeared intended to reveal a major shift in Soviet Cold War foreign policy. Many foreign economists attended. Representatives from Soviet Bloc countries presented studies encompassing volume projections of potential East-West trade attainable in the next few years. The caveat rested on the removal of Western artificial trade barriers. Western economists saw it as a not very subtle way of expanding trade on Soviet terms. Nonetheless, it represented a fundamental shift in Stalin's Cold War trade policies.

Not lost on western economists was the success of the Marshall that recently concluded bringing aid to Western Europe. During its four years of assistance, European countries outside the Soviet Bloc saw industrial output return to well above 1948 levels. The economic stimulus of the Marshall Plan now fueled continuing economic gains. The Soviet Union and the Eastern Bloc countries under Soviet influence still struggled with recovery from the devastation of WWII. Stimulating trade with the West could improve the lagging Soviet economy.

The conference occurred at a time when East-West military tensions showed no signs of easing. The conflict in Korea remained stalemated after two years of war while negotiations continuing with little progress. A Soviet gesture toward improved trade appeared out of geopolitical context.

However, the opportunity allowed Baranovsky to address western economists directly. He delivered a captivating speech outlining the economic benefits for both East and West of increased trade while pointing out the facilitating process inherently would reduce political tensions. He made no reference for Soviet demands to remove security-related western barriers. Although deeply anti-Soviet, Baranovsky genuinely believed economic engagement could be the first step in détente with the West.

However, the Soviet clumsy approach made relaxing trade restrictions unlikely with no resolution to the Korean conflict. Baranovsky's secret correspondence with his friend Dimitri Galyorkin locked inside the closed city of Arzamas-16 working on a new generation of nuclear weapons was a truer expression of increasing international tensions. The West must undoubtedly know of Soviets efforts to expand their nuclear weapons arsenal. The increasing threat of another world war between the United States and the Soviet Union overshadowed all international relations.

* * *

Vladimir Mishnyov showed up at Nikolai Baranovsky's office at Moscow State University after calling the previous day suggesting they have lunch. With their wives close sisters, they saw each other often, however this was somewhat unusual. The excuse was Mishnyov's need for advice on a personal matter. Purposely vague, both understood no one discussed confidential matters over the telephone. Especially someone in a sensitive position in the foreign ministry.

It was May and the weather turned warm with a clear sunny day. As they left the university building, Mishnyov turned to Baranovsky, "I do need to speak with you, but not at a restaurant, Nikolai. What I must discuss is best done away from someone possibility overhearing. We can walk about the botanical garden. Perfectly natural on this fine spring day."

Baranovsky's responded with an expression of concern on his face. Letting out a deep sigh, "That sounds ominous. What is it, Vladimir?"

"We talk frankly about our disgust over life in repressive Soviet society. For you and me, doubly distressing since we see what life is like in the West. Every trip to Western Europe I return depressed. As I have described, even abroad I am under surveillance by the state security apparatus." Mishnyov stopped walking. "I decided I must do something. Something frightening. Difficult to explain, but it nonetheless provides a feeling of satisfaction. Taking back control over my life."

"Vladimir, you are scaring the hell out of me? What have you done?"

"I approached someone in Paris. Family. Someone I can trust."

As Mishnyov paused searching for the right words, Baranovsky interrupted. "Trust to do what?"

"Pass the secret diplomatic material I deliver to our embassies to the Americans."

The shock evident on Baranovsky's face. Shaking his head, "You cannot do that, Vladimir. It is far too dangerous."

"I already started. I am sick of living like this. Look at us. Talking out here because it is not safe inside. We get together with you and Natasha usually at your place because Dasha and I cannot trust that state security has not bugged our apartment because of our sensitive government positions. Say something against the government means risking a knock on your door in the middle of the night. Interrogation. If serious enough, you end up in Siberia for doing nothing more than privately speaking your mind."

"What you are talking about is more serious. Spies are shot, my friend."

"Who is this person in Paris?"

"Dasha and Natasha's Uncle Oleg."

Baranovsky knew of Oleg Leonov. A legend in his wife's family. A White Russian with a colorful military background.

"I thought you said you passed the information to the Americans. Oleg Leonov is a French Army officer."

"He believes he can pass my information to the Americans. I only met with him once. At my next meeting he will explain more details."

"Then you have not yet begun this dangerous venture?"

"I have. To convince Uncle Oleg and the Americans, I handed over something very secret. Something hopefully to convince the Americans I am not a Soviet double agent."

"Does Dasha know what you are doing?"

Mishnyov nodded. "It was actually her idea."

"What about Natasha? Do I tell her?"

"You can tell her. She has a right to know what her sister is getting into. Dasha agrees. I wanted to tell you first. Natasha has the same disgust for the repressive measures we live under in Russia. Not certain how she will view this kind of direct dissent. For that matter, I do not expect you to agree, Nikolai. But our friendship compels both Dasha and I to tell you. We understand the risks."

Only eighteen months different in age, Dasha and Natasha were exceptionally close. They grew up as best friends as if twins. Dasha's seven-year old daughter Mara treated her aunt as a second mother. Natasha was more sensitive and less confident than Dasha.

Baranovsky said, "I believe it best to withhold telling Natasha. Not sure she could handle the anxiety well. Tell Dasha to say nothing to her."

Because of their close association, Vladimir and Dasha's action also put him and Natasha at risk. Since Mishnyov already made the move, there was nothing Baranovsky could do to change the circumstances.

Baranovsky nonetheless respected Vladimir and Dasha's bold commitment. Sharing their same disgust of living under the thumb of the oppressive dictatorship of Joseph Stalin, he often fantasized about defecting to the West. Those feelings became overpowering during trips abroad. The problem was getting Natasha out of the country. Even if there were a way for both to defect, his parents and his two siblings would undoubtedly suffer retaliation by the government. His connection to Vladimir Mishnyov would destroy their careers. His mother-in-law also caught up in the fallout. His high-profile defection might even send Dimitri Galyorkin to the Siberian Gulag. Their encrypted correspondence might not stand up to intense decryption efforts or the secret police simply declare it was a complex cipher.

Those previous musings now harbored very real concerns for all of them. If discovered, Vladimir's spying was far worse than the defection of an economist. Everyone now close to Vladimir would suffer in the collective purge. No one would escape sentencing to Siberian forced labor camps. Rationalized from that prospective with Vladimir inadvertently putting those around him at risk, caused Baranovsky to revise his own thoughts about defection.

* * *

It was Oleg Leonov that solved the problem of inserting someone into Orly Airport. "Boris Antonovich's son might be a possibility, Yuri. Boris and I talk often about our experiences in the Russian Civil War. I know his son Grigori. He recently completed his trade apprenticeship and is now a journeyman electrician. I believe he works in maintenance somewhere."

Boris Antonovich was a key figure in Rozovsky's network. A staunch White Russian, he still had contacts in Russia that periodically smuggled out material. Running an importing business of Eastern European liquor and packaged food provided the ability of secreting information concealed within the shipments.

"No question about Boris' commitment. I do not know the son though," Yuri said. "This assignment becomes more sensitive than for anyone in our group, Oleg. Mishnyov and your niece's life are at stake."

"I cannot say I know Grigori that well."

Rozovsky said, "I will speak with Boris. His son sounds right for the job. He will of course know this is about spying. We must be sure of his commitment to observe absolute secrecy."

To vet Grigori Antonovich for this delicate work, Rozovsky had no choice but to share with his father Boris what this was about. For the elder Antonovich it was an honor that he and his son could take a greater role in subverting Stalin.

Although active in the Russian expatriate community because of his father's stature, Grigori Antonovich was not an active participant in Rozovsky's network. He did however know that his father secretly received letters from extended family in Russia. Conditions under Soviet rule were a constant source of anguish and hatred toward Stalin for those living in Paris with connections to Russia.

Meeting with Boris and Grigori privately Rozovsky said, "I have discussed something of great importance with your father. Something that must remain secret. It is no exaggeration that lives are at stake. Your father believes you may wish to offer your services. Before I explain what this is about, I must ask for your solemn word to never divulge what you are doing to anyone, even if you choose not to participate."

Surprised, Grigori Antonovich looked first to his father who nodded approvingly. "Yes, Sir. Since my father thinks this is important, I will do what I can to help. I swear not to repeat whatever you tell me to anyone."

"Thank you, Grigori. What are your feelings toward Russia?"

"It is my heritage. I am Russian."

"Do you share your father's feelings toward the Soviets and Stalin?"

He vigorously nodded. "Papa receives letters from Moscow. Smuggled letters because communication outside Russia is subject to censorship. We still have family there. I feel badly for them. Months ago we learned the secret police arrested a cousin my same age. They do not know why or what happened to him. Asking too many questions might also bring trouble down on their heads.

"I hate everything about the Soviet Union. Stalin is an old man. I hope he dies soon. Preferably by a bullet to the head. What is it you want me to do?"

Sufficiently convinced after talking to Grigori Antonovich, Rozovsky said, "I want you to be the courier for smuggling secret information out of Russia. Something entirely different from the smuggled information you father receives in shipments from Moscow. Someone is risking his life to bring out information damaging to the Soviet Union. We need you to pick up that information at Orly Airport without being seen."

"Sounds easy enough."

"Not quite that simple," Rozovsky said. "The person bringing the information periodically disembarks a foreign flight. He must deposit the information in a certain hidden location before entering through passport control. He cannot trust that once beyond passport control that Soviet security might be watching him. Your job is to retrieve the information hidden in a special place. To do that you must always have access to the international terminal.

"You are an electrician. It requires getting a job in airport facilities maintenance. When there is a delivery you are to retrieve it by the following day."

"How will it be hidden?"

"I will explain that later. Are you willing to change jobs?"

Grigori nodded. "Yes, if I can help you and Papa. What happens to this information? How does it become useful?"

"You are not doing anything illegal under French law. You are smuggling information, not contraband. You will become part of an elite espionage system spying on the Soviets. The information eventually finds its way to American intelligence."

Rozovsky chose to be candid rather than allow for Grigori to speculate. "Communism and democracy divide the world today. The United States and the Soviet Union emerged from World War Two as the most powerful nations. Now locked as enemies in this Cold War. There is no middle ground. No neutrality. You have chosen to join your father and me along with others to work against the Soviet Union. Welcome to our conspiracy against Stalin, Grigori."

Rozovsky would work his many contacts to help in securing the position for Grigori Antonovich at Orly Airport.

* * *

Once Leonov suggested an electrical outlet box as the drop, Rozovsky enlisted Inga Jansons to accompany him on a reconnaissance to Orly Airport. They needed a photograph to duplicate the outlet box exactly. Not only Jansons' specialty but she also managed dead drops during the Nazi occupation.

Jansons and Rozovsky needed to observe the secure area for disembarking international passengers. To do so they booked a flight to London allowing them to examine any opportunities for a dead drop at London's Heathrow Airport. Turning around to take a return flight to Paris, they took their time walking the segregated passageway funneling disembarking international passengers to pass through passport control.

Oleg Leonov's suggestion of a fake electrical outlet box was brilliant. Along the wall of the passageway near the floor was a line of several externally spaced outlets along a wall. Somewhat exposed, but if Mishnyov bent down shielding the view from others walking behind him, he could deposit the film inside in a couple of seconds.

"There Yuri. See the outlets along that wall. That is where we install our drop box. Substitute for one of the live boxes. When it does not work for powering the floor polishers, they just plug into another outlet."

With Rozovsky shielding her from view, Jansons surreptitiously snapped several close up photos with the Minox camera purchased for Mishnyov. The developed enlargements would provide the craftsman every detail including the manufacturer's logo to construct a fake duplicate.

A week later in his office at the Sorbonne, Rozovsky picked up the metal box that arrived earlier that day from Oleg's friend at the machine tool company. Obviously intended to hide something disguised as a normal object, his friend never asked any questions.

Rozovsky was specific with the specifications. The appearance meant to appear as a common electrical outlet box. The type used for external mounting. Mounted with the conduit containing disconnected power with a receptacle on the cover. The unique feature was the ability to quickly open and close the cover with a concealed internal spring hinge. The door must release quickly without the mechanism being obvious or subject to accidental opening. Rozovsky left the details to the technical skills of his friend.

Rozovsky opened and closed the cover repeatedly marveling over the ingenuity of the design. A completely normal looking electrical receptacle box. Any attempted use by plugging in an electrical cord will simply appear as something wrong with the circuit. The cover-mounting screws were dummies. One screw acted as a release button. Depressing it released the spring-loaded hinged cover.

Things were coming together. His committed group of Russian expatriates might accomplish something official Western intelligence agencies failed to achieve according to Viktor Neiman. Specifically a highly placed spy with direct access to sensitive material from within the Soviet Foreign Ministry. If Neiman could convince Swedish military intelligence to act as the source, they were in business. An extra layer of security also provided for the other sources of his loosely assembled network in Russia. If his efforts proved successful, the network could proceed without outside interference.

Chapter 13

Paris & Stockholm | June 1952

Two nights after receiving a call from Vladimir Mishnyov, Oleg Leonov arrived at the same hotel used before. After spending an hour at the bar, he visited the toilet to retrieve Mishnyov's room number. Avoiding the des
]k clerk, he took the service elevator and entered Mishnyov's room without knocking.

Before either said anything, Mishnyov turned the radio to a music station and increased the volume. The usual precaution against any imbedded listening devices.

After embracing, Leonov said, "You made quite an impression on my associates. The information on the American-backed coup d'état to replace Farouk in Egypt convinced the Americans you were probably not a Soviet double agent. Not that Egypt is that important but the information suggests Moscow has penetrated American intelligence. Do you have any knowledge about that?"

Mishnyov shook his head. "No. Such things are not shared with Soviet diplomats. Perhaps not a penetration of the CIA but possibly British MI6. The Americans and British are very closely allied. Look at this. It describes where the British intend to conduct their first nuclear bomb test."

TOP SECRET AMBASSODOR EYES ONLY

From: Andréy Vyshinskiy, Foreign Minister USSR

To: Soviet Union ambassadors to United Kingdom and France

Subject: Western Powers nuclear weapons aggression

The British intend to detonate their first nuclear bomb test before the end of the year. Sources report the test location will be the Montebello Islands off the west coast of Australia. The weapon will be a plutonium device the same as first tested by the United States and that dropped on Nagasaki, Japan in 1945.

The United States Strategic Air Command completed construction of Nouasseur Air Base near Casablanca, French Morocco. Sources report the first contingent of U.S. B-36 bombers and possibly their newest turbojet B-47 long-range bombers will begin arriving soon. From this location, these aircraft have the capability of striking Moscow without refueling.

The importance of this information is to prepare your positions toward the British and French governments. That position is to denounce publically these threatening actions by the West once these events materialize. Such overtly aggressive actions unnecessarily increase international tensions. The stance of the Soviet Union to maintain a buffer zone of conquered territory from the Axis powers in WWII is therefore justified by the combined threat of the Western powers to isolate the Soviet Union by nuclear threat.

Leonov said, "I see what you mean. If we assume western intelligence contains Soviet spies, you must be cautious to pass along only information that is known to a wide range of people so suspicion does not fall on you."

"What about the camera? There are other documents of interest."

Leonov reached inside his suit jacket and extracted the tiny Minox model III camera. Handing it to Mishnyov, he removed several film cassettes from another pocket. "This camera is capable of photographing documents from a close distance. All you need is decent lighting."

Leonov took the camera and showed Mishnyov the shutter and how to advance the film. "These are the film cassettes. Load them like this." After loading the camera, Leonov handed it back to Mishnyov. "Thirty-six exposures to each cassette. Each advance loads a new exposure. The film does not use sprockets so you can quickly take many exposures."

"Excellent," Mishnyov said.

Leonov said with an expression of concern. 'You realize possessing this camera brands you as a spy. If searched when you return to Moscow, it is a death sentence."

Mishnyov nodded. "I know that. Been returning countless times going back to the war years and never searched yet. I have a false bottom in my briefcase where I hide these hand-written transcripts. The camera will fit inside there. Good enough to pass a basic search short of dismantling the briefcase."

"Very well. Now to the method for passing along the film. Take a look at these photos. These are close ups of a fake electrical outlet box. Constructed to look identical to actual electrical boxes at Orly Airport. Opens by pressing one of the screws that acts as a release button. The hinged cover opens with enough space inside to hide several film cassettes. Just close the lid and it snaps shut.

"These photos show the location of your drop box. The second from left as circled. Located on this stretch of wall where all international passengers pass by before arriving at passport control. The box is near the floor. Bend down as if tying your shoes shielding the box from view. You can make the exchange in seconds. New unexposed film will always be there when you make a drop."

"Very ingenious. Have you already made contact with American intelligence, Uncle Oleg?"

"Yes. Through a close friend of mine. Also an expatriate who fled Russia with his family during the Civil War. My friend was a leader in the French Resistance during WWII. That is where he met someone now connected with American intelligence."

"Is this friend in French intelligence?"

"No. He is a professor of economics at the Sorbonne. A Russian. A White Russian like me. His name is Yuri Rozovsky."

"How do you know my material is getting to the Americans?"

"Because I have met Yuri's American friend. I cannot reveal his name but he works for American intelligence."

"Good. If you are convinced then I am satisfied my information is reaching the right people,"

"I will make certain that other precautions are set in place. This espionage business is complicated. Many people involved. Both sides running spies. The material you already provided shows the Soviets have sources within western intelligence agencies. Different intelligence services also compete, sometimes even within the same country. The Soviet Union has the Ministry for State Security that keeps close watch over your movements when abroad. Then there is the *Glavnoye Razvedyvatelnoye Upravlenie*, the GRU, representing military intelligence that competes with the MGB. The Americans have several intelligence services which also do not always work in the collective interest of their country."

"Why is this important in my situation, Uncle Oleg?"

"Because it is important for maintaining your security. The American intelligence service responsible for running spies is the Central Intelligence Agency. My friend's contact is with a different agency. If he goes directly to the American CIA, he fears they will take over controlling you. Too many people will know about you. Right now, only a few people know that you exist. The American wants to keep it way. He already assigned you a code name. When passing along any of your information, it is identified as coming from Hermes."

"I do not understand. How does Rozovsky's American friend intend to pass along this secret material to American decision makers?"

"He plans on secretly enlisting an allied intelligence service of another country. I promised to keep the name confidential. It is difficult to explain why the necessity for the smoke and mirrors, but it allows your information to reach the Americans at the highest level while insulating you for added security. Trust me on this, Vladimir. We are as committed as you to fighting against Stalin and avoiding another world war."

"Very good, Uncle Oleg. I do trust you. I will miss these visits with you. Dasha sends her love. Your sister is well. She knows nothing of what we are doing."

Leonov nodded. "Best to keep it that way. One more thing. Here is a telephone number. When you have a delivery, call this number. Someone will answer as *bureau récepteur* 24-hours a day every day. Say only, *I rang the wrong number.* The reply, *understood* confirms receipt of your message. That means you will deposit a delivery sometime within the next twenty-four hours. Those answering the phone have no idea what this is about."

Mishnyov nodded and sighed. "I guess this is the last time we will be meeting. Goodbye, Uncle Oleg. Thank you for everything you are doing."

Leonov's eyes teared as he embraced Mishnyov. Having witnessed all manner of courage in war, his niece's husband was risking a fate possibly worse than death on a battlefield.

* * *

Viktor Neiman arrived in Stockholm this time circumventing announcing his arrival to the American embassy. No need to encourage speculation among the staff why he was again in the city again meeting with Swedish military intelligence. Immersed in this clandestine operation acting beyond the portfolio of his position made him oversensitive. Hiding information from other American intelligence services left an uncomfortable feeling. Yet once again operating in the field, he reverted to wartime trade-craft.

His welcome by Konstantin Lindström, Swedish deputy director of T-kontoret, was particularly cordial. "Good to see you again, Mr. Neiman. I have some interesting news to share with you."

"Excellent. I requested this meeting because I have some interesting information to share with you also, Colonel."

"Then this should prove productive for both of us. Let me start off by saying that your offer of sharing American intelligence gathered on the Soviets in exchange for claiming it is our intelligence product is a bargain we cannot refuse. That is a direct quote from Director Palm. Your cooperation proposal met with enthusiastic approval from the Prime Minister and the Foreign Minister. For security, we are limiting knowledge of the arrangement to just that small group."

"Thank you, Colonel. Hoping that to be the case, I came prepared to demonstrate the value of our joint cooperation by sharing some recently acquired sensitive information."

Neiman handed Lindström an envelope. "This is from a new source code named Hermes. A walk-in source. We have vetted him. He is genuine. This is his first offering. Typed transcripts of his hand-written copies of Soviet diplomatic traffic to their West European embassies."

After reading Mishnyov's material, Lindström, said, "Enlightening. It reveals a serious Soviet penetration of American and British intelligence services."

"One of the reasons we believe Hermes is genuine not a Soviet double agent. The substance of the documents is accurate. Not likely the Soviets would reveal such important penetration to their ambassadors simply for the purpose of inserting Hermes as a double agent.

"There is something else Hermes represents. Perhaps the best-placed Soviet espionage source we have. Obviously, he is a Soviet Foreign Service officer. He approached us through our diplomatic channels. Because of my position, I was the first informed. For various reasons my superiors in the U.S. State Department agreed with my recommendation to retain control of Hermes rather than hand him off to our Central Intelligence Agency. All the more reason given evidence of Soviet penetration. Therefore, this new arrangement with T-kontoret provides the perfect mechanism to insulate Hermes with both me and your organization acting as cutouts, Colonel."

Lindström raised an eyebrow. "Not sure I understand what you mean, Mr. Neiman."

Neiman smiled. "Hermes becomes a source developed by Swedish intelligence. I become the conduit passing the product of Hermes deliveries directly to T-kontoret. You in turn ostensibly pass it back to me. My superiors at the State Department in Washington pass it to CIA. The cover reason portrayed as Swedish demands to keep this in the realm of foreign relations rather than intelligence service channels. Everyone benefits. The information gets to Western intelligence. Hermes remains concealed under a new layer of security. Sweden benefits by becoming a full partner in jointly sharing intelligence with the Americans."

Lindström smiled. "An amazing scheme of duplicity, Mr. Neiman. Portrayed as a Swedish intelligence operation, your State Department avoids the inter-departmental warfare for circumventing your government's protocols. How high does your authorization for this subterfuge go?"

"Secretary of State Acheson personally authorized my overtures to Swedish intelligence. He also has the President's ear."

Neiman chose not to disclose that Hermes and Rozovsky's unofficial espionage network remained unknown to Acheson or even Neiman's direct superior, the head of INR.

Lindström continued, "Yet this is an election year in the United States. If a new president comes into office, will there not be a new secretary of state? What happens then?"

"I will deal with that later. Once in place and delivering high-grade intelligence a new secretary of state will be disinclined to change what is working well. Besides, this is a Swedish operation. I trust your foreign minister shall make a forceful case."

Lindström nodded with a smile. "A pleasure conspiring with you, Mr. Neiman. How do you propose to deliver information to us?"

"Have not yet given that serious thought. I want to keep my involvement under the radar. The less people that can connect me to Swedish intelligence the better. Any suggestions?"

"Perhaps. Your background indicates you are accomplished in fencing. Going back before the war. You rejoined your former fencing club Salle d'Armes Coudurier at 6 Rue Gît-le-Cœur when you returned to Paris. My information states you are very proficient."

"Sufficiently accomplished to give a good account of myself. You are well informed, Colonel."

"Considering your unusual proposal, we made a most thorough examination of your background and habits. Even your marriage to a photographer and former member of the French Resistance. Is there a story behind that?"

Neiman smiled. "Oh yes. I will share that with you later over a drink."

"I will enjoy that. To your question, we discovered your enthusiasm for fencing led me to a solution of how to exchange information regularly without raising suspicion. Our resident agent in Paris works under the cover of trade secretary at our Paris Embassy. Obviously speaks French fluently. He is a former Olympic medal winner in fencing. Los Angeles in 1932 and Berlin in 1936. He is about your age. I do not know if he is still active in fencing, but perhaps he could reacquaint with the sport."

"What type of fencing?"

"Type?"

"There are different fencing weapons. Foil, épée, and sabre. Each uses different techniques"

"Sabre I believe recalling his file. Does it matter?"

"Not really. However, since I also fence sabre that makes it natural to strike up a personal relationship. Allows us to meet regularly without attracting attention."

"My agent's name is Sven Norberg. Here is his photo."

Neiman looked at the photo thinking for a moment. "When he is ready to meet at Salle d'Armes Coudurier, have him call or leave a message at my office in the U.S. Embassy. Use the code name *Monsieur Sabreur*. In English, Mr. Swordsman. Specifically a sabre swordsman."

"Now that those particulars are settled, how do you wish me to pass along this material to the Central Intelligence Agency?" Lindström asked.

"No need. We provided Hermes with a Minox camera to photograph original documents. I will pass on the undeveloped film to Norberg. You simply develop the film and provide me copies. I will forward to Washington in the diplomatic pouch. Hermes becomes a Swedish source. You will actually see the material before I do. The CIA receives the information from the U.S. State Department in Washington.

"This preserves the arrangement of the source remaining under State Department control. Washington will immediately forward the material to CIA headquarters. In turn, the CIA will likely share the information with the British. Perhaps edited versions also shared with other allied intelligence services like France, Belgium, the Netherlands, Denmark, and Norway.

"The CIA will probably protest directly to your foreign ministry. I need your government to hold firm to the fabrication this is a Swedish operation. Follow the script that Sweden needs to preserve the appearance of political nonalignment as much as possible by keeping this in the realm of foreign relations. It is Sweden that contacted the U.S. State Department and holds firm to sharing the intelligence channeled in this manner."

* * *

The Rozovsky group gathered immediately after Neiman returned from Stockholm.

"Swedish military intelligence is onboard," Neiman said. "Too good a deal for them to pass up. They also bought into my reasoning to use me as the conduit. I give them Mishnyov's undeveloped film and they return developed photo enlargements which I send to Washington."

"How do you pass the information to the Swedes?" Leonov asked.

"To a Swedish intelligence agent in Paris."

"Where do they believe Mishnyov originates from?" Rozovsky asked.

"A walk-in. Someone obviously within the Foreign Ministry by the nature of the intelligence."

Rozovsky said, "Excellent. Mishnyov has photos of the drop box and its location taken by Inga. Oleg passed along the instructions for notifying his next arrival. No more meetings with Oleg."

"What about recruiting someone with access at Orly to retrieve the material?" Neiman asked.

"Soon to be in place. A young man, an electrician. Oleg and I both are acquainted with the man's father. A fellow White Russian from the time of the Russian Civil War. Already involved with receiving smuggled material from Moscow.

"The electrician agreed to leave his current job and seek a position with Orly facilities maintenance. That has not yet happened but we are confident of his acceptance. One of our associates has a close friend with a brother in the Orly Airport personnel department. Our fellow already submitted an application and passed an initial interview. If selected, he must go through a background check and pass another interview with the hiring manager. We expect him to be in place at the airport very soon and install the fake electrical outlet box."

* * *

Returning to Moscow, Mishnyov now had a miniature Minox camera and several film cassettes concealed in the false bottom of his briefcase. He realized exhibiting any sense of unease would invite an inspection. His diplomatic passport meant nothing to the MGB. The hidden bottom of the briefcase would not stand up to a determined search. If he intended to traffic in espionage, he must find the emotional discipline to compart-mentalize his fear.

To do that he focused on exhibiting a calm demeanor of de-tachment. A touch of arrogance emphasizing his role of handling sensitive information as evidenced by the small aluminum atta-ché cast handcuffed to his wrist.

The following day he strolled with Nikolai Baranovsky in the botanical garden near to Moscow State University. He was anx-ious to share details of the trip with his close friend Nikolai Bar-anovsky.

"I have fully taken the plunge, Nikolai. Look at this?"

Shielded from view although few other people were walking in their proximity, he showed Baranovsky the small Minox cam-era in the palm of his hand while they stood close together.

"I will photograph the documents in my office and deposit the undeveloped film in a drop location disguised as an electri-cal box after I disembark my plane at Paris. Before passing through passport control and before security from our embassy puts me under constant surveillance."

Baranovsky realized how far his friend's dangerous inten-tions had advanced. Uncle Oleg apparently did have access to American intelligence. Vladimir was now a committed spy. An exciting but frightening thought. Should the MGB discover Mishnyov's activities, Baranovsky and his wife could also find themselves in dire circumstances with state security.

With their wives as sisters, Baranovsky's frequents trips abroad would provoke serious security concerns. Difficult to contemplate Dasha Mishnyov enduring intense interrogations. Perhaps physical abuse. Everyone knew the reputation of what went on in the Lubyanka. The secret police always assumed con-spiracy. If they could not uncover the involvement of others, the MGB would manufacture a conspiracy.

Mishnyov's venture into espionage decidedly curtailed thoughts of Baranovsky's defection as his means of rebelling against Soviet oppression. Defecting now would compromise Mishnyov, his wife, his daughter, and their mother-in-law as the secret police sought to purge everyone closely connected to them. He and Natasha might escape to a new life in the West but at the cost of destroying so many lives. That included abandoning Dimitri Galyorkin. Essentially imprisoned in a closed city working on a super bomb. Increasingly despondent, he remained his friend's lifeline in preserving his deteriorating mental state of mind through their clandestine encrypted correspondence. Nikolai Baranovsky understood he must stay the present course.

Chapter 14

Sarov (Arzamas-16), Russia | July 1952

The ancient city of Sarov was a holy place of the Russian Orthodox Church noted as the home of the 17th century Saint Seraphim. Located 400 kilometers east of Moscow, the government removed all but essential citizens and renamed the city Arzamas-16 in 1947. It became home to the All-Soviet Scientific Research Institute of Experimental Physics, abbreviated VNIIEF. Arazmas-16 became the Soviet Union's principal research and development center for nuclear weapons. It also became a closed city. Everyone within worked for the nuclear weapons program or in some supporting capacity. Heavily guarded by state security personnel, there were no visitors allowed other than those authorized on official business. No one assigned to Arzamas-16 left without specific authorization. Sarov/Arazmas-16 was removed from all official maps. A virtual prison for all those relegated to its confines.

Everyone within the nuclear weapons program enjoyed a better quality of the physical comforts of living than elsewhere in Russia. Better food, liquor, clothing, and medical care. Cultural entertainment was however lacking. Opera and theater absent since those required outsiders into the secure environment made the movie theater the only available entertainment venue.

Yet this state-provided generosity could not mask the fact that freedoms of normal life held constraints little different from a prison. Scientific and technical personnel could not choose to resign and leave the program. Security was so intense, everyone assumed the MGB compromised their living quarters with listening devices. Since the Soviet Union successfully penetrated the Manhattan Project and the highest level of the British Foreign Service and Secret Intelligence Service, dictated the necessity for special security arrangements to guard the Soviet Union's most important secrets.

For the majority of scientists and engineers, work consumed their existence. Typically working twelve-hour days six days a week, the restrictions on personal freedom were a small sacrifice. Careers could greatly advance should their collective work achieve Soviet objectives for producing nuclear weapons giving parity to the United States.

Dimitri Galyorkin may have once shared this devotion to his work as part of a team of the most gifted scientific minds in Russia, but that progressively diminished since arriving in Arzamas-16 in March 1951. As a closed city, this isolated backwater hundreds of miles east of Moscow felt unwelcoming from every perspective.

Arriving in the city by bus after the flight from Moscow, the first impression of Arzamas-16 was that of a prison. In large part, it was also a conventional prison. The majority of thousands of construction workers were inmates of Stalin's Gulag of forced labor penal camps. Political prisoners. The construction was never ending. Scientific laboratories, workshops, roads, and housing for employees from scientists to those necessary to support daily living continued unabated since Galyorkin arrived. Every morning, long lines of men marched to work under heavy guard from men on horseback and others holding barking guard dogs.

While Galyorkin was part of the theoretical physics group headed by the brilliant Igor Tamm and the scientific director of the Soviet nuclear weapons program was the respected physicist Igor Kurchatov, Lavrenti Beria welded overall political authority. Everyone attributed the dark aspects of the closed environment, the use of political forced labor prisoners, and the pervasive intrusion of state security into every aspect of life at Arzamas-16 to Beria.

Former head of the NKVD, the predecessor of the MGB, active participant in Stalin's Great Purge, rumored serial rapist, now one of the most powerful figures in Russia, Beria was evil personified. Yet apart from his repulsive image as a human being, Stalin recognized Beria's extraordinary organizational abilities. He did Stalin's bidding with ruthless efficiency. There was no higher priority than development of a nuclear weapons program to rival that of the United States. It received unlimited funding and Lavrenti Beria closely oversaw the program.

After a year locked away behind the security perimeter, Galyorkin's thoughts turned constantly to leaving weapons work and leaving Arzamas-16. For him, the place was not only a prison, but also a place of repressing his growing disillusionment with everything about the Soviet system. His clandestine correspondence with his friend and confident Nikolai Baranovsky became his only means of staving off deepening depression.

* * *

The Soviet Union tested their first nuclear bomb in August 1949. It was a plutonium-based design, the same as the first atomic bomb Trinity detonation by the United States in New Mexico in 1945. The same design as dropped on the Japanese city of Nagasaki. The Soviets had the benefit of detailed design details of the American device provided by the Soviet spy Klaus Fuchs a British scientist working inside the ultra-secret American Manhattan Project as a senior physicist.

The design and other technical information related to the manmade element plutonium greatly accelerated Soviet nuclear weapons development. The fissile component of the first nuclear weapon dropped on Hiroshima, Japan consisted of uranium-235. While the physical principles of the U-235 isotope were well known, it is difficult to produce in significant quantities. Used for the Hiroshima bomb only for the reason the simpler design assured it would perform. The Trinity implosion design successfully detonated from a tower rather than dropped from an aircraft. Concerns of something failing with the far more complex design dictated going with the assured Hiroshima gun-barrel uranium-235 bomb.

U-235 naturally occurs in uranium ore but only in a 0.72 percent concentration. The remainder is U-238 that is not capable of sustaining a nuclear chain reaction. Therefore, uranium ore required *enrichment* to increase the percentage of U-235 to 80% or greater. Enrichment processes are difficult and costly. Eventually the United States produced enough U-235 to assemble a nuclear bomb. The design to achieve critical mass sufficient to release the atomic binding energy was mechanically simple. So straightforward, it became the weapon first used against Japan without prior testing.

Plutonium is produced as a byproduct in a nuclear reactor consisting of both U-238 and U-235. Plutonium offers the advantage of producing a weapon requiring less fissile material that is easier to produce than highly enriched uranium. The complexity arises from the need for a more complex weapon design involving conventional chemical explosives to generate a spherical implosion. The precision mechanical construction and the electrical detonation system were exceedingly challenging to achieve uniform compression of the plutonium core to create a critical mass causing the release of energy through nuclear fission.

The Soviets benefited from espionage-acquired technical information from the Americans and British since known uranium reserves in the Soviet Union were scarce following WWII. Producing plutonium provided a faster developmental process and avoided research efforts already expended by the Americans. Nonetheless, when the United States detonated Trinity, the Soviet nuclear program remained years behind.

By 1949 after the Soviet Union achieved their first successful atomic bomb test, nuclear arms technology began turning toward a new generation of weapons with exponentially greater destructive power. A thermonuclear super weapon theoretically held the possibly of releasing energy through atomic fusion. Fission is the nuclear process of releasing energy by splitting two heavy, unstable atomic nuclei into two lighter nuclei. Fusion is the combining of two light atomic nuclei under enormous temperature to produce the nucleus of a heavier element. This nuclear synthesis releases energy on an exponentially vaster scale than possible through fission alone.

While pursuing their PhDs at the Lebedev Physics Institute in Moscow, known by the acronym FIAN, Dimitri Galyorkin and his friend Andrei Sakharov began working under the direction of Igor Tamm. Appointed head of a theoretical group researching development, Tamm assembled a senior working team of brilliant theoretical physicists then relocating to Arzamas-16. Galyorkin initially felt energized as part of such an elite group working at the cutting edge of his field with the best minds in Russia.

The most outstanding of this group of brilliant physicists was his close friend Andrei Sakharov. Andrei Sakharov advanced a breakthrough idea for creating a super weapon. In 1948, he proposed a design in which alternating layers of deuterium and uranium are placed between the plutonium fissile core and the surrounding chemical high explosive. Called *Sloika*, translated as 'Layer Cake', his design was analogous to the same idea developed independently by American physicist Edward Teller.

Teller was the earliest champion of creating a super bomb utilizing nuclear fusion. While a senior scientist as part of the Manhattan Project, Teller began making calculations as far back as 1942 while the collective efforts of the other scientists focused exclusively on constructing the first nuclear fission bomb. Not as gifted as Igor Tamm and Andrei Sakharov, Teller however was tenacious. Obsessively anti-communist, his singular efforts spurred American development of a super bomb following WWII.

The only method of achieving temperatures in the millions of degrees required for fusion to take place could only occur through nuclear fission. This led to Teller's theoretical idea that deuterium, the heavy isotope of hydrogen, could undergo nuclear fusion if subjected to high enough temperature. Pressures only achievable through nuclear fission. However, further calculations suggested nuclear fission generated pressures in the magnitude of only thousands of atmospheres. Nuclear fusion of deuterium required pressures in the millions of atmospheres. Creating a super weapon utilizing nuclear fusion therefore required a more complex approach.

Sakharov's design was not truly a thermonuclear device but rather an enhanced fission weapon of much greater yield than through fission alone. Sakharov named it the *First Idea* to distinguish it from the *Second Idea* attributed to another scientist on Tamm's team a year later. That approach came closer to a true thermonuclear secondary fusion weapon. That design substituted lithium deuteride for liquid deuterium alone. When bombarded with neutrons through primary nuclear fission, the lithium yields tritium, another isotope of hydrogen. At an achievable pressure, the tritium fuses with the deuterium generating a greater energy release by a secondary fusion process. As an isotope of hydrogen, deuterium became the basis of the second generation of nuclear weapons hence the term hydrogen bomb came into common usage.

By the end of 1948, the Soviet Union had a workable design for a hydrogen bomb. This was before its first test of a plutonium fission bomb of essentially the same design as the United States first atomic bomb tested in New Mexico. Much empirical work however remained to progress through the sequential stages of development.

The year before, Tamm together with Sakharov also proposed a system to realize the potential of controlled thermonuclear fusion as a sustaining energy source using what they termed a toroidal magnetic thermonuclear reactor. The prospects for peaceful use of nuclear fusion-produced energy theoretically unlimited. Being an integral participant of this group of the best creative minds was an invigorating experience for Galyorkin.

However, Stalin postponed any work on nuclear energy application until achieving a nuclear weapons arsenal sufficient to compete with the United States. Arrival in the oppressive environment of Arzamas-16 to work solely on weapons immediately dampened Galyorkin's scientific enthusiasm. Unlike most of his colleagues, his professional work could not compensate for other factors weighing down his thoughts. He enjoyed Sakharov's friendship and their stimulating technical conversations, yet it did not serve his emotional needs. Corresponding with Nikolai Baranovsky allowed him to express his philosophical feelings. Even encumbered by the laborious task of encryption, their special relationship maintained the ability of unrestricted interaction with someone with a shared history of expressing philosophical thoughts. Views considered reactionary by a system of government that removed all individual expression under threat of reprisal.

* * *

Walking back to their office after sharing lunch in the cafeteria with his colleague and friend Andrei Sakharov, Sakharov said. "I must share with you something disturbing I learned today. Ever wonder what happens with all these political prisoners once they serve out their sentences?"

Galyorkin shrugged his shoulders. He and Sakharov arrived in Arzamas only three months earlier. "Not really. I assume they are released."

"Not exactly. I never thought about their fate either but I learned the truth last night. Yakov Zeldovich woke me in the early hours of the morning. He was in a high state of agitation. Asked if I could lend him money. Perhaps you may have noticed his interest in that pretty prisoner Olga Shiryaeva."

"I know the one. Saw her painting the recreation clubhouse."

"Well I believe the sociable Zeldovich has more than a passing interest in her. Tells me Shiryaeva was an artist and architect by profession. Arrested for anti-Soviet slander. Having served her sentence the State will not allow her return to Leningrad. Instead, they are exiling her to Magadan. He wants to give her money. I gave him everything I had. She just learned she is to leave tomorrow."

"Where is Magadan?"

"Zeldovich says Magadan is in Eastern Siberia on the Sea of Okhotsk. It is the administrative center for the forced labor penal camps of the gold and mineral mining operations in the Kolyma Region. An exceedingly cruel fate but logical from the perspective of state security. She knows too much about this place. Knows the names of those of us working here."

"So essentially she remains in the Gulag system." The disgust in Galyorkin's voice obvious. "To be expected with someone like Beria in charge. Does that mean none of us can ever leave this place?"

Sakharov made no reply. Saddened by Zeldovich's distress, he also found Galyorkin's rhetorical question profoundly troubling.

Returning to his room, Galyorkin spent several hours encrypting a letter to Nikolai Baranovsky. His last letter soon after arriving in Arzamas-16 alluded to the dismal observation that this felt like a prison. The circumstances recounted by Sakharov suggested this was in fact a prison. They all were nothing more than a privileged class of inmates.

He began the encrypted letter with nothing to arouse suspicion by MGB censors. The encrypted content disguised in brief comments of discussing a chess game as practiced with Baranovsky over several years. The cipher he and Baranovsky developed employed the memorized shorthand alphabet in Russian and an additional set of mathematical operators to communicate equations. Although Galyorkin became a theoretical physicist and Baranovsky an economist, both are brilliant mathematicians. That shared talent provided a unique bonding by offering a means of communicating an understanding of the fundamentals of their unrelated fields to each other.

The appearance as innocuous communication distinguishes their cipher. Given the repressive police-state environment and Galyorkin's sensitive secret work, everything that passes between them comes under intense scrutiny. To accomplish this they created a cipher based on their shared passion for chess. This provides the appearance of chess-related commentary while providing a two-tiered method for conveying an encrypted message.

The encryption allows using the moves of any documented chess match to represent any shorthand character or mathematical operator. This is accomplished by converting the numerical identified board position for a move to represent any memorized character by its assigned number. That conversion disguises the communication by using three or four-word phases defining encryption sets that convert to a simple table that provides a numerical value. That value converts the board position number of a move to any desired character or mathematical operator.

Practiced over years by two outstanding minds with prodigious memories, their complex construction provided the secrecy of a one-time cipher while hiding in plain sight as something entirely non-political.

Nikolai,

Hope you and Natasha are well. I miss you both. My research work is interesting and important. Perhaps one day I can share more about what I do. My workdays are long. I also miss playing chess with you. Occasionally I can find a competitive game but our schedules often make it difficult to allocate sufficient uninterrupted time. Our discussions of great chess games through correspondence provide a stimulating substitute. Here are my observations of the world championship match round 10 of 8 February 1910 in Berlin between Emanuel Lasker and Carl Schlechter.

1W Classic Slav Defense opening. 2B Black avoids usual E6. Better than c6 played. 6B Defending Queen's Gambit? An original new approach? 8B Questionable move series. Leaves isolated pawn. 14W Avoids playing safe? 15W Behind in match score? Starts attack kingside. 15B Playing Lasker's tempo? Ahead in match score, why not draw? 23B Worked out

*badly. 35B A bad sacrifice. e5 seems better move. Why not
draw? 37W Starts remarkable progression. 47W Moves this
knight, for first time. Lasker displays precision. Schlechter
holds firm. 64B Exchanging queens fatal. Perhaps an oversight? 67W Game is over. 67B Why not resign? 71W A great
game. A remarkable historic struggle.*

The short phrases associated with comments about a chess
match provided the mathematical key to the encrypted content.
The decrypted content reads in the condensed style of a telegram
by removing unnecessary words for economy. Many chess
matches number 40, 50, or more moves. Using both white and
black's moves separately, this creates adequate opportunities for
constructing most messages. A lengthier message could add another match with some relation to the first such as the same
player or a comparison of the same opening giving the appearance of narrative continuity.

This letter continued required progressing to another match.
Another match in 1918 between the same players Lasker and
Schlechter also employing the Queen's Gambit Declined. A laborious task to draft the encryption using appropriate moves to
make it appear coherent if read by a chess-savvy censor.

Decryption was faster by someone well practiced in the process. They used the same reference collection of great matches to
trace the sequence of moves. Memorizing the shorthand characters and mathematical symbols became similar to writing and
reading in another language. For security, they never documented the cipher's construction. All the characters associated by
identifying numbers and the code key multiplier matrix memorized.

The decrypted portion of Galyorkin's letter revealed the dis-
piriting nature of his circumstances since arriving at Arzamas-
16.

*I learned a colleague began romance with female prison-
er. She completed sentence for anti-Soviet slander. State
forbids her return to Leningrad. Knows too much about
this place. Exiled instead to Siberia. Still imprisoned in
the Gulag penal system. I am scientist but no better off.*

Arzamas-16 is just another labor camp. Not working on science to benefit mankind. Instead, developing super bomb. More destructive than first atomic bomb tested in 1949. We work to provide madman Stalin the ability for starting WWIII and destroying mankind.

We understand the physics to create such a weapon. Far more powerful than a fission bomb. Called a hydrogen bomb because it fuses the heavy hydrogen isotopes deuterium ^2H and tritium, ^3H under extreme pressure and temperature forming a nucleus of helium, ^4He, and a neutron while releasing immense energy through the fusion process. Physically creating the bomb remains challenging. The process formula is $^2H+^3H\rightarrow^4He+n+17.59MeV$.

Everything is depressing. How can I rationalize doing such work? You remain my lifeline to sanity dearest friend. Dimitri

Aware of the nature of Galyorkin's work in the Soviet nuclear weapons program for some time, this was the first time Galyorkin provided specific details. This was only the second letter received from his old friend since relocating to Sarov now absorbed into the vast Soviet nuclear program as a closed city with a new name. From Galyorkin's remarks, the term closed city was a bureaucratic euphemism for a special kind of confinement. Galyorkin was already in a poor state of mind before this. Ever since joining the nuclear weapons program they saw little of each other the first year when Galyorkin worked in Moscow. They resumed their regular encrypted correspondence with Baranovsky learning of the extraordinary restrictions.

Now into Galyorkin's fourth year in the nuclear program, Baranovsky could mark his friend's abrupt progression toward depression since relocated to Arazmas-16. The freedom afforded in their clandestine correspondence since theirs days at the university continued to reflect a shared hatred of Soviet restrictions. Since beginning work in the weapons program, Galyorkin's criticisms became more virulent. Undoubtedly, isolation played a part, but his letters reflected his sense of disgust over the nature of his work contributing to his growing malaise.

Baranovsky drafted a letter in response. He chose another match with the Queen's Gambit Declined opening that went 85 moves affording ample opportunity for creating phrases to define encryption characters. There was nothing he could say to ameliorate his friend's darkening views. They were all too real. Baranovsky's trips abroad showed him Russia was on the wrong side of 20th century history. He chose instead to reveal he too had reached a point of taking a more active rebellion.

Dimitri,

I understand your feelings completely. Communism is a failed aberration of socialism. Socialism can exist within democracy but by definition communism is an autocratic system. Marxist philosophy pronounces communism as the dictatorship of the proletariat. Any fool can see that leads to despotism no different from fascism. Stalin is leading Russia to ruin. Russian people still suffer while war-ravaged Western European recovers. Yet Stalin spends on military and declares America as an enemy. Why? Because he is a megalomaniac craving power. He aspires to become a modern day Peter the Great, but rules with the demented brutality of Ivan the Terrible

I think often of taking Natasha and defecting to the West. That is not possible without hurting many people, including you Dimitri. I must dissent by different means. I may have discovered a way to communicate Soviet secrets to the West. Are you interested in participating? Nikolai

Chapter 15

It was Nikolai Baranovsky's turn to invite Mishnyov for a secluded stroll in the botanical garden near to Moscow State University.

Baranovsky said, "Now that you have advanced things so far, there is no turning back, Vladimir. Does Dasha remain just as committed?"

"Yes. Difficult to describe, Nikolai, but rebelling against Soviet oppression gives us a feeling of value. Instead of hopelessly living under fear, rebelling restores a measure of independence. We are individuals exercising our will. Perhaps a small measure of silent dissent, but meaningful to us."

"Hardly small dissent, Vladimir. Although you can never know what it possibly accomplishes, it is a major step at retaliating against the Soviet system. A process by which the State seeks to destroy the individual. I can appreciate your satisfaction in actively resisting. What if I said I was interested in joining you?"

Mishnyov stopped walking. "What do you mean?"

"I mean, what if I gave you confidential information to pass on to the Americans?"

Mishnyov remained silent for a moment wondering what Baranovsky meant. What secrets did he possess that might interest American intelligence?

"What sort of confidential information, Nikolai?"

"You probably wonder what of interest an economics academic might have to offer to the West?"

"That is not what I meant, Nikolai. You must have information of great interest to the West. But is it worth risking your life and Natasha's."

Baranovsky smiled his usual engaging smile and put his arm around Mishnyov's shoulder. "I have come to the same conclusion about doing something. For the same reason this brought you to take such bold action.

"Like you, I feel a pawn living a lie when I secretly revile everything about living under this oppression called the Soviet State. Stalin has twisted an already flawed Marxist socioeconomic system into a totalitarian ideology. From the beginning, it was no different under Lenin. Had Lenin lived longer, the outcome probably the same. Lenin like Stalin craved power. Stalin however is not only evil but quite possibly a madman. He rules as a despot. Like Hitler, he has delusions of empire. A greater Russian empire."

"If you feel that way, why not defect? You travel abroad."

"I am not that trusted, Vladimir. My trips require approval. Expenses paid by the university. Unlike in the West, not an independent institution. Natasha cannot accompany me. More than that, should I defect it would destroy too many other lives. You and your family. Dasha and Natasha's mother-in-law. All of us are too tightly connected. Secret police retaliation would reach everyone around me."

"What information do you have worth risking your life and Natasha's?"

"Information as highly secret as what you handle. Information supplied by someone from my past. Should that person be willing to pass along secrets, I will provide more details at a later time, my friend. I first need to know more about how your material gets to the Americans. Uncle Oleg is a senior officer in the French Army. How does he get the information to the Americans? I do not wish to raise concerns, Vladimir, but how does he know he is dealing with American intelligence?"

"I trust Uncle Oleg. He is genuine. Also someone worldly and not the sort to risk the lives of his sister and nieces without assurances," Mishnyov said forcefully.

"Yes, of course. I should never have raised such a concern. Yet if I am to participate, I need to know more about whom we are dealing with. How did Uncle Oleg say the information gets to the Americans?"

"He said only that he arranged that with a trusted friend. A fellow White Russian living in Paris. A former leader in the French Resistance during the war. His name is Yuri Rozovsky. Like you, a professor of economics. He reconnected with an American intelligence operative he met in occupied Paris during WWII."

Rozovsky's name was vaguely familiar to Baranovsky. Yet the alarmed the scant details Mishnyov possessed while already risking his life was alarming. This seemed too amateur. Everything built around trust. The trust of Uncle Oleg perhaps was understandable but to extend that to trusting someone Mishnyov did not know? Then another unknown connection to someone this Rozovsky claims is an American intelligence operative.

The connection to the French Resistance also raised concerns for Baranovsky. Many of the French Resistance groups were communists. Was Leonov's trusted friend a genuine White Russian or a covert agent of Soviet intelligence? As a French Army officer, was Leonov possibly passing the information to French intelligence rather than the Americans? Everything beyond the Leonov connection needed clarification for Baranovsky.

Both stood silently looking at each other. "What exactly do you want me to do, Nikolai?"

"I need to be sure of the exchange of transferring the information. That is the most dangerous aspect of what you are doing. The more people involved knowing your identity or even enough about you to identify you increases the risk of discovery exponentially.

"I need to make an exploration the same as you did before committing."

"I could convey a message," Mishnyov offered.

Baranovsky shook his head. "No. I want to make an independent arrangement. For your sake as well as mine."

Mishnyov said, "You travel regularly to Western Europe. Are you being watched on these trips?"

"I do not believe so. Perhaps a casual surveillance reporting on my official movements. Still a possibility that I am under less obvious scrutiny. The MGB might simply want to conceal their surveillance. Looking for material for later use as blackmail."

"What about meeting with Uncle Oleg?"

"Way too risky if I am under surveillance. Old NKVD records might identify him as an enemy of the Bolsheviks. I would also prefer to speak directly with the American connection.

"My trips always involve some symposium or academic venue centered on economics. That is the only reason the government allows my travel abroad. What if the Americans arrange a meeting at an upcoming event? Perhaps the European Economics Symposium in London next month? A meeting with this Yuri Rozovsky. On your next trip can you contact Uncle Oleg?"

Mishnyov answered, "I suppose so."

"Very well. Explain my shared depth of anti-Soviet feelings. Request that Yuri Rozovsky meet me in London prepared to speak in specifics about what happens to the information. Particularly how are identities are protected."

Mishnyov said, "What is the reason I give for introducing you into the mix of transferring information to the Americans, Nikolai? I need something to interest them. Something also to convince the Americans this is not MGB misinformation."

"Very well, I understand. I have not yet discussed this with my old friend. I know his feelings but I do not know if he is willing to go this far. He has access to Soviet secrets of great interest to the Americans. You see my friend is a senior scientist inside the Soviet nuclear weapons development program."

"What! Are you serious?"

"Totally serious. An old friend from days as a university student. A fellow mathematics major. We pursued different fields in graduate school. Then the Nazis invaded separating us during the war."

"This friend is willing to give nuclear secrets to the West?"

"I believe so. He shares our disgust of living under Soviet oppression. Especially working on a Soviet super bomb."

Mishnyov looked at Baranovsky dumbfounded. "Do you see this old friend frequently?"

Shaking his head, Baranovsky said, "No. I have not seen him for years. He works in an ultra-secret location. His travel is prohibited."

"I don't understand. How do you communicate?"

"Through letters. Using an encryption cipher we developed while attending the university. A way of sharing our anti-Soviet thoughts without fear of denunciation."

Mishnyov starred at Baranovsky uncomprehendingly.

Baranovsky explained, "You see even back then both of us rebelled against the Soviet system. We pursued different fields in our graduate studies. Economics for me while my friend went to a scientific institute. He became a theoretical physicist.

"Attending different graduate schools, we developed a means of writing that disguised our encrypted code by appearing as a discussion of chess. Being mathematicians, we put our brains to the task of devising a cipher that allows using the moves of a chess game to encrypt any message we wish."

"How does that appear as a discussion of chess?"

"The system allows using written language as a part of the process. Somewhat complicated. It involves memorizing several hundred characters represented by different numbers. Much like learning a new language. The details are not important. It allows us to communicate candidly under the very noses of censors. You can imagine the security scrutiny my friend endures. We have communicated for years this way.

"WWII interrupted our studies and we separated. I remained in Moscow while my friend went to a munitions plant in the East. After the war, he disappeared into the nuclear weapons program. A virtual prisoner because of his work."

Mishnyov said, "Are you sure you want to involve yourself directly, Nikolai?"

Baranovsky nodded. "If I am going to take this plunge then I must know everything about what happens to the information. Is it of any practical value? How can it be used against Stalin?"

Mishnyov let out a sigh. "Very well. I can try telephoning Uncle Oleg my next trip. I can make calls from airports unobserved by any MGB observers before passing through passport control. What am I supposed to tell him?"

"Essentially what I told you. I am as much family as you are since I am married to his other niece. Doing this for the same reasons you are. Arrange for Rozovsky to meet me at the London conference prepared to discuss how information gets to the Americans. I must assume the MGB assigns local Soviet embassy staff to observe me. Everything I do must be explainable.

"The conference is a three day event starting on 6 August, running three days Wednesday to Friday. I address the conference on Thursday. Arrange a meeting with Rozovsky for Friday over lunch. Some public place. Have Uncle Oleg brief Professor Rozovsky. He should approach me Friday morning as the conference convenes with no one within earshot. I will not recognize Rozovsky so after introducing himself, he needs to say, *I listened with interest to your speech yesterday. A relative of your family suggested we have lunch. A French officer by the name of Colonel Leonov.*"

"This is unnecessary to expose yourself, Nikolai. Why not just let me photograph the information your scientist friend provides and transfer it along with my diplomatic material?"

"If I am taking this step, I am not satisfied with accepting Uncle Oleg's explanation of the connection to American intelligence. He is in no position to understand American methods. All of this is too vague. Understandable for security reasons unless the Americans have a reason for keeping you in the dark. I do not like unknowns."

"What do you mean?"

"I mean we cannot blindly trust the Americans. They must harbor some suspicion about your unsolicited offer to spy for them. A possible Soviet trap. I need to evaluate the circumstances better for the sake of both our families, Vladimir."

"Very well. I understand. I leave next week for a quick trip to the Scandinavian capitals. I will try to reach Uncle Oleg by telephone. It might take a couple of attempts to reach him."

Baranovsky had another reason for making direct contact with the Americans. This espionage undertaking might not last. If Soviet intelligence had sources within Western intelligence organizations, they would soon conclude the West had access to confidential Soviet information at the highest level. Even without knowing the sources, it would undoubtedly create a counter-intelligence witch-hunt within an already paranoid MGB. No telling the effects of the fallout. Spies undoubtedly had a limited professional life. The constant stress must also take a toll. Best to prepare contingency plans with options.

Mishnyov's disclosure of his spying did not extinguish Baranovsky's thoughts of defecting. Living in the West could become a reality. It could become the escape plan for him and Mishnyov, their wives, and Mishnyov's daughter should something happen giving them enough warning. Spying might provide reason for the Americans to create the means for both families to defect.

A tall order for the United States to execute in the closed environment of the Soviet Union. For the extraordinary intelligence provided, they should however consider it well worth any effort.

"By the way. Have the Americans assigned a code name for you, Vladimir?"

"Yes. *Hermes*."

"Appropriate. The Greek god of messengers."

"Since I am joining you in this dangerous undertaking, I also need a code name. Instruct Uncle Oleg to keep those that know my name to just the very few that need to know. Since it is Greek gods they prefer, henceforth communications should refer to me under the code name *Janus*, the Greek god of beginnings and choices if I correctly recall mythology. Seems appropriate don't you think?"

Mishnyov nodded with a weak smile, "One other thing, Nikolai. Does Natasha know what you are doing?"

"No. She also knows nothing about what you are doing, Vladimir."

Mishnyov said, "Do I tell Dasha about you joining us in this in this venture."

"No reason she need know. Difficult enough for her not to share with Natasha what you are doing. Besides, I need to go first to London and meet with Rozovsky. If satisfied, I then tell my scientist friend that I have the means to transmit his secret work to the Americans. That should rank as far more than dissent against Stalin's criminal state."

* * *

Oleg Leonov called Yuri Rozovsky one evening. "I must see you and Neiman immediately. Something important just came up. Something not for discussion over the phone."

Convened in Rozovsky's living room later that night, Leonov related the substance of a call received from Vladimir Mishnyov.

"Do you know Nikolai Baranovsky?" Neiman asked Leonov.

"I know Baranovsky and Mishnyov only through occasional letters from their wives, my nieces."

"How does he know my name?" Rozovsky asked.

Slightly irritated, Leonov replied, "Because Mishnyov is risking his life, Yuri. He was not about to accept just a reference of a friend as the contact to American intelligence. Would you?"

Rozovsky raised his hand. "I apologize, Oleg. No harm done. It may actually be helpful if Baranovsky proves to be a source with access to Soviet nuclear secrets."

Neiman said, "Everyone, let's step back a moment. This does not feel right. All the earmarks of a Soviet disinformation operation or attempt to insert a double agent. Baranovsky is an economics professor like Yuri. How could he possibly have access to Soviet nuclear secrets? "

"I met twice with Vladimir Mishnyov. If he was working for the Soviets, he is a consummate actor. I cannot accept he could be working for the Soviets," Leonov said.

Neiman responded, "You are probably right Oleg. However, we cannot ignore the possibility that both Mishnyov and Baranovsky might be acting under duress. Threats to their family can be very powerful. The MGB is a ruthless secret police organization. Life is of no importance. Status within the Soviet system is meaningless unless accompanied by power. Neither of your nieces' husbands possesses power. Yet both could be particularly useful against the West.

"Planting disinformation among Mishnyov's diplomatic dispatches could be useful. Then of course Baranovsky's implausible assertion that he has access to nuclear secrets could be an elaborate fiction."

"I see Viktor's point," Rozovsky said. "I attended the International Economic Conference in Moscow in April of this year. Baranovsky delivered a speech. He is inexplicably a celebrity technocrat in the Soviet Union. A brilliant mathematician noted for his complex modeling of integrating market-driven variables into surprisingly useful explanations of economic factors in Western democracies. This from someone in a rigid communist country operating under a command economy."

"Does he promote communist decree-driven economics as a better alternative?" Neiman asked.

"Not really. I don't know his work that well, only his academic reputation. Western critics sometimes characterize his position as a clever communist shill. He apparently avoids making meaningful statements about communist economics by vaguely citing inconsistent historical parallels with the West during the 20th century. The many exceptional catastrophic circumstances befalling Russia."

"Okay. Baranovsky is a clever guy. Yet how does he access Soviet nuclear weapons secrets? He and his friend Mishnyov team up to feed secrets to the West originating from entirely different sources? Stated that way it sounds preposterous. Preposterous enough that it might be real. Hard to believe any MGB senior official would authorize something like this."

Inga Jansons asked. "Aren't the same reasons Mishnyov cited enough for his friend Baranovsky to participate?"

"Certainly could be," Neiman said. "What I meant was for this to be a Soviet intelligence operation requires very high authorization. For that to work, it requires the Soviets to give up some real secrets for the ability to insert disinformation or establish the trust of a double agent. A delicate calculus fraught with great risk to the MGB official authorizing the scheme. If acting under threat, it would also require extraordinary acting skills on the part of Mishnyov and Baranovsky to play out the deception."

"So you are inclined to pursue this?" Rozovsky asked.

Neiman replied, "Of course. Look at what we have. We have a Soviet foreign service official willing to photograph diplomatic documents. Could be a charade, but so far we have invested very little. We have a friend married to the sister of the foreign service guy's wife. The economist has the unusual ability to travel to the West. The economist offers to pass Soviet nuclear weapons secrets to America. A scenario so implausible that it might be genuine. Plausible however if he is acting with a connected third dissident. If so, we have two sources with astounding access to the Soviet Union's most sensitive information."

Neiman paused gathering his thoughts. "Now that Baranovsky becomes a second walk-in spy, he becomes critical for corroborating the legitimacy of this exceptional opportunity. Selling us on the legitimacy of accessing nuclear secrets will take some doing. Everything now becomes bound together. We have no choice but to proceed."

"For that we must rely on Yuri. Perfect for this role," Inga Jansons said. "I worked for him for four years running the Druids during the German occupation. He understands people, spying, and he can be ruthless."

Yalena Rozovsky smiled and patted the back of her husband's hand. "Inga is correct. He has a heart of gold and the mind of a conspirator. That is how we survived while spying on the Nazis. He is well-qualified to determine if Baranovsky is real or working a double game."

"Very well. It happens that I already considered attending the London conference," Rozovsky said. "Might I suggest that you accompany me, Viktor?"

Neiman thought for moment. "I would like to but I can serve no purpose. What if Inga went?"

Inga looked puzzled.

"She stays in the background. Members of the press will undoubtedly be there. She can claim to be a freelance photographer for some financial publication or newspaper. My guess she can forge press appropriate credentials. She is also practiced in espionage tradecraft from her days in the Resistance."

Turning to Inga, he continued, "Take as many photographs as possible of Baranovsky. Get some close-ups with a long-range lens."

To Rozovsky and Leonov, Neiman said. "I am impressed with your adhoc intelligence network. Among the windfall material coming from Hermes, we can add the random leakage coming out of Russia through Yuri and Oleg's expatriate Russian Paris-Moscow network. If Baranovsky, let's begin calling him Janus, provides access into the Soviet nuclear program, that will be a spectacular intelligence coup. Unequalled by any western intelligence organization."

* * *

The following week, Neiman solidified the final element in the circuitous communications channel to obscure the origin of intelligence gathered by the Rozovsky network.

Taking a call at his embassy office from Konstantin Lindström, Deputy Director of Swedish T-kontoret, Lindström said, "I trust arrangements are progressing satisfactorily on your end."

"Better than expected, Colonel. I anticipate a more consistent flow of information in the next several weeks."

"Excellent. Then my news comes at an opportune time. Sven Norberg is now a new member of the Salle d'Armes Coudurier fencing club in Paris. He suggests you call him at our Paris embassy. Two foreign service officers enjoying their shared interest in competitive fencing. Norberg knows your background. Looks forward to meeting you. Says he is out of practice but will do his best to give you competition."

"Considering he is an Olympic medalist, it is me who should be concerned."

Chapter 16

London | August 1952

The British hosted the European Economics Symposium in London. Held at the elegant Ritz Hotel on Piccadilly, the British wanted to make a visual statement that they were once again a center of international banking. Something to emphasize the beginning of a period of British renewed prosperity.

Yuri Rozovsky found it difficult for the economic conference to hold his attention. Having attended the International Economic Conference held in Moscow in April, he recognized Baranovsky among the panel of speakers. A handsome fellow of medium height with a charismatic presence as Rozovsky witnessed when hearing him speak.

The first day Rozovsky circled about the attendees observing Baranovsky but avoiding making an introduction. He wanted to get a sense if he could discern if Baranovsky was under security observation. On the second day, he listened to Baranovsky deliver his remarks in excellent English with a captivating delivery. His subject was a cautionary theme concerning recovering market-driven economies. Subsidized vast public spending on public works, the increase of public debt, and other volatile factors could eventually contribute to unintended consequences. He cleverly punctuated his comments with statistical data supporting projections based on his acclaimed mathematical models.

According to plan, on Friday Rozovsky arrived early to find his opportunity of approaching Baranovsky as soon as he appeared. The opportunity came as Baranovsky exited the hotel elevator before proceeding to the banquet hall hosting the conference.

Approaching Baranovsky, Rozovsky introduced himself. Baranovsky stopped, smiled, and shook hands. In Russian, Rozovsky delivered the coded signal, "I listened with interest to your speech yesterday. A relative of your family suggested we have lunch. A French officer by the name of Colonel Leonov."

Baranovsky answered, "Of course. Perhaps somewhere close by but away from interruption by other attendees."

"I agree. There is a British pub only a short walk. I suggest we break out before everyone else and make our way uninterrupted. You are a popular figure. I will meet you just outside the hotel's front entrance."

As they walked into the conference auditorium, Baranovsky said, "My reputation comes from being an anomaly. A Soviet Russian lecturing on market-driven democratic economics."

Rozovsky smiled. "I have read your publications and listened now to you deliver two speeches. Interesting how you successfully walk that tightrope yet still enjoy support from a Soviet communist leadership."

Both suffered through the boring presentations anxious to get to the purpose of their meeting.

A warm summer day, Rozovsky met Baranovsky outside the Hotel Ritz before the lunch break.

"Are you under surveillance by Soviet security?" Rozovsky asked.

"I do not believe so. At least not obvious. Yet I am always prepared to explain any of my actions on my trips outside the USSR. Should I be observed having lunch with you, easily explained as professional interaction with another economist and fellow Russian."

"Your offer came as a surprise coming soon after your friend Hermes approached us."

"I can well imagine. I suspect your associates in American intelligence fear this might be a Soviet intelligence operation."

"The question did arise."

"How are you associated with American intelligence? Colonel Leonov was rather vague when explaining to my friend."

"I have a close friend. Someone I met in Paris during the Nazi occupation in WWII. At the time, he was American OSS. I ran a French Resistance network in Paris. This friend works in the intelligence branch of the American foreign service. One of several American intelligence agencies. He is an analyst. A specialist in Soviet affairs. A Russian like me. We both fled the Bolsheviks during the civil war although he is much younger."

"So he is not associated with the American Central Intelligence Agency?"

"He does not work for the American CIA, which is the intelligence service directly involved with conducting foreign espionage. However, he sees all the CIA's intelligence product in his function as an important analyst of the Soviet Union. For our situation, that offers certain advantages. I shall explain more fully over lunch."

Once seated having placed orders for a couple of pints of beer and the pub's lunch special beef stew, Rozovsky continued explaining the arrangement, careful to avoid revealing anything unnecessary while vetting Baranovsky.

"This started with Hermes approaching Colonel Leonov, your wife' uncle. Oleg Leonov is also a close friend of mind. Both of us are Russian coming to France because of the civil war against the Bolsheviks. He knew of my wartime espionage background."

"I do not understand. Where is the advantage dealing with this foreign service person rather than the American Central Intelligence Agency?"

"According to my friend, once the CIA learns of Hermes and now you, they will demand taking over control of both of you as their sources. My friend fears too many more people learning of your identities compromises security. He says the CIA is inexperienced in running agents in the Soviet Union. He therefore believes retaining control within the U.S. State Department is safer. Your information still reaches the highest level in the U.S. government with as few people as possible knowing your identities. My friend prepares confidential intelligence summaries on the Soviet Union."

Baranovsky considered Rozovsky's explanation. Already committed, it was the best he could do. "Very well. Security is our principal concern.

"Hermes said you have access inside the Soviet nuclear weapons program? You are an academic, an economist. How is that possible?"

Baranovsky sipped his beer. "In the same manner that this entire affair has come together. Through another friend. An old friend from my undergraduate days at the university. We resented the intellectual restrictions imposed by the government. Enforced by a secret police turned our disgust into youthful rebellion. Separated at different institutions while pursuing graduate studies in different fields, we needed a way to indulge our private dissent."

"You received your PhD from Moscow State University. Where did your friend study?"

"At the Lebedev Physical Institute of the Russian Academy of Sciences. A prestigious scientific research institute specializing in physics. Also in Moscow but a four-kilometer walk from Moscow University. Being young with good minds, we invested our energy in devising a means of secret communication to continue unrestricted discussions critical of the Soviet system. Then Germany invaded. Separated then by a much greater distance, our covert correspondence became even more important."

"So you developed some sort of coded communication?"

"Yes. However, our method incorporated a decidedly different feature. We needed to communicate in plain sight of the censors. Using an obvious cipher was not possible. Therefore, we needed a method appearing as normal communication. Something non-threatening to the Soviet system, yet capable of communicating any thoughts."

"And this encryption method is sufficient to pass secrets from inside what must be the most sensitive area within the Soviet Union?"

"Yes. We have exchanged many letters for several years. All of which subject to MGB censorship. The ones I receive are even stamped *approved for transmitting.*"

"So your friend is joined in this effort to send Soviet scientific secrets to the Americans?"

"I believe so. He is increasingly depressed locked away in a government controlled closed city. No one within the city, even important theoretical physicists like him, can leave. He describes the environment as no different from a prison. Like me, he hates Joseph Stalin. We believe Stalin is leading Russia to ruin. Possibly to another world war. Helping Stalin achieve a super atomic bomb, what my friend terms a thermonuclear bomb, is deeply troubling."

"And you agree?" Rozovsky asked.

"Yes. My disgust for communism is the obvious observation made from my chosen career. A democratic market economy not only provides human rights but also is vastly more economically successful than communist command economics. Marx's label of a dictatorship of the proletariat by practical definition requires some select group at the top to run things. As in any dictatorship, the system serves to benefit those holding power then repressing dissent to maintain that power.

"I not only see the evidence in my travels outside the USSR, but the study of economics clearly demonstrates that. Communist economists attempt ridiculous contortions to explain the economic failures of communism. The entire basis of communism is flawed since it runs counter to human nature. People do not willingly give up their identity to the State. Destruction of the bourgeoisie, the middle class, doomed Russia. Going from a near-feudal absolute monarchy with a secret police to decisions made by committees controlled by a small elite group requiring an even more repressive secret police did not give Russians a better life."

"Yet you seem to be a favorite technocrat to the current Soviet regime. How do you manage that?"

"That also amazes me. I am an expert in western economics based largely on my mathematical models. I became expert in the inherent difficulties of market economics. My Soviet minders see this as critical of western economics. I carefully avoid responding to questions about Soviet economic failures. I use exaggerated historical references embellished by comments consistent with Soviet propaganda. The leadership hears what it chooses."

Rozovsky smiled. "An impressive accomplishment in a house of mirrors where facts are distorted. About this secret communication method you and your physicist friend use. How does that work."

"I cannot discuss details without first consulting with my friend. It is something personal between the two of us. We developed it jointly. If he agrees to become a source, I will demonstrate the method fully. However, I will attempt to explain enough to satisfy you that it is possible. I realize that is central to explaining how getting out secrets from an ultra-secure location is possible.

"Our rebellion against restrictions took the form of looking into encryption methods. Our cipher avoids the vulnerability of letter frequency inherent in any language. We learned that even advanced encryption could be decrypted. Therefore, we approached that challenge like any mathematical problem. Ciphers are largely exercises in mathematics. Our research into cryptology pointed to a method called a one-time pad cipher as the most secure. Our method achieves the equivalent result.

"The most difficult problem is concealing the encryption by making our letters appear as something else. Something that makes perfect sense while concealing an entirely different encrypted message. For us, it became like learning a new language. It requires exceptional memory skills. Until my scientist friend agrees, I prefer to leave it at that."

Rozovsky nodded. "Do you propose to give your material to Hermes for passing to us?"

"Yes. Typed material. My transcription. It will be my friend's words and equations. Largely meaningless to me. Hermes now has this spy camera you provided. He will photograph my material and burn the originals. I will leave the text in Russian so as not to introduce my attempt at translating technical terms into English. I am no expert in theoretical physics."

"Is there anything else?" Rozovsky said.

"Yes. One more request. "My affinity for the West has often prompted thoughts of defection. Because of family and friendships, an unrealistic fantasy. I could never abandon wife Natasha and she has no means of traveling with me. Even if possible for both of us to defect, the secret police would retaliate against all those closely associated with us. Standard practice as a warning to others. A very effective deterrent.

"Embarking on this dangerous journey however makes defection a necessary contingency plan should something go wrong. I know nothing of espionage but evading continual risk plays against the mathematical odds of beating discovery indefinitely. I realize American resources in Moscow are limited or nonexistent. However, Oleg Leonov told Hermes that you and he were active in the Russian expatriate community in Paris. Perhaps you have contacts in Moscow that might be called on for assistance in an emergency?"

"Defection for you and your wife?"

"Yes. The same also for Hermes, his wife, and young daughter. Escape is unfortunately not realistic for my physicist friend. Already locked under tight security, should he fall suspect he can expect a bullet to the base of the neck."

Rozovsky responded, "You understand exfiltrating someone out of Russia is exceeding difficult. Each of you represents a different set of challenges. All of you represent an enormous undertaking behind enemy lines. However, it is a reasonable request in view of your risks. Since you travel outside the Soviet Union, you can telephone me directly at my office at Paris University. Since two-way communication is difficult with our arrangement with Hermes, telephone me every time you are outside the Soviet Union. At least to give me the status of yours and Hermes situation in Moscow. Also the circumstances of your physicist friend. Use a public pay telephone. Do not trust hotel switchboards. I will begin work on a contingency escape plan right away."

Rozovsky handed him a business card. "Probably time we return to the conference."

Both got up from the table and shook hands. Baranovsky said, "Give my regards to Oleg. Hope someday to meet him. A pleasure meeting you, Professor Rozovsky. I look forward to talking to you again on my next trip."

* * *

Rozovsky immediately convened his group of conspirators following his and Jansons' return from London.

Jansons spread out enlargements of photographs she took of Baranovsky on the Rozovsky's dining table. "Handsome fellow. Looks more like a European, the way he dresses, his poise, the way he spoke at the conference."

"Charismatic is the word," Rozovsky said. "Confident, articulate. Convincing in his explanation for the motivation to do this. Seems devoted to his wife and Mishnyov and this unknown physicist friend working in the nuclear program."

"What is the story there, Yuri? Neiman asked.

"He spoke at some length about him. Prefers not to reveal his name. Says they met as undergraduates. Math prodigies although they pursued different fields in their post-graduate studies. Baranovsky remained at Moscow State University while his friend went to a scientific academy."

"Did he say what scientific institute?" Neiman asked.

"Yes. The Lebedev Physical Institute of the Russian Academy of Sciences. Specializing in physics."

"Nikolai Baranovsky sends his regards to you Oleg. Any background that might shed light on who this scientist might be?" Rozovsky said.

Leonov shook his head. "Their infrequent letters only make general references to their husbands. Proud of marrying successfully, but avoiding specifics as you might imagine."

Neiman asked Yuri, "Did you learn anything more about this secret method of communication between Baranovsky and his scientist friend? For someone locked away in a top secret government installation, all communications must come under intense scrutiny."

"Baranovsky preferred not to reveal details until consulting with his physicist friend, and things move forward. I pressed him since it sounded remarkable that they could communicate under intense MGB scrutiny looking for illicit encoded information. He would only say it avoided the inherent weakness of codes subject to deciphering based on letter frequency of a given language. Says their cipher employs the same security as a one-time pad cipher. Not sure what he is talking about."

Neiman replied, "I do. Early OSS training. The real question is how do they disguise their letters as appearing something other than encrypted code. Ciphers almost always take the form of sets of numbers."

Rozovsky continued, "Baranovsky said they found a way to convey their messages that otherwise appeared as acceptable normal correspondence. Said he would reveal in detail how this works if his friend agrees to participate. Is it that important we understand how Baranovsky communicates with his physicist friend?" Leonov asked.

"Not so much we understand the exact details, but that we are satisfied it is possible to regularly pass censorship." Neiman said.

"If we are not convinced how they accomplish this do you mean that leaves open the possibility this is a MGB trap?" Rozovsky said.

"Unfortunately yes. It is critical to understand how they accomplish what seems to be an extraordinary deception."

"If this is an MGB trap then Vladimir Mishnyov is also compromised," Leonov said.

"Let's not get ahead of ourselves," Neiman said. "I simply mean we need to understand as much as possible before accepting everything at face value. I am an intelligence analyst. That means not only evaluating the content of intelligence but also assessing the credibility of the information. I inherently question the substance of all intelligence, including the motivation of the source.

"Oleg you have met Mishnyov and Yuri has met Baranovsky. Both appear genuine. Mishnyov's material so far backs that up. However, we know very little about this theoretical physicist working on Soviet atomic bombs. Has he been coopted under duress by the MGB? Is the MGB composing his letters using his and Baranovsky's secret coding method?"

"Where does that leave us then, Viktor?" Rozovsky asked.

"No different than before. If somehow the MGB is involved then the Mishnyov channel is already blown. Should that be the case then the only danger lies with passing on Soviet disinformation. Therefore, we proceed while viewing all information with a critical eye."

Rozovsky said, "If we understood the details of how Baranovsky's encryption method works, would that improve your confidence in the material, Viktor?"

"It might. I am no expert at ciphers and encryption though. Nor how codes are broken. However, if any of us could see how their method works it would go a long way. Think about it. You are locked away in an ultra- secret installation where everything is under intense MGB surveillance. How do you write letters that have the ability to convey any hidden message while appearing as entirely unobjectionable correspondence?"

Leonov interrupted. "I remember Mishnyov's wife, my niece Dasha, mentioning one time something about Natasha's husband Baranovsky. She commented that Vladimir prided himself on his chess abilities but Nikolai was in a class far beyond him. Vladimir could never beat Nikolai. Might that be involved?"

Rozovsky said, "Baranovsky did say his method of encryption involved exceptional memory skills. I play chess but not at the level to which Mishnyov describes Baranovsky's proficiency.

Chess masters have the ability to envision many possibilities for several moves in advance. That requires a spatial memory far beyond my abilities. Baranovsky also referred to their encryption method as something like language."

Neiman said, "Well, chess might offer possibilities for discussing chess games in letters. Chess might provide some mathematical basis for constructing their cipher. Lots of possibilities to work with while appearing as innocent communication. If the game under discussion is identified then that could be interrupted as something like a one-time pad that you said Baranovsky mentioned."

"What exactly is a one-time pad?" Rozovsky asked.

"Where the sender and receiver of a coded message use a different code key reference known only to them and used only the one time for each message."

"Baranovsky is to call me his next trip. What if I tell him that American intelligence needs to understand how their cipher works in order to demonstrate that such communication is possible while under intense scrutiny?"

Neiman responded, "Good idea but let's wait and see what material comes our way first before concluding we do not totally trust the information. We do not want to scare Baranovsky off. I have the ability to access the opinions of American scientific experts regarding information on Soviet nuclear weapons development."

* * *

It was only the second time that Neiman and Sven Norberg of Swedish intelligence met at the fencing club. They were about the same age. That first time they worked out together since their mutual weapon was the fencing saber. Norberg confessed to being out of practice. After medaling in the Los Angeles 1932 and 1936 Olympics, he was off and on about maintaining that level of performance. He had not picked up a saber since posted to Paris two years ago.

Even so, Neiman recognized he was not in the same league as Norberg. While Norberg's timing was off, by the end of an hour's workout, Neiman could see the skills of a master swordsman returning. Norberg's exceptional reflexes were sharp enough to cover the mistakes of being out of practice.

This second session two weeks later, Neiman put up good competition, but Norberg clearly took command. Toweling off after showers, Neiman said, 'Let's go for a drink. I have a package to give you."

At a café, Neiman said, "After that workout I deserve a couple of Scotches." Passing Norberg an envelope, "My first delivery." Norberg placed the envelope in his inside jacket pocket. "I have no idea what is on the film. That is the arrangement. Our source makes delivery to a dead drop. How soon can you get this to Stockholm?"

Neiman did not reveal that the dead drop was in Paris.

"Tomorrow. I should have the prints back to you within the week," Norberg said.

"Good. Tell Colonel Lindström we may have struck gold with this walk-in source. It appears he has others interested in using him to transmit Soviet secrets to us. In the envelope are typed notes referencing information from other sources identified only by code names. We have no way of verifying much of the information so tell Lindström to be his own judge.

"More than that, our source says he may have someone with access to something of greater significance than anything provided to us already. I say this only to prepare Lindström for the pressure exerted by the American government. These sources are more important than anything the CIA or British MI6 has. The CIA and probably others in our government will not appreciate Sweden holding out by insisting to go only through the State Department. They will increase their pressure for taking this over. No different from their clumsy attempt in 1948.

"It is also an election year in the United States. Truman will not run again. That means a new administration. A new secretary of state. I might be replaced as the channel for this information. Regardless, T-kontoret must remain in control of this operation. Do not trust the CIA to manage this intelligence gold mine. Keeping the charade of this originating with Sweden works to your advantage. It gives Sweden full representation within the Western intelligence community while seeing the raw intelligence product."

"I understand. Politics and bureaucratic infighting is the same everywhere."

***

Neiman received the developed prints back from Stockholm. Mishnyov was productive. Perhaps too productive. Looked as if he photographed everything in his diplomatic pouch without considering some of the documents as unimportant.

Nonetheless, Neiman had to play his contrived role and pass this on to Washington without editing. This was a Swedish intelligence operation.

Two weeks later came the first evidence of the shit hitting the fan. Aggressive CIA Director General Walter Smith went on the attack recognizing President Truman as a lame duck and therefore his antagonistic Secretary of State Acheson. Smith began applying backroom pressure in the Senate. Even more effectively, he could use his close wartime relationship with General Dwight Eisenhower, likely the next president in the November election. The Republican Eisenhower did not harbor the same reservations toward the CIA as the Democrat Harry Truman.

Neiman's old adversary Frank Landers, CIA head-of-station Paris approached him. The two barely acknowledged each other although their offices in the Paris Embassy were on the same floor. Stepping into Neiman's office without knocking, Landers walked up to Neiman's desk. "Rumor at Langley says you are running some kind of espionage operation. Is that true?"

"Good morning to you also, Landers. And what does the gossip at Langley say?"

"You have something going with Swedish intelligence."

"What the fuck does that mean?"

"The Swedes are feeding you intelligence, bypassing the CIA."

"Bypassing? You receive their intelligence product without editing. What's the issue?"

"Why do they use you?"

"I have no idea what you are talking about."

"Director Smith suggested I might have an informal talk with you about how this came about."

"Really? Smith should take that up with the Swedes. He is just sore because the Swedes have better sources on the Soviet Union than the CIA. All Langley has is the useless Gehlen Organization. Gehlen's merry band of former Nazis is just jerking the CIA around by feeding you meaningless information from the Eastern Bloc. The CIA has no important sources inside the Soviet Union. Like many of us, the Swedes see the CIA as adventurers. Operational cowboys still fighting WWII. The CIA knows nothing about conducting espionage, just fucking up things around the world.

"Tell Director Smith you talked to me. Now, unless you have something else to discuss, Frank, get the fuck out of my office."

Chapter 17

Sarov (Arzamas-16), Russia | September 1952

Sarov ceased to exist as a normal city in 1947. This ancient Russian holy place became part of the vast Soviet nuclear program following WWII. Having defeated Nazi Germany, Joseph Stalin envisioned a new Russian empire. He was not about to relinquish territory occupied in Eastern Europe. Instead, he set his sights on further Soviet expansion. As the post-war dominate world power, the United States stood in the way of realizing Stalin's ambitions. Having punctuated their new international dominance by creating and using nuclear bombs to defeat Japan in 1945, they became Stalin's new adversary.

Located 400 kilometers east of Moscow, Sarov was isolated yet sufficiently assessable from the Soviet seat of power and the many scientific institutions supporting Soviet nuclear research. Literally sealed off, the government renamed the city Arazmas-16 using the name of another town some 75 kilometers from Sarov. The All-Russian Scientific Research Institute of Experimental Physics became part of a vast network of renamed locations. Removed from maps and assigned names usually associated with the Soviet administrative region to obscure the actual locations of laboratories, processing plants, and reactors comprising the Soviet nuclear weapons development program.

By 1952, Arazmas-16 was the scientific center of nuclear bomb development. All the principle scientists in weapons design, research, and warhead assembly worked there. Having successfully tested their first atomic bomb in August 1949, two more tests followed closely together in September and October of 1951.

The 1949 Soviet bomb was very similar in design and yield to the United States *Fat Man* plutonium bomb of the Trinity test in New Mexico and the bomb dropped on Nagasaki, Japan in 1945. The subsequent Soviet tests in 1951 used different *boosted* designs doubling the explosive yield of the 1949 bomb. All these tests still represented nuclear fission as the principal source of the energy release. The Soviet development effort currently focused on achieving a super bomb employing a secondary fusion detonation using a hydrogen isotope triggered by a primary fission detonation. Over two years earlier, U.S. President Truman announced the beginning of the development of a hydrogen bomb. The Soviet Union had no choice but to do the same.

Security forces constructed a perimeter fence creating an exclusion zone 80 square kilometers manned with guard towers surrounding Arazmas-16. Soon after relocating much of the population of Sarov, new construction started. The first buildings erected were facilities to house the forced-labor construction workforce. As with all of Stalin's massive projects, the Gulag system provided unlimited manpower. That labor force eventually amounted to tens of thousands political prisoners employed at Arazmas-16. Augmented by military construction battalions, construction never stopped. Laboratories and factories rose up, some with additional specific security barriers within the larger confines of the closed city. Security provided by the Soviet army required facilities equivalent to supporting a large military base.

Scientific and technical personnel required new housing along with facilities such as commissaries and movie theaters to provide personal amenities. Arazmas-16 required a large supporting service sector. Additional forced labor inmates filled that need.

Travel outside the perimeter prohibited even for scientific staff and their families. Access into the city required high-level authorization.

Like all the entire scientific team, Galyorkin's work stretched to twelve hours each day at least six days a week. A day a week was set aside for relaxation but occasionally demanded work if engaged with a particular problem or experiment. Whereas other theoretical physicists of Andrei Sakharov's team often spent much of their off-hours discussing work, Galyorkin preferred to withdraw into his own diversions.

Those diversions consisted of reading and drafting encrypted letters to Nikolai Baranovsky. He increasingly felt the desire to remain indoors. With the autumn weather turning colder, the environment of Arazmas-16 only added to his depression. The architecture of the new construction was utilitarian. Drab and seemingly designed to appear aesthetically unappealing. Various areas fenced off with armed security guards dampened any enjoyment of being outside. Everything reinforced the feeling of imprisonment.

Galyorkin was by nature quiet and introverted. Congenial to his colleagues, he nonetheless communicated poorly on an emotional level. Andrei Sakharov was a singular exception.

Sakharov possessed a personality similar to Nikolai Baranovsky. Both charismatic and engaging, both brilliant, yet with personality traits reaching far beyond their professional abilities. Both recognized Galyorkin's exceptional mind but also his emotional sensitivity and reserved personality. Galyorkin responded differently when interacting with Baranovsky and Sakharov that naturally developed into genuine friendships.

Reading the official Communist Party newspaper *Pravda* increasingly irritated Galyorkin. Even without a Western publication counterpoint, any Russian could see it was distorted propaganda nonsense. No attempt made to disguise ridiculous assertions. To any thinking Russian, the Soviet system offered nothing to the proletariat, the working class. The system served only those in Soviet leadership. The communist ruling class was nothing more than former bourgeois assuming absolute power under the pretext of representing a state devoted to the proletariat. Disguised as something more closely resembling religion, in practice Soviet communism represented something closer to feudalism where the state owned everything.

Even those holding great power such as scientific director Igor Kurchatov, were likely expendable should they not deliver the next generation nuclear bomb to Stalin. Such a purge would likely extend to every level of those connected with the program. A repeat of Stalin's Great Terror of the late 1930s. The casting of blame to mask Stalin's many personal leadership failures had a long history.

Working with Galyorkin in the laboratory was a new female engineer. Her function involved calibrating various measuring instruments and monitoring experiment progress. Galyorkin noticed her when she arrived weeks earlier. About his age, she caught his attention. In those weeks, they exchanged only professional greetings. Galyorkin's shyness usually causing him to avert his gaze as their eyes met.

One afternoon he became deeply involved in an experiment. It was well past the usual mid-day time when he concluded. Well past the time when most of the scientific staff broke for lunch.

Working alongside him, engineer Talia Zubarev took the initiative as they shut down the experiment. With no one else within hearing, she said, "We both missed lunch. Would you like to join me in the cafeteria, Dr. Galyorkin?"

Flustered, he stumbled over is words covering his reaction to her unexpected overture. "Why yes. So sorry. I lost track of time."

In the cafeteria, the cooks and workers were taking lunch after the technical staff finished eating and returned to work. Galyorkin felt all eyes looking at them as if he and Zubarev were interrupting their brief period of relaxation. They were not technically prison inmates however there was little difference. Selected for their skills such as these food service workers and induced by higher wages. Perhaps never to return to their homes in Western Russia. Conscripted into the Soviet nuclear Gulag comprised of dozens of facilities and factories. Places where they often labored alongside those serving prison sentences. Exiled eastward to remote scattered locations in the endless Russian steppes in the name of state security.

One worker got up and went behind the food service counter. She served Galyorkin and Zubarev as they pointed to their food choices without exchanging any words.

Returning to a remote table with their trays of food, Galyorkin said, "Obviously they are not happy we disturbed their lunch."

"Unfortunately, this is not a happy place for any of us," Zubarev said. "Apart from doing our work, this is a dreary place."

Galyorkin nodded. "I agree. I certainly would prefer Moscow. Where did you come from?"

"I grew up in Smolensk. Studied electrical engineering at the Moscow Power Engineering Institute. Graduated just as the Germans invaded. Spent the war working in a factory producing military radios."

"I spent the war working at a munitions laboratory in Ulyanovsk. Still further to the east of here on the Volga River," Galyorkin said. "Where did you work?"

"Gorky. Also on the Volga but closer to Moscow. A big city. Prettier than Moscow. Was Ulyanovsk a good place to work?"

"Never thought about it that way. Like you, work dominated your life during the war. Not much different from our lives stuck working here. Outside of our work, there is little joy in living locked away behind fences with armed guards."

Zubarev took a mouthful of food to avoid immediately responding. This was dangerous talk. Although attracted to this scientist, she knew nothing about him. Was he just being kind by accompanying her to lunch or was there something more?

"We are doing important work so the security precautions are understandable. What do you enjoy doing in your spare time?" she said steering the conversation to safer territory.

"Reading mostly. Playing chess when I find a willing opponent."

"Are you a skilled player?"

"At a level where I believe I can provide accomplished players challenging competition."

"Is anyone here capable of beating you?"

"Not yet." Galyorkin smiled with pride but also with slight embarrassment. He did not want to sound boastful. "I enjoy difficult matches the most. It draws my concentration so deeply that time seems suspended. Unpleasant thoughts temporarily become shut out."

"I play chess. I think of myself as a competent player, but I sense you are much better."

"That does not matter. Perhaps we could play sometime?"

"Of course. Playing you might improve my skills. Perhaps you could teach me how to better my game."

"I look forward to that, Comrade Zubarev."

"If we are to be friends, please call me Talia."

Galyorkin mostly ignored his food. Normally shy around women, this pretty woman seemed to enjoy his company.

"I would like that Talia. Please call me Dimitri."

Talia reached over offering her hand, "Pleased to know you, Dimitri."

Galyorkin made an attempt to take a few mouthfuls of food but preferred continuing the conversation. "Do you enjoy reading, Talia?"

"Oh yes. Novels. The great storytellers. Pushkin, Gorky, Tolstoy. Tolstoy is my favorite. The settings in difficult periods of Russian history. Something to escape our difficult times in the 20th century. Escaping being forced to see life only through political ideology."

Dangerous territory again but she sensed something about this quiet man that emboldened her.

For Galyorkin, he needed little prodding to share his inner feelings.

"My favorite novelist is Dostoevsky."

"Oh my. You must be attracted to the dark side."

"Never thought of it that way. I just find Dostoevsky characters deeply absorbing. Yet not everything I read is like that. I also appreciate Tolstoy. In fact, Tolstoy appreciated Dostoevsky. I am equally absorbed in the works of William Shakespeare."

"Oh my. That is impressive. I found Shakespeare somewhat difficult. Do not see why he is held in such high regard."

"Are you reading Shakespeare in English?"

"No. I do not read English. And you do?"

"Yes. My education began in mathematics which turned later into theoretical physics. Much of the technical body of knowledge is in foreign languages. I therefore learned to read English and German. It often is important to read in the original language to avoid distortions through translation."

"That makes sense. You have a surprising range of interests outside your scientific work, Dimitri. I am so glad the experiment delayed our lunch. Gave us the opportunity to become more than just professional associates."

"I enjoyed our lunch immensely, Talia. I look forward to a game of chess whenever you are interested."

Her phrase of *more than just professional associates* evoked emotions rarely experienced by Galyorkin.

"Of course I am interested. Whenever your busy schedule allows. I room in the single women's dormitory building number Я-231. You can leave me a message by telephoning the building clerk's number."

* * *

Over the next few weeks, their relationship rapidly progressed. Talia Zubarev was the more assertive finding opportunities for sharing meals and spending time playing chess in the library or enjoying a movie at the theater.

While not at the same level of proficiency as Galyorkin, Zubarev was a solid chess player. She absorbed Galyorkin's instruction in chess strategy by displaying evident improvement. Galyorkin was delighted to find someone so intellectually talented. Clearly, a budding romance developed within the confines of this restricted environment. More poignant given Galyorkin's inexperience with the opposite sex.

His dour mood quickly brightened. Noticeable in his improved temperament at work. He became more engaging with his professional colleagues.

Andrei Sakharov remarked to him one day, "Since you found a girlfriend, your disposition is much brighter. However, we miss your participation in social activities. Those informal activities are important to our work, Dimitri. Creativity is cultivated when freed from formal constraints. Sharing a non-threatening exchange of ideas with colleagues is important to our cutting edge work. Women can be a distraction."

Easy for Sakharov to say since he had a family to provide some normalcy. He married a laboratory assistant in 1943 when he and Sakharov worked at the munitions laboratory during the war.

Out of character for Galyorkin, he responded more forcefully than he intended. "Talia provides an essential balance to my life. I understand your point about the informal collaboration fostering creative thinking. So does moving away from the problem, clearing the mind before returning."

"I appreciate that also, Dimitri. Yet your associates on the team often remark about your preference to leave your work in the laboratory and go off with your sweetheart. We have important work to complete. Since you speak of balance, you need to also balance your professional obligations, Dimitri."

This was the scientist Sakharov asserting his position as team leader. Galyorkin realized he lost sight of that seeing Sakharov as more a friend that happened to be a colleague.

Subdued but angry, Galyorkin responded, "I shall be more diligent, Andrei."

* * *

Weeks later, Talia Zubarev was absent from her current place in the laboratory one day. Concerned, Galyorkin called her dormitory that evening. The reply from the Talia's dormitory desk clerk when he telephoned dealt a blow almost physically painful.

"Talia Zubarev is no longer a resident here."

"What does that mean? Where has she gone?"

"I do not have that information."

"Is she still within the city?"

"I am sorry, I have no information."

"Did you see her leave?"

"Comrade, I am not authorized to discuss anything about our residents."

Galyorkin immediately rushed to Sakharov's apartment. Sakharov responded to the repeated knocking on his door.

When Sakharov opened the door, Galyorkin said, "Andrei, Talia is gone. I have no idea where. What am I to do?"

"Step inside for a moment but say nothing to my wife. I will get my coat and we can talk outside."

It was well into the evening and turning bitterly cold with a wind coming up. Sakharov's children were making a great deal of noise so it made sense to talk outside undistracted.

However, that was not Sakharov's reason. He never discussed anything involving work with his wife.

With collars turned up to shield out the wind, Sakharov put his hand on Galyorkin's shoulder. "Talia Zubarev is gone, Dimitri. She is no longer here in Arazmas-16."

"Where has she gone?"

"That I do not know. Security reasons do not allow imparting such information unless there is a need to know. She is an excellent technician. My guess they reassigned her to another related location engaged in our work."

"Who has the authority to just move people around with no warning?"

"Who? There are many with that power. I am only a team leader."

"Was this Kurchatov's doing?" Referring to the overall scientific director.

"Listen carefully, Dimitri. Because you are a friend, I will tell you more than I should. You must keep secret what I am about to tell you. If you protest, it will destroy your career. It might also be dangerous. None of us are indispensable."

Galyorkin nodded. "I must know what happened to her, Andrei."

"I do not know where they sent her. I only know the reason for her removal because Igor Tamm confided in me. I could even say rebuked me for not bringing you under better control. The old man said it was becoming obvious you were not devoting sufficient attention to your work. Equally obvious to all of us on the team, the reason was this woman. The solution self-evident. She was more expendable than you."

Galyorkin constrained himself to avoid an ugly exchange with the only person he considered a friend. He also knew that Sakharov had no way of preventing this. Sakharov counselled him to find some middle ground. Spend more time informally with his professional colleagues. Best not to burn bridges and make his situation any worse.

Galyorkin feared saying anything more. He bit his lip as his eyes teared up. Sakharov again put his hand on Galyorkin's shoulder.

"Go home. Take some vodka. Get a good night's rest. Everyone will be expecting you in the lab tomorrow. Stay focused. Do not let anyone sense your emotional pain is effecting your work. Do you understand, Dimitri?"

"Yes. I understand. Thank you for telling me, Andrei. I will be all right."

As Galyorkin left Sakharov, he was anything but all right. Deeply wounded, he barely held his rage in check. Instinctively he wanted to lash out at those responsible for this outrage.

Emotional discipline dictated if he was to survive he must redirected his anger to hardening his resolve. Find refuge in the technical challenge of his work. Devote his full intellectual efforts to contributing to the development of the next generation of nuclear weapons. He had no alternative but to participate by fully applying his skills. However, he would not forget losing Talia to a system that held no regard for him as an individual.

Galyorkin blamed everything comprising the structure of the Soviet Union and Joseph Stalin as its creator. A sociopolitical system so perverse and barbaric it rivalled the evil of Adolf Hitler and Nazi Germany. He was an individual not an instrument of the State. Committing himself to the most serious act of opposition possible seemed the only way to preserve his sense of self in the dystopian Soviet state.

* * *

Deprived of a relationship with Talia Zubarev, Galyorkin profoundly changed following the exchange with Sakharov that cold night. He vowed not to allow the bastards to defeat him. Smart enough to compartmentalize his hatred he would play the long game by appearing to fall in line by concentrating on his scientific work. All the while subverting Soviet secrets by providing them to the Americans. The Soviet Union was the enemy. That included everyone in authority at Arazmas-16, even Andrei Sakharov.

The next day following Sakharov's revelation about Talia, Galyorkin returned the curious stares of his colleagues with a smile accompanied by forced friendliness. As days passed, those around him believed he had come to his senses. Appearing newly engaged in his work, Dimitri Galyorkin appeared a changed person. His behavior substantially modified from the prior introverted quiet intellectual. Exhibiting this deception made possible through his festering hatred while plotting revenge.

Within days, he began composing a series of letters to Baranovsky explaining the current status of Soviet nuclear bomb development. A lengthy body of encryption requiring many chess games to define the quantity of required encryption keys. Since he would send these letters in succession only several days apart he needed to explain this increased correspondence output to avoid arousing suspicion by the security censors.

The answer was to choose a single grand master with the most games documented in his catalog. That proved to be the Russian-born Alexander Alekhine. Most fittingly, Alekhine left Russia for France in 1921 when the Bolsheviks came to power. Noted for his imaginative attacking style, he matches should provide ample opportunity for commentary from which to construct the encryption keys.

The first letter began with an upbeat commentary and introduction to his series of letters to put off any suspicions that these were nothing more than the ramblings of an obsessive chess enthusiast.

Dearest Nikolai,

Hope you are doing well. Been working long hours. Much of my spare time spent playing chess. Several of my associates provide challenging competition. Chess provides a perfect outlet for relaxing after working long hours. I recall our days together at the university.

I began looking at some of Alexander Alekhine's great games. I realized he was extraordinary even among the great chess masters. A theoretician that produced a range of chess opening innovations. I begin with the earliest game in my catalog. A 1910 game against Rubinstein in the Vilnius All-Russian Masters tournament. From there I progressed through all ten of the games included in the catalog. I became fascinated with his brilliance. Sufficient to absorb me for weeks.

From that introduction, Galyorkin began his analytical chess move comments to construct the encryption. When decrypted by Nikolai Baranovsky, the concealed message read:

The same thing that happened to my colleague Yakov Zeldovich that I wrote about to you earlier. I also met a woman. An engineer named Talia Zubarev. She worked on instrumentation with me in the laboratory. Unlike a prisoner like Zeldovich's woman, Talia was no different from me. I felt human being with her. Now she is gone. Sakharov told me our boss ordered her relocation because she was distracting me from my scientific work. Neither she nor I is any different from a political prisoner. The State governs everything in our lives. I will no longer live like this.

Have no fear about me harming myself. That cannot appease my hatred. You spoke of a way to smuggle secrets to the West. I am ready to reveal everything. I shall follow with encrypted material explaining important information on the sta-

tus of Soviet advances toward designing a thermonuclear fusion bomb. Get the information to the Americans.

Chapter 18

Paris | September 1952

Nikolai Baranovsky arrived at Orly Airport in Paris. He was an invited speaker at the annual conference of the Parti Communiste Français, the PCF. French communists comprised a significant percentage of those actively serving in the French Resistance fighting German occupation during WWII. However, following liberation in 1944, the provisional government headed by Charles de Gaulle excluded communists. With creation of a new constitution, the French Fourth Republic came into being. Under its first president Vincent Auriol, the PCF was again excluded from government. Like their comrades in the Italian Communist Party, both French and Italian communists followed ideological direction from Moscow. Communist political ideology proclaimed a collective international view subjugating nationalistic interests.

The communist parties of both France and Italy remained a powerful socio-political force. They remained influential in all sectors of the workforce capitalizing on a sense of disenfranchisement from the prosperity as Europe recovered from WWII. The insecure governments of both countries therefore had little choice but to tolerate the communists that could still exert substantial electoral support. Under pressure from Moscow, the PCF distanced itself from other French political parties by focusing on political agitation from their membership within the powerful trade unions.

Baranovsky was here to deliver a speech titled *Exploiting Market-Driven Economic Weaknesses.* Backed by his mathematical models, the content explored how Western Europe prosperity could eventually experience difficulties from excessive debt, increased interest rates effecting access to capital, and other factors causing inflationary pressure.

His remarks would conclude with, "Circumstances deem this a perfect time for aggressively demanding higher wages and improved benefits. In market-driven economies, those at the top of the economic hierarchy continue to benefit at the expense of the working class. Demand for skilled labor is high. Recovering from the war torn economies creates vast opportunities for increased profits. The proletariat must exercise all possible means to share in those profits."

While doing nothing more than exhorting the working class to use their leverage to improve their economic stature, it did not condemn democratic market economies. To the contrary, he could recast the textual content as a cautionary blueprint to avoid inherent pitfalls as a bull market cycle inevitably tapers off. By slanting the language for delivery to the PCF, the presentation pleased those in Moscow reviewing the content of his remarks prior to authorizing his trip.

When meeting Yuri Rozovsky in London a month ago, he agreed to call during his next trip abroad. This trip afforded an unexpected opportunity to meet again with Rozovsky but without providing advance notice of his coming to Paris. Baranovsky assumed he would have little ability to sneak off for a meeting with Rozovsky once he was among the PCF leadership. Yet there was the opportunity to meet with Rozovsky before met by PCF members and possibly a MGB operative sent by from the Soviet Embassy.

To make that happen he arrived at the airport in Moscow early in the morning. His scheduled flight did not depart until 2:00pm. At the last minute, he changed his reservation for a ticket on the 9:00am flight to Paris. This avoided a PCF welcoming delegation at Paris Orly Airport sent to whisk him off to a dinner in his honor.

Arriving at 1:45pm Paris time, he called Rozovsky's office number after clearing French customs. In Russian he said, "Professor Rozovsky, this is Nikolai Baranovsky."

"Good afternoon. This is a surprise. Where are you calling from?"

"Here in Paris at the airport. An unexpected trip with no way to alert you. Can we meet right away? I am to speak at a PCF conference tomorrow. Expected to arrive on a later flight. The next couple of hours offer the only opportunity to meet unnoticed."

"Yes, certainly. I understand. Let me think of a place where we can talk. Where are you staying in Paris?"

"The Hotel Karlotta on Rue Boussingault in the 14th Arrondissement. Not far from where I am to speak. Some large union hall. I gather this is a working area of Paris?"

"Yes. I know the street's location. A southern district of central Paris. There is a park in the 14th. Parc Montsouris. Accessed from Rue Gazan on your way north from the airport. The taxi driver will know the location. I can be there in less than one hour. There is a pond close to Rue Gazan. I will meet you on the east side of the pond."

Rozovsky immediately called Neiman. "Baranovsky just arrived in Paris. I am to meet him within the hour near the pond in Parc Montsouris. Can you join me? It will allow you to make an assessment about Baranovsky's ability to communicate with his scientist friend. You can also directly assure him of his information getting to the Americans."

"Yes of course. How he pulls off coded communications with someone in the most secret Soviet sector still raises concern. What about Oleg? Should we try to include him?"

Rozovsky replied, "Might be helpful. He is extended family by his connection to the wives of both Baranovsky and Mishnyov. Baranovsky will likely be interested how we might provide an escape for their families should something go wrong. We of course do not want to be specific."

"Have you made any progress thinking how you might use your extended contacts in Moscow?"

"Given it much thought but it seems impossible. Contacts in Moscow are only known through their individual associations among our loose group of expatriates. To my knowledge, none of those in Moscow knows any of the others leaking out information. You cannot even call our group a network. No one directs activities. Those in Paris just collect what comes their way."

"The CIA has no assets in Moscow," Neiman said.

"What about your friends in Swedish intelligence?" Rozovsky asked.

"Perhaps, but too premature to raise the issue with them. Perhaps if Baranovsky's nuclear secrets prove as important as he claims, I can explore the subject in earnest with them. Speaking of the Swedes, Baranovsky is to know nothing of their involvement. Keep it simple. The U.S. State Department believes it better to directly manage him and Mishnyov for reasons of their own security by limiting knowledge of their identities."

Rozovsky said, "Understood. Can you try to contact Oleg? If he is not available, you at least need to join me."

"If I can reach him, I will pick him up and meet you at Parc Montsouris within an hour."

* * *

Neiman, accompanied by Leonov, found Rozovsky seated on a bench near the walkway surrounding the pond. They recognized Nikolai Baranovsky seated next to him from Inga's photographs.

Rozovsky saw them approaching. "Mr. Baranovsky, I asked Oleg Leonov and Mr. Jones my associate in American intelligence to join us."

Baranovsky stood up shaking hands with Leonov then embraced him saying, "A pleasure finally meeting you, Uncle Oleg."

In Russian, Neiman said, "I am Mr. Jones, United States Department of State, intelligence branch."

Baranovsky and Leonov spent a few minutes exchanging information about Leonov's sister and his two nieces.

Eventually, Rozovsky interrupted, "I appreciate how much you wish to share personal information, however we have limited time and much to cover. Shall we get to the reason you requested this meeting, Professor Baranovsky?"

Baranovsky nodded. "My physicist friend's name is Dimitri Galyorkin. He currently works in the closed city designated Arazmas-16. The former city of Sarov east of Moscow. Dimitri is a brilliant theoretical physicist working on the development team of a thermonuclear super bomb employing nuclear fusion.

"Our friendship began before WWII when both of us were undergraduates studying mathematics. As I explained to Professor Rozovsky in London, Dimitri is increasingly depressed. He feels himself no better than a prisoner. Denied the ability to use his skills toward applying nuclear energy for peaceful uses. Forced instead to develop atomic bombs that are even more powerful for a madman taking Russia on a path of destruction.

"A recent personal incident profoundly affected him. I came here to communicate that directly to Professor Rozovsky. Dimitri wishes to do more than simply exercise dissent. His sense of outrage now turned to revealing all he can about Soviet nuclear weapons technology progress to America."

"In your meeting with Professor Rozovsky, you were vague about how you communicate to each other," Neiman said.

"I understand how that might be troubling. How can Dimitri possibly smuggle the most secret information out of perhaps the most secure Soviet installation where travel is prohibited for those working there? Now that Dimitri agrees to proceed, I will explain how our method works. I presume that is necessary to ensure this is not some disinformation scheme of the Ministry of State Security?"

"Precautions are necessary within the intelligence business. I appreciate your understanding, Professor," Neiman said.

"Let me first explain by an overview of our cipher. Developed years ago between the two of us while still university undergraduates. It provided a safe means of exercising our dissatisfaction for restrictive life under the Soviet communist system. I will then demonstrate by using examples. Everything we created is committed to memory.

"I first discovered a shorthand method developed a hundred years ago in Germany. Translated into Russian using a phonetic Cyrillic alphabet, it became popular for stenographic transcriptions. For me, highly useful method for taking lecture notes. I taught Dimitri and we began exchanging personal notes. Much like learning a new language.

"Somewhat secret except for someone also proficient in shorthand. We needed something secure to express views that otherwise would result in arrest and exile to a Siberian penal labor camp. Therefore, we turned to studying encryption techniques. Our problem went beyond creating a cipher. We needed to disguise the cipher as appearing to be correspondence of something unthreatening to Soviet ideology.

"The concept is fairly straightforward. Eliminating the fundamental problem of letter frequency for a given language was the first challenge. With even the most advanced ciphers, that represents the risk of unwanted decryption. I discover in my research that if the cipher code key becomes a text known only to the sender and receiver, this logically overcomes that problem. This avoids the inherent vulnerability of techniques involving even complex letter substitution techniques. We also wanted that common base text to be a definable variable instead of a fixed reference. The greatest challenge was how to accomplish this while disguised as normal communication. As avid chess players, we fixed on a method of using chess as a basis to solving the problem.

"The result is a cipher that allows using any chess game to encrypt any message. Accomplished through describing chess moves with phrases that convert the board position of a given piece following a move to any required number. That number then identifies a shorthand character or mathematical operator. Requires memorizing approximately three hundred characters by their associated number. Easily accomplished and reinforced with practice."

Neiman, Rozovsky, and Leonov all exhibited expressions of incomprehension.

Baranovsky said, "Expressed verbally, it is difficult to understand. Remember for Dimitri and I, this is second nature. Fluency in our special language practiced over years. Let me show you."

Baranovsky extracted a notebook from his briefcase. "Let's say I wish to communicate the sentence, *I am glad to be in Paris*. In Russian, that requires only these few shorthand characters to express. Phonetically based therefore it eliminates letter frequency association. I select a chess match and draft a textual content commenting on specifically identified moves. The first letter of the words in that textual content converts to a number key using a simple table of the Russian Cyrillic alphabet. That number becomes a multiplier of the board position for a selected move of a specific chess piece thus converting to any desired number corresponding to one of the three hundred shorthand characters or mathematical operators."

Neiman commented, "Do I assume the difficulty comes from composing these comments associated with a move?"

"Precisely. Decoding is faster than composing the text to generate the required code key multiplier. Takes some practice to contrive phrases that produce the desired result while sounding realistic enough for even a censor proficient in chess. Not only are we accomplished chess players but we each use a catalog of great chess matches accompanied with expert comments from which we base our appropriate phrases to create a number that transforms the board position number. Let me show you.

Baranovsky scribbled an equation. $^2H + {}^2H \rightarrow {}^3He + n + 3.27 MeV$. "According to Dimitri, this a basic equation for the energy released by deuterium-deuterium fusion. Deuterium is a hydrogen isotope with a nucleus consisting of one proton and one neutron and expressed as ^2H. A key component of a thermonuclear fusion bomb, hence the name hydrogen bomb. He transmitted this to me using a specific document chess match. A sequence of board positions used consisted of *54, 36, 44, 66, 33, 57, 53, 37, 51,* etcetera. Applying a multiplier derived from text phrases restates these numbers as *2, 34, 11, 2, 34, 7, 11, 40, 11,* and so forth. These numbers then correspond to shorthand characters or mathematical operators in this example."

"Give me an example of the textual content that produces the key that transforms the board position into the value representing the required encryption character," Neiman said.

Baranovsky nodded scribbling, *35B A bad sacrifice. E5 seems better move. Why not draw? 37W Starts remarkable precision. 47W Moves this knight, for first time. Lasker displays precision. Schlechter holds firm. 64B Exchanging queens fatal. Perhaps an oversight? 67W Game is over. 67B Why not resign? 71W A great game. A remarkable historic struggle.*

"I recall this from the last portion of Dimitri's latest letter expressing this equation. The actual matrix used is the Russian Cyrillic alphabet using 30 letters. The first letter of each word in the phrase produces a multiplier to three decimals to transform the board position number to integers identifying the required shorthand character or mathematical operator. You can see the number 11 appears several times indicating the plus symbol but in each case is derived from a different board position number by the multiplier key."

Rozovsky looked at Neiman who responded to Baranovsky, "Impressive. I trust that neither of you has any of this written down anywhere?"

Baranovsky smiled. "No, of course not, Mr. Jones. We know full well the consequences of our actions. So does Vladimir Mishnyov. Should we make a mistake it is a death sentence after prolonged interrogation under torture.

"It is impossible to relate Soviet oppression on every facet of life to someone living in the West. Mishnyov and I are among the privileged few that experience what it is like to live somewhere free from fear of a secret police."

Neiman said, "I understand, Professor Baranovsky. I was born in Moscow. Although a boy, I fled the Bolsheviks during the civil war, as did Professor Rozovsky and Colonel Leonov. My parents stayed in Russia to care for their parents. Stalin murdered them during the Great Terror in 1938."

Baranovsky nodded then reached into his briefcase. "I assumed you might want some good faith gesture that I was offering information of importance. These are some recent decrypted communications from Dimitri over the last several weeks. My typed transcriptions of his letters. I chose to keep it in Russian rather than attempt translating into English. I am not a physicist and I do not want to misstate Dimitri's technical meaning."

As Neiman read each message from Galyorkin typed on individual pages, he passed them to Rozovsky and Leonov. No way to tell if the information was genuine or of importance. That would take specific scientific expertise.

The first transcript included the details of the second and third Soviet detonations of atomic bombs a year earlier in the autumn of 1951.

By the autumn of 1951, our secret facility KB-11 located within Arazmas-16 produced 29 bombs of the RDS-1 design with a blast yield of 22 kilotons. A solid plutonium-core implosion device. The test of RDS-2 followed on 24 September employing an advanced design of the explosive lens, increasing the yield to 38 kilotons using the same fissile core mass. The equations in addendum #1 explain the enhanced yield performance.

RDS-3 detonated 18 October used the improved explosive lens with a composite fissile core of plutonium within a uranium shell yielding 41.2 kilotons. With modifications, RDS-3T began mass production this year.

RDS-4 development is underway to reduce the size of the warhead from 3200 kg to 1200 kg while still achieving a yield in the area of 25 kilotons. Such a device enables ballistic missile delivery. I have listed the pertinent design details in addendum #2 attempting to explain the reduced size without the ability of providing a diagram.

The next transcript dealt with the developmental effort to create a thermonuclear super bomb.

As early as 1946, Soviet efforts focused on developing a thermonuclear weapon employing nuclear fusion of light elements. The *foundation for achieving the temperature and pressure to insti-gate fusion only possible through nuclear fission. Igor Kurchatov is the overall scientific director of the Soviet nuclear program. Igor Tamm heads the theoretical group. They soon discovered that creating the necessary pressure to fuse the hydrogen isotope deu-terium, ^2H, was not achievable by a fission detonation. Calcula-tions indicated that $^2H + ^2H \rightarrow ^3He + n + 3.27MeV$ occurred at tens of millions of atmospheres rather than hundreds of thousands gen-erated by a fission release, therefore making fusion unachievable.*

In 1948, Andrei Sakharov proposed what he called the First Idea. The concept involved placing alternate layers of deuterium, triti-um, and uranium-238 in a fission bomb between the fissile core and the conventional high explosive lens. The primary fission stage produces the enormous pressure and temperature required to instigate a secondary fusion stage of hydrogen isotopes deuterium ^2H and tritium ^3H. The deuterium-tritium fusion cycle reaction becomes $^2H + ^3H \rightarrow ^4He + n + 17.6MeV$, with the two hydrogen iso-topes fusing to produce helium, ^4He, and releasing vastly greater energy. Tritium however does not occur naturally because of its short half-life decay rate into helium. Tritium is therefore im-practical and cost-prohibitive to produce, requiring specifically designed reactors.

In 1948, Vitalii Ginzburg proposed a solution to resolve the triti-um problem by using a compound of deuterium and lithium-6 instead of deuterium alone to produce tritium as a byproduct of the fission detonation. This Second Idea used lithium deuteride, $^6Li^2H$, a chalklike solid easily produced and handled. When bombarded by neutrons released from a primary stage fission det-onation, lithium deuteride absorbs a neutron breaking up into helium, ^4He, deuterium, ^2H, and tritium, ^3H. The reaction be-comes $^6Li^2H + n \rightarrow ^3H + ^4He + 4.7MeV$. The deuterium then fuses with the produced tritium in a fusion reaction with the full po-tential energy release expressed as $^2H + ^3H \rightarrow ^4He + n + 17.6MeV$. This breakthrough of producing tritium as part of the fission detona-tion process redirected design efforts for a thermonuclear hydro-gen-based second stage fusion bomb. From a theoretical perspec-tive, the Soviet Union possessed a workable thermonuclear design concept before the first atomic test of a fission bomb in 1949.

Perhaps years of work and extensive testing remains to produce a functional design for a two-stage thermonuclear weapon using the full energy release potential of nuclear fusion.

"None of us are experts but if this is new information to American intelligence than it certainly appears to be of great importance," Neiman said. "This suggests the Soviet Union is within reach of having a staggeringly powerful atomic bomb. Dreadful news but better to know of it in advance. I assure you this information will make its way to the right people in the American government."

"Do you have an excuse for evading your reception delegation at the airport?" Rozovsky said.

"Yes. I needed to prepare for my presentation tomorrow. Spent the afternoon at a café reviewing my notes before the dinner commitment tonight."

"Before we depart, we are exploring how to develop a contingency plan to exfiltrate you, Mishnyov, and your wives out of Russia, should the need arise," Rozovsky said. "A difficult problem but understandable if I were in position,"

Neiman said, "Will your future transmissions be through Mishnyov?"

"Yes. He will photograph my transcriptions of Galyorkin's information and burn the originals."

Neiman added, "Going forward, never identify yourself or Galyorkin by name in any form of communication with us. I understand you chose the code name *Janus*. Mishnyov is *Hermes*. Dimitri Galyorkin is to be *Poseidon*. Professor Rozovsky is *Raven*. Colonel Leonov is *Cavalier*."

"And you are?" Baranovsky asked.

"Jones," Neiman replied.

* * *

Baranovsky appeared genuine to the extent possible for Neiman to evaluate. Final assessment would come from expert evaluation of Galyorkin's information. Was it sufficiently compelling that made it unlikely to be Soviet disinformation? No other choice but continue under the assumption that it was genuine for the time being. Inexorably connected with Mishnyov's independent espionage efforts unfortunately made for security concerns. Yet Rozovsky's network now had highly placed sources in the Soviet Foreign Ministry and the All-Russian Scientific Research Institute of Experimental Physics developing the next generation of Soviet nuclear weapons. A remarkable intelligence penetration.

There were rarely absolutes in intelligence. Always looking at an incomplete picture and often unsure of sources. Neiman would continue playing this out for as long as possible.

The election in November will bring in a new administration and new secretary of state coming into office in January of 1953. That will undoubtedly mean Neiman's return to his intelligence analytical role and transfer back to Washington. That will not happen. Refusing to leave Paris likely meant leaving U.S. government service. He needed to rethink what he might do. Perhaps returning to the art world.

For the time being, he needed to provide assistance to these dissident Russians before leaving government service. Given his personal hatred for Joseph Stalin, his contribution to Rozovsky's espionage network proved rewarding.

The material handed over by Baranovsky required special handling to explain the origin of this new intelligence source. That meant a face-to-face meeting with Konstantin Lindström. Two days later Neiman was again in Stockholm at T-kornet headquarters.

"As I said over the telephone, we have a new development, Colonel. Seems our walk-in source has associates through personal association. We now have a highly placed source inside the Soviet nuclear weapons program. Someone part of the scientific research and development group. We received these first transmissions hand-delivered."

Neiman handed the typed sheets to Lindström.

After reading through Baranovsky's material, Lindström said, "You believe these are genuine?"

"Circumstances suggest they are. Depends on what the scientific experts say."

Lindström said, "I am aware of the tightest possible security placed at every location in Soviet nuclear work. How is it possible for this source to smuggle information out?"

"My question also. The person that handed these to me in Paris travels outside the Soviet Union periodically. We assigned him the code name *Janus*. The actual source is a theoretical physicist and long-time friend of *Janus*. We code-named him *Poseidon*. *Janus* and *Poseidon* developed a remarkably inventive cipher disguised as innocuous communication to smuggle the information out right under the noses of MGB censors. *Janus* personally demonstrated the method to my general satisfaction. Seems they developed the communication method years ago while in undergraduate school as a means of protesting Soviet repression. Both *Janus* and *Poseidon* are brilliant mathematicians."

"How will Janus communicate with you in the future?"

"Through *Hermes* using microfilm. *Janus* decodes the encrypted letters from *Poseidon* and types out his transcriptions in Russian."

"So all three of these sources are personally connected?"

"Yes. An uncomfortable security circumstance emphasizing extreme caution on our part. Please keep the details I just told you from any direct inquiries from the CIA, MI6, or any allied intelligence service. Maintain this as the most sensitive Swedish penetration."

Lindström smiled. "Of course. Director Palm relates he has already received indirect pressure applied through the Swedish Foreign Ministry for greater intelligence cooperation with the American CIA. The resentment over channeling the information through you is clear when reading between the lines. With this added valuable source, pressure will increase."

Neiman smiled. "I trust you and Director Palm to maintain this is as the product of Swedish intelligence efforts. Shared with American intelligence for mutual objectives while still bound by the limits of maintaining Swedish neutrality."

"Spoken like a professional diplomat," Lindström said with a laugh. "Is the arrangement with Monsieur Norberg proving satisfactory?"

"Definitely. We are good friends. He also provides exhausting workouts at the fencing club. He seems to have quickly recaptured his Olympic competitive form."

Chapter 19

Paris | September 1952

Mikhail Nikolayev looked out the window from his office in the Paris Soviet Union Embassy. A massive ugly building in an architectural style better suited to Moscow than to Paris. Situated in the 16th Arrondissement west of the Eiffel Tour it was somewhat shielded by other buildings more Parisian-centric. Nikolayev's office looked toward the west over the vast green expanse of the Bois de Boulogne. In diplomatic status, he was officially the third secretary of the embassy dealing with trade matters. His real function was as resident Paris head-of-station for the Soviet Ministry of State Security, the MGB.

Posted to Paris fours earlier, he fell in love with the city. Perhaps a self-fulfilling result. Learning English at Moscow State University before WWII seemed a vital asset for advancement in the Soviet Union. Realizing an aptitude for language with success at English, he tried his hand at French because of the sheer elegance of spoken French. This led to an appreciation of the architectural charm through photographs of Paris. Reading of the French devotion to life's pleasurable pursuits made him a Francophile.

The MGB became the successor secret police and intelligence agency of the former NKVD and NKGB of the Soviet Union following WWII. Its mission included a broad portfolio with functions divided among various directorates. Nikolayev held the rank of full colonel in the First Directorate. Its function included foreign intelligence infiltrations into governments, political parties, and other influential social institutions. Additionally, the First Directorate maintained surveillance over Soviet foreign service personnel stationed abroad.

The Second Directorate focused primarily within the Soviet Union acting as the counterintelligence branch combating foreign intelligence penetrations. The Third Directorate discharged an intrusive policing function of the armed forces ensuring conformity to Soviet ideology. A role growing out of the brutal counterintelligence repression exercised by political commissars over Soviet armed forces in WWII.

Policing all those living within the Soviet Union through pervasive fear was the function of the Fifth Directorate. Stalin's secret police. Charged with supervising every aspect of behavior for the entire citizenry regardless of position. Government, science, industry, academia, and every social organization. No one was immune to scrutiny or arrest for anything deemed as anti-Soviet behavior.

The MGB Fifth Directorate exercised its power without oversight except for the hierarchy of the MGB and Joseph Stalin himself. They could arrest and impose prison sentences in the forced labor camps in Siberia and even executions without trial. The most feared place in Moscow was MGB headquarters in Lubyanka square. It also served as a political prison with facilities designed to administer torture to extract confessions. Once entering the Lubyanka, people might disappear without a trace.

Nikolayev studied a recently decoded message from Moscow.

To Colonel M. P. Nikolayev
USSR Embassy Paris, France

We have uncovered a foreign network of reactionary traitors operating in Moscow. Four perpetrators are currently under arrest undergoing interrogation. We continue gathering further information as the investigation expands to identify the sources of this espionage.

Those arrested confess to passing Soviet state secrets to individuals in the Russian expatriate community in Paris. Information acquired from what appear to be lower-level functionaries suggests this might be an unaffiliated government operation led by former White Russians of the civil war era. The more likely scenario indicates this group is acting as a proxy for a Western intelligence service. We discovered the conspiracy through an informant identifying how information is smuggled out of the USSR. The confidential material concealed in the packing material of vodka and tinned Russian food delicacies. The consignee in Paris is Délices d'Europe de l'Est in the 19th arrondissement at 178 Avenue Jean Jaurès.

Headquarters requires all intelligence available including ownership of this establishment and the composition of the Paris expatriate Russian community. Advise efforts to initiate useful covert action from sources and assets under your control in Paris. Report to this office and your appropriate authority in the First Directorate.

Colonel R. V. Sedelnikov
Chief of Staff
Fifth Directorate
Ministry of State Security

An unusual message. Unusual because true foreign espionage activities were rare inside the USSR. Of greater concern were foreign agents turning Soviet diplomatic staff working abroad into sources. However, Nikolayev knew quite a lot about the Paris expatriate community. A group thought to be relatively harmless, noted more for their virulent opposition to the influential French Communist Party. He nonetheless had a source close to the group. A French citizen of Russian heritage. Born in Paris to parents fleeing Tsarist reprisals after the first Russian Revolution of 1905. The source was also his mistress.

Angelique Plisetsky was an attractive woman in her early forties. Educated as a lawyer, she was an activist for women's rights. A writer for center-left publications, she was an aggressive advocate for progressive issues. Being a clandestine committed communist, she actively spied for the Soviet MGB. With her political leanings, those in the PCF accepted her as a sympathetic socialist.

Although she was not a vocal critic of the Soviet Union, the Paris expatriate Russian community accepted her based on the general circumstances of her parents fleeing violent political turmoil in Russia. In 1905, political and social unrest erupted against the absolute monarchy of Nicholas II and the ruling class. Almost three hundred years of Romanoff rule retarded economic and social progress. The industrial revolution bypassed Russia under Romanoff rule leaving the vast country a relic of the 19th century. Peasant unrest, worker strikes, and military mutinies set against a hated monarchy fresh from a humiliating defeat by Japan in the Russo-Japanese war that same year.

Her father was a human rights activist lawyer often opposing the Tsarist regime and her mother a teacher. Plisetsky could therefore claim a similar heritage of fleeing the revolt of a radicalized working class the same as White Russians fleeing during the civil war following the Bolshevik Revolution of 1917. This along with fluency in Russian allowed her to move within the Russian expatriate community.

Angelique Plisetsky provided her lover and Soviet intelligence an insider's assessment of attitudes and opportunities within both the French Communist Party and the Russian anti-Soviet expatriate community. Two groups holding polar opposite political views as it relates to the Soviet Union made her a valued resource and her looks a desired romantic companion to Nikolayev.

Angelique augmented her usefulness further by recruiting her twenty-one year old daughter Monique Plisetsky a year ago. Employed within the French Ministry of the Interior records sector provided Nikolayev with access to all manner of confidential information on French nationals. Passports, driver's licenses, business licenses, marriages, criminal records, military records, and other related data. French bureaucracy kept extensive records.

Monique Plisetsky proved an important asset. For her part, she enjoyed the secretive dual life she shared with her mother. A freethinker and supremely confident woman like her mother, she expanded that behavior to relationships with men. Monique enjoyed sex while using it to exercise control over men. For her romance was adventure. With that came an appreciation of the finer material things in life. What better place to exercise her skills and enjoy life than in Paris.

Monique's father was a predecessor of Angelique's current lover. An officer in the NKVD, the Soviet intelligence-secret police agency of that time, stationed at the Paris Embassy. Recalled to Moscow in 1939 for critical remarks against aligning with the Nazi Fascist regime after Stalin signed a nonaggression pact with Adolf Hitler. When Nazi German attacked the USSR in 1941, he became an intelligence officer in the Red Army. Captured while serving on the Eastern Front, he returned to Russia in 1946 after surviving two years in a German POW camp.

Stalin became notoriously paranoid of thousands of former soldiers having spent time outside insular Soviet Union. Upon repatriation, most received forced labor prison sentences, considerably growing the inmate population of the Siberian Gulag forced labor camps. Many years still remained on the sentence of Monique's father.

That disturbing personal history however did not dampen either Angelique's or Monique's devotion toward international communist ideology directed from the Kremlin. Like others recruited by Soviet intelligence as spies living in the West, not experiencing life under Soviet repression allowed ideological commitment to remain unclouded by reality.

While the French intelligence service, the SDECE, undoubtedly knew Nikolayev was a Soviet intelligence officer, they were less antagonistic toward the Soviet Union than the United States or United Kingdom. Several reasons account for this. Not the least of which was the political influence of the French Communist Party, particularly at local levels. It was the largest leftist party in France. Communists represented a significant percentage of those actively involved in the French Resistance during WWII. Although excluded from government following the war, the PCF remained influential among French labor unions.

The United States and Britain knew French communists infiltrated the SDECE to some unknown degree. Western intelligence also knew the PCF as an organization followed directives from Moscow. Nikolayev observed the appearance of a foreign diplomatic official but held little concern of exposure as a Soviet spy and declared persona non grata by the French. However, unsure how close SDEEC counterintelligence might monitor his activities, he nonetheless observed caution when making contact with his sources. The exception was Angelique Plisetsky. Given her left-leaning status and associations with the Russian expatriate community did not rise to the level of active espionage against the French state. For this reason, they frequently appeared together in public.

The daughter Monique on the other hand unquestionably conducted covert espionage by providing confidential information as a French government employee. Although Monique knew her mother and Nikolayev were lovers, and he was a Soviet spy, she passed her information through her mother to maintain security.

Nikolayev ran a well-developed espionage network of illegals throughout France, but principally Paris. He was careful to avoid clandestine contact whenever possible. When necessary, he employed rigorous espionage tradecraft. Information usually passed through dead-drops or some secure means. Like Angelique and Monique Plisetsky, other French nationals supplied information of varying degrees of importance. Several were in French government service and the French military. Additionally he had a small direct staff mostly devoted to counterespionage of Soviet diplomatic personnel stationed in Paris.

After receiving the inquiry from Moscow, that night Nikolayev asked Angelique Plisetsky if she knew of this Paris importer Délices d'Europe de l'Est.

"If you are a Russian in Paris of course you know of it," she replied as they were enjoying wine at her apartment in the Left Bank. "North of here in the 19th. Been there several times. The owner is a leading figure in the expatriate community. Boris Antonovich. A White Russian relic of the civil war."

"Seems this establishment receives sensitive Soviet information concealed in liquor and food shipments from Moscow. Arrests made in Moscow are widening in scope. Would you mind paying a visit to make an initial reconnaissance of this enterprise? Use the excuse that you are helping to arrange food and liquor for a gathering. East European journalists or some such thing. Looking for authentic ethnic food goods."

"Of course. What kind of information are you looking for?"

"From your visit, just what you can observe. Size of the place. Sources of his imported goods. Number of employees. Name of the manager. I also need Monique to dig up whatever exists on the owner Boris Antonovich. Immigration details. Passport details. Family. Business license information."

* * *

Monique Plisetsky's job in the records section of the Ministry of the Interior provided access across a broad range of personal information. Her responsibilities required researching government records to provide inquiry information for various functional branches of the ministry. The ministry held responsibility for the Gendarmerie and the National Police, granting of government documents, immigration, and coordination of the state's appointed representatives to French administrative departments. Hers was a repetitive administrative job enriched by the occasional clandestine request from Nikolayev communicated through her mother.

She understood the illicit nature of providing information to Soviet intelligence. As a committed communist that presented no moral dilemma. The extra money funded indulging her habit for stylish clothing.

Dressing well allowed her to show off her attractive body. Flirtatious and promiscuous, that in turn added to attracting men willing to spend money on fine dining and entertainment. She enjoyed the pick of handsome men with the means of supporting her habits in exchange for sexual favors.

The simple request to research records for all information on Délices d'Europe de l'Est, its owner Boris Antonovich, and the shop manager was a simple request. Within days, she assembled all available information on the business, Boris Antonovich, the manager, also Russian, and Antonovich's only a son. The twenty-four year old son, Grigori held a union certification as a journeyman electrician. Currently employed in facilities maintenance at Orly Airport.

The information provided basics from which to launch a deeper investigation. At his disposal, Nikolayev had a number of communist PCF members willing to do low level surveillance tasks. Several were former WWII Resistance veterans with some experience operating secretly. With economic times remaining difficult, the extra money as important as pursuing their political ideology in some direct manner. It was this group he assigned to conduct surveillance on the three names produced by Monique Plisetsky. The objective was to determine the additional players involved in the Paris end of the operation. Who becomes the recipient of the information? Who is running this intelligence operation? What is the scope of their sources inside Moscow?

Nikolayev disliked counterespionage work. Trying to uncover spies for the other side was police work. He much preferred the creative challenge of recruiting and running agents against the enemy in their home country. This however was a highly unusual circumstance. Not some Soviet official coopted by the West but possibly a foreign intelligence operation within Moscow with connections extending to Paris. Practiced in reading the tone of messages from the Kremlin, he sensed this might be something more than Russian dissidents. Should that be the case, an opportunity existed to advance his career by accomplishing something important.

Several days of surveillance led nowhere for the shop manager or the son of the owner. However, several contacts observed by the owner Boris Antonovich provided other leads to pursue. Two individuals in particular stood out. A professor at the Sorbonne and a French Army officer. Both Russians, According to Ministry of Interior records, both these White Russians fled Russia during the civil war. Both well known in the Paris expatriate Russian community.

With further assistance from Monique Plisetsky, Nikolayev found government archival information suggesting these individuals were capable of involvement in an anti-Soviet conspiracy using connections inside Moscow as sources.

Professor Yuri Rozovsky headed a French Resistance network in Paris known as the Druids. A subnetwork of the larger Alliance resistance network. The Druids and Alliance were highly successful acting against the Nazi occupation. That made Rozovsky experienced in covert espionage.

Colonel Oleg Leonov had a long and colorful military career. Fought on the Eastern Front in WWI. As an officer in the Imperial Russian Army, he then fought against the Bolshevik Red Army during the ensuing civil war. Eventually Leonov fled to France when part of his command became trapped and evacuated on the Black Sea. Joining the French Foreign Legion, he served thirty years in various French conflicts. Currently an instructor in unconventional warfare at the École Militaire. Not a background in intelligence but he might have informal connections to the French SDECE.

Interesting possibilities but nothing substantive. Nikolayev switched surveillance to Rozovsky and Leonov.

A week later a more promising lead materialized. A weeklong surveillance on Professor Rozovsky led to identifying another connection. An American diplomat. Monique Plisetsky provided the information that elevated Nikolayev's interest to a new level. Viktor Neiman was more than just another foreign service office. His diplomatic credentials read senior officer United States Department of State Office of Bureau of Intelligence & Research.

Intelligence? Nikolayev did not realize the American foreign service had an intelligence branch. He immediately sent a message to Moscow requesting information on this obscure intelligence service. He also requested all information available on Viktor Neiman.

Awaiting that information, Nikolayev assigned two of his staff to learn everything possible about Neiman's associations and movements.

***

Two weeks later, Nikolayev sat in his office reviewing the assembled material on Viktor Neiman. Far more background information than available for Rozovsky, Antonovich, and Leonov from French government records. The level of detail suggested the Soviet MGB had sources reporting from within sensitive areas of the United States government.

Viktor Neiman was very much involved with intelligence. The information went into considerable detail about the function of this obscure American intelligence service known by the acronym INR. Neiman was the senior officer assigned to preparing intelligence briefs related to the Soviet Union to the American president and key U.S. government officials.

The information likely from confidential personnel records outlined Neiman's background making clear his unique qualifications. Born in Moscow in 1911 to a family of non-practicing Jews, he fled Russia during the civil war. As educated bourgeoisie, obviously fleeing the Bolsheviks. Parents remained in Russia. Imprisoned in a Siberian forced labor camp during the Great Terror, presumed diseased.

Neiman served in the American wartime intelligence service the OSS. Holds dual American and French citizenship. Little question about his sentiments toward the Soviet Union.

From Nikolayev's own staff, he learned that Neiman lives with a French woman. A Latvian refugee and former member of Rozovsky's French Resistance network operating against the

Germans during the occupation. She is now a successful photographer.

Monsieur Neiman is therefore experienced in the ways of espionage. Ethnically Russian and quite possibly connected to this discovered intelligence penetration of which Moscow provides no details other than an address in Paris.

Is this an American intelligence operation? Neiman's position with the United States Department of State is inconsistent with managing foreign espionage sources. That was the responsibility of the United States Central Intelligence Agency. The CIA was the principal American intelligence adversary of Soviet counterintelligence.

Still, too many points of connection to ignore. Nikolayev needed more information than what was possible through surveillance and accessing French government records. He needed to infiltrate this Paris importation business as a known conduit of smuggled intelligence out of Moscow. Looking at photographs taken by his surveillance people, the son of the owner of the importing firm might present that opportunity.

Grigori Antonovich was a handsome young man only a few years older than Monique Plisetsky. Both ethnically Russian. Monique spoke Russian fluently providing options for making an advance toward the young man. Should Monique successfully seduce the younger Antonovich, she might be able to uncover further information. Are these Parisian Russians part of an espionage network operating in Moscow? Perhaps working for the Americans?

Regardless, he could make an interim report to Moscow about covert assets assigned to infiltrate the expatriate Russian community. Other than maintaining surveillance on the American intelligence officer, there was nothing further he could do until Moscow provided more information obtained from those arrested in Moscow.

Chapter 20

Paris | October 1952

Grigori Antonovich liked his new job at Orly Airport. Better pay and working conditions than his previous job, although it meant a seventeen-mile commute from his apartment in the 11th Arrondissement. However, the excitement of participating in actual espionage was addictive. He understood his father's work involved smuggling out information from Moscow in shipments of packaged food and liquor. His father never revealed the nature of the information, only that people in Moscow risked their lives passing information to the West. Nor did his father reveal what happened to the information.

Grigori was as staunchly anti-communist and anti-Soviet as his father was. As French-Russian, he grew up in Paris among a community of anti-communist expatriates. Parents and grandparents forced to flee the Russian Civil War or Stalin's Great Terror of the late 1930s. Firsthand accounts of brutality and death were common topics among his parent's generation. Participating in fighting directly against the enemy embodied by Joseph Stalin in this Cold War provided immense satisfaction.

He worked the night shift as part of the larger maintenance crew to perform repairs during the off-hours with fewer passengers. Installing the fake electrical outlet box was an unnerving twenty minutes as a new electrician doing something without a work order. Periodically servicing the dead drop still required a degree of careful stealth to avoid fellow airport staff noticing. He developed a routine for checking other equipment in the area to avoid singling out the dead drop that never appeared on his worklist.

Most weekends were free. Helping out at the Délices d'Europe de l'Est allowed him to keep his Russian language skills free of a French accent. He liked helping out his father and mother. Always rewarded with a good dinner. Usually followed by drinking vodka with his father often with his father's friends. Witnessing the esteem in which the community held his father was a personal source of pride.

He enjoyed the comradery of his father's generation. The tales of revolution, civil war, and world wars. The guarded talk of a select few that spoke of the difficult life in Moscow. Indiscreet references of their current activities that Grigori understood to mean smuggled information in Russian foodstuffs shipped to his father's shop.

Mother was not above frequently inquiring about his love life. Was he seeing a particular girl? Commenting that most young men his age were married or at least engaged. Some already starting families. She could not conceal her yearning for grandchildren reminding him that he remained their only hope for producing the family's next generation.

Grigori liked girls and girls liked him. Finding sex was not difficult. Avoiding young women looking for husbands pushed him to seek female companionship in venues less suited toward matrimony.

* * *

Angelique and Monique Plisetsky walked into the Antonovich shop on a Saturday morning. Grigori was stocking shelves. A Nikolayev agent surveilling Grigori confirmed his presence. The Plisetsky women waited for the confirmation telephone call before proceeding to the shop. Both women dressed in a stylish manner sufficient to turn heads without overtly flaunting sexuality. Mother and daughter well practiced in catching the attention of men.

Seeing Boris Antonovich behind the counter, Angelique called out in Russian, "Boris Sergeyevich, good to see you again." Although having met him before, she still used the formal address of his first and patronymic middle name."

Looking up, he recognized the attractive middle-aged woman. "Angelique Stepanovna. It has been a long time but one does not forget a beautiful woman."

"Ah, you are such a gentleman. Let me introduce my daughter Monique Feliksovna."

Antonovich nodded to Monique. "Mademoiselle. Welcome. And what brings you ladies to my shop this morning?"

"Your wonderful delicacies from the Motherland. I am responsible for catering a gathering of journalists. I wish to present a traditional Russian feast."

Antonovich noticed his son staring at the daughter from the other side of the shop. He smiled while motioning with his hand, "Would you help me here, Grigori?"

Grigori quickly stepped over.

"This is my son Grigori. Let me introduce Madame Plisetsky and her daughter Monique."

Grigori responded in Russian making a slight bow. "A pleasure meeting you. I am at your service."

Angelique said, "Excellent. Perhaps you can educate Monique about Russian liquor while your father helps me fulfill my list of food items. I wish to serve good Georgian wine and of course your best vodka. We shall follow your recommendations."

Grigori was only too glad to assist the alluring daughter. "Let us then first select your wine. Please follow me, Mademoiselle. "

Monique displayed her sexual attraction through attention to the style and tailoring of her clothing. Accentuating her full figure and long legs accomplished through selecting clothing still accepted as good taste. Her mother taught her how to apply makeup and style her hair for best effect.

"What do you like to drink, Grigori?" Monique asked addressing him in the familiar on purpose.

"I like vodka of course, but mostly I drink beer or wine. French wine."

"What is Georgian wine like?"

"Very different. Considered natural wines. French wines are aged in oak barrels. This allows oxygen into the wine and the tannin's in the wood to effect aroma and flavor. Georgian red wines are aged in large clay pots just like in ancient times. Georgia has made wine for 8,000 years. I am no expert like my father, but he says aging in clay allows for some oxygen into the juice but the clay does not impart additional flavor."

"You know quite a bit. Do you like it?"

"Some. I favor the bold reds."

Monique laid her hand gently on his arm, "Show me some that you like. I will impress Mother."

Her touch electrified him. Difficult to take his eyes off of her especially as she smiled while appearing absorbed in everything he said.

"Very well. I particularly like this one. So does Father. A deep inky color. Full bodied. Delicately aromatic."

"What grape variety is this?"

"*Shavkapito.*"

"Excellent. I shall take four bottles. What about another red? Like you, I like bold reds."

"Here is one my mother particularly likes. A blend. Highly acidic with flavors of black cheery and raspberry."

"Give me two bottles of that. Now that I choose what I like, show me some others that will give Mother's guests a variety."

For the next twenty minutes, she and Grigori talked more about personal topics than Grigori's commentary on wines.

After settling on a light red wine, a white wine, and Grigori's recommended vodka, they shared enough personal interaction for Monique to set the stage.

"This has been a wonderful adventure coming here today. I expected Mother was just dragging me along on my day off to help her shopping for her gathering. Before we rejoin my mother and your father, I have a personal question I would like to ask."

"Of course."

"Having just met you, I hope I am not sounding too forward. You see, I have two tickets to see Josephine Baker at the Folies Bergère on Rue Richter in the 10th. The tickets are for the ten o'clock performance tonight. I intended it as a surprise for Mother's birthday, but did not know of her professional obligation. I cannot go alone. You said you liked American jazz performers. I hate to miss the performance so you would be doing me a favor."

She paused biting her lip in an expression of concern while flashing her expressive eyes. "Oh my. I carried away in the moment without asking if you might be in a serious relationship. I certainly do not wish to upset your personal life."

Nikolayev's surveillance reported he lived alone with no indication of a particular woman in his life.

He could not believe his good fortune. Watching a show of partially clad beautiful woman while escorting a sexy woman. Grigori smiled broadly. "There is no girlfriend. And I would be delighted to go as your escort, Mademoiselle Plisetsky."

"That is wonderful. Then you must call me Monique."

"Of course. Might I be then so bold as to then ask you to dinner?"

"Oh my. Not only handsome but a real gentleman. Of course. We shall have a grand evening."

"How about you pick a restaurant convenient to the Folies. Perhaps make a reservation for eight o'clock? I have a car and will pick you up."

Possessively as if absentmindedly she touch his upper arm, this time giving it a squeeze while looking directly into his eyes. "Wonderful. I will give you my address. I have my own apartment in the 9th."

As she and Angelique left the shop after arranging delivery of their purchases, Angelique said, "Successful?"

"Oh yes. He was undressing me with his eyes. I am sure that after tonight I will own him."

* * *

Unlike her more conservative attire that morning, Monique Plisetsky dressed provocatively for the Folies Bergère. Something to compete with Josephine Baker's backup dancers. She wore a knit shape-hugging black pencil dress with a plunging neckline, slit up one side, with open-toed pumps.

Arriving at her apartment, Antonovich's jaw dropped when she opened the door. "You look magnificent, Monique."

"Thank you, Grigori. Please come in. I am ready, just need to freshen my lipstick. I am famished. You will like the restaurant. Not far from the theater."

Returning to Monique's apartment after midnight, events progressed as Grigori hoped and as Monique planned. Instead of just a kiss at her door, she touched his cheek and said, "Care to come in for a late drink?"

After closing the door, they never got to the drinks. Monique embraced him giving him a passionate kiss. Running his hands over her body, her sustained kiss became more demanding in its urgency. Breathlessly she hurriedly loosened his belt. Opening his fly, she grasped his erection feeling it respond to her touch.

Pulling down his trousers and underwear, she guided him backwards to a comfortable chair. Once seated, she dropped to her knees and took him into her mouth. Working him slowly, it was not long before she could sense he was close to orgasm. Slowing the rhythm with her mouth, she increased the pressure with her lips while pulling the length of his erection mumbling, "Not yet. Make it last."

Saying that of course made it impossible to forestall his release. Using his underwear to collect his ejaculation, she said, "Now it is my turn. Let's go to bed. Will you do that to me?"

She removed her clothes letting him watch her as he sat on the bed. She moved closer letting him touch her breasts before grasping his head bringing it down to her pubic area. Hoisting one knee onto the bed, she opening her vagina.

Quickly realizing he was inexperienced in giving a woman oral sex, she laid back on the bed spreading her legs. "Come here. I will show you what I like."

Following instructions, her groans of pleasure eventually bringing her to orgasm aroused him fully erect again. Entering her, he sustained her extended orgasmic pleasure before ejaculating a second time.

She thought he could prove an adequate lover. Handsome with a good body, all he needed was coaching. This might prove a pleasant assignment after all. Yet only until she uncovered more details of this espionage network using Délices d'Europe de l'Est. Nikolayev was specific. Who was the recipient of this intelligence smuggled into his father's shop? Names of others involved? The relationship to sources in Moscow?

She enjoyed the challenge to her sexual and manipulative skills. The sense of mystery. Acting in a real-life drama as an actual spy. If caught, did she face execution like Mata Hari during the Great War? Death by firing squad or guillotine? The possible danger only added to the thrill. After this first night, she controlled Grigori Antonovich. The feeling of conquest was intoxicating.

* * *

After several weeks, Monique Plisetsky became frustrated with her lack of progress in gathering new information. One evening relating the difficulties of importing goods from the Soviet Union, he unexpectedly revealed something he thought might impress her with his worldliness.

"There are those in Moscow that find exporting Russian liquor and packaged foods a convenient method of concealing secret information sent to those they know in the West."

"What kind of information?"

"I never see any of it, but father says it is anti-Soviet stuff. Some of it secret. If caught, it would mean a sentence in the Siberian labor camps. Not something done without serious thought."

"What happens to this information?"

"Father will not say."

"Do you know Russians in Paris that maintain contact with those in Russia?"

"A few. They are very secretive though about what actually goes on."

Another week of Plisetsky's probing produced the names of three people close to his father that Grigori believed maintained secret contact with those in Moscow. He continued claiming he had no idea what happened to the information they received, but Monique sensed he knew more than willing to reveal. She reported the names of those involved with Boris Antonovich to her mother.

Such information seemed trivial to Monique Plisetsky but would prove useful to the MGB. They would identify the family tree of these expatriate Russians. Regardless of any proof, the secret police would arrest or put under surveillance every relative in Moscow. Charges ranging from espionage to anti-Soviet behavior. Those arrests in turn would spread outward to ensnare others.

The expanding human damage set off by her actions never entered Monique's thoughts. She was just exercising her role as a Soviet spy. She held little concern for the possible consequences of her actions. Nothing more than a contest against spies working the opposing side. Stories about brutal oppression within the Soviet Union were too remote to impact her. She was a narcissist and self-absorbed adventuress. Whatever actually became of her father held no emotional meaning.

Tenacious, Monique conspired with her mother to apply greater pressure on Grigori.

They typically spent the weekends together. Arriving midday on a Saturday at Monique's apartment looking forward to the weekend, Grigori instead found her crying.

"What's wrong?"

"It is about my father."

"Your father? I thought you said he died years ago?"

"No. That was just easier for Mother and me to say. He was a Russian diplomat caught up in Stalin's Great Purge in the late

1930s. Recalled to Moscow. Sentenced to a forced labor camp. Part of the Soviet Gulag in the Kolyma region of Siberia. Rarely does my mother receive a letter. Two years since last hearing from him. We thought he might be dead. Then she received this letter just days ago."

She altered the real story to portray her father as a diplomat rather than an intelligence officer. Easier to explain his recall to Moscow as part of Stalin's universal great terror than the more complex events leading to him to the Siberian Gulag.

She handed Grigori a soiled sheet of butcher paper. A short hand-written letter in pencil in Russian.

Handing the letter back to her, "I do not read Russian very well. Read it out loud, Monique."

Dearest Angelique. I write many letters but never know if they make it to Paris. I have taken ill. It is turning bitterly cold early. Even felling trees does not keep me warm. I believe I have pneumonia. Confined to my bed in the barracks. Cold even inside. The barracks heated only by a single stove. No medicine available. My food rations reduced because I am too sick to work. I think of you always. I fear I will not survive the coming winter. Care for our beautiful daughter. Should I die, remember me fondly, Angelique. Stanislov.

Grigori embraced Monique, trying to calm her after she began sobbing uncontrollably. A convincing performance. The letter was a fake produced by her mother. The butcher paper retrieved from her trash. The writing executed with a shaky hand with a blunt pencil.

Now also crying, Grigori held her until her crying subsided. Leaving her, he found a bottle of vodka in the kitchen and brought it over with two small glasses.

Pouring each a drink, "Here, drink this."

They both downed the contents in a continuous swallow Russian fashion.

Sitting down next to her on the sofa, "What happened? How did your father wind up in the Gulag?"

"It was 1939. My father was second secretary in the Paris Soviet Embassy. The signing of the Molotov–Ribbentrop Pact between Nazi Germany and the Soviet Union made him furious. I was only eight years old at the time but Mother told me how angry he became. For the Soviet Union to align with a Fascist dictator was unthinkable. According to her, Father said Hitler clearly had imperialistic ambitions to the east of Germany. Said as much in his ridiculous book *Mein Kampf*. This was Hitler's plan to buy time before then invading the Soviet Union."

She withheld from Grigori the fact that although officially second secretary, he was no diplomat. Like her mother's present lover, his position was a cover for his actual function as the resident Paris chief of the NKVD, predecessor to the current MGB.

"He apparently made indiscrete comments too freely. Recalled to Moscow. Accused as a Trotskyist they sentenced him to twenty years hard labor in the Gulag. It was the time of Stalin's Great Purge. Tens of thousands executed or sent to the camps. Appears now my father will probably die in Siberia."

"I am so sorry, Monique. Seems we both share a hatred for Josef Stalin. Your loss much more personal. For me, it is about losing grandparents and extended family. Those of my parents' generation of the revolution then the civil war fighting the Bolsheviks."

"Well at least your father and his friends do something by seeking revenge against Stalin." Waving the letter theatrically, "This makes me feel guilty for living a good life while my father dies alone as a prisoner in a freezing Siberian labor camp."

Grigori remained silent for several moments. Considering whether to tell Monique that he understood how she felt. That he was doing something bold to retaliate against Stalin. That he and his father were part of an espionage network. Part of a conduit to channel stolen secret Soviet information to American intelligence. The people sourcing Soviet secrets were true spies. The person bringing out the tiny rolls of film deposited into the airport dead drop was the boldest of those spies.

Seeing her anguish over the fate of her father and desire to do something weighed on him to explain that *he was doing something*. Perhaps she could be of service to the network.

"I also felt that way until my father confided to me that he and others were doing something directly against Stalin. What I am about to tell you must never be divulge. Not even to your mother. Will you promise me that?"

"You are frightening me, Grigori. What are you trying to say?"

"You must promise total secrecy, Monique. Quite literally, lives are at stake."

"Yes, of course. I promise."

He let out a long sigh before proceeding.

"First of all, what we do at the shop is vital. What is called an intelligence operation directed against the Soviet Union. We act as a channel for spies to transmit their material safely across the border to the West. Difficult and dangerous since the secret police have informants everywhere."

"What happens to this secret information?"

"It goes to American intelligence."

"Oh my. That is something. How does that happen?"

"My father handles that. For security, even I do not know the details."

Monique smiled. "Thank you for sharing that. I wish I could join your network as you call it. Doing something would help my frame of mind."

She reached over drawing his face closer to give him a kiss. "I am so proud of you, Grigori. Who would have thought my boyfriend is a spy?"

He beamed at her compliment. "Not really a spy, but perhaps something close enough."

She smiled. "What do you mean?"

He paused again, a flash of uncertainty but there was no turning back now. The prospect of impressing her with his real intelligence work too compelling.

"I do something quite different. I recover information placed in what spies call a dead drop. A hidden place to deposit something retrieved by someone else. I am that someone else."

"And who is this spy?"

"That I don't know. That is part of the security for the spy."

"How does this dead drop work?"

"That is why I work in the facilities maintenance department of Orly Airport. Someone arrives on an international flight and places small rolls of film in a fake electrical outlet box."

"Film?"

"Rolls of miniature undeveloped camera film."

"Then what happens?"

"I give the film to my father who gives it to American intelligence."

"Do you know who the American is?"

"No. Part of the security. Everyone knows only what is necessary to do their part."

"This film is secret information on the Soviet Union?"

"Yes. That is the only reason I would risk doing something like this."

"What do you mean? This is France. The Soviets cannot touch you."

"Fairly sure I am breaking French laws. Participating in espionage for another country from within France must be a crime. In this case, spying for the United States. Even though we are not spying against France, we are still probably breaking some French law. All of us understand that. You must promise to keep this absolutely secret, Monique. You cannot tell your mother."

"I promise. I am very impressed. You make me feel proud. Wish I could be part of this. Now let us make each other feel good in bed."

Chapter 21

Russia | October 1952

On a brisk Moscow autumn day, Nikolai Baranovsky and Vladimir Mishnyov again walked through the park close to Baranovsky's office at Moscow State University. Baranovsky just returned from the speaking engagement to the PCF in Paris and asked Mishnyov to meet him at their usual place. Unlike their political dissent discussions, this conversation could not involve the wives. Although Mishnyov's wife Dasha knew what her husband was doing, she did not know that Nikolai now joined his friend in the dangerous venture. Nor did her sister Natasha, Baranovsky's wife, know that her husband and brother-in-law were engaged in espionage for the West.

"As planned, I met Yuri Rozovsky just days ago in Paris. I also met the American intelligence officer that receives your material, Vladimir. Mr. Jones. Obviously not his real name. Also met Uncle Oleg. He vouches for the American."

"Are you sure you were not under surveillance?" Mishnyov asked.

"No. I was careful. Arrived by an earlier flight so no one from the PCF met me at the airport. The meeting took place in a remote Paris park. Rozovsky and the American made sure the location was secure."

"Did you learn more about what happens to the material?"

"Oh yes. It goes to the American Central Intelligence Agency. Not directly, but perhaps that is even better."

"What do you mean?"

"Mr. Jones is with the intelligence branch of the American foreign ministry. They convinced me that routing our material through that channel instead of the American Central Intelligence Agency is more secure for us. Less people know of us. Safer from possible Soviet intelligence penetration into Western intelligence services."

"That is good news," Mishnyov said.

"Yes. With you supplying sensitive diplomatic material and with me providing nuclear weapons secrets, we are very important spies for Western intelligence. I therefore took the opportunity to make a request from the American."

Mishnyov looked questioningly at him.

"I requested they develop a contingency plan to exfiltrate us from Russia should something go wrong."

Mishnyov's expression changed to one of doubt. "I could never leave Dasha and Mara."

"Nor could I leave Natasha behind. What I asked was for them to make a plan to get us all safely outside the Soviet Union."

"Is that even possible? All of us? What did they say?"

"Both Rozovsky and the American acknowledged that would be difficult. Yet they agreed to work on the problem. You and Dasha of course realize that what we are doing cannot go undiscovered indefinitely. The odds against maintaining that are too great. If the MGB or GRU has spies inside western intelligence services, they will know that serious security leaks exist. Our activities become the highest Soviet counterintelligence priority. We must be sensitive to any hint we are under suspicion. You most of all. Even if Rozovsky and the Americans can devise an escape plan, we must make preparations for immediately going into hiding somewhere safe."

"What do you mean? None of us can travel without papers."

"Of course not. However, there are arrangements we can make regardless what assistance might come from Rozovsky and the Americans. We should prepare an emergency escape list of essentials. Important papers and as much cash as possible. Do you or Dasha know someone that is not among your circle of acquaintances or family? Someone you could trust here in Moscow?"

"For what purpose?"

"To temporarily hide Dasha, and Mara. A precaution to prevent their arrest. Provide time for any plan the Americans can put together to get them out of the country."

Baranovsky continued. "You are at the greatest risk, Vladimir. Not only photographing secret documents but also couriering them to the Americans. Should something unfortunate happen, you need a means of getting a warning to me. I can perhaps help Dasha and Mara. However, should you be discovered, I will fall immediately under suspicion because of our close relationship. Natasha and I must consider escaping as well.

Mishnyov said, "I understand, Nikolai. Should I come under suspicion while outside the Soviet Union, there is nothing I can do to warn you or Dasha. I shall at least give you notice as to each trip and my scheduled return. If legitimately delayed, I will call Dasha from abroad and have her call you. Otherwise, if you not hear from me immediately according to my return schedule, you must assume the worst."

Baranovsky nodded. "We both must devise a plan to go into immediate hiding without raising suspicion should this become a false alarm. Getting to someplace that is not associated with our usual routine. Someplace allowing for fabricating a normal explanation should everything be a false alarm."

Mishnyov nodded, letting out a deep sigh as he absorbed the unlikely success of escaping the Soviet Union with his family.

Baranovsky concluded with, "If I do not receive your expected call upon return to Moscow, I will act under the assumption that your circumstances are compromised."

Mishnyov replied, "Agreed. Let us hope it never comes to that, Nikolai. Relying on Rozovsky's connections and the Americans to even get us out of Moscow seems a difficult undertaking."

***

Since physicist Vitalii Ginzburg's proposed the use of lithium deuteride in 1948, this became the foundation for all thermonuclear bombs to achieve the fusion phase of detonation. Plutonium-239 became the principal fissile bomb material. While still a bomb component, uranium-235 became important for fueling breeder reactors necessary for producing plutonium. Extensive uranium enrichment processes therefore remained essential.

Many of the younger physicists on the team had never seen the actual production facilities for these essential materials. In October 1952, Project Director Igor Kurchatov and senior physicist Igor Tamm took a select group of younger physicists to the main production location. Dimitri Galyorkin was among this select group that boarded an Ilyushin Il-12 twin-engine transport aircraft for the long flight to the city of Ozyorsk located in the Chelyabinsk Oblast 1000 kilometers further east of Arazmas-16.

They landed at a small military airfield. As with Arazmas-16, no commercial flights allowed. By air was the only practical way into the city. The bus transporting the scientists entered the city through two levels of fencing with guard towers and patrols with dogs. As a closed city, Ozyorsk ceased to exist. Designated Chelyabinsk-40, it now resembled an immense industrial complex.

Rumor among the scientists told of the crash construction of the vast complex. Started in 1945, construction has never ceased. The original work consisted of building a gaseous diffusion plant for uranium enrichment and five nuclear reactors to breed plutonium.

Ginzburg's breakthrough *Second Idea* represented the next generation of nuclear weapons by employing nuclear fusion to increase the energy yield exponentially. The most recent construction added a production facility for lithium deuteride as the essential component for delivering a secondary fusion detonation.

The required lithium-6 isotope existed as only 7% of naturally occurring lithium. For weapons use, it requires enrichment to 95%. Deuterium known by its chemical symbol ^2H is the heavier isotope of hydrogen. Hence the term hydrogen bomb. Manmade like plutonium in reactors fueled by enriched uranium-235, producing sufficient quantities of lithium deuteride also requires various processes.

Lithium deuteride, expressed as $^6Li^2H$ used in nuclear weapons is a compound consisting of lithium-6 and deuterium, or heavy hydrogen. Lithium and deuterium are the essential elements for constructing a thermonuclear bomb through a nuclear fusion reaction. In a nuclear weapon, lithium reacts to neutron bombardment caused by nuclear fission in the primary phase of detonation. Absorbing a neutron breaking up into deuterium, helium, and another heavy hydrogen isotope tritium with the chemical symbol ^3H. The tritium then *fuses* with deuterium releasing extraordinary amounts of energy through nuclear fusion. The result makes possible energy release in the megaton range, and the ability to miniaturize a warhead with yields beyond that possible only through a fission weapon.

A workforce of 40,000 consisting of Gulag prisoners and German POWs provided construction labor. Stalin appointed Lavrentiy Beria to head the entire Soviet nuclear weapons effort. His cruel disregard for the welfare of forced labor inmates was widely rumored to have cost the lives of thousands. Stalin's hatchet man, Beria was no less indifferent to the scientists and technicians. Virtual prisoners themselves, they felt the weight of fear under Beria's implicit threats. Should the project fail to achieve the objective of creating weapons rivalling those of the United States, it was the end of their careers, possibly imprisonment. As a production location, remote Chelyabinsk-40 felt even more like an extension of the Gulag system with its ugly industrialized environment with limited amenities for the technical staff.

As they toured the vast complex, the implications of their science took on physical form. As a theoretical physicist working in the abstract, Chelyabinsk-40 produced a profound jarring effect on Galyorkin.

Captivated by these massive processing installations, his friend Andrei Sakharov unexpectedly said in a hushed voice with his head close to Galyorkin, "Did you know that Kurchatov suffered a dangerous level of radiation exposure a few years ago here?"

"What?"

"In 1949, a failure in one of these reactors caused an unexpected chain reaction. The building began filling with radioactive gases. Everyone knew the dangers of exposure. Regardless, Kurchatov supervised alongside those inside saving the uranium load. He prevented further damage that would have severely delayed the production of plutonium."

"How much exposure did he experience?"

"I do not know. There is no official mention of the accident. However, some estimate significant numbers of those working to save the uranium rods have already died. Hard to keep that totally secret."

Galyorkin wondered if their scientific leader might be suffering long-term effects of radiation poisoning. "Why did anyone remain in the contaminated environment?"

Sakharov said, "As project head, Kurchatov understood if the uranium rods were destroyed, it would set back the schedule by months. By staying to supervise the extraction of the rods, everyone else stayed. No telling how many received dangerous levels of exposure. "

Sakharov looked around to ensure no one else was within earshot. "Be glad, you work in research at Arazamas-16 instead of this production hell hole, Dimitri. Inadequate underground storage exists for radioactive waste. In the last three years, they dumped tens of millions of cubic meters of radioactive waste into the Techa River feeding into lakes and swamps. All contaminated with caesium-137, ruthenium-106, strontium-90, and iodine-131. People in the region rumored complaining of various illnesses and symptoms consistent with radiation poisoning. But you will never hear any official reference to the problem."

The environmental disaster clearly troubled Sakharov. For Galyorkin, another example of Stalin's indifference to suffering of the Russian people. As he walked through the reactor rooms, he also realized none of the working staff wore dosimeters to measure accumulated radiation exposure. This environment un-doubtedly contained abnormally elevated radiation levels. Ap-parently it was better those working here did not know the ex-tent of risk to their health.

The visit to Chelyabinsk-40 provided Galyorkin with a wealth of statistical information on production outputs and in-ventory levels of key bomb-making materials. Upon his return to Arazamas-16, he composed a series of encrypted letters to Bara-novsky. To avoid raising suspicion for an unusual flurry of cor-respondence, he mailed them over a period of weeks.

* * *

Galyorkin's encrypted letters contained a wealth of scientific information on the state of Soviet developmental efforts. Much of the information conveyed in the form of equations providing expansive explanation in condensed form. The last of these se-ries of letters disturbed Baranovsky for what it said about his old friend's mental state of mind.

'There is no end to this nightmare. We will forever build bombs that are more powerful. I know too much about our weapons program. They will never allow me to resign to pur-sue a different professional path. Even peaceful pursuits for us-ing nuclear energy are deemed secret. Difficult to go forward with no hope for a better life. You remain my lifeline, Nikolai.'

Dismayed, Baranovsky became concerned about the possibil-ity of Galyorkin contemplating suicide. He immediately com-posed a letter with an encrypted reply.

'All is not lost Dimitri. The government cannot forever keep its top scientists virtual prisoners. You must find a way to divert your attention. Interact with your colleagues. Do not succumb to withdrawing or you will not survive. Engage in chess matches as often as possible. Chess and the interaction with others must become your lifeline. You are not alone feel-ing entrapped in this endeavor.'

Galyorkin took Baranovsky's advice to heart. When he lost Talia Zubarev, seeking others to engage in chess sustained him for some time. He allowed depression to cause him to fall back in the habit of avoiding the company of his colleagues. Although his circumstances would not likely soon change, he chose to survive. If for no other reason than to continue active rebellion against Stalin. He took Baranovsky's advice to use chess as a means of forcing himself into interaction that is more social.

Stalin lay behind everything he hated about the Soviet system. Not satisfied with defeating Nazi Germany, Stalin could not constrain his imperialistic ambitions. Instead of reaping the economic benefits of peaceful coexistence with Western democracies, he chose confrontation. All peoples under Soviet rule suffered. The need to establish parity in nuclear weapons with the United States became a natural consequence of his megalomania.

* * *

On 1 November 1952, the United States upped the nuclear arms race with the Soviet Union by detonating the first test of a thermonuclear hydrogen bomb employing a secondary fusion reaction. The measured yield was equivalent to 10.4 megatons of TNT. Over 500 times the energy released by the Nagasaki fission bomb of 1945.

The detonation took place on the Pacific island of Elugelab in the Enewetak atoll. The test fulfilled the commitment made years earlier by President Harry Truman to develop a U.S. super bomb. It was intended as a signal to the Soviet Union of U.S. advanced technology, serving as a counter to continuing Soviet nuclear weapons development. The test occurred only days before the 1952 U.S. presidential election.

Unlike other nuclear tests held secretly without advance public notification, the code-named Ivy Mike test was a very public affair. Over 11,000 military and civilian personnel witnessed the test.

From a scientific perspective, the test was a major scientific leap. The American scientists determined that using lithium deuteride surrounding a fissile core could not produce the full potential of a fusion reaction. For that to take place, a fully separate fusion detonation must take place. The Ivy Mike test set out to confirm a new approach named the Teller-Ulam design. For that reason, this test did not resemble a bomb. It was more like a small two-story building. Inside was a device weighing 82 tons. This included a massive cryogenic chamber containing 1000 liters of liquid deuterium cooled to near-absolute zero.

This was not a deliverable weapon. It was to confirm if focused X-rays generated by a primary fission detonation could produce the required pressure and temperature to cause the fusion detonation produced by lithium producing tritium then fusing with the deuterium.

**

In the library set aside for the scientists at Arzamas-16, Galyorkin was in the end game of a match with Vitalii Ginzburg. Galyorkin held the advantage when he moved his rook calling out, "Mate."

Ginzburg sighed. "I enjoy the challenge of playing you, Dimitri, however it is discouraging never to win or even play to a draw against you."

Andrei Sakharov walked in and seeing them took a seat at their table. Looking at the board, "Do I assume you are playing black, Vitalii?"

Ginsburg nodded, "Hello, Andrei. Good to see you back. Dimitri is the best player here."

"I agree. And there are those among us that are very good."

Galyorkin smiled at the compliment. "What do you think of the American test in the Pacific, Andrei?"

Covered by international journalists, the Soviet knew of the test. Even the American press releases provided much information.

Sakharov replied, "Very interesting. This stationary equipment meant they were trying to prove some new design concept. Seems to have worked if the published yield estimates are accurate."

"Yes. Ten megatons is almost unimaginable. Any idea how they achieved that, Andrei?" Ginsburg said.

"Your *Second Idea* using lithium deuteride remains a brilliant concept, Vitalii. Yet it presents challenges to configure a design to achieve a fully secondary fusion reaction. Perhaps the Americans have solved that problem."

Galyorkin said, "That is why our efforts are prioritized on developing the device for next year's test using your layer cake concept, Andrei, along with Vitalii's lithium deuteride."

Sakharov nodded, "And we also have two additional tests scheduled to test other design features. After all, we have only tested one bomb. Essentially the same as the first American bomb. We have a lot of practical engineering ground to make up before attempting to produce results through a full fusion detonation. For example, one test next year is an airdropped bomb. Our first such test. The Americans have already executed many."

"So does this American test suggest they discovered how to achieve a significant secondary fusion reaction?" Galyorkin asked Sakharov.

"Considering the yield result, it seems they did. At least in terms of the concept. Whatever they discovered however might prove difficult to replicate in a deliverable weapon."

That evening, Galyorkin composed another encrypted letter to Baranovsky relating Sakharov's comments. Realizing the tone of his last letter must have conveyed a stronger expression of the state of his mind then he intended, he softened the impression in this letter.

'*Forgive my selfish comments in the last letter. Did not mean to worry you. Took your advice about engaging in chess. Situation is now better. Discussed American test in Pacific with Sakharov and Ginzburg. Consensus is Americans testing approach for achieving a fully independent secondary fusion reaction was successful. Much work remains to engineer the approach into a deliverable bomb design. Does not alter our continuing work to increase yields through employing fusion effects in various layered design configurations using lithium deuteride. Three tests scheduled for the last half of next year at Semipalatinsk-21 test site in northeast Kazakhstan south of the valley of the Irtysh River.*'

Chapter 22

Moscow | October 1952

After months of spying for the Americans, the strain was telling on Mishnyov. Sleep was difficult whether home or abroad. His wife was also feeling the strain. Just as much at risk, she also suffered the uncertainty when her husband travelled abroad. Both worried about the fate of their daughter should their spying be discovered. A constantly troubling reexamination of their decision to work actively against the Soviet system. That compelling motivation ran counter to the emotional imperative to protect their child.

Life at home changed. He and Dasha talked less. Lovemaking became rare. He ate less and drank more. Nikolai was right. This could not go on indefinitely. Even if not discovered by the secret police, they could not survive the stress that contorted every aspect of life. The unimagined practical consequence of acting on their ideological principals. He avoided sharing his state of mind with Nikolai. Did not want to frighten him since he now joined in this dangerous endeavor.

However, he would turn more attention to Nikolai's suggestion of planning their escape from Russia. Perhaps without waiting for something to go wrong which might be too late. Relying on Rozovsky's espionage network and the Americans remained too uncertain. Putting their lives completely in the hands of others represented further risk. Yet the problem seemed insurmountable. The Soviet Union was a closed country. All the borders sealed preventing Soviet citizens from leaving. The best evidence for condemning Soviet oppression.

The most nerve-wracking part of spying was the photographing of documents. Assembled over days at the foreign ministry, he locked the latest diplomatic pouch in a safe each night. As he received new documents often accompanied by a briefing from his superior the deputy foreign minister, he must photograph them back in his office. Always the risk that someone might catch him in the act.

Then of course concealing the Minox camera was a constant risk. No way to hide it within his office meant he must bring it back and forth from his apartment before preparing for a courier trip. Security guards searched his brief case entering and leaving the building but the false bottom never aroused any interest.

The thin profile of the camera allowed it to fit in the modified interior bottom of his briefcase when he first embarked on smuggling secrets. Stitched to the outer leather was a heavy piece of leather acting as a stiffener. Removing the stitches on one end and side provided a narrow space sufficient to hide the thin camera and several film cassettes. With Dasha's help, they affixed concealed snap fasteners on the underside to allow easy access. Replacing what now amounted to dummy stitching made the bottom stiffener appear untouched yet remaining in place unless firmly lifted by one end to disengage the snaps.

Surprisingly, accessing the fake electrical outlet box at Orly Airport proved easy. With other disembarked passengers, he walked toward passport control. The dead drop was the first in a series of outlets mounted low on the wall. Stepping out of the flow of passengers, he then bent down appearing to tie his shoelaces. Shielding view of the box with his body, he pressed the cover-mounting screw that acted as a release button. The cover sprung open and he inserted the undeveloped small film cassettes. The transfer took less than ten seconds.

Mishnyov's trips to western European capitals increased in frequency. Much was going on in the world in 1952. Soviet embassies became outposts in what the Kremlin termed enemy territory.

The United States would soon have a new president. The bombastic U.S. Senator Joseph McCarthy stoked anti-communist furor with his unsubstantiated claims of communist infiltration of the U.S. government. The diplomatic ramifications of the successful test of the American hydrogen bomb of unprecedented destructive power signaled increased military advantage over the Soviet Union. The North Atlantic Treaty Organization dominated by the United States threatened the Soviet Union militarily.

The United States also began construction on the first nuclear-powered submarine. A scientific breakthrough to miniaturize a nuclear reactor to harness atomic energy for uses other than warheads. The military implications of nuclear-powered submarines with unimagined extended underwater capabilities added another threat to the Soviet Union.

The United Kingdom successfully tested its first atomic bomb on an island off the west coast of Australia. Now the third country with a nuclear weapons capability. A country hostile to the Soviet Union and closely allied with the United States.

Now in its second year, the war on the Korean peninsula continued in a state of stalemate. The conflict a microcosm signaling the demarcation of the world order divided between democracies and communism.

Within two weeks after returning to Moscow, Mishnyov was off again with stops in London, Paris, Stockholm, and Copenhagen. Arranging a meeting with Baranovsky, they met at the park near Baranovsky's office as usual.

"Day after tomorrow I am off again," Mishnyov said.

Baranovsky nodded then looked around to see if anyone was watching. "Inside this newspaper are several transcriptions. My physicist friend has been productive. The Americans assigned him the code name *Poseidon*."

"Important material?"

"I assume so but I cannot tell. Considering it is a condensed series of encrypted letters, seemed like my friend is delivering a broad assessment of the Soviet nuclear weapons development program. He broke it up into separate letters to avoid suspicion of too lengthy a letter making it appear suspicious when disguised as something innocuous. Most of the material consists of nuclear related equations which are beyond my technical understanding."

Mishnyov took the newspaper.

Baranovsky said, "About making a contingency plan for our escape. I gave it much thought. The problem breaks down to two key elements. Let us assume that we are proactive. Defecting before waiting for some indication that something is wrong."

Baranovsky understood that Mishnyov was the most exposed in this venture. Baranovsky's unspoken plan was to engage in spying only long enough to obligate Rozovsky and American intelligence to assist in their exfiltration from the Soviet Union. Being proactive allowed the best chance for defection aided by help. Once outside Soviet borders they could fabricate a story to the Americans that certain red flags prompted the emergency message. A modest deceit that might save their lives.

"First is the matter of traveling. Couples traveling abroad raise an impossible security obstacle. Air travel is out. More likely, we reach the border by rail or automobile then find a way of crossing the border. With American outside help of course. The problem there is we have no travel papers to reach the border."

Mishnyov commented, "Far too dangerous. Takes far too long to reach the border. Once we go missing, there will be a massive search."

"Yes, I know. That is why I am asking the Americans to also provide all of us with new identifications and travel authorizations under false names. At least sufficient for use within Soviet borders. Travel for couples to leave the country together using false identities becomes far too complicated to be considered realistic."

"Why?" Mishnyov asked.

"Because that is most unusual, it subjects us to unusual security questioning. Families do not leave the Soviet Union together. That also means rehearsing a new identity sufficient to pass security questioning. You and I could do that but not Mara. She is only seven. Risky even for Dasha and Natasha. The method of getting across the border then becomes the second problem. Concealing us in a truck or slipping across some poorly guarded border sector requires serious resources.

"Inside the newspaper is the request to the Americans with the necessary particulars. New identities and necessary documents for internal travel. Undated for future use. A plan for crossing the border and a telephone number in Moscow in case of emergency. Everything for passing on to the dead drop. I included photographs of Natasha and me. Take photos of Dasha and Mara for your new identification papers. All this is just a precaution to be prepared to act at some future time should we need to act."

"What about our mother-in-law?"

Baranovsky shook his head. "Should we have to leave without warning, there is no way to prepare her to leave her home and country."

"Leaving her behind will devastate Dasha and Natasha."

"Our survival will be difficult enough. There simply is no way to include her, Vladimir."

"Sounds as if you are concerned about me being discovered," Mishnyov said.

Baranovsky put his hand on his friend's upper arm. "You described how risky it is each time you photograph the diplomatic documents. Every time is a potential for discovery. No matter how careful, you cannot beat the odds indefinitely. If Soviet foreign intelligence has sources within Western intelligence services, MGB counterintelligence knows there are spies accessing top-secret Soviet Foreign Ministry information. Security will intensify. Possibly has already. We cannot risk waiting for some catastrophic event before making our move."

Mishnyov nodded his understanding. "I did not realize the toll the stress of spying takes on your life. Do you believe there will be a time when we are living free in the West, Nikolai?"

"Yes, my friend. We just need to be careful and choose the right time. Make ourselves valuable so Rozovsky and the Americans will help us make that journey when the time comes."

* * *

Viktor Neiman and Inga Jansons sat in Yuri Rozovsky's study on a Saturday afternoon. His wife Yalena served coffee. The purpose was to act on the request just received in the latest dead drop by Hermes. Rozovsky passed the request and the photos to the others.

Rozovsky looked at Inga Jansons. "Can you produce Soviet identity documents, Inga?"

Jansons examined the photographs Baranovsky provided for his and his wife's identity cards, Soviet passports, and travel authorizations. "Should be possible. But I need to see actual Soviet documents from which to replicate every detail in the forgeries."

"That might take some doing," Rozovsky said.

Neiman asked, "What about people we can trust in Moscow to help hide our sources should the need arise, Yuri?"

"Obviously we have sources supplying information. For security, only their contact here in Paris knows their identity. Might be possible but these people in Moscow do not know of each other. They are only individuals not a group."

Neiman shook his head. "No way for us to organize a group from people unfamiliar with each other."

"Boris Antonovich uses an exporter in Moscow that is part of his smuggling operation. They receive information from sources unknown to them then conceal them in the shipments to Paris. I have no idea how many people are involved, but it is a starting point."

"We have no better option, Yuri. That means confiding in greater detail to Antonovich. We need to reveal that an important asset exists. Should that person fall under suspicion, we need to find a way for him and his wife to escape the country."

"Could be four adults and a child according to Janus' request," Yalena Rozovsky said. "Is that even realistic to think it possible to escape the Soviet Union? Just getting to any border from Moscow is a lengthy journey. Secret police checkpoints along the way and using false papers. Then getting that many across the border." Yalena raised her eyebrows.

"Let's start with a manageable number. Even with resources in Moscow, attempting to simultaneously exfiltrate five people starting from Moscow becomes impossible. Should an eventuality arise, it should affect either Hermes or Janus, not both immediately. We deal with one couple at a time," Neiman said. "I should also point out that exfiltrating Oleg's sister will be impossible. She knows nothing of her daughters' involvement in espionage. Leaving her home and country at her age, she might balk. Should escape become necessary, it must happen quickly. For planning purposes, we must exclude her."

Rozovsky said, "Very well. I will meet with Boris Antonovich. Best to be straight with him. Without revealing any details, I will explain we have an important intelligence source in Moscow. Should his situation become compromised, we want a contingency plan to get him out of the Soviet Union. Can those already involved with smuggling out sensitive material be called on to help? Depending on what Boris is willing to provide, I will go from there."

Jansons said, "Should they even make it to the border, what then? How do they get out of the Soviet Union?"

"Getting across a Soviet border is even more a problem. With flying unrealistic, Finland becomes the only country that offers an acceptable possibility of crossing the border on the ground. Every other country is part of the Soviet Union or a closely allied Eastern Bloc communist state.

"Is that true, Yuri?" his wife asked.

"Never thought about it. Let me get a world map."

Retrieving an atlas, Rozovsky placed it on the coffee table opening it to Europe.

The pre-WWI map only defined Russia not the expanded Soviet Union. Neiman pointed to Russia. "What started out as Russia now includes many other states forming the Soviet Union." He traced his finger to approximate the boundaries. For practical reasons we must rule out the Far East. Russia is so vast that travel by ground or even air to these areas is impractical. The borders also do not offer friendly states.

"Therefore, that leaves only the western border of the USSR. Unfortunately, occupation and coercion following WWII extended Soviet communist influence well beyond its official borders. The Eastern Bloc presents no possibilities for safe haven." Neiman pointed to each country on the map, "This includes Ukraine, Belarus, Poland, Czechoslovakia, Rumania, and Bulgaria. Closest to Moscow are the Baltic States of Estonia, Latvia, and Lithuania. All with Soviet communist governments under the thumb of Moscow. That leaves only Finland."

Rozovsky said, "I see what you mean. It seems the only possible destination."

"For an overland route, yes. Leningrad is the logical waypoint. Something like 700 kilometers from Moscow. Then it is still about 150 kilometers to the Finish border according to the map. Also reachable by sea to the southern coast of Finland or further to Sweden."

"Why is air travel not an option?" Jansons asked.

"Spouses are prohibited from travelling abroad. The Soviet hold on those like Hermes and Janus from defecting. Their wives cannot travel separately because they have no professional reason to travel abroad. They cannot even obtain passports. Fabricated identities present the same problem."

Rozovsky said, "Until we can think of something better than an escape plan to Finland from Leningrad, it is not necessary for my preliminary discussion with Boris Antonovich. We first need to establish if we have reliable assets in Moscow willing to hide Hermes and Janus accompanied by their wives.

* * *

Yuri Rozovsky entered the Russian food and liquor market Délices d'Europe de l'Est. His friend Boris Antonovich was behind the counter.

"Yuri, my friend. Good to see you. Winter is in the air. What brings you here on this rainy afternoon?"

"Some special business, Boris. Can we speak in your office?"

"Of course. Come this way. We shall have coffee to warm us."

For a specialty importer of Russian and East European consumables, Antonovich's spacious office looked more like that of a prosperous lawyer. An expensive Louis XIV style desk with matching round table and bookshelf. Books about Russia from novels to history, mostly in Russian. Photographs and paintings of Mother Russia.

"Our American friends are seeking assistance in a matter of some importance. They value us as a partner aligned against Stalin. They confided to me that they have a highly placed spy operating in Moscow. This source now transmits material using the dead drop serviced by your son. This spy is important enough that should he fall under suspicion, they want to extract him out of Russia."

Antonovich set down his coffee cup. "Good lord. How do they propose to do such a thing?"

"They have not shared all the details but the contingency plan involves getting the spy and his wife to Leningrad. From there the Americans would attempt to smuggle them out of the Soviet Union."

"To Finland I assume?" Antonovich asked.

"Possibly, but they have not said. At any rate, that part of the operation is in their hands. They are looking for help in hiding these individuals should an emergency arise. Then assisting in getting them to Leningrad if possible."

"That is a tall order. Once this person disappears, the secret police will begin a manhunt. How can he and his wife even travel from Moscow to Leningrad?"

"The Americans have the technical expertise to provide false identifications and the necessary travel internal documents. Do you have resources you can call on to hide these people should that become necessary?"

Antonovich thought about his contact in Moscow that exported his food and liquor shipments. Yet he knew only of the export firm owner's participation in the information smuggling. Perhaps he was the only person involved. This plan to rescue spies should they fall under suspicion required many people. Antonovich could not risk compromising his pipeline to Moscow.

Antonovich also had no way of knowing that the exporter was currently under constant surveillance by the MGB. Arrests of two individuals sending secret material to those in Rozovsky's Paris expatriate group confessed under torture. They gave up the names of several other sources and explained how they smuggled information out of Moscow.

Antonovich paused for a moment before answering, "For such an operation, this requires individuals practiced in deceiving the government."

"Do you know of any such individuals in Moscow?" Rozovsky asked.

"Possibly. A have a close family connection. My wife's brother-in-law. My wife is Ukrainian you know. This individual despises the communists but he has no reason to risk his life to help people he does not know."

"Why is he then a possibility, Boris?"

Antonovich silently debated for a moment whether he should go down this path. "Because Bohdan Zinchenko is an important figure in the Moscow black market."

"That is interesting. That means he has some sort of organization. Knows how to manipulate the system. Might he do this for money?"

"I do not know. Perhaps for a great deal of money? The risk is far greater than his black market activities."

"The Americans should be willing to pay whatever is required," Rozovsky said. "Do you have a way to communicate with him?"

"Yes. I periodically ship coats for him and his wife. A valuable commodity in Russia. The coats offer bulk and have linings. Sewn inside the lining is a piece of cloth with a written message.

My wife prepares the garment. The message written on the cloth is undetectable by feeling the material of the coat. Zinchenko has his own means of smuggling letters out of Russia to us. If you wish, I will send a message inquiring as to his willingness to provide assistance in the event of emergency. Should I offer payment? He will also want to know who is paying."

"By all means. Make him an offer. We have no other options. Offer Zinchenko a retainer of the equivalent of 2,000 US dollars every month, in any currency he chooses. Should the need arise, offer 10,000 dollars for his services and an additional 10,000 for delivering each person to Leningrad."

"That is a great sum of money. Will the Americans agree?"

"They have no choice either, Boris. One more detail. Should that emergency ever occur our spy requires a telephone number to call to activate his and his wife's escape. He will simply say, *"An old friend named Boris told me to contact you. To discuss a profitable opportunity.* The reply will be, *"You must come into the office to discuss your business."* An address for a safe location is then provided."

Antonovich nodded. "Very well. I will make immediate arrangements to send the message, Yuri."

Bohdan Zinchenko was an ethnic Cossack anti-Soviet White Russian unable to escape Russia during the civil war. A clever entrepreneur, he evaded reprisal from the victorious Bolsheviks by providing illicit goods for anyone willing to pay. In the chaos following the civil war, Zinchenko relocated to Moscow, successfully obscuring his White Russian past.

Chapter 23

Paris | November 1952

Mikhail Nikolayev sat in his Paris Embassy office reading the latest coded dispatch from MGB headquarters in Moscow.

Reliable information confirms serious penetration by unknown foreign intelligence into sensitive Soviet areas. Our source is from within the British Secret Intelligence Service. The information concerns the Soviet foreign ministry and nuclear weapons development program. No further details are available. Not believed to be a British intelligence operation. Your recent uncovering of an unidentified intelligence conduit in Paris, possibly an American operation may therefore have wider implications. Direct all available efforts toward expanding knowledge of those involved with the Paris importer in question. Surveillance continues on the associated exporter in Moscow.

Passing instructions to his mistress Angelique Plisetsky to pass along to her daughter Monique produced surprising results two weeks later.

Monique called her mother the morning after Grigori Antonovich made the revelation of his servicing an intelligence dead drop.

"Mother, I have something of importance to report. I need to see you today."

"Come by after work, dear."

"It is more urgent. What about lunch? You may wish to ask Mikhail to join us. He may have questions after hearing what I have discovered."

"Very well. How about noon at Café L'Avenue near your office on Avenue Montaigne?"

"I will be there."

As Mikhail Nikolayev's mistress, Angelique Plisetsky had the perfect cover for calling the Soviet Embassy second secretary.

At noon, Monique arrived. Too cold for sitting outside, Angelique arrived earlier to secure a table a table better suited to their conversation out of hearing of others. Seated with her was Nikolayev.

Nikolayev stood and kissed Monique on both cheeks then motioned the waiter to bring another glass of wine.

Speaking in Russian, he said, "Your mother reports you have important news?"

Waiting for the waiter to leave after serving her wine, "Mother provided the opportunity to play on Grigori Antonovich's sympathies. He is infatuated with me. Willing to do anything to impress me. Mother wrote a fake letter made to look as if it came from my father dying in a Siberian forced labor camp. After I broke down crying and read the letter to Grigori, he told me he was spying. I looked suitably surprised. To make himself look important, he proceeded to tell me about his job at the airport which he described as *servicing a dead drop*."

"He used those words?" Nikolayev asked.

"Yes. He works in maintenance on the night shift at Orly Airport. Provides access to international arrivals before passing through passport control. When a delivery is to be made, he receives a telephone call. He then empties the dead drop on his next shift."

"The airport is a busy place. How is the dead drop made secure?"

"He says it is a dummy electrical outlet box. Made to look perfectly normal. Opens by touching a screw that acts as a release button to open the cover."

"What does find inside?"

"Undeveloped film. Very small in size. He calls them cassettes."

"What does he do with the film?"

"Takes them immediately to his father."

"Does Grigori know what happens to the film?"

"His father does not say but Grigori knows the Americans are behind this."

Angelique placed her hand over her daughter's hand. "That is remarkable work, Monique."

Nikolayev said, "Most definitely. You were born to this. I will see to an appropriate monetary reward. It is important for you to pursue this further. How often are deliveries made? Where is this fake electrical box located? Is it visible? How does the person depositing the film avoid being observed? Most importantly, we need to know the date the next delivery occurs. We must catch this traitor capitalist spy."

Nikolayev extracted a pen and business card from his suit jacket. He wrote a telephone number on the back. "Your information is sufficiently important that I want you to keep me informed directly of progress even if you have nothing new to report. Should you learn any further details, no matter how trivial, call me day or night. The number on the back is my residence. If calling the embassy, say only this is Mademoiselle Circe calling. *Circe* is your code name. I will leave instructions to put your calls through without question. If you cannot reach me, leave a message and number where I can call you."

Monique smiled and nodded her understanding. A code name. She knew Circe as the goddess and enchantress from Homer's *Odyssey*. The code name suited her vanity. She loved this intrigue and excitement. This was more about that than an ideological political commitment to communism.

She knew her life was decidedly better in beautiful Paris rather than anywhere in Russia. Her mother's political fervor only superficially affected Monique. Soviet propaganda was nonsense. Even her mother spoke of life being difficult in Russia. Then again, her mother might simply embrace the excitement of her chosen life. After all, Monique's father was Soviet NKVD and her mother's current lover was MGB, the current incarnation of the NKVD. Maybe she too was like the moth, dangerously attracted to a flame.

For Nikolayev, Monique Plisetsky's seduction efforts meant a professional success of unimaginable proportion. This newly discovered conduit might prove to be the link to the intelligence penetration mentioned in the dispatch weeks earlier. If his efforts could lead to identifying the courier making the drop at Orly Airport then this might lead back to identifying the actual spies. Obviously, a wide Western intelligence penetration given that the leaked intelligence came from different sectors of the Soviet government.

Nikolayev knew that no sector within the Soviet Union was more secret than the nuclear program. Headed by Stalin's most powerful subordinate, the feared Lavrenti Beria still exercised oversight over the MGB from his position within the Politburo. A source from inside the insular nuclear program was a spectacular security failure. If uncovered, Stalin might call on Beria to purge the MGB leadership for gross negligence.

* * *

Returning to the embassy, Nikolayev personally encoded a message to his superior in Moscow.

TOP SECRET - Two hours ago received first-hand information from agent code named Circe. The product of a honey trap, Circe reports Grigori Antonovich revealed to her his servicing of a dead drop located in the international arrival area of Paris Orly Airport. Antonovich is the son of the owner of the importation firm of Russian food delicacies identified in earlier reports as receiving confidential information smuggled out of Moscow. The younger Antonovich receives a telephone call notifying of a delivery. Delivers undeveloped microfilm cassettes retrieved from dead drop to his father. Antonovich claims his father delivers the film to American intelligence but did not reveal particulars to Circe.

Target sexually obsessed with Circe. Revealed information as way to impress her. Circe directed to obtain further details. Dead drop disguised as an electrical outlet box. Cover opens by concealed release. Depositing film accomplished within seconds while shielded from view of other passing passengers. Not possible to gain observation of dead drop because location is within transit security area of arriving international passengers before entering French passport control. If Circe can obtain advance notice of next delivery from Antonovich, agents on standby could fly into Orly locating and retrieving the contents of the dead drop prior to Antonovich's arrival for work shift at 10pm. Will keep headquarters advised of further progress. Advise instructions. M. Nikolayev, Resident Chief MGB Paris.

* * *

Viktor Neiman had no way of knowing the Rozovsky espionage network suffered a serious breach with the MGB identifying the Antonovich importing business as receiving smuggled intelligence from inside the Soviet Union. The loss of several sources ceasing to communicate intelligence for smuggling to Paris would take time before discovery. Even Rozovsky knew little of the loosely organized network in Moscow. The unconnected group of extended family and former friends did not know each other. The only commonality was the Moscow export firm that concealed sensitive information in shipments of foodstuffs to Paris.

Yet Rozovsky's network evolved into something far greater with the walk-in defection of Vladimir Mishnyov photographing sensitive Soviet diplomatic traffic. Mishnyov's action then led to his close friend Baranovsky offering extraordinary access from inside the Soviet nuclear weapons development program by another connected dissident.

Neiman saw all U.S. intelligence on the Soviet Union. That also included intelligence from allied western intelligence services. No intelligence penetration reached as deeply inside the insular Soviet state as Hermes, Janus, and Poseidon.

Neiman inadvertently stumbled into Rozovsky's espionage network of anti-Soviet Russians. It was not an American intelligence operation. He had even gone to great lengths to keep the CIA from taking operational control. With that came the risk of amateurs playing a deadly game. Other than himself, only the Rozovskys and Inga Jansons possessed espionage backgrounds. Their field experience coming from seeking actionable intelligence against the Germans in WWII occupied France a decade earlier.

All realized that fighting the Cold War was different in many ways. A strategic confrontation with continually changing objectives. A war where understanding enemy secrets became the measure of progress. What remained the same was individual motivation. Ideology and national identity still mattered. Rozovsky mined the personal motivations of his network of spies to enlist against the Soviet communist enemy. The Soviet communist totalitarian system employed the same motivations but reinforced through repressive measures and fear. The United States and the Soviet Union avoided direct military confrontation resulting in unconventional proxy wars with the two superpowers seeking advantage. This was the nature of the Cold War.

The Western democracies were at a disadvantage to the Soviet Union in conducting espionage. The Soviets had a thirty-year history of refining foreign espionage while employing tactics of a secret police eliminating effective dissent of peoples under their control. Rozovsky's amateur network was all the more exceptional given the paranoidal society of their Soviet adversary.

Yet the Paris group possessed insufficient resources for instituting professional oversight controls. The unknown catastrophe of Grigori Antonovich succumbing to a Soviet honey trap might remain hidden until the MGB rolled up the entire Rozovsky network. The loss of the adhoc collection of dissidents in Moscow randomly smuggling out material to Paris was a disaster for those sources in Moscow, but not a serious loss of high-value intelligence for the United States. Yet discovery of the Orly Airport dead drop could lead to the discovery of Mishnyov then to

Baranovsky then to Galyorkin. A mortal blow to the single most productive Western intelligence penetration of the Soviet Union.

* * *

Neiman always shared intelligence drops made by Mishnyov with Rozovsky's leadership group before passing on to Washington and ultimately to the CIA at Langley. This included Yuri and Yalena Rozovsky, Oleg Leonov, and Inga Jansons. this was their operation. Neiman was just the consulting intermediary conveying the material to American intelligence. Photocopies of the undeveloped film came by way of Swedish intelligence agent Sven Norberg handing a package off to Neiman at their fencing club. Neiman therefore was just as astounded by the sensitivity of the documents as anyone else. The material dispelled any uncertainty about this possibly being a Soviet reverse-intelligence operation.

The next delivery a week later was an extensive batch of material including pages of technical material on the nuclear program from Poseidon.

Neiman remarked to the group, "Means very little to me. I do not understand the science or the broader arch of the Soviet weapons program. Once I eventually learn what this means after scientific evaluation I will share that with you."

Rozovsky commented, "Considering how tightly security surrounds Soviet nuclear technology, it is remarkable how Poseidon communicates this stuff to Janus. Right in plain sight under the noses of the secret police."

Neiman commented, "It also represents an intelligence penetration of extraordinary proportions. Should this ever be discovered, heads would literally roll within Soviet security. Let us hope it never comes to that. Of all the spies, Poseidon is the most exposed. He can never expect exfiltration. "

"Ah, here is something specifically for us to deal with," Neiman said. "Something I will not forward to the CIA."

He passed the photograph of Baranovsky's request for false identifications to Inga Jansons. "Take a look at this and tell us if this is possible, Inga."

After considering the identification documents required, she passed the photo to Rozovsky. "Possible but difficult. For passports or internal identifications, or anything other than a typed letter of authorization, I need to examine actual documents. Forged documents are all about duplicating the paper, and getting the ink and stamps right. Even down to the feel. That is always the failure of bad forgeries." Looking at Rozovsky, "Can you get me actual Soviet identity documents? Including a passport?"

Rozovsky replied, "Not sure how to accomplish that." Turning to Neiman, "What about your friends in Swedish intelligence, Viktor?"

Neiman nodded. "Possibly. I will look into that. What about assets in Moscow for hiding Hermes or Janus and their wives, Yuri?"

"I approached Boris Antonovich who I believe has the best connections in Moscow. I was correct. At least he offered a possibility that made sense. Assuming this person is willing to risk his life."

"Someone already connected with smuggling out the information that arrives at Antonovich's shop?" Neiman asked.

"No. Actually his wife's brother-in-law."

"Why would he consider doing this? Is he already involved somehow with anti-Soviet activity?"

"Not exactly. I asked Boris the same question. He said he did not know if his brother-in-law would help. If so, it would be for money. The fellow's name is Bohdan Zinchenko. A Ukrainian Cossack. A successful black marketer. All Boris knows about his politics is that he hates communists."

Everyone pondered the idea.

Jansons said, "Maybe a good option. The guy knows how to circumvent the police. Probably pays bribes. If he agrees, we understand his motivation. His extended family connection to Antonovich gives him credibility. Should we need to exfiltrate either Hermes or Janus, we need someone resourceful and street smart."

"Assuming we can induce him with enough money," Rozovsky said. "I already suggested a figure to get his attention. 2,000 US dollars or equivalent currency retainer each month. 10,000 dollars should we need his services and another 10,000 for each person successfully delivered to Leningrad. From there it becomes our problem how to get them across the border into Finland. Will American intelligence provide that kind of money, Viktor?"

A small sum for the United States government but awkward to arrange given his special status as an employee of the State Department. Unlike the CIA, he had no access to discretionary funds. Swedish intelligence might possibly provide the funding. After all, they benefit handsomely by this special intelligence-sharing arrangement.

"I believe that can be arranged, Yuri. How can Boris communicate with Zinchenko?"

"Boris and his wife already communicate regularly. They send him coats with messages sewn inside the lining. He sends messages out of Moscow somehow and Boris receives in Paris in the mail. Boris is sending Zinchenko our proposal."

"That leaves it to us to figure a means of escape from Leningrad," Neiman said. "Something by water seems a better option than a remote border crossing into Finland. Still a long way into the Baltic before leaving Soviet waters. Finland is closer but Stockholm offers assistance from our Swedish friends. I will look into that further."

To Rozovsky, Neiman said, "Let me know when Boris hears from Zinchenko. If we can put together a viable exfiltration plan, it will go a long way to encouraging Hermes and Janus."

* * *

As the Republican candidate, former General Dwight Eisenhower won the presidential election of the United States in a landslide victory over the Democratic candidate Adlai Stevenson. The departure of the unpopular Truman presidency meant not only a change of administration but also a different international view. For Viktor Neiman, his unique position as special advisor to the secretary of state was likely to change abruptly with transition to a new secretary in the next couple of months.

The change could not happen at a worse time. Hermes and Janus intelligence output began increasing. A new secretary of state might force the transfer of their control to the CIA. Neiman thought there could be no more aggressive proponent of the primacy of the CIA within the U.S. intelligence community then current Director Bedell Smith. A telephone call from his boss Paul Kline, head of the State Department's INR, proved him wrong.

"A bit of bad news, Viktor. Eisenhower's likely new secretary of state will be John Foster Dulles. The good news is that Dulles is hardline anti-communist. No one more hawkish toward the Soviet Union. The bad news is his brother Allen."

"The Deputy Director of Central Intelligence? Smith's right-hand man. The architect of most of the CIA's screwball misadventures?"

"Right. Word floating around Washington is that big brother is lobbying hard for his appointment as the next Director of Central Intelligence."

"Shit."

"But it gets worse. Rumor also has it that Bedell Smith might move to the state department as an under secretary. So your special arrangement with Acheson will soon be in real jeopardy."

"That is troubling news, Paul. Got any advice?"

"Secretary Acheson wants to have a conference call tomorrow with just you and me. With this new intelligence from within the Soviet nuclear program, the CIA increased pressure on Acheson. They are pissed off that the material comes through State first. They want Acheson to convince Sweden to cooperate in a joint intelligence operation directly with the CIA. Acheson wants our thoughts how we manage this."

"Fine. I tell you, Paul. If we hand these golden assets over to the CIA, they will fuck it up. Since it involves the Soviets, they might even turn it over to that prick Gehlen and his organization of former Nazis that produce nothing but unverifiable crap."

Seated in his embassy office, Neiman began preparing a plan to propose to outgoing Secretary Acheson.

The following morning, Acheson greeted him, "Good morning, Mr. Neiman. I understand Paul already briefed you on the lay of the political landscape in Washington. Your special assignment will be coming to an end. Your job function is intelligence analysis not conducting field operations. It likely means your recall to Washington."

"I am aware of that, Mr. Secretary. I am more concerned about maintaining the integrity and security of this extraordinary intelligence penetration that fell into our laps. The Soviets may already suspect they have a serious intelligence leak. They undoubtedly have sources in the West. Possibly in sensitive U.S. or British intelligence and foreign services branches. Regardless of Joseph McCarthy's unsubstantiated allegations, some Soviet sources may actually exist. Not in large numbers as McCarthy insists, but a few well-placed sources can make a difference. Look at the output of our Hermes, Janus, and Poseidon."

"Neiman's point, Sir is by turning these sources over to the CIA risks far too many people learning their identities," Paul Kline said.

"Diplomatically put, Paul. However, I believe Mr. Neiman has a deeper distrust in CIA capabilities."

"That is true, Mr. Secretary. However, Hermes, Janus, and Poseidon are such important spies that risking them to satisfy partisan bureaucratic interests is misguided."

Silence for a moment before Acheson responded, "Since you are soon to have a new boss, what do you suggest, Mr. Neiman?"

"Actually turn this over to Swedish intelligence. Provided my expat Russian associates in Paris agree. This network is an independent organization. It is not an American intelligence operation. We do not even fund it. Our involvement comes only from the United States being the logical recipient of intelligence against the Soviet Union."

Once Neiman thought about it, turning this over to Sweden became the only logical solution. All he needed was Acheson's agreement before approaching Swedish intelligence. He also needed Acheson's cover before he left office. Neiman did not want to risk violating U.S. national security interests by divulging the identities of intelligence sources covered under classified information to a foreign power.

Acheson reflected on Neiman's surprise proposal before saying, "What is your reaction, Paul?"

Kline did not know beforehand what Neiman might suggest. Although surprised, personally, Kline wanted to return to the analytical business of the INR rather than running agents outside the scope of the U.S. Department of State's charter. As a senior civil service employee, he was not a political appointee. He still had a job in the next administration.

"Seems the best solution. Turning this over to the CIA also raises the problem of our complicity in this subterfuge. We may be in some legal trouble. Even you, Mr. Secretary. We do not have President Truman to give us cover from the shit storm if the CIA discovers we were aware of the real origin of this independent intelligence operation then concealed our active participation."

As a lawyer, Dean Acheson understood the messy ramifications should their subterfuge become known. Neiman's proposal therefore satisfied several problems. Should their involvement ever become known, there was enough plausible deniability to muddy the issue. Only the three of them officially knew of Neiman's operation. None of them committed anything related to this secret off-books espionage operation to writing. Only documentation reference existing was Neiman's authorization to share specific intelligence with Sweden in exchange for their reciprocation by providing high-value Swedish intelligence on the Soviets.

"Very well, Mr. Neiman, I also agree. Proceed to make the transfer if those involved agree. I assume the Swedes will gladly accept taking control of this spy network. Keep Paul and I informed. Good luck."

PART THREE

Kremlin & Saint Basil's Cathedral, Moscow

Chapter 24

Paris | November 1952

Monique's Plisetsky's mother told her Nikolayev was intensely interested in exploiting what she discovered. This was direct evidence of western spies operating in Moscow. If managed correctly, it could lead from discovery of the courier up the chain to the spies.

Motivated to conclude this affair with this naive young man and move on, Monique began subtly working on Antonovich to reveal further information about the dead drop. She adopted a tactic of feigning that the intrigue of his spy activities sexually excited her. A foolish assertion, but it played into enhancing his lust.

Two days after the meeting with Nikolayev, Grigori Antonovich arrived at her apartment after the end of his night shift on a Saturday morning. She had the whole weekend to work on him.

When he arrived, she opened the door and kissed him. Shutting the door, she kissed him again pressing her breasts against his chest. She wore only a robe and he knew she slept nude adding to the effect of feeling her body.

"I woke up early. Could not sleep. Thinking about you. Do you want coffee or sex?"

He slipped his hands inside her robe. As he ran his hands down her bare backside then moved to her breasts, she said,

"Thinking about your spying arouses me, Grigori. Being close to you somehow makes me feel a part of it. Does that sound silly?"

Breathing heavily from his arousal, "Not silly at all. Just my good fortune."

"Did you find any delivery in the dead drop this morning?"

"Not today. Never received a call, but I checked anyway in case I missed the call."

"Too bad. You must show me next time, Grigori. Promise?"

Shedding her robe, she pulled him into the bedroom. As he pulled off his clothes, she stroked his erection. "Will you show me?"

"Yes. Next time," he said breathlessly.

* * *

About this same time, a MGB agent flew into Orly. His purpose was to locate the electrical box and confirm it could serve as a quick-access dead drop. After disembarking a flight from London, the agent located the box in a line of several boxes spaced at intervals along the corridor funneling arriving passengers to French passport control.

He set his briefcase on the floor out of the flow of passenger traffic. Opening the briefcase, he pressed each of the screws holding the cover until the cover opened. Nothing inside.

From inside the brief case, he produced a subminiature German Minox camera to photograph the open fake receptacle box. Elapsed time less than fifteen seconds.

Within two hours of arrival, the agent stood before Mikhail Nikolayev in his Paris Embassy office making his report. The embassy possessed a fully functional darkroom with enlarging equipment.

Looking at the photo enlargements of the fake electrical box, Nikolayev immediately encoded a message to Moscow. Evidence that this purpose-constructed dead drop existed confirmed it as a conduit for a foreign intelligence operation targeting the Soviet Union. Things were coming together. All he needed now was for Monique Plisetsky to squeeze out more information that could lead to identifying the courier.

*　*　*

The following week, Grigori Antonovich knocked on Plisetsky's door at seven o'clock in the morning of a workday. Opening the door in her robe holding a cup of coffee, "This is a surprise. Do you miss me that much?"

He smiled giving her a quick kiss then closed the door. "Something to show you. Promise me again you will never tell anyone what I am about to show you."

Wondering if it was what she thought, "Yes, I promise again. Now show me. Please, Grigori."

Sure enough, he extracted two film cassettes from his coat pocket.

"Oh, my god! Are there really Soviet secrets on the film?"

"So I am told. Give me your hand. You can hold them."

Cradling them in one hand, she set down the coffee cup to examine the cassettes more closely.

"They are so small. Did you receive a call about the delivery?"

"Yesterday."

"How often do they make deliveries?"

"It varies. Every couple of weeks lately."

"This is real spy stuff. You are an important part of a spy ring, Grigori. How exciting. Where to now?"

"I must get these to my father immediately."

She set the film cassettes on the table next to her coffee cup. Untying and opened her robe. "Like what you see?"

He nodded smiling broadly.

"I have time for quick lovemaking before I get ready for work if you drive me to work."

Thirty minutes later, she was in the shower.

The lovemaking put Antonovich in a buoyant mood. Pleased with himself doing exciting work alongside his father with this spy network working against the Soviets. A relationship with a beautiful woman that enjoyed sex.

He poured a cup of coffee and looked about Monique's apartment while she showered. A small bookshelf held a stack of fashion magazines on the top shelf and a row of books on the lower. He looked at the titles. Novels. His familiarity with literature extended only to required-reading in school. Enough to recognized most of the titles because they were classics by French authors. *Le Comte de Monte-Cristo* and *Les Trois Mousquetaires* by Alexandre Dumas. *Les Misérables* and *Notre-Dame de Paris* by Victor Hugo. *Madame Bovary* by Gustave Flaubert. Interesting reading tastes for a young 20th century woman.

At the end of the line of books was a title that caught his eye. *The Second Sex*. He did not recognize the author's name of Simone de Beauvoir. Pulling it off the shelf for a closer look, he noticed the corner of something sticking out from between the pages. A business card.

Looking at the card froze him in place. In French it read, *Comrade Mikhail Nikolayev, Second Secretary, Paris Embassy, Union of Soviet Socialist Republics*. Unable to process the ramifications, he stood there for some time staring at the card. Turning the card over, the same information repeated in Russian Cyrillic. Also a handwritten telephone number. Monique knew this person.

Monique was still in the shower by the sound of the water running. What did this mean? How should he confront her? Could there be an innocent explanation? Something to do with her father in the Gulag. The card read *second secretary*. Some sort of diplomatic official. Then darker thoughts flashed through his mind. A lover? A Soviet spy?

That possibility brought a stab of intense fear. What had he done? Was it possible Monique worked for the Soviets?

The sound of running water stopping brought him out of his stupor. He examined the business card one more time before slipping it back inside the book and returning it to the shelf.

As Monique returned from the bathroom, she walked by the open bedroom door. She stopped and dropped the towel wrapped around her letting him look at her. "Making love this morning was nice."

He tried for a smile but failed, instead saying, "Can I see you for lunch today?"

"I am having lunch today with Mother today at the Café L'Avenue near my office. You can come by when I get off work tonight. I will make you dinner. Now I have to get dressed and put my makeup on. Must not be late for work. How about getting me some coffee?"

The time alone while she got ready allowed him to compose himself. Although quiet, he put on a normal face as he drove her to the interior ministry building. As he watched her walk from his car into the building, his thoughts turned to what to do next. The fear of the unknown so oppressive it blotted out everything except terrifying imagined thoughts.

He drove to the address of the Soviet Embassy. For no particular reason other than adding to his intense anxiety until he could confront Monique. Looking at the massive building sent a shudder through him. The massive structure was architecturally out of place. Intimidating in its Stalinist Soviet style situated between two large boulevards to the west of the Eiffel Tower. For Antonovich, it conjured a malevolent presence feeding his imagination of dread.

* * *

Arriving at her office building, Plisetsky used a payphone in the lobby to avoid using the office switchboard to make an outside call.

In Russian, she said to the Soviet Embassy operator, "Comrade Nikolayev, please."

"Who is calling?"

"Mademoiselle Circe."

A short pause then, "One moment please."

"Yes?" Nikolayev answered.

"Circe calling. I must see you. I have important new information. Can you meet me at Café L'Avenue on Avenue Montaigne at noon today?"

"I will be there."

* * *

After delivering the film to his father, Antonovich backtracked to the west locating the Café L'Avenue not far from Monique's Ministry of Interior building. Parking nearby, he found a public phone and left a message that he would not be into work today. With a couple of hours to waste, he walking up and down the broad tree-lined Avenue Montaigne brooding over what to do. He found a good vantage point from which to observe the café while concealed behind a tree. Only a couple of blocks from her office, he expected Monique to walk back to her building just blocks away after lunching with her mother.

After debating when and where to confront Monique, he settled on intercepting her as she returned to work. Not ideal but further waiting was beyond his capacity to endure the anxiety any longer.

Promptly at noon, he observed Monique walking toward the café then entering.

After several minutes passed, he approached hoping to observe her through the café windows. Using a newspaper to conceal his face, he took furtive glances inside.

When he spotted her, the shock almost caused him physical pain.

She was sitting not with her mother but a man. Someone older. Both engaged in conversation with their heads close together as if discussing something very private.

After several minutes, Antonovich resumed his position from behind the tree.

Surprisingly, Monique and the man exited the café after only a short time. They parted walking away in opposite directions. A brief meeting, but not lunch. What might that mean?"

Making a quick decision, Antonovich decided to follow the man rather than confront Monique as planned. Crossing to the other side of the boulevard, he kept a distance from the man far enough ahead to keep him in sight. As they walked west almost three kilometers, Antonovich's heart sank. His worst fear materialized as he watched the man walk through the gate of the Soviet Embassy. Likely, this was Mikhail Nikolayev from the business card.

Walking back to his car, Grigori Antonovich's thoughts progressively turned darker. Having not eaten for some time he stopped for a sandwich and beer as he walked back to his car. Forcing down the food appeased his hunger but did nothing to improve his state of mind.

By the time he entered his apartment, his anger escalated to something far more extreme. By telling Monique the details of his participation in spying, he betrayed those that trusted him. Especially mother and father. Sworn to secrecy, his character was so flawed he allowed a woman to seduce him into breaking faith with everything he held dear.

He must confront Monique and force the truth from her. Yet more than that, he must atone for his betrayal. So must Monique.

* * *

When Monique arrived at her apartment at six o'clock, Antonovich was waiting nearby out of sight. She carried what appeared as a grocery bag. Remembering she spoke about making dinner, he nonetheless turned his thoughts to what he must do. Fifteen minutes passed before knocking on her door.

She opened the door and gave him a quick kiss, "Did not expect you this soon. Just got home myself. Got us something for a nice dinner and a good bottle of wine. How about opening the wine?"

Instead, he grabbed her arm turning her back toward him. "How was lunch today?"

Surprised by his rough gesture, "Good. Mother was in good spirits. Excited about some new publishing project."

Antonovich shook his head bringing a puzzled look to her expression.

"What is it?"

"You did not have lunch with your mother. You met a man. Spoke for a short time then left the café separately. Care to tell me who the man is?"

Realizing Antonovich followed her, she could not deny the rendezvous. Thinking quickly, she said, "It is not what you think. I met with my mother's lover. They had a quarrel. He wanted me to try to intercede on his behalf."

Antonovich went to the bookshelf extracting the business card from the book.

"Your mother's lover is Mikhail Nikolayev?"

Cornered, Monique quickly attempted to fabricate an acceptable reason. "Yes, but let me explain."

"Go ahead," he said sharply.

"Mother fell in love with Mikhail some time ago. He is a diplomat. He has been trying to help my father suffering in the labor camp. I showed you my father's letter."

"I do not believe you Monique. Whether this man is really a Soviet diplomat or more likely a Soviet spy makes no difference. He is the enemy. You used me. I told you secrets I should never have revealed to anyone. Are you using those secrets to bargain for your father's life?"

Grigori gave her an idea of what to say next. She sat down in a chair and began to sob uncontrollably. "I am so sorry, Grigori. I know I was wrong, but I believe father might die in his condition."

He shook his head and bit his lip. "You are lying? Nikolayev put you up to this. Told you to seduce me. Let me fuck you until I told you what I was doing at the airport."

"No, Grigori, that is not true."

His anger boiling over, he ceased listening to her.

"Your mother is also part of this. She brought you into my father's shop. Perhaps she is not even your mother. Why are you doing this? For money? Are you a communist?"

"No, no. You have it all wrong, Grigori. It was to help my father. He is dying."

Her eyes widened as he pulled a revolver from his waistband. A gift from his father. A WWI Nagant 7.62 made in Belgium for the Russian military.

"I will give you the opportunity to clear this up. Call Nikolayev. Tell him you need to meet him urgently at eight o'clock this evening at the same café. Say nothing more and hang up."

At least it could buy her time. Grigori would not dare shoot her in public. Getting through to the embassy, she gave her name as Circe. Delivering the message to Nikolayev in a breathless call with her voice halting, she whispered, "I cannot talk right now." She hung up as instructed.

"He agreed. You will see I am telling the truth when you speak with him."

"No. You are a Soviet spy and I gave you secrets that will cause people to die. I have betrayed all of them. Betrayed my family. Nothing can redeem me. You gave me your word then betrayed me. Nothing you say justifies what you did."

Consumed by his own conviction of her betraying his espionage activities to Soviet intelligence proved too much to bear. As she looked up at him, Antonovich shot her in the forehead. The look of surprise on her face as he stared at the obscene bullet hole in her forehead made him physically sick.

Leaving her apartment immediately, he drove across the city and parked near the same café. Arriving early, he paced the street across from the café waiting for Nikolayev to show up. Thirty minutes later, Nikolayev walked up to the door of the café and entered after looking up and down the street. From behind the same tree used earlier, Antonovich waited several minutes before entering.

Following the waiter leading him to a table, Grigori Antonovich stopped abruptly as he passed Nikolayev's table. Pulling the revolver from the back of his waistband, he turned toward at Nikolayev now staring at the weapon with eyes widened in fear. Without hesitation, he shot Nikolayev in the chest. As Nikolayev fell back off his chair, Antonovich stepped closer firing two additional shots into Nikolayev.

Women screamed. Tables and chairs overturned spilling dishes and food as people and staff rushed to escape. Standing alone in the café, Grigori Antonovich put the revolver to his temple and pulled the trigger.

Chapter 25

Paris | December 1952

The murders made the Paris newspapers the following day. When police knocked on the door of Boris Antonovich's apartment early that morning, the news of his son's death became more distressing when told his son was the murderer. A double murderer with the discovery of Monique Plisetsky by her mother.

Viktor Neiman picked up a copy of Le Monde before entering the U.S. Embassy. By the time he entered his office he already read the entire newspaper article and immediately called Inga at her photography studio.

Summarizing the newspaper report, he told her, "Get in touch with Yuri. Have him see Boris Antonovich as soon as possible. Learn what he can about this woman shot in her apartment. I will try to get more information on this Soviet diplomat. The implications are all too apparent.

"Tell Yuri that Hermes must be warned off from making any drops. When he makes his phone call prior to a delivery relay the message, '*Abort. Mission compromised. Contact Cavalier.*' Have Yuri contact Oleg to prepare him for a call from Hermes."

"I will. What do you make of this Soviet diplomat?" Inga asked.

"I suspicion Comrade Nikolayev might not have been a diplomat. Probably MGB. That is the way intelligence services work. They place an agent in their embassy with diplomatic status to control covert assets. The murder of the young woman makes that a possibility."

"You mean she might have been a Soviet spy?"

"That is what I need to find out."

Neiman than walked down the hall knocking on the open door of Michael Pierce, resident security officer for the state department's Diplomatic Security Service.

The Diplomatic Security Service was a little known U.S. law enforcement agency. Responsible for the safety of U.S. diplomatic staff and security of U.S. assets also involved a counterintelligence function. They collaborated closely with foreign police and counterintelligence services of friendly countries.

Throwing the copy of Le Monde on Pierce's desk, "Seen this, Mike?"

"Morning, Viktor. Have a chair. I am already working with French police to understand the background of the murdered woman. I can tell you that Mikhail Nikolayev was MGB. Known to us and the French SDECE for some time."

Neiman nodded, not surprised. "Which suggests this woman might be one of his assets?"

"Possibly. She is an employee of the French Interior Ministry. Records section. French police and counterintelligence are taking this seriously."

"Will you keep me informed?"

"Sure. You are INR. What's your interest?"

"Something highly classified that might be indirectly affected. Sorry I can't tell you more."

Two days later Pierce updated Neiman. "Interesting background of the murdered woman Monique Plisetsky. Born in Paris 1931. Her father was the resident Soviet NKVD chief in Paris before the war. His mistress was a woman by the name of Angelique Plisetsky. A socialist journalist now suspected as a possible Soviet spy. Currently in custody undergoing questioning.

"Monique Plisetsky's father got crosswise with Moscow for critical comments after Stalin signed the non-aggression pact with Hitler in 1939. The interesting piece of information however is that her mother Angelique Plisetsky was also the mistress of murdered MGB Paris chief Nikolayev."

Neiman commented, "Pointing to the probability of these Plisetsky women being long-time Soviet assets working for different incarnations of Soviet intelligence. What about the shooter that put a bullet in his head?"

Neiman withheld revealing he knew of Grigori Antonovich. Neiman's involvement with the Rozovsky network must remain known only to his boss Paul Kline and Secretary Acheson.

"Guy's name is Grigori Antonovich. Works as an electrician at Orly Airport. Neighbors say he might have been a boyfriend of Monique Plisetsky. French police are investigating. Shooter's father owns a firm importing Russian foods and liquor from Russia. The elder Antonovich is prominent in the Paris Russian expatriate community. An old White Russian that fled during the Russian Civil War. Not a likely candidate for a communist spy."

"What's the speculation by the SDECE?"

Pierce shrugged. "Too early to tell. I'll let you know when I learn more."

***

That afternoon, Neiman, Inga Jansons, and Oleg Leonov met at the Rozovsky's apartment to postmortem the disaster.

"What do I tell Hermes when he calls me?" Leonov said.

Rozovsky said, "Tell him the dead drop may have been compromised. Something happened to the person picking up his deliveries. Possibly unrelated but he cannot afford the risk until we find out more. Cease all his activities. Try to reassure him.

"Tell him not to panic. Contingency exfiltration plans are not yet in place. Going underground is not an option."

Leonov said, "Very well. What do we think made Grigori Antonovich do such a thing?"

Neiman answered, "Could be domestic but circumstances suggest otherwise."

Rozovsky stated the obvious question, "The larger concern is did Grigori Antonovich reveal something to his girlfriend who appears to have been working for Soviet intelligence."

"Yuri is right, Oleg," Neiman said. "If Antonovich revealed anything about the dead drop to the girlfriend then Hermes will undoubtedly come under intense scrutiny because of his frequent trips to Paris. His only chance is to hold firm by maintaining his innocence. His identity is not known."

Rozovsky added, "If Antonovich compromised the dead drop, no evidence was ever found. He delivered film from Hermes last delivery to his father the day of the murders which I received within hours."

Inga Jansons said, "How is Boris Antonovich holding up, Yuri?"

"As good as could be expected as a father losing his only son. Yet he is also a realist. His son murders his girlfriend and a Soviet diplomat then takes his own life. What else could drive him to such an extreme than something related to the spy network?"

Jansons said, "Has he heard back from this black marketer in Moscow yet?"

"I will ask him. It did not seem the time to bring it up when I saw him earlier today," Rozovsky said.

Neiman added, "Inga is right. If Grigori told his girlfriend what he was doing then Hermes could be in immediate jeopardy. That could lead to Janus and Poseidon. Janus may want to pull the plug and get out of the Soviet Union."

"Yes, of course. I will see Boris as soon as we conclude here and find out the status if this Zinchenko fellow agrees to help."

"If Zinchenko agrees and should exfiltration become necessary, ask Boris to tell Zinchenko that he must make some telephone arrangement for contacting him. Should his services be required, we must have the means of telephone communication to coordinate activities."

Rozovsky nodded.

"Yuri. Apart from this setback, there is another pressing issue. In Another two months, there will be a new American president. That means a change in the administration. Which means I get a new boss. All indications point to the incoming secretary of state to be someone named Dulles. That likely means this special arrangement routing the intelligence of your network through me will come to an end."

"Why is that? American intelligence still receives everything we produce," Rozovsky said.

"Because the brother of the new secretary of state is the number-two guy at the Central Intelligence Agency. Strong possibility he will become the new director. Even if he does not, the American State Department will press Sweden to deal directly with the CIA."

"Well that still works does it not?"

"If Sweden agrees to maintain the subterfuge. They might just want to hand off your network directly to the CIA's to avoid conflict. If that happens then Hermes, Janus, and Poseidon come under CIA control. You must then of course cease passing on your intelligence, Yuri. Better for everyone if you continue working directly with the Swedes assuming they agree."

Neiman chose not to add that under a new secretary of state, meant his probable recall to Washington.

Having already discussed that with Inga, he assured her he had no intention of leaving Paris. Thinking for some time about leaving government service. Holding dual citizenship, made it easy enough to remain in Paris. Returning to a career in the arts field. Having helped foster this espionage operation, he felt obligated to help with damage control to this possible MGB counter-espionage effort.

Inga encouraged him to pursue his former career. Leave intelligence work. Return to the Louvre? What about the Musée d'Orsay? Her photography career exceeded all expectations. With international interest in visual Paris, she landed several lucrative commissions. Those further increased her professional exposure. She wanted him to become a full-time part of her world and leave concerns about Cold War intelligence to others.

Neiman said, "If you agree, Yuri, I will propose the idea to my contacts at T-kornet."

"What do you think, Oleg?" Rozovsky said to Leonov.

"Probably have no other choice according to Viktor. We cannot abandon Hermes, Janus, and Poseidon. Their work is too important."

"Very well, Viktor. Approach the Swedes and feel them out about working directly with them."

Neiman nodded. "I will fly to Stockholm as soon as possible. I also need to discuss exfiltration contingency plans. At least we are talking about exfiltration from Leningrad rather than Moscow. That allows the possibility of crossing the Soviet border by sea. Still difficult but maybe it offers the best option."

Neiman paused. "There is also something else. We need to remain positive. That means arranging a new dead drop for Hermes once safe to resume deliveries. Assign the task to Swedish intelligence. They should be able to create the same dead drop we used at Orly or something equally suitable at the Stockholm Airport. I will even make a reconnaissance when I fly there probably in the next couple of days. I recall you saying Hermes itinerary included stops in the Scandinavian capitals. Am I correct, Oleg?"

Leonov nodded then asked. "Should all this blow over, how do we advise Hermes to proceed and deliver information?"

Neiman said. "Tell him we are making arrangements for a new dead drop at some different location. Do not tell him yet it might be the Stockholm Airport. He should inform Janus what has happened. When it becomes possible to resume, we will contact Janus. His international standing allows Yuri to have a communication related to economics. "

Neiman said to Rozovsky, "The most immediate task is getting Zinchenko's participation and a contingency plan for hiding these people. I will fly to Stockholm as soon as I can arrange a meeting."

* * *

The change of administrations combined with this apparent MGB counterintelligence penetration into Rozovsky's network made circumstances urgent. Little time remained for Neiman to do what he could to salvage the network and the lives of these spies using his official capacity. That same night, he met Sven Norberg at the fencing club. No time for a workout tonight, they went to a café several blocks distant. Perhaps paranoid, Neiman wanted to make sure no one was following. No telling how much Nikolayev's agents might have found out from the Plisetsky woman.

"You saw the headline in the newspapers yesterday, Sven?"

"Of course. What can you add?" Norberg asked.

"The shooter that committed suicide at the scene was one of ours. The person that retrieved the film deposited by our source in the dead drop."

"That is very bad. What does this mean?"

"It means our sources must temporarily go dormant until things settle down. We must establish a new dead drop. That is where T-kornet can help. However, there is another factor requiring a change in our arrangement. A change T-kornet and the Swedish government should find attractive. Time has come to actually turn over operational control of this spy network to Swedish control."

Neiman explained the ramifications of a new American administration coming into office in January. After Neiman answered his questions, Norberg said, I will call Lindström tonight as soon as I return to the embassy."

"Excellent. Tell Colonel Lindström I will be at his office the day after tomorrow. Time is urgent."

***

The next day some welcomed news. Bohdan Zinchenko indirectly contacted Boris Antonovich by telephone. The call coming from one of his associates calling from Budapest, Hungary relayed the message, '*Your friend in Moscow expresses interest in your business proposal for a retainer of 4,000 USD monthly, and should his services become necessary for the fee of 20,000 per person for lodging and another 20,000 for travel expenses to the agreed on destination. Method for transacting payment to be determined. Emergency telephone number is Moscow 18-72558.'*

Rozovsky telephoned Neiman. After repeating the message, Rozovsky commented, "Our mercenary friend understands the market value for his unique services."

Neiman replied, "At least we understand his motivation. We have no choice but to trust Boris Antonovich's instincts. Zinchenko is the only option should we need to rescue our sources."

"Will the money be a problem?"

"Don't think so. Small expense for the Swedes in exchange for handing them high-value spies already in place. I am flying to Stockholm tomorrow. Laying out the details of my proposal. Outlining the reasoning behind the change. If they agree, I shall give them your name, Yuri. Their Paris agent I work through will undoubtedly want to meet you. Tell Oleg to provide Hermes with the Moscow emergency telephone number."

Rozovsky nodded in agreement.

"Don't be discouraged, Yuri. You of all people understand espionage operations suffer setbacks. Regardless of the need for a new arrangement, this will be a positive move. Still feeding Soviet secrets to the Americans while keeping your work under European control.

* * *

Neiman's meeting in Stockholm included only Sven Norberg from Paris and Colonel Konstantin Lindström Swedish deputy director of Swedish T-kontoret.

Lindström opened the meeting by saying, "Mr. Norberg briefed Director Palm on your proposal, Mr. Neiman. He is not joining us because he wants the details to remain as closely held as possible. Even among our own staff. Director Palm, Minister of Foreign Affairs Undén, and Prime Minister Erlander are the only others that know of this .... Not sure how to characterize this double dealing among allies. Both Minister Undén and Prime Minister Erlander want to maintain plausible deniability following the changes in the American government with a new president."

"Sometimes compartmentalization is necessary in bureaucracies, even between intelligence services," Neiman commented.

Lindström continued, "At any rate, the less the number of insiders that know of the origin of these intelligence sources the better. We shall stay as close to the actual story as possible. The only difference will be substituting you with Sven Norberg. The cover story becomes a walk-in source to the Swedish Embassy in Paris. That source becomes Yuri Rozovsky. Stockholm instructed Mr. Norberg to channel the intelligence to the Americans through his friendship with you as an American foreign service intelligence official. A logical conduit given our preference to keep this cooperation within the confines of our respective foreign services.

"We shall continue to provide the Americans the product of these Soviet sources through the U.S. State Department as a means of plausibly maintaining our unaligned status while sharing with the Americans and Western Europe."

"Excellent. Makes perfect sense, Colonel. As I explained to Mr. Norberg, my status may change very soon with a new administration coming into power. Yuri Rozovsky is ready to make the transfer as soon as possible."

"Arrange a meeting with Monsieur Rozovsky as soon as you both return to Paris. Make this a seamless transition."

"I agree, Colonel. Best for everyone concerned. There is one remaining detail. Our high-value sources in Moscow understandably requested an exfiltration plan should something go wrong. I do not believe they have any illusions that should Soviet counterintelligence suspicion their activities, there will be no warning before arrest. Even with time to plan for such an operation, getting them out of a police-state like the Soviet Union will be difficult."

"Are we speaking about all three sources? Hermes, Janus, and Poseidon?"

"Not Poseidon because he is already beyond our reach in one of the nuclear closed cities described by Janus. However, it includes Hermes, Janus, their wives, and one young child."

"We have the services of a first rate forger, but do not have access to Soviet passports, identity documents, or vital Soviet travel authorizations to use as templates. I thought T-kornet might help with that. Here are photographs and personal details on the five people," Neiman said passing an envelope including the material provided by Mishnyov and Baranovsky.

"That is not the problem. How do you plan mounting an exfiltration? We have no assets in the Soviet Union capable of mounting such an attempt," Lindström said.

"Neither do the Americans. However, Rozovsky and his associates in Paris are resourceful. They made an arrangement with a well-connected Moscow black marketer. Someone related to someone in Rozovsky's circle. Not an ideal option but the best we can devise."

"How is this black market person going to get five people from Moscow to a border with a receptive country then across a tightly secured border out of the Soviet Union?"

"He is not offering that. Only to hide the fugitives and get them from Moscow to Leningrad. Getting them out of the country is our problem."

"You mean Sweden's problem?" Lindström said with a sour expression. That is also no easy feat. Why Leningrad?"

"The closest border from Moscow offering possibilities for exfiltration is the Baltic region. Leningrad is a port city. Offers options for smuggling these people out by sea."

"Depending on the time of the year. The Port of Leningrad becomes iced in for a couple of months during winter," Lindström remarked.

"Nonetheless, geographically it is our best bet. Should an emergency arise, let us hope it is during warmer weather. Even without an escape by sea, Finland is a neutral country with a border with Russia. At any rate, we need Sweden to fund this black marketer. He is looking for a retainer of 4,000 USD per month and 40,000 for each person to hide them and get them successfully to Leningrad."

Lindström grimaced. "The fellow thinks highly of his services."

"A good bargain for giving these spies some hope for getting out of Russia alive should the need arise. Unless both Hermes and Janus collectively get cold feet, it might not be five people. Should something go wrong, it becomes more likely to involve only one of the families. Arrest without warning leaves the other party to decide if they must risk trying to escape"

"Very well. The obligation obviously goes along with making them our responsibility," Lindström remarked.

***

Vladimir Mishnyov arrived at Orly Airport. He was on edge after reading the London Times before departing Heathrow Airport that morning. The front page reported the murder of a Soviet diplomat in Paris. Familiar with the senior Paris Embassy staff, Mishnyov knew that Mikhail Nikolayev was actually the resident MGB chief. Upon disembarking, he made his usual call to the Paris number. After the person answered as *bureau récepteur*, Mishnyov gave the usual response of *I rang the wrong number.* Instead of receiving the usual reply response of *understood*, the person said, *Abort. Contact Cavalier.*

The call disconnected before he could ask what this meant. Shocked, Mishnyov dialed Oleg Leonov, code named *Cavalier.*

Fortunately, Leonov answered. Keeping the message short, Leonov said, "The dead drop is possibly compromised but you are not knowingly connected. Destroy any materials you are carrying. Should you feel under serious suspicion the Americans arranged a rescue plan. Only to be used as a last resort for you, Dasha, and Mara. It means defection to the West. A dangerous journey that could cost lives of everyone. Not a decision taken lightly. Call Moscow number 1872558 to activate such a move. Cease all activity indefinitely until we feel comfortable for you to resume under a new transfer arrangement. Raven will advise

Janus when it was safe to resume. Be advised the Soviet Embassy in Paris is in turmoil due to the murder of the MGB station chief. Happened days ago. Appears possibly domestically related. Be prepared when you arrive at the embassy but stay calm. The MGB cannot connect you to the dead drop except by the general circumstances of your access to sensitive material and frequent trips through Orly Airport.

Leonov was torn. He understood that was disingenuous. Trying to give Mishnyov a thread of hope was not being honest. The MGB would likely be all over Mishnyov. He was in for a rough time and Mishnyov knew that. The sensible advice was for Mishnyov to defect immediately before leaving the airport. However, Leonov knew that would doom his niece Dasha and their daughter Mara.

Leonov changed his mind. That decision must be Mishnyov's not his. "Vladimir. Because of your unique circumstances, you will undoubtedly become the principal subject of suspected espionage. You know better than I do the possible consequences of that. You have one chance to decide immediately to defect. I understand what that means for Dasha and Mara. The reality is that should things go badly for you their fates are already sealed. Only you can assess your chances of surviving intense secret police interrogation."

Mishnyov remained silent for several moments. Everything in his mind focused solely on thoughts of Dasha and Mara. "My survival no longer matters, Uncle Oleg. As you said, their fates are already determined. I could never live with the thought of saving just myself. I must play this out regardless of my chances. Goodbye, Uncle Oleg."

Overcome by emotion, Leonov could find no words to dissuade Mishnyov, "Good luck, Vladimir." After a long silence, the call disconnected.

Shaken to his core, Mishnyov held the payphone receiver for several moments while rooted in place. After regaining control, he began making his way with other passengers toward passport control. He ventured a quick glance as he passed the fake electrical box. Nothing seemed out of place. How then did the MGB discover the dead drop? How is the murder of the MGB agent connected?

***

Nikolai Baranovsky answered his office telephone. Unexpectedly, it was Yuri Rozovsky. Probably not good news going outside security protocols. Hoped Rozovsky could communicate in some indirect manner. He must assume the MGB monitored all international calls through the telephone exchange.

After consulting with Neiman and Leonov, Rozovsky took the initiative to alert Nikolai Baranovsky of the potential threat resulting from events in Paris. Should things go badly for Mishnyov, it might become too late for Baranovsky to react without prior warning.

"Wanted to wish you a joyous Christmas, Professor Baranovsky," Rozovsky said in French.

"Thank you. Most kind of you to think of me."

"Got to looking at the exchange rate between the French franc and Soviet ruble. Wanted to get your read on what this meant for improved trade between our countries. A problem you addressed in your speech at the International Economic conference in the spring. So given the holiday season, I decided to call."

Playing along with no idea what Rozovsky was getting at, Baranovsky said, "Not good for French industrial exports to the USSR. Seems more a problem for France. What is happening to moderate the strengthening franc?"

"Little that France can do. I recommend the Soviet Union should sit on its natural resources until the situation improves."

Still uncertain what Rozovsky was attempting to convey with these contrived economic references, Baranovsky replied, "Not that easy. We cannot simply dial down economic activity without causing serious consequences. As a fellow economist, what would you suggest?"

"I believe we spoke about such a contingency affecting trade activity when we met at the conference. There is an alarming compromise in French confidence regarding balance of trade. Should things become worse, look at the numbers. The current exchange rate is about 1.87 rubles to the franc. I project that will worsen by 2-5% per month given the trend line. The Soviet government needs to reverse that by realigning spending to increase non-military industrial output by as much as 5-8 % annually. You are a mathematician. Put the numbers together."

Look at the numbers? Put the numbers together? Did sitting on natural resources mean intelligence coming from Galyorkin or Mishnyov's activities? Contingency? Was Rozovsky communicating a Moscow telephone number to call to activate an exfiltration plan as Baranovsky requested? What did the unusual phrase *alarming compromise* mean? Something must have happened that made this more urgent than waiting to send a message through Vladimir through the dead drop. Was the dead drop compromised? Was Vladimir compromised? Stringing the numbers together gave the number 1872558. This had the correct structure for a Moscow telephone number.

"I will look at those numbers and give you my thoughts."

"I am working on completing a more comprehensive study that will be available soon. That will build on these broader figures I just gave you," Rozovsky added referring to forged identity documents necessary to facilitate travel once the Baranovskys came under Zinchenko's protection. He hoped Baranovsky made the connection. With Zinchenko on board, they had the ability of delivering the forged papers.

"Very good talking with you Professor Rozovsky. We should talk more often."

"You and your wife enjoy the holidays," Rozovsky said and disconnected the call.

The implications of Rozovsky's call unnerved Baranovsky. Vladimir Mishnyov was out of the country. Due back in two days. Dasha should be at her office in the Foreign Ministry. He immediately placed a call to ask if she had heard from Vladimir. Instead of reaching Dasha on her direct line, another woman answered. Baranovsky said, "May I speak with Dasha Mishnyov please?"

The reply came, "Comrade Mishnyov is out of the office to-day after calling in sick. Can I leave her a message?"

Baranovsky disconnected the call immediately and dialed the Mishnyov apartment. The phone rang repeatedly without answer.

Chapter 26

Paris & Moscow | December 1952

Within the span of minutes following arrival at Orly Airport, Vladimir Mishnyov felt overwhelmed and trapped. While reading of Nikolayev's murder before Uncle Oleg told him, it did not seem threatening to him personally. Learning of the MGB discovery of the dead drop changed everything. He did not have the chance to ask Leonov how that came about. Whatever the circumstances, it confirmed the existence of an active spy penetration by the West. He would undoubtedly fall under suspicion. Both as source and with the means of transferring the information.

After disconnecting the call from Oleg Leonov, his first concern was disposing of the film cassettes in his pocket. Once he passed through French passport control, the embassy driver would be waiting. As he walked along with the other passengers, he withdrew the film cassettes from his pocket. Placing them inside the folded London Times, he dumped the incriminating evidence into the first trash receptacle before approaching the passport control queue.

Passing through passport control was routine. Holding a diplomatic passport with multiple French entry stamps identified him as a frequent traveler to Paris. He immediately spotted his usual driver. As the man stepped toward Mishnyov, two other men advanced next to him. Undoubtedly, MGB like the driver. Mishnyov's heart sank realizing the implications of three MGB waiting to escort him to the Soviet Embassy. Thoughts of Dasha and Mara dispelled any thought of taking the last opportunity for defection.

As they drove toward the Paris Embassy, no conversation passed between the MBG agents. At every Soviet Embassy Mishnyov visited, security personnel were the same. Blank unfriendly unsmiling faces yet with some deference to his status. The expressions of these three exuded only malice.

Instead of escorted to the first secretary's office as normal after arriving at the embassy, one of the MGB said, "Your presence is required by the chief of security." The man took his arm roughly.

Escorted not to an office, but to a sterile room with a single table and two chairs confirmed his worse fear. He needed to focus his thoughts to avoid exhibiting signs that might indicate his guilt. Play this as an expected consequence following the murder of the resident MGB chief. Deny any accusations about spying while displaying confident arrogance.

Alone for several minutes, a uniformed major Mishnyov recognized from prior visits entered the room.

"I trust you are aware of the murder of Comrade Nikolayev, Comrade Mishnyov?"

"I read of it just before boarding my plane in London. The killer apparently took his own life. Is the motivation known?"

The major ignored the question. "There is a larger security concern more important than the murder of Comrade Nikolayev. Moscow has ordered your immediate return."

This was clearly something more than the MGB lashing out blindly.

"I am scheduled to fly to Copenhagen then on to Moscow. I carry important confidential documents." Mishnyov replied in a manner expressing his status while gesturing toward the small briefcase secured by handcuffs to his left wrist.

"My orders are specific. I am to take custody of your brief-case and put you on a plane to Moscow tomorrow. You shall spend the night here at the embassy, Comrade."

A long night without sleep passed. Mishnyov's imagination played through every imaginable scenario possible. He understood that he must demonstrate his indignation by forcefully denying any accusations. Whatever they suspected, he must assume they had no evidence. Certain that he did not make any mistakes in photographing documents. The miniature Minox camera well hidden in the apartment. To maintain his resistance during sustained questioning, he must believe that he is a target only from circumstantial factors.

If he was wrong and the MGB did have evidence, it was all over. Nothing he said could mitigate his fate. His principle objective was providing Dasha the emergency telephone number given by Oleg Leonov. If a possibility existed for Dasha and Mara to escape the country that provided a measure of hope should his situation deteriorate. Then of course, he might be underestimating Dasha's current circumstances. Might she already be under arrest?

Hard to tell what evidence the MGB possessed. Yet, Mishnyov understood the true power of the MGB in Stalin's police state. Evidence was irrelevant. The secret police generally assumed suspicion equated to guilt. If mistaken, the accused suffered the same fate unless someone of elevated stature intervened. The theory being that everyone was expendable in the service of the state. Better to condemn those innocent few than to let anyone guilty escape unpunished. It fed the ideology of the primacy of the state over all other considerations. The environment of terror further enhanced the power of the state. Joseph Stalin was the State. Those anointed as his chief deputies served only to execute Stalin's broader directives. Even they could fall victim to Stalin's capricious nature.

That night spent at the Paris Embassy was a forerunner of what he might face in Moscow. A room with its own toilet but locked from the outside. Already under detention. His stature as a senior foreign service officer trusted with state secrets and allowed travel outside the Soviet Union became irrelevant. If there was a chance he was spying for the West, he became expendable.

His Aeroflot flight to Moscow was under armed escort. One of the same MGB agents that met him at Orly. Arriving in Moscow, he immediately understood the serious nature of his circumstances.

Two other MGB agents met him as he disembarked. Bypassing passport control, they escorted him to baggage claim. Brought to a customs table, MGB agents emptied his suitcase. Every article of clothing thoroughly searched and thrown in a pile. Contents of his toiletry kit dumped out.

The final indignity as passengers filed past averting their eyes was as an MGB agent ripping out the lining of his suitcase.

They found nothing incriminating. This was the first step in instilling fear in the victim by suggesting they knew something incriminating. Humiliation played a key factor in Soviet interrogations.

From the airport, wedged in the backseat between two MGB agents, they drove to Lubyanka Square. MGB headquarters with its dreaded prison occupying the lower levels of the large ugly building dominated the square. They arrived in the early evening. The exterior lighting made the building appear more ominous.

Without any further explanation of his circumstances, the MGB escort brought him into the building. Removing Mishnyov's handcuffs, the MGB agent said to a uniformed guard behind a desk. "Vladimir Ivanovich Mishnyov."

Locking at list, the guard behind the desk responded, "Cell 127," then motioned to two other guards standing nearby. "Prisoner is to remove his overcoat, belt, tie, and shoe laces. Empty everything from your pockets. Remove your watch and ring."

A final indignity. Already a prisoner.

They escorted him down two flights of concrete steps. This was early January and the place was cold and damp. Already he missed the warmth of his overcoat.

They walked half way down the long brightly lit corridor stopping at cell 127. A solid steel door with a small hinged-port for guards to look inside.

Pushed inside the windowless two-by-three meter cell, the door closed with a metallic clank behind him. Then the turning of a key. A metal frame bed suspended from the wall held a thin rolled up mattress and a blanket.

A stainless steel toilet and sink occupied the end wall. A single light protected by a wire cage protruded from the high ceiling. A small rectangular vent on either sidewall presumably supplied heating and ventilation.

A place designed to remove all hope for the prisoner. Let the victim reflect for a time before facing interrogation. Another long night ahead of him to organize his mental defenses.

Having fallen into an exhausted asleep for only an hour, the sound of the heavy cell door squeaking open brought him awake.

A guard came over and grabbed him by the arm. "Stand up and come with me."

Walking him up the stairs to the next level with another guard stood beside an open door. Pushed inside, the guards pushed him into a heavy wooden chair bolted to the floor. Once seated, he faced a large wooden table with two chairs on the other side of the table. To Mishnyov's dismay, the arms of his chair were fitted with straps along with the front legs of the chair.

The guards stepped back taking up positions on either side of the door. Overhead was the same type of light fixture as in his cell. On the table stood a desk lamp with a flexible arm.

Minutes later two uniformed MGB officers entered.

Mishnyov was not sure of the insignia of rank, but thought the officer holding a folder might be a colonel. The other younger man held a notepad.

The colonel extracted photo enlargements from a folder placing them on the table. Mishnyov recognized the images. The fake electrical outlet box at Orly.

"Do you know what this is?"

Mishnyov pretended to look intently at the photos. "No. Looks like some piece of machinery."

"An electrical outlet box. The photo taken at Orly Airport in Paris. The location not accessible except to arriving international passengers and airport employees."

Mishnyov remained silent.

The colonel continued. "You photographed secret government documents and used this fake electrical box as a dead drop on your trips to the Paris Embassy. You place a telephone call before making a delivery. An employee of the airport then removes the undeveloped film you deposited in the dead drop. We know all this because this airport employee confided to one of our agents. Your espionage network no longer exists, Mishnyov."

"I have no idea what you are talking about. I did not betray my country."

The colonel smiled and shook his head. "You will ultimately confess, Comrade Mishnyov. You have access to sensitive foreign ministry material and the means of delivering it to our enemies. I assure you that you will unnecessarily endure much unpleasantness unless you provide us with details and names. In the end, everyone confesses.

The questioning went on for several hours. Deprived of sleep and without natural light, Mishnyov lost all track of time. Allowed water and an opportunity for a brief escorted visit to the toilet, the interrogation resumed. This time with a fresh officer pursuing the questioning. They had yet to subject him to overt physical torture but the threat was implicit if did not confess.

Nearing collapse, the interrogators then left Mishnyov alone with only the guards by the door. His head dropped to his chest succumbing to sleep. Moments later, another guard entered carrying a plate of bread and cheese. Looking at the food, Mishnyov withheld the impulse to satisfy his hunger by waiting to see what this meant. The colonel returned within a short time carrying a bottle of vodka and two glasses.

The colonel shook Mishnyov awake. "Come. Eat something before we begin again. I brought vodka. You must be thirsty. We shall talk as men that understand the realities of a difficult world."

After hours deprived of water, of course he was thirsty but not for vodka.

Mishnyov ate the bread and cheese knowing it was nothing more than a change in tactics but necessary to preserve his strength to resist.

The colonel poured two glasses of vodka handing one to Mishnyov. "Drink with me, Vladimir Ivanovich."

The colonel downed his glass. Mishnyov took a sip moistening his dry lips but avoiding swallowing too much and then set down his glass.

"I am trying to help you, Vladimir. You must think about your wife and daughter. We know you are guilty. However, you still have some leverage. If you provide us everything you know, then I can promise it will benefit your family's circumstances."

"Do they know I have been detained?"

"Oh, more than that. We also arrested them. Your wife is also undergoing questioning elsewhere in this same building. Your daughter is in a special facility for children of parents under arrest."

Tears flowed freely down Mishnyov's cheek. There remained no hope now for saving them. Dasha knew everything and they will subject her to harsh treatment. Should she survive the torture, it meant exile to a forced labor camp in Siberia. Mara's life destroyed after condemned to an orphanage, labelled the daughter of foreign spies.

The colonel seemed in a different mood drinking his vodka. Perhaps just a temporary change of tactics. Then he asked Mishnyov a new question. "You have a good friend. Your sister-in-law's husband to be exact. A noted academic. Professor Nikolai Baranovsky. His wife Natasha is your wife's sister."

"Yes."

"We of course have questioned all your friends and associates. Except for the Baranovskys. Their whereabouts is unknown. They are not at home. Neither of them showed up at their offices at the university the last couple of days. Neither left any messages explaining their absence. What do you make of that?"

"I have not talked with Nikolai for over week. From before I left the country. He never mentioned any travel plans."

"Yes, like you, the renowned Professor Baranovsky also travels out of the country. He therefore must have contacts in the West. Are we to assume he and his wife have found a way to defect?"

Mishnyov's head jerked up. "He has no reason to defect. He could have done that during any of trips abroad."

"True, but not with his wife. Then again, maybe there is something more to his disappearance. If we believe you are spying, Vladimir Ivanovich, why not also your close friend Baranovsky?"

"Nikolai is an economist. He does not handle sensitive information."

"Possibly. Yet you must agree his disappearance along with his wife becomes a remarkable coincidence with our discovery of a spy ring involving his closest friend. You can appreciate our interest in talking to him. If you cannot tell us anything about Baranovsky that is unfortunate. Unfortunate for you. It could prove of value in helping your wife and daughter."

While the MGB had no direct evidence of Mishnyov's spying, he was among only a handful of those within the foreign ministry with access to the broad range of Soviet intelligence acquired by Western intelligence. Both the MGB and the GRU had sources in British MI6 and the British Foreign Ministry. Sources with access to not only British foreign intelligence but also intelligence shared by the United States. Yet the Soviets did not believe this to be a British espionage operation casting further suspicion this was an American venture.

Adding to the focus on Mishnyov was discovery of at least two people in Moscow confessing weeks earlier to smuggling confidential information to Paris. The recipient was the father of Nikolayev's killer and the person servicing the dead drop. The connections suggesting Paris as a conduit for perhaps multiple Western assets operating in Moscow working for the Americans.

The MGB spy-hunt began when the evidence first pointed to the Soviet foreign service. Mishnyov at that time was among many under scrutiny. What made him the principal candidate was the discovery of the dead drop in Paris. Few people had the access combined with the means of delivering information to Western intelligence.

Yet the MGB still could not account for the more recent flow of technical intelligence that must originate from within the Soviet nuclear weapons development program. Information not possessed by the Soviet Foreign Ministry. That would take further unraveling of what might be a widespread espionage network. As a close friend of Mishnyov, the disappearance of Baranovsky and his wife took on importance.

In the uncertain environment of senior officers of the Soviet state security service in which the colonel served from before WWII, he well understood the pitfalls of failure. Breaking Mishnyov and his wife and uncovering the wider conspiracy could make him a general. Failure might find him a prisoner in the Lubyanka or a bullet to the back of the head. Such was the precarious reality in the uncertain environment fostered by Joseph Stalin. Trained in manipulating interrogation victims made him somewhat of an authority on the human mind. The violence and unpredictable actions of Comrade Stalin might suggest tactics to prevent those closest to him from achieving enough power to become a threat. Viewed through that lens, helped the colonel navigate the dangers of his position. Flying too close to the sun, as the Greek mythological Icarus, could prove fatal.

Chapter 27

Moscow | December 1952

The day before Rozovsky's unexpected telephone call, Nikolai
Baranovsky read in Pravda of the murder of a Soviet diplomat in Paris. The official newspaper of the Communist Party of
the Soviet Union, Pravda obviously made no mention that Mikhail Nikolayev was MGB. Yet Rozovsky's alarming coded telephone call providing him with an emergency Moscow number
suggested something more was going on. Was Mishnyov's dead
drop compromised? An emergency number implied some sort of
exfiltration plan existed for him and Natasha. Did Rozovsky's
call coming before Baranovsky even knew an exfiltration plan
existed mean something unexpected happened in Paris?

If Mishnyov is blown then he comes under serious suspicion as
Mishnyov's closest friend. The thought of abusive interrogators
in the Lubyanka torturing Mishnyov and Dasha made him
shudder. The use of torture was common knowledge circulated
by rumors attributed to survivors held at the Lubyanka. Would
Vladimir and Dasha reveal his and Natasha's subversive views?
At best, their careers would end. More likely sentenced to forced
labor in the Siberian Gulag.

Baranovsky thought of what this meant for his friend Dimitri
Galyorkin. Far removed from what was happening yet as much
a part of this as he and Mishnyov. With Baranovsky's demise

then Galyorkin fell under suspicion because of their correspondence. No way to prevent that but he must warn him. With Galyorkin's fragile state of mind locked away in a closed city doing work he despised, losing his only meaningful contact would be devastating. He doubted his own ability to withstand harsh secret police interrogation much less torture.

Baranovsky immediately drafted an encrypted letter. Building on Galyorkin's selection of the chess match used to encode his last letter, Baranovsky selected a complimentary chess match to use for this letter. The encrypted content read, '*Delivery conduit for your information believed compromised. My situation uncertain. Cease all communications. Expect intense scrutiny by MGB. Reveal nothing. No evidence exists of your involvement if they cannot decode our correspondence. Hold your ground. Admit to nothing. You have not seen me for a couple of years. Will contact you should circumstances improve. Stay strong. Good luck old friend.*'

Too late to question joining in Mishnyov's crazy act of rebellion, Baranovsky must make an immediate decision. Once he called the emergency number there was no turning back. Defection to the West provided he and Natasha could escape the Soviet Union. Something dreamt of but he knew nothing of what planning might be in place. They as yet possessed no fake identification papers. Travel to any border region within the Soviet Union was highly restricted, requiring specific authorization. To make the move now meant placing their fate entirely in the hands of unknown persons.

Natasha knew nothing about his espionage activities. Nor that of her brother-in-law. While Dasha Mishnyov knew fully what Vladimir was doing, she never shared it with her sister.

Natasha Baranovsky held the same critical views of her husband and the Mishnyov's. She only voiced criticism of the Soviet system with her husband and the Mishnyovs. Nikolai never once expressed to her any desire to leave Russia. She seemed reconciled to their relative good life in Moscow and mistakenly assumed the same of her husband.

He was unsure how she would react when he announced they must abruptly leave with only what they could carry in a suitcase. His explanation understandably terrifying. Everything in her ordered life overturned. Her very existence in jeopardy as a wanted fugitive. Fugitives without any reasonable expectation of escaping the Soviet Union.

Baranovsky's decision came down to doing nothing on the chance Mishnyov was not compromised. If wrong, it meant the end of his and Natasha's lives. Once falling suspect to the secret police there would be no opportunity for escape. The alternative was to act immediately and attempt a perilous escape. Either option represented a life and death decision.

Allowing more time to gather more information was not an option. He called the Moscow number provided by Rozovsky.

A man answered, "Warehouse services."

"An old friend named Boris told me to contact you. To discuss a profitable opportunity."

After a long pause came a reply, "You must come into the office to discuss your business. The address is Ulitsa Seregina 5. Just north of Leningradsky Prospekt. Name on the sign reads Logistics Services. Press the buzzer."

Baranovsky grabbed his briefcase and left his office. For the last time. No turning back now. It was mid-afternoon. Since Natasha also held a faculty position at Moscow State University, he began walking hurriedly to her building housing the humanities department. They must leave immediately. Having acted, he now experienced the concern of having acted too late. Much relieved when he found her in her office preventing further delay.

As he walked in she said, "This is a surprise." Carrying his briefcase, she thought perhaps he wanted to leave early. Theater? Dinner and a romantic evening? "Celebrating something?"

"Something important has come up, Natasha. We must get home immediately."

Frightened, she said, "What is wrong? Has something bad happened?"

"I will explain on the way. Get your coat. We must leave now."

He hurried her along the pathway toward the car clutching her by the arm. His urgency increasing her sense of dread.

Once inside the car, she demanded, "What is going on, Niko-lai?"

"I believe something may have happened to Vladimir."

"Oh no! What?"

"I do not know. Not able to reach Dasha. Someone said she called in sick when I called her office, but she is not at her home."

"Vladimir is in Europe on one of his usual trips."

"I know."

"Then what is it?"

"No time right now to go into all of the details but I believe it has to do with Vladimir's involvement with something outside the country."

"Like what?"

"I will tell you what I know when we get home. Right now it is important for us to pack for being away from home for a few days."

"Why? You are making no sense, Nikolai. Tell me what this is about."

"Vladimir is involved with something dangerous in Europe."

"A woman?"

Nikolai shook his head vigorously realizing why she might think that was what he meant. "Not another woman, Natasha. Spying."

Her face went white. Vladimir and her sister both worked in the foreign ministry. Moments passed before she said in quiet voice, "Is he spying for the Americans?"

"Yes. I fear the MGB might have discovered his activities."

"Why must we leave?" she said before realizing the implica-tions. "Because we might be implicated by association?"

"Yes, but more than that. I have known for some time. Even-tually I joined him."

"Oh my god! Are the secret police going to arrest us?"

"Probably. That is why we are leaving. Going into hiding. Arrangements have been made. People to provide assistance."

"Assistance? For what?"

"To get us out of the country. We are defecting to the West, Natasha. We can resume our careers living a better life. A life where we can speak our mind without fear of secret police pounding on the door in the middle of the night."

He laid a hand on her arm. "I am so sorry but we shall get through this."

Back at the apartment, he said, "Pack only one suitcase. Take warm clothing. Your jewelry. Anything important that you can fit into the suitcase. We shall not be returning."

She stood motionless for a time before he placed both hands on her shoulders. "Now, Natasha. There is not much time."

She pushed his hands away saying nothing then began pulling undergarments and warm clothing from her dresser drawers.

He did the same using his small suitcase for short trips. In the kitchen, he pulled a screwdriver from the drawer and pushed aside the bed. Invisible except by very close inspection, he inserted the screwdriver into a slot between the floorboards and pried up a small section of wood flooring. Inside was a metal box several inches deep seated in a hole through the subfloor. A modification he made himself to hide emergency cash.

He pulled out a sizeable wad of Soviet rubles and foreign currency pocketing the cash. Natasha looked at him silently, consumed by fear for her life and their future. Fear for her sister and niece. Anger for Nikolai for never confiding in her. Lastly, she pulled a thick volume of Shakespeare's collected works from the large bookshelf. All her other beloved books she must leave behind. She taught Shakespeare. She would not leave Shakespeare behind.

Natasha was crying silently as they left the apartment and got into the car. She said nothing to Nikolai as he drove to the nearest Moscow Metro subway station. At the subway station, he deposited the letter to Galyorkin in a postal box. First Vladimir and Dasha. Now losing Dimitri added to his sense of personal loss.

Once on the subway, it was a short ride to reach the subway station on the major thoroughfare Leningradsky Prospekt closest to their destination. In the twilight, Nikolai and Natasha made their way on foot through a falling light snow.

Withdrawn into herself, Natasha said nothing since leaving the apartment.

Finding the address of a nondescript small storefront, he pressed the buzzer. Looking at her, Nikolai could see she was no longer crying. Her blank stare suggested reconciliation to an unknown terrible fate. Her sadness broke his heart.

* * *

A man opened the door saying nothing only motioning with his head for them to enter. He ushered them through a darken office to a room in the back. A cluttered area with a couple of chairs and a small table in the center. A cot with a folded blanket on one wall. Against the other wall, a small refrigerator with a cabinet and counter alongside with hotplate and coffee pot. A single light bulb hung from the ceiling. The place was dirty with a stained concrete floor but at least warm. No windows, only a steel door presumably to the outside.

The man said, "You will stay here tonight. There is food and coffee. Toilet through that door. Keep all doors locked. Keep office in front dark. I will return in the morning."

"What happens then?" Baranovsky asked.

"I do not know. I must leave you now. If the telephone rings in the office, do not answer. No one must know you are here."

The man left through the heavy steel door and locked the deadbolt.

Sitting at the small table, Natasha spoke for the first time. "Tell me why, Nikolai. Is your disgust with the Soviet system worth risking our lives?"

"Yes. In a manner of speaking. Unfair of me though to make the decision without consulting you. Difficult to put into words. A festering hatred since my early days. Living through Stalin's Great Purge. Watching how it twisted my parents' lives. Constantly afraid of saying something that might be used against them. Everyone fearing denunciation as reactionary or counter revolutionary. Anti-intellectual nonsense as a means of totalitarian control. You feel the same. Think of all our discussions with Vladimir and Dasha."

At the mention of her sister, she asked, "What was Vladimir doing?"

Nikolai sat down. Relieved to unburden what he regretted keeping from her. "Stealing secrets from the ministry. Taking pictures of documents with a special camera provided by the Americans. Not sure what happened, but I believe something may have gone wrong with transferring the information."

"How did you discover something happened?"

"A telephone call yesterday from someone I met when in Europe warning me."

"Why you, Nikolai? What is your involvement?"

"Because I was doing the same thing as Vladimir. Also using him to deliver my material when he made his regular courier trips to Western Europe."

She looked incredulous. "You are an economist. What secrets do you have of interest to the Americans?"

He took a deep breath before answering. "An old friend. From my days as a student before we met. As you know, my undergraduate work was in mathematics. That is where I met Dimitri Galyorkin. Mathematics brought us together. Dimitri's skills are astounding. Although we pursued different disciplines in our graduate work, we remained close. Dimitri became a theoretical physicist. He works in nuclear weapons development."

She shook her head with an expression of disbelief. "So Galyorkin is part of this? Where does he work?"

"Hundreds of kilometers east of Moscow. What is called a closed city. Sealed off with exceptional security measures. He calls it a prison. No one is allowed to leave."

"How is it he is able to pass you secret material?"

Anxious for the diversion, he wanted her to know the importance of what he, Mishnyov, and Galyorkin did. Something tangibly subversive toward the Soviet regime. More than mere intellectual discussions.

"Let me show you." Opening his suitcase, he withdrew a well-used book of great chess matches.

"Through a method of encryption Dimitri and I devised when in different graduate schools. A way of secretly communicating disguised as something else. That something else was a discussion of chess matches. Dimitri is a much stronger player than I am. Let me show you how it works."

Sneaking into the dark office, he located a note pad and returned to Natasha.

"Write something and I will explain how it works."

She wrote a passage from Shakespeare's Hamlet. *'Doubt thou the stars are fire. Doubt that the sun doth move. Doubt truth to be a liar. But never doubt I love.'*

He leaned over to kiss her cheek recognizing her gesture. She reciprocated by touching his cheek communicating forgiveness.

"Whoever is writing the letter identifies a documented chess match. This becomes the key to converting phrases describing the chess moves to become the key for the encrypted portion of the letter. The letter then appears to be a related discussion between two knowledgeable chess aficionados.

"This takes a few minutes to compose. First, I translate this into Russian. Then I select a chess match to use as a base. Let me write down a sequence of chess moves." Drawing a table on the note pad, "I then convert the moved piece to a numeric position on the board. In the next column, I assign a number that becomes a multiplier to the board position number that corresponds to a memorized table of shorthand symbols identified by a number."

"I follow so far, but what do you mean shorthand symbols?"

"Shorthand is a rapid method of taking notes. Uses easily written symbols representing words or syllables phonetically. We assigned numeric values to these shorthand symbols. Once we added mathematical operators, we have a list of less than 300. Enough to communicate any message. Dimitri and I memorized the list."

"Not sure I follow, but then what?"

"The key is the multiplier. This comes from a short table converting the Russian alphabet to numerical values. From there requires some creativity is required to assemble a sequence of phrases to identify this multiplier key. Phrases of which the first letter of each word equates to a number.

"For example if I use the phrase *black's attack fails,* the first letters of each word generate a three digit number."

He showed her his handwritten matrix. "To encode the message, I create three or four-word phrases commenting on moves, board position, or something related to produce whatever numeric value is necessary to convert the board position number to the required shorthand form. Except for Dimitri or me, to anyone else reading our correspondence the content looks like annotations explaining a chess match. No obvious suggestion that this is a code. The underlying shorthand characters are phonetically based which removes the relationship of individual letter frequency in any language which is the weakness of most codes"

She nodded while raising her eyebrows in an expression suggesting she did not fully understand. "You and Dimitri memorized everything so only you know how this works?"

"No different than learning a secret language. We have years of practice. Nothing written to incriminate us. Here is the last letter I mailed to Dimitri yesterday before I encrypted the sensitive content."

He handed her a folded typewritten page. "Emotionally difficult for me to write. A farewell letter. I probably will never see him again. The encrypted commentary on this chess match incorporates the phrases necessary to convert the chess piece positions of this particular match to generate the hidden message."

Out of habit never committing to writing anything that reveals the basis of their code, he instead verbally translated what the hidden message said to Natasha.

With a heavy sigh she said, "Did Vladimir approach you to join in this?"

"He confided to me what he was already doing. Vladimir's distress over not doing something substantive to rebel against Stalin's mad imperialistic ambitions made a deep impact on me.

With my hatred for Stalin, difficult not to also take an active part in this subversion with my connection to Galyorkin."

"And my sister. Did she know what Vladimir was doing?"

Nikolai took her hand. "According to Vladimir, she encouraged him. Said Dasha did not tell you because it would not be fair to involve you."

She pulled her hand away. "Is that why you never told me, Nikolai?"

"I suppose so. A mistake. I should have told you. Rationalized that should Vladimir ever become discovered, we therefore become dangerously implicated because of our close relationship. That provided the incentive for me to also do something. Yet I also felt compelled to actively take part in rebelling against Soviet repression."

"Was Vladimir discovered?"

"Everything points to that. I believe that was why I was warned. That is why I sounded the alarm."

"What are our chances?"

"I truly do not know. The people working with us will do everything possible. The Americans are behind this."

***

Giving the cot to Natasha, Nikolai fell asleep hunched over the table with his head resting on his arms. As a key rattled in the backdoor before sunrise, he came awake switching on the light.

In walked a large man in his sixties dressed in working clothes smoking a cigarette. In a loud voice he announced, "I am Bohdan Zinchenko. And you are?"

Nikolai instantly stood up hearing the key in the door. "I am Nikolai Baranovsky and this is my wife Natasha."

"No others? I was warned there might be five."

"No. Just us."

"Are the police looking for you?"

"If not, they will be soon."

"I agreed to get you and your wife to Leningrad from there it becomes the problem of those you are working for. Promised new identity papers for you but have received nothing yet. Leningrad is in a border region. Travel there is restricted. Requires individual authorization."

Nikolai said, "Can it be done without papers?"

Zinchenko crushed out his cigarette in an ashtray on the table and lit another. "Everything is possible. Until I figure this out, we must hide you in a safer place outside Moscow. More comfortable for Madame Baranovsky. You will leave this afternoon. I shall make contact with the Americans and determine how to proceed. I brought hot food for you."

* * *

Boris Antonovich received a telephone call from Istanbul. The caller said, *"I have a message from your friend in Moscow. The two professors arrived last night. Moving them to a safe location until travel arrangements can be determined. Without new papers, the journey to the specified destination becomes difficult. Will advise progress. Advise arrangements on your end. Reply to this telephone number. I will relay messages to Moscow."*

The caller gave Antonovich an Istanbul number to call any time of day or night.

Boris Antonovich called Rozovsky immediately who then contacted Neiman.

"Did Janus reveal anything about Hermes?" Neiman asked.

"No. At least not to Zinchenko," Rozovsky said.

Neiman said, "Perhaps Hermes was already under suspicion. He may have shared that with Janus triggering his going into hiding after receiving your warning. No way for us to know. At least Janus and his wife got away. Hard to gauge if his disappearance jeopardizes Poseidon through their correspondence."

"Depends if the Soviets believe the discussion of a chess match is a code," Rozovsky said.

Neiman said, "No code is absolutely secure. Depends if the deception that it is about chess proves sufficient to discourage a serious effort attempt to break the cipher by dedicated cryptologists. Poseidon might not endure intense interrogation that might include harsh physical abuse. Even if the MGB cannot break the code, they may simply proceed by declaring it to be a code and batter Poseidon into submission. Whatever happens, he is beyond our reach.

"Right now we must concentrate on how to get the Baranovskys out of Leningrad should they make it that far. I will fly to Stockholm tomorrow. Need to work on this directly with the Swedes."

"Take Inga with you. She was good at this sort of thing during the German occupation. Supervised getting you out of France." Rozovsky said.

Chapter 28

Stockholm & Moscow | January 1953

Neiman and Jansons arrived in Stockholm accompanied by Sven Norberg. A car was waiting to deliver them to T-kornet headquarters. By telephone, Neiman and Norberg explained the circumstances probably compromising Hermes and the dead drop at Orly Airport. Those events in Paris likely forced Janus and his wife to go into hiding in Moscow preemptively. They represented the only link to the nuclear weapons source Poseidon. Their exfiltration from the Soviet Union becomes vital to preserve the security of Poseidon. Nikolai Baranovsky's exfiltration makes possible a reconnection with Poseidon at some future time.

Escorted to a large conference room, Deputy Director Konstantin Lindström stood up to shake hands along with another man.

"This is Major Ostergard. I brought him into our small circle because this now involves his sector," Lindström said. "Major Ostergard is head of operations. We still however want to limit those that know anything about our special arrangement with American intelligence. Can you bring us up to date on what transpired with Hermes and Janus?"

"Certainly, Colonel. Let me first explain Miss Jansons' background and the reason for her presence here today. She is an active part of the independent espionage network working out of Paris. That network produced Hermes, Janus, and Poseidon. Walk-in sources to an already established independent anti-Soviet dissident group that smuggle confidential information out of the Soviet Union. The members of this group are expatriate Russians. First or second generations with ties to the Russian Civil War or with Stalin's Great Purge of the late thirties.

"Miss Jansons is a professional photographer. Born in Latvia, she is fluent in Latvian, Russian, French, and English. During German occupation in WWII, she was a member of the French Resistance group known as the Druids lead by Yuri Rozovsky who created this anti-Soviet espionage network. Her specialty was forgery, taught by one of the best during the war. Among many duties, she aided in hiding allied operators from the British SOE and the American OSS. Experienced operationally. She saved my life during the war."

Turning toward her, "Now she is my wife. I trust he her implicitly. Since exfiltration will undoubtedly involve forging various documents, she can work alongside your experts.

"The current situation is the possible arrest of Hermes. He of course is both courier as well as source. He and his wife hold positions in the Soviet Foreign Ministry. Hermes is a diplomatic courier to Soviet Embassies in Western European. Including Stockholm."

"Are you certain of his arrest?" Lindström asked.

"Not certain although he might be under serious suspicion depending on how much the MGB learned from the apparent woman spy killed by the person servicing the dead drop. Yuri Rozovsky contacted Janus in a guarded call communicating only that the dead drop was compromised. Perhaps Janus learned something more about Hermes circumstances. Whatever transpired, it proved enough for Janus to declare an emergency and go into hiding. A decision not taken lightly."

"How did you learn of Janus going into hiding?"

"By way of the black market operator, Bohdan Zinchenko. Unfortunately, this emergency happened before we put together a viable exfiltration plan. As we speak, Janus and his wife are in hiding somewhere in Moscow under the protection of Zinchenko.

"Given his sensitivity to the secret police, Zinchenko's informers report heightened search activity in Moscow for Baranovsky."

"Thank you, Mr. Neiman. As you say, the timing is certainly unfortunate. Yet as you know in the intelligence world, setbacks often occur at the worst time," Lindström said. "When you first spoke about the need to develop an exfiltration plan for Hermes and Janus, Leningrad appeared the best option to escaping the Soviet Union. As a busy Baltic port, an operation by sea did offer better options than a crossing by land into Finland. However, with winter closing in, the port of Leningrad is closing down because of heavy icing conditions already developing. Typically, the port suspends commercial sea operations in winter until April."

"Leningrad is still the best option geographically," Neiman responded.

Lindström nodded in agreement. "Does Zinchenko have the ability to transport Janus and his wife to Leningrad?"

"Says he does. He is our only option. The problem is this happened before we could fabricate new identities with the necessary documents to allow travel to Soviet border regions. Without such papers, it greatly multiplies the risk if the MGB is already searching while they remain in Moscow. Does Swedish intelligence have assets inside Russia that can deliver new identity papers to Moscow?"

Pausing for a moment before responding, Lindström finally said, "There is another problem I must explain, Mr. Neiman. T-kornet is under strict orders not to conduct any covert operations within the Soviet Union. Even using proxies such as Finland must be done with the utmost caution. Then only with the ability to invoke plausible deniability. The prime minister was adamant about avoiding any possible international incident with the Soviets. We can render support only from outside Soviet territory."

This was a severe blow to Neiman's plans.

"Are you saying you cannot even offer assistance for getting Janus and his wife across the border if they reach Leningrad?" Neiman asked.

"Regrettably, that is the case. Short of crossing into the Soviet Union, we are authorized to do everything we can to assist in this exfiltration."

"Makes the situation vastly more difficult, but I understand, General. We will improvise with what resources are at our disposal. The most immediate issue is arming Janus and his wife with new identities and travel documents. Miss Jansons has their photographs."

Jansons said, "I would have already begun but I did not have Soviet passports, identity cards, or travel authorizations from which to copy. Photographs of these documents are inadequate for duplicating the correct materials. I assume you have originals of the necessary Soviet documents?"

Major Ostergard responded, "That will not be a problem, Miss Jansons."

"What about documents for other nationalities?"

Ostergard answered, "Depends on the country. Not a problem for countries within the Baltic region. What are you suggesting?"

"To early to tell. However, since we have not yet devised how we get these people across the border should they make it to Leningrad, additional false documents for another country might prove useful."

Ostergard nodded. "A good point. We can create excellent reproductions of any documents used by any of the Scandinavian countries."

"How soon can we produce Soviet documents to get into Zinchenko's hands? Getting these people out of Moscow soon seems to be a pressing issue. I can offer my services," Jansons said.

"I will leave that question to you and our documents team, Miss Jansons. They will welcome your assistance."

"How long are you and Miss Jansons planning to remain in Stockholm, Mr. Neiman?" Lindström asked.

Neiman looked at Inga. "As long as it takes to successfully get these assets out of Russia."

* * *

Zinchenko's people placed the Baranovskys in a truck with a concealed space behind the cab. The cargo area contained a sturdy framework structure for hanging beef and pork quarters. There was a twenty-four inch wide enclosed section running the width of the truck next to the cab housing the refrigeration system. Requiring only a portion of the space left a twenty-four by sixty-inch area the full height of the truck empty.

The truck served a dual purpose. It allowed for Zinchenko to purchase meat from slaughterhouses for the same price paid by the state-owned commissaries. Under law, only the Soviet state legally engaged in retail commerce in the state-controlled economy. Nevertheless, illegal black market commerce functioned as an essential private commercial system in urban centers commodities experiencing chronic shortages.

Zinchenko purchased the best quality meats at state-fixed prices offering a bonus of other difficult to obtain black market goods in trade to the meat producer. Distributed through outlets servicing higher-end consumers, provided lucrative profits even after paying bribes.

The concealed section in the cargo area served to transport other black market commodities. Especially difficult to obtain foreign items or items of superior quality to universally inferior Soviet produced goods. Clothing, watches, jewelry, women's lingerie, and especially cigarettes. The concealed section could carry a sizeable quantity of these smaller high-value goods.

Access was through a tall exterior panel secured with screws. Easily accessed from outside by turning several false screws that acted as latches allowing the panel to swing open on internally concealed hinges. Never intended to transport people it nonetheless allowed perfect concealment for two people to stand. A vent at the top provided ventilation to the area making for adequate air supply. The obvious problem was claustrophobia for the occupants.

In the afternoon under a dark sky light snow was falling. The truck backed up to the rear of the building. Zinchenko entered. "Time to leave. We are not traveling far but you will find it somewhat uncomfortable. You must stand up in a confined space. Plenty of fresh air but no heat. Regrettably a dark area. You may feel claustrophobic. The best I can offer is a flashlight."

Once ready, Zinchenko opened the door then grabbed a chair from inside the building. Zinchenko placed the chair to serve as a step to get into the truck. Switching on the flashlight, he directed the beam into the interior of the dark space.

"Natasha gasped, "Oh my god! I cannot go in there."

Nikolai took her arm. "We must do this, Natasha."

"How long must we be in there?" she asked.

"Less than an hour," Zinchenko said then motioned with his head for Nikolai to hurry his wife.

Going first, Nikolai climbed on the chair pushing his suitcase in then stepping up into the truck. Reaching down he took Natasha's suitcase then reached for her hand. With Zinchenko's assistance and pulled by Nikolai she climbed into the truck.

Zinchenko handed her the flashlight then closed the door. Standing on the chair, he closed the three concealed latches. Once closed, the door looked like a service panel. Easily explained as access to the refrigeration equipment that had another identical service door on the opposite side.

Forty minutes later the truck arrived at Krasnogorsk, a suburb 25 kilometers northwest of central Moscow situated on the Moskva River. Pulling inside a warehouse, the Baranovskys exited their confinement none the worse for the short trip.

Zinchenko took them into a small cluttered working office inside the warehouse with only a desk.

"Let me explain the problem," Zinchenko said. "It appears your disappearance has aroused considerable attention among the secret police. I agreed with those you are working with to get you to Leningrad. They were to provide new identifications for both of you along with travel authorizations allowing travel to a border region. I have received no such new identifications.

Seems whatever caused you to declare an emergency happened too suddenly.

"It is 700 hundred kilometers from Moscow to Leningrad. Flying is out of the question. There is no way to make that trip hidden in that truck. That means by train is the only practical means. Yet you cannot travel under your real names. At every leg of the journey, police will check your papers. Therefore, we must wait until your foreign friends provide us with new identifications.

"I am as unhappy as you must be. This was not what I bargained for. Whatever the MGB wants you for also puts my people at risk. I do not know how long before I can get you on your way to Leningrad. The danger increases if you are together. The MGB are searching for a man and woman. They will soon distribute your photographs. Every ordinary policeman, every postal worker will know your faces. You must separate until new identification documents arrive. Even then, that means traveling to Leningrad separately."

Natasha shook her head vehemently, "No! I will not leave my husband."

Nikolai put his arm around her shoulders. "You ask too much, Mr. Zinchenko."

"I ask what is necessary to save your lives. And for those risking their lives to help you. Do you understand what happens if you are caught? You are American spies. Likely torture then death by a bullet to the head. Perhaps your wife might escape the bullet only to die a slow death in a Siberian labor camp."

Natasha shuddered at the image. Forced to endure an uncertain escape without Nikolai at her side overwhelmed her sense of dread more than Zinchenko's frightening warnings.

Nikolai did not know what to say. He understood the pragmatic necessity to split up but he too found the thought of separating from Natasha unbearable. "Is there not a way we can remain together until ready to begin the journey to Leningrad?"

"I am afraid not. I am sending your wife to stay at the home of my local business associate. The man that operates this warehouse. After dark, I will drive her to his home on the outskirts of this town. She can stay in an attic apartment in their old farm-house. Where his children slept when they lived at home. Now it is just he and his wife."

Turning to Natasha. "You cannot leave their house even to go outside. But you will be warm and well fed. They also have an indoor toilet. The woman's name is Raisa. She will have a meal ready for you when you arrive at her home tonight. As for your husband, I will take him later tonight to an apartment over a bar. The apartment is home to the bar owner who lives alone.

"I provided each of you suitable clothing in those packages in the corner. You must blend in as working class. Before you leave here tonight, change and leave the clothes you are wearing in this office. I will now leave you alone together until I return after dark."

* * *

As difficult as it was separating from Natasha hours later, Nikolai at least felt they should be temporarily safe. While de-layed, their escape process at least began. Zinchenko seemed to know what he was doing. Possibly connected with Rozovsky's network but Nikolai suspected his profession involved the black market. That meant Zinchenko knew how to evade police.

As an economist, Baranovsky understood the importance of the *second economy*. The Soviet command system could not func-tion without this shadow capitalistic process that provided vir-tually all urban dwelling Russians the ability to survive with a means of access to essential goods. A reprieve from standing hours in lines to obtain essentials at state-operated stores. Any items of quality available only through the black market.

Successfully functioning in the black market explained Zin-chenko's unique resources such as access to a warehouse, a truck rigged for hiding contraband, and an underground network. Although a paid mercenary, it was more than Nikolai Bara-novsky might have hoped for in engineering an exfiltration from Moscow hundreds of kilometers from any Soviet border.

Zinchenko transported Baranovsky in the truck and waited until Pyotr the bar owner closed well after midnight. A tough looking fellow with a shaved head and bulging biceps.

After a brief conversation with Zinchenko, Baranovsky followed Pyotr up the external stairs to his apartment. A squalid dump. With only a filthy sofa to sleep on, Baranovsky had no choice but to spend the next couple of hours drinking vodka with the talkative Pyotr.

Pyotr never asked why Baranovsky was running from the secret police but enjoyed the ability to talk frankly. While relaxing and getting drunk, he regaled Nikolai with his exploits in the Red Army as a senior sergeant during the war.

He realized Pyotr's anti-Soviet political slant when he recounted one incident with particular relish.

"Best kill I ever made was a fucking asshole Red Army captain. The battalion political commissar. Responsible for our political education. A hated sonofabitch always looking to use his power. Wrote a damaging report over something my captain said. A good officer we all liked.

"Found my opportunity to remove this thorn in the unit's ass when the prick got too far in front while we advanced on a German position. Pushing my stragglers from the rear, this political commissar wound up ahead of me. It was an easy head shot from only five meters to remove the irritating piece of shit."

With that closing story and slightly drunk, he threw Baranovsky a blanket and pillow that looked none too clean. "I sleep late but feel free to make yourself coffee if you are up before me. Bread and eggs in the icebox. Toilet is that door. Just don't go outside."

* * *

Two days passed before Zinchenko received word that new documents for the Baranovskys were ready. Yet it meant that it would be several more days of delay using one of his means of smuggling foreign goods to get the documents to Moscow. MGB efforts searching for the fugitives had grown more intensive.

Further delay in getting the Baranovskys to Leningrad placed his organization at unacceptable risk. It also delayed his payment. This was business. He might hate Soviet communism, but he long ago found a way to prosper in spite of police state oppression.

Zinchenko would therefore improvise to provide the Baranovskys new identities. Without the means to create forged documents, the only alternative was using existing identity documents with photographs that could pass scrutiny. He had a source for such identity documents. The night supervisor of the morgue of the largest Moscow hospital always had a useful supply of identity cards stolen from the dead. A black market commodity of value to criminals.

Zinchenko did not have resources with the expertise to substitute photographs. That required the ability to duplicate the official stamp and perforations that fixed the photograph to the identity card. For the Baranovskys he therefore needed identifications with photographs close enough to pass general security examination. In their case, security checks would focus attention on the name. If the photograph bore enough general facial resemblance and the hair looked right, chances were good it would not provoke closer scrutiny. The critical factor was dressing and acting the part of the false identity. For the Baranovskys it also meant traveling apart on the journey to Leningrad.

Having made arrangements with the morgue supervisor, Zinchenko showed up at the hospital at midnight. While Zinchenko sat at the desk, the man said, "As you instructed, I prepared two piles of identification cards for men and women in their thirties and forties."

"Let me see the men first."

The man dumped a pile of ID cards from a shoebox.

Not as many as Zinchenko hoped for, he quickly began segregating those with possibilities. The result netted several possibilities. None however bore a strong likeness. The best was the face of a working man wearing wire-rim glasses.

Baranovsky had blond hair, easily changed by dying. The black and white photos made the facial structure more important. Adding glasses would create a touch that would draw the attention of someone scrutinizing the image. It would have to suffice.

The selection for Natasha Baranovsky yielded an acceptable likeness, and more importantly indicated the place of residence as Leningrad. That eliminated the need for a separate travel authorization which the guy at the morgue apparently saw no value in saving.

The transaction cost Zinchenko a hindquarter of good beef. Enough for the man's family with enough left over to trade for something else on the black market.

* * *

Armed with false identifications, Zinchenko began preparations for getting the Baranovsky's to Leningrad immediately. His plan called for Nikolai to leave first by truck. The same truck and driver used to move them to their current hiding locations. Baranovsky would ride in the cab with the driver. A two-day trip requiring a layover one night in the city of Novogorod about eight hours from Moscow. Zinchenko's meat transport company held travel authorization to Leningrad.

Natasha would leave the following day by train. Armed with the identity of a citizen of Leningrad did not require travel authorization. Escorting her would be Zinchenko's personal secretary and mistress. Someone he could trust to hide the reunited Baranovskys until handed off to those working with the Americans. She also held travel authorization to Leningrad as an employee of various Zinchenko enterprises. As the second largest city in Russia, Leningrad was an important black market trading location for Zinchenko.

Zinchenko arrived at the bar the following evening. Pyotr saw him enter and both went outside to take the stairs to the apartment. Zinchenko carried additional clothing for Nikolai packed in a canvas duffle bag.

Entering with Pyotr, Zinchenko said, "You are to leave early tomorrow morning for Leningrad. You shall travel by truck. The same truck that brought you here will pick you up before sunrise. Be ready."

A look of shock came over his face.

"Not in the concealed space but in the cab with the same driver you met before."

"And Natasha?"

"She will leave the following day by train."

"No. We must travel together."

"That is impossible. The secret police are looking for you. Your photographs distributed widely to all police. You must leave Moscow immediately."

Baranovsky shook his dead. "I cannot leave without Natasha."

"You have no choice. Too many are risking their lives to help you. You will do this my way," Zinchenko said sharply. "You will follow my instructions. Here is your new identity. Memorize the name. The date of birth, the address of your residence. Be prepared by creating other details of your life should you be questioned."

"I look nothing like this fellow in the photo. Who is this?"

"A dead fellow. The best I can do. Pyotr will help you change your appearance enough to hopefully pass scrutiny." Turning to Pyotr, handing him the ID. "Help him cut and dye his hair to make him look like this."

To Baranovsky, he handed him a pair of wire-frame reading glasses. "Put these on when encountering checkpoints along the highway. A day and a half's journey. You will stop tomorrow night at Novogorod and continue on to Leningrad the following morning. In this bag are a warm coat, hat, and workman gloves appropriate for your new identity."

"And Natasha?"

"She likewise has a new identity. I will explain everything to her after I leave here. She will carry the identity of another dead person. A citizen of Leningrad that allows her to travel there without special authorization. A woman I trust will accompany her on the train to Leningrad. She will hide both of you until handed off to those working with the Americans that will get you out of the Soviet Union."

Zinchenko extended his hand. "I shall not be seeing you again. I wish you and your wife luck. Keep your head and you have a good chance of making it out safely."

After Zinchenko left, Pyotr said. "I do not know the reason they are hunting you. Remember the secret police use torture to extract information. My advice is never let them catch you. Better to die a clean quick death."

Pyotr then went into a cabinet in the kitchen and pulled out a revolver from behind some pans. "Take this. A German Luger. Took it off a dead German officer. Still loaded. Just in case things go wrong."

"I have never fired a gun before. Not sure I could hit anything."

Pyotr exhaled a deep sigh. "All you need to do is release the safety on the grip to fire. I give it to you to make sure you have that quick clean death if things go badly. Just put it to your temple and squeeze the trigger."

* * *

Pyotr took a liking to Baranovsky staying up after closing the bar drinking vodka then waking early to make Baranovsky breakfast before the truck arrived before dawn. Sending him off with a thermos of coffee, Pyotr gave him an affectionate bear hug with his massive arms. "May God be with you."

The main highway stretched 700 kilometers northwest from Moscow to Leningrad, with few cities along the way. A vital link between Russia's two largest cities, the road was clear of snow. Twice while in route, they stopped for security checkpoints.

The first stop rattled Baranovsky's nerves. Unknown to the driver, the Luger was in his waistband at his back underneath his sweater. Not forgetting to fix the glasses in place, he handed over his identification to the regional police officer standing on the driver side. Another officer stood beside his door holding an assault rifle.

As the driver opened the cab door to go to the rear of the truck to open the cargo doors, Baranovsky saw the police officer looking at Baranovsky's false identification. Being on the opposite side of the cab possibly helped to accept his appearance as matching the identification photo.

Once the driver was back behind the wheel, the police waved them forward. A second checkpoint stop also went without incident. After eight hours on the road, they pulled up to a warehouse in the industrial sector of the only sizeable city on the route, Novogorod. The driver stepped out to unlock a door and go inside. Slowly he hoisted up the rolling door.

The driver who said nothing to Baranovsky during the entire trip, pulled the truck inside the building then said, "We are to spend the night here in the truck. I have blankets. Bohdan says I am to watch over the cargo. I have food and beer in the back. There is a toilet over there."

Baranovsky wondered if by cargo the driver meant the load of meat or him?

The warehouse had some source of heating keeping the temperature up to a bearable five degrees Celsius. With his warm coat and wrapped in a blanket he was reasonably comfortable. The food and beer helped relax his physical tension. However, nothing could mitigate his overwhelming anxiety about Natasha. She must be suffering unbearable anxiety being alone. All this was his making.

After falling asleep for a couple of hours, the blaring of the truck's horn jarred him awake. The driver's door was open. Someone yelling was attempting to pull the driver by his arm from the truck.

Everything began happening simultaneously. He saw the driver reach down under his seat pulling out a large caliber automatic pistol from under a rag. Pointing it at the attacker, he shot the man in the face.

Another attacker pulled Baranovsky's door open as Baranovsky reached under his coat extracting the Luger from his waistband. Catching it in his shirttail caused a slight delay allowing his assailant to shoot first.

Baranovsky felt the impact of the round in his abdomen. Realizing he was shot, he stayed focused enough to recall Pyotr's admonition to avoid capture. He fired two rounds knocking down the gunman.

However, the end came when additional gunmen appeared out of the dark. One shot the driver in the head splattering blood throughout the interior of the truck. Another gunman on the other side of the truck fired repeated rounds hitting Baranovsky. Any of several wounds might have proved fatal.

Nikolai Baranovsky died quickly and cleanly.

* * *

Bohdan Zinchenko learned of the hijacking of his truck in Novogorod the following morning. The truck was missing. Four dead bodies left inside the warehouse. No police activity yet evident. His associates were certain this was the work of criminals not the secret police. Eventually word would leak implicating the perpetrators when they sold the cargo of meat.

The black market was only a criminal enterprise because of Soviet law prohibiting private retail business. Even government officials turned a blind eye to the necessary function of the black market. Prosecutions were rare. The hijacking was ordinary armed theft. Zinchenko and his black market associates would eventually learn the perpetrators identity and extract justice.

The immediate necessity was to distance any involvement from the wanted fugitive Nikolai Baranovsky. He ordered the bodies removed and dumped in a remote location far from the warehouse. If the MGB identified Baranovsky as one of the victims, that might prove helpful in quieting the intensity of manhunt leaving only the wife at large.

The loss of his truck and cargo was a cost of doing business. He did not mourn the death of Nikolai Baranovsky only the financial loss. However, Bohdan Zinchenko possessed a fierce sense of honor. Although for reasons beyond his control, he still failed to deliver Baranovsky to Leningrad. He must do everything possible to deliver the wife to fulfill his contract. To accomplish that required her active participation. For that reason, he must withhold the information of her husband's death. However, he must inform those working with the Americans immediately since it would affect plans for getting her out of the Soviet Union.

Chapter 29

Receiving Nikolai Baranovsky's letter delivered a shock to Dimitri Galyorkin. The thought of never seeing or corresponding with his old friend had a profound effect. Did he bear some responsibility for encouraging Nikolai by providing him the most deeply protected of Soviet secrets?

Apart from Galyorkin's critical introspection, he was now truly alone. Nikolai was his sole interpersonal link. Congeniality toward his colleagues now more than even forced only out of necessity. His despair now so advanced as to inhibit normal emotional feelings even toward those he liked, including Andrei Sakharov.

A day after receiving Baranovsky's letter, Galyorkin's situation worsened.

Igor Tamm, the head of the theoretical group, approached Galyorkin working in the Laboratory. With a severely troubled look, Tamm said, "Dimitri, there are people here from the Ministry of State Security to talk to you. Please follow me."

Had Tamm been more observant, he might wonder why Galyorkin said nothing and appeared calm as they walked to a small conference room. Two MGB officers in uniform were waiting as he entered. Tamm left closing the door behind him.

Galyorkin was neither calm nor frightened. Simply reconciled and ready to end everything.

Without any introduction the senior officer said, "Please sit down, Dr. Galyorkin."

The one in charge was a major, the other younger officer a captain. Once seated, the major launched into his interrogation. He spread out several photographic enlargements on the table in front of Galyorkin. Close up photos of Nikolai Baranovsky.

"Do you know this person?"

Galyorkin did not have to fake his shock. Removing his glasses to wipe away a tear and exhaling with a deep sigh, "Yes. An old friend I have not seen for a long time. Nikolai Baranovsky. What happened?"

"Killed a couple of days ago by gunshots. You said you have not seen him for a long time yet you regularly correspond with him. You were therefore close?"

Thinking the MGB shot Baranovsky, Galyorkin fortified his resolve to resist any allegations vehemently. He would not play a victim to their accusations. Express grief and outrage instead. Easy enough given his blind hatred for Stalin's secret police.

"Very close. Since attending Moscow State University together."

"Yet you have not seen him for a long time."

"How could I while locked away for the last couple of years in this closed city?"

"You sound angry, Dr. Galyorkin."

Galyorkin said nothing but stared back at the major defiantly.

"These letters you exchange. What are they about?"

"Mostly about Nikolai's work. He was a noted economist. We both shared a passion for chess going all the way back to school. Difficult to play a match through correspondence that would take forever, we choose instead to discuss great matches. A form of competing indirectly by using our analytical skills. I received a letter from Nikolai only yesterday."

The major paused. He threw down photographs of several past letters authored by both on the table. "As you can see, we are well aware of the nature of your correspondence. However, we believe these to be a code. What do you say?"

"I say that is ridiculous. Who says this is a code?"

"I say it is a code," the major said slapping his palm loudly on the table.

Uncharacteristically to his typical demeanor, Galyorkin went on the attack. "Do you play chess, Major?"

"Of course.

"How is it you see a code in comments related to a chess match?"

"We have experts trained in deciphering codes. They say it has all the appearance of a code. After all, chess has possibilities for apply mathematics. You and Baranovsky are both mathematicians."

"Your experts say it *appears* to be a code. Yet they are unable to break it because it is not a code. So why do you insist it is a code? If somehow they believe mathematics are involved then there must be some method of communicating numbers in a textual message. I am no expert at ciphers but using different chess matches seems an unlikely basis for encryption. Mathematics does not have a direct application to chess. Chess is about using spatial visualization to project possible board positions several moves ahead."

Having lost control of the interrogation, the major could only press forward with threats and bombast.

"Are you denying knowing nothing about Baranovsky's spying?"

"Spying? That makes no sense. He is an economist. Allowed even to travel abroad. Held in high regard by the government. Why should he be suspected of something as bizarre as spying?"

"Do you know someone named Vladimir Mishnyov?"

"No."

"Seems the wives of Baranovsky and this Mishnyov are sisters. Baranovsky and Mishnyov are also known as close friends. Mishnyov and his wife are currently under arrest for spying. Spying for the imperialistic Americans."

"I do not know these people named Mishnyov but Nikolai Baranovsky has no reason to spy for the Americans. For what reason? He and his wife are respected academics leading privileged lives in Moscow."

There was little else to ask Galyorkin during this initial session. They would of course interview all those he worked with to learn of any political missteps perhaps revealed in the course of working so closely with fellow scientists and engineering technicians. Locked within the closed city of Azarmas-16 limited avenues of inquiry. The Baranovsky connection might be a red herring. Baranovsky might not be a spy, just trying to defect with his wife because of his close connection with Mishnyov. The leak from within the nuclear program might be someone other than Galyorkin.

Unlike most interrogations conducted by the major, he was under certain constraints in this situation. Dimitri Galyorkin was an important scientist working in the most sensitive Soviet scientific program. That meant if Galyorkin were guilty of espionage, it required irrefutable evidence. Unless tangible evidence could be uncovered, that meant he could not resort to enhanced physical stress interrogation methods.

Such evidence did not yet exist. The cryptologists closely analyzed what they called the *chess letters* without success. They could find no means of even theorizing a method for using different chess games to communicate encrypted messages. Attempts made by a team of cryptologists to devise various encryption techniques failed to yield anything meaningful when applied to the Galyorkin-Baranovsky letters.

Only his relationship with his old friend Baranovsky singled out Galyorkin for suspicion of the nuclear information leaks. Even then, Baranovsky's complicity only suspected by his close relationship with Mishnyov and his disappearance. A thorough background check confirmed that Galyorkin never knew Mishnyov. As for leakage of nuclear secrets, the nuclear program employed hundreds with access to confidential information. A few of the most senior scientists even traveled outside the insular security environments. Galyorkin only traveled occasionally between other secure sites in the program, and then under close security surveillance.

Without proving how Galyorkin communicated highly technical secrets with Baranovsky, the MGB's case lacked any tangible or explainable hypothetical evidence. Under different circumstances that might not be relevant. The theory that any suspect was expendable did not apply to Dimitri Galyorkin. Every one of the theoretical physicists working on nuclear weapons enjoyed unique status. The program ranked as the highest priority receiving unlimited funding. Galyorkin was not expendable without clear cause. Accusing him without proof might damage the collective morale of the theoretical physics team.

* * *

For the next few days, Galyorkin sensed the uneasy glances of colleagues. An entire team of MGB agents remained at Azarmas-16 interviewing all those that worked with him. Several told him of their questioning, encouraging him to stand firm. Most avoided unnecessary interaction with him. Galyorkin reverted to his natural inclination toward introversion reinforced now by an obvious excuse for privacy.

His hatred for everything Soviet and for Joseph Stalin now dominated his entire being. Every individual existed only for the good of the State. He continued his work out of habit and training. Any thoughts of sabotaging calculations or experiments rejected as insufficient to satisfy his desire to do something of consequential damage. Any mistake could be mistaken as sabotage and thereby indirectly give credibility to allegations of spying for the West.

Mentally Galyorkin turned a corner with the death of Nikolai. He had no future even if ever allowed to leave this accursed place. His career in nuclear physics wasted on working to achieve weapons that are ever more powerful. Miniaturizing warheads to facilitate use with different types of delivery systems.

A final round of interrogation sessions only fortified his resolve to find the means of striking back with something worthy of sacrificing his life.

The major began the session by stating, "Further inquiries reveal you engaged in a romantic involvement with a female colleague. An engineer named Talia Zubarev. What did you discuss with her?"

"The usual things. Our work. Music. Literature. Chess."

"Not politics?"

"Of course not."

"Why of course not?"

"What is there to discuss?"

"As a good communist it is necessary to continually increase your political awareness."

"My job is to increase my technical contribution through continual discussion with my colleagues."

"Were you in love with this woman?"

"I was fond of her. Enjoyed her company."

"Did you have sex with her?"

"I refuse to answer questions about her character."

"Regardless how you viewed your relationship, it distracted from your work."

"Is that what others say?"

"Yes. Including the head of your theoretical section. Seems you neglected social interactions with your scientific colleagues."

Galyorkin remained silent.

The major waited for a response. "Well?"

"What is your question?"

Exasperated by Galyorkin's stubborn resistance, the major continued trying to provoke him. "When she was transferred did you become angry?"

"Disappointed."

"Others say you were more than disappointed. Were you angry enough to do something foolish? Perhaps providing your old friend and chess correspondent with secrets of your work?"

"You read my correspondence. I did not share my personal problems. Under the intense security of this place, I had no means of communicating secret information. The assertion that somehow our correspondence concealed information in code has no basis fact."

* * *

Galyorkin was actually just one of several suspects in the nuclear weapons development program under scrutiny from various locations. Only his connection to Baranovsky placed him in a special category of suspects. Baranovsky's close relationship to the Mishnyovs represented the only solid lead for what appeared a Western intelligence penetration into the most secret sectors of the Soviet government. With Baranovsky dead and the whereabouts of his wife unknown, the MGB possessed nothing directly incriminating against Galyorkin.

The political leaks clearly were the work of Vladimir Mishnyov and his wife. The source of the nuclear secrets leak however remained unresolved. The MGB general in charge of security for the nuclear program ordered Kurchatov and Tamm to sideline Galyorkin into non-critical work until further investigation verified his loyalty. While the secret police struck fear in every Soviet citizen, it equally struck fear of failure for MGB senior officers.

Galyorkin became further infuriated when his immediate superior Sakharov reassigned him to areas of routine engineering work. Insulting and demeaning by wasting his skills working toward solving the intractable problems associated with creating advanced thermonuclear weapons.

Sakharov was apologetic, "Tamm assures me this is only temporary until they clear you."

"I understand, Andrei. The MGB are knuckle-draggers. Everything they do is by brute force. There is no oversight to their power therefore their stupidity prevails."

"Do not repeat what I am about to tell you. I strongly protested to both Tamm and Kurchatov. Told them you were a vital part of my team. Losing your contributions will hamper our efforts. I explained work on specific problems where you are an essential contributor. They appeared to listen. Told me they would see what they could do. Just give it a little time."

Galyorkin gave Sakharov a weak smile. "I will carry on with my new work assignments. I appreciate your efforts on my behalf, Andrei."

A week later, Sakharov pulled Galyorkin aside. "You are back doing your regular work rather than getting your hands dirty. Both Kurchatov and Tamm apparently believe you are vital to our work. They went to Beria personally. He not only heads every aspect of nuclear program, he still indirectly controls the MGB. The following day Beria ordered the MGB to cease further questioning of you unless they discover something substantively incriminating."

Galyorkin nodded. "That is good news."

It mattered little to Galyorkin's frame of mind. The intellectual work no longer meant anything except as a possible means for inflicting revenge.

Chapter 30

Leningrad | February 1953

Zinchenko sent a message to Rozovsky through his normal channel of shortwave to his agent in Istanbul who then telephoned Boris Antonovich in Paris who relayed it to Rozovsky.

The message shocked Rozovsky. *'Male package shot dead during hijacking a load of meat while in transit. Repeat, criminal perpetrators, not secret police. Regret loss. Female in transit using false identification to destination by different route. Arrival expected tonight local time. Arrangements made for her safety until advised of handoff arrangements. Package is located at Ulitsa Tkachey 1, apartment 305. Telephone 2655917. A woman will answer. Say the big fellow gave me this number. Time is critical to preserve her safety. BZ'*

Rozovsky called Viktor Neiman in Stockholm at a number provided by T-kornet. The switchboard immediately put the call to *Mr. Jones* through to the conference room taken over as the command center for the closely guarded exfiltration operation.

After Rozovsky relayed Zinchenko's message, Neiman asked, "No other details?"

"That is everything, Rozovsky replied. "If Janus died by some criminal activity rather than the MGB, that is at least some good news."

"Maybe. Depends where the MGB finds Janus' body. If discovered in Leningrad then not so good because they will intensify their search there looking for his wife. That of course depends if

365

they identify him. Perhaps gives us more time if Zinchenko armed him with false identification. Regardless, we put must together a plan quickly to rescue this woman. Time is short. Inga and I will be working through the night with our Swedish colleagues. Will keep you informed of progress, Yuri. Stay by your phone."

Neiman repeated Zinchenko's message to the three Swedish intelligence officers and Inga Jansons.

"The first issue to settle on is the method of exfiltration. Let's start there?" Neiman said.

"A sea passage out of the Soviet Union is not possible," Major Ostergard said. "Commercial vessel traffic is already minimal with the Port of Leningrad already icing in. Only ships designed to handle the ice with the main channel opened with icebreakers are in service. Limits the opportunities for locating a cooperative captain. Time is too limited.

"Using even first-rate forged identifications, exfiltrating a single woman of the same age as the subject of the nationwide search presents unacceptable risk. Emigration from the Soviet Union is allowed only under rare circumstances. No matter the quality of false documentation, Soviet border security would seek confirmation. A border crossing by air or rail presents unacceptable challenges."

Neiman nodded acknowledging Ostergard's assessment. "Then that leaves only a crossing on foot into Finland at some remote location north of Leningrad. It that a possibility?"

"Theoretically yes. Provided you can overcome the practical problems. Foremost is the weather. Temperature probably around minus twenty Celsius at night. The Neva river is already frozen. The obvious location to make a border crossing is somewhere 30 kilometers west of Vyborg. The only city of some size in that region. Snow might be over a meter deep in places from wind driven drifts. Then of course, you must evade Soviet border patrols. They use tracked vehicles equipped with high-intensity lights looking for telltale tracks in the snow."

Neiman said, "Colonel Lindström, you made clear that Sweden cannot provide assistance inside the Soviet border. Can you at least provide assistance with Finland?"

Lindström answered. "I believe that is possible. We have good relations with Finnish intelligence. The Soviet Union is an even greater threat to Finland. If you can make it across the border, you will be safe there."

Thinking ahead, Neiman asked, "Might that cooperation extend to creating a diversion at the border?"

Lindström smiled. "That might also be possible. Regardless what help we provide from outside Russia, how do you propose to accomplish this with the Baranovsky woman hidden in Leningrad? Still a long way from the border. You require suitable equipment for a foot trek of several kilometers assuming you start from the only main highway in the region. Then you still have the problem of getting from Leningrad to the jumping off location to start the trek to the border.

"After that, the problem becomes time. You risk the Soviet border patrol vehicles discovering your tracks in the snow inside the exclusion zone before reaching the actual border."

Lindström paused not wanting to discourage ideas for overcoming what appeared insurmountable obstacles. "Do you have any resources you can call on in Russia?"

With Swedish intelligence unwilling to operate inside the Soviet Union, this placed the responsibility on Neiman. He could not abandon Natasha Baranovsky. Although this was Yuri Rozovsky's network, Neiman actively participated and connected Hermes, Janus, and Poseidon directly to American intelligence. He therefore bore a share of responsibility to save Natasha Baranovsky.

Neiman understood there was only one possibility. Bohdan Zinchenko. Rozovsky must seek his help using Boris Antonovich as intermediary. Even if Zinchenko agreed to help, it required someone from outside to directly participate and attempt the border crossing with Natasha Baranovsky. That left only him to go to Leningrad and take charge of the Russian side of the operation.

"Only one possibility. The black market operator Bohdan Zinchenko that is getting the woman to Leningrad."

Major Ostergard, head of Swedish operations said, "The same fellow that lost the husband?"

"Yes. If we accept that Nikolai Baranovsky's death came at the hands of criminals hijacking a load of valuable meat, we need to accept that as a circumstance beyond his control. Zinchenko might be willing to help us further as a way of compensating for Baranovsky's death. Maybe willing if offered his previous fee for the delivery of Baranovsky to Leningrad in exchange for his helping exfiltrate the wife. Can I count on Sweden for that?"

Lindström nodded.

"Thank you. I will get a message to Zinchenko immediately. We must also find a way to communicate with him or his people directly. We need real-time communication with Zinchenko. His current method going through Paris will not work for rescuing Natasha Baranovsky."

Neiman understood that to coordinate the exfiltration, they must be able to communicate directly with Zinchenko. The MGB monitored all international telephone calls. That is why Zinchenko communicates with Paris by sending messages to Istanbul by shortwave then relayed by telephone from beyond the Iron Curtain. Even if Zinchenko communicated with Stockholm by shortwave it was still not secure unless in code. They had no such code. More than that, they needed the means to work alongside Zinchenko's people to pull this off.

Neiman understood he was the only person available to do that.

Yet it was a terrible risk. Since he left Russia as a child, he never set foot in the country. Using false identification, if caught he was legitimately a spy. Likely to face execution. Not likely to be exchanged by the United States. They would disavow his actions as a rogue foreign service employee engaging in an independent venture with Russian dissidents. Yet he still felt compelled to try to save Natasha Baranovsky.

Neiman said, "We have a long night ahead. I suggest we take a break. Can we get some sandwiches and coffee?"

Telling Inga would be difficult. The break afforded the opportunity for him to speak with her alone.

"What do you think?" he asked her standing in the hallway near the toilets.

"I don't know. We know very little about Zinchenko. He is doing this for money. With the loss of Baranovsky he might just want to cease helping."

"I am hoping he has a sense of responsibility. He also has a financial incentive. Boris Antonovich speaks well about him. However, one thing is certain. Someone needs to get to Leningrad and coordinate with Zinchenko."

Letting the comment settle in, she looked into his eyes sensing what he was thinking. Exhaling deeply, she said, "You mean you?"

He nodded. "I have a personal responsibility to rescue Natasha Baranovsky from almost certain death. I speak fluent Russian. I can pass as French, German, or English with high-quality forged identifications to support some cover story. There is nobody else."

"You are not the only one. I have those same qualifications."

"No, Inga. I cannot risk you going into Leningrad much less finding your way through the snow to cross into Finland."

"I don't need to. That is your job while I take care of Natasha Baranovsky."

He stood silently transfixed for several moments absorbing what Inga was suggesting.

"Listen, Viktor. I first fell in love with you during the war then had to see you leave not knowing if you got to London safely until weeks later. Those weeks I spent worrying were terrible. Then our separation and being apart again years later. I understand why you must do this. You must understand why I must go with you."

They embraced and kissed until interrupted by someone coming out of the toilet.

Wiping tears from her eyes, Inga said, "Now that we settled that, let's figure out how to pull this off."

Returning to the conference room, Neiman announced, "The only way to get Natasha Baranovsky out of Russia is with Zinchenko's assistance. With time of the essence, we should proceed on the premise that he can be convinced. I will attempt to make contact as soon as possible. Miss Jansons and I will be the ones to go to Leningrad and coordinate operations on the ground."

The three Swedish intelligence officers looked up in surprise.

Lindström said, "I believe that is unwise." Looking at Jansons, "Do you understand the risk?"

"I do, Colonel. I worked for years undercover fighting the Nazis during the occupation. Mr. Neiman and I are the only people qualified for doing this. Will you help us?"

After a pause, Lindström nodded, "Of course. What do you need?"

Jansons replied, "The most urgent need is quality false identifications and a cover story for getting us into Leningrad."

"Once inside Russia, we must rely on Zinchenko to provide everything we need to make the exfiltration. He is a mercenary. I need cash. A great deal of cash to buy his help," Neiman said.

"That is not a problem," Lindström replied.

Ostergard said to Jansons, "Do you have an idea for a cover story? What nationality will you require?"

Neiman answered, "Along with speaking Russian, we both speak French, German, and English sufficiently to hold passports masquerading as nationals in one of those languages. As to a cover, what about something commercially related?"

Ostergard replied, "I agree. Most Soviet imports are manufactured goods. The majority of trade however comes almost exclusively from East European communist countries. Shipbuilding might be an area offering a possibility. Producing military vessels dominates much of Soviet shipbuilding. Yet growing the Soviet merchant marine fleet is an economic priority. What do you think?"

"Maybe. The United States and United Kingdom both have excess shipbuilding capacity since WWII. Even with Cold War tensions, merchant marine vessels should be non-political. Both shipbuilding contracts and marine equipment like engines should be an opportunity for pursuing sales opportunities as a cover. What might that entail to pass scrutiny?"

Ostergard embracing the challenge said, "What about acting as a representative for a fictitious marketing firm representing various shipbuilders and marine equipment manufacturers? In addition to passports, business cards and letters of introduction from shipbuilders authorizing your representation should complete the cover. The Soviet visa process will take time and means their checking the authenticity of this fictitious firm. We do not have that kind of time.

"We must therefore forge the visa. Gets you into the country but the clock is ticking. You cannot rely on your cover holding for more than several days."

Neiman digested Ostergard's idea for a moment then replied, "Let's do it. How long to produce the documents?"

"Which nationality for the passports?" Ostergard asked.

"United States I think. I can pull strings and obtain original passport blanks from our Stockholm Embassy tomorrow. Does that help?"

"Certainly. With Miss Jansons' assistance we can put together the full documentation package within 48 hours."

Neiman looked at Inga. "I agree. You are the salesman, what am I?"

"My secretary and interpreter of course. I claim having poor written fluency in Russian. I can fake a terrible accent while speaking poor Russian. We work out of an office in London close to the European markets still rebuilding from the war."

* * *

Given the time difference between Stockholm and Washington, Neiman reached his boss Paul Kline. After bringing Kline up to speed on the cascading sequence of setbacks, he said, "I am sitting here with our friends in Swedish intelligence trying to hatch a plan to rescue Natasha Baranovsky. This is my final participation before handing off what remains of our Soviet espionage penetration. Poseidon might still remain undiscovered but no way for us to know. Regardless, this removes U.S. involvement with Rozovsky's network and cleans up our fingerprints before a new secretary of state takes office.

"To clean up this mess, I need to get into Leningrad undercover and supervise the extraction of the Baranovsky woman."

"Are you out of your mind? If caught, it creates an international incident. You officially become a spy. Big show trial to display the imperialistic actions of the United States. Then they execute you."

"That is my risk, Paul. This is the fucking Cold War."

"You're still nuts to do this." After a pronounced sigh, "So what is it you need?"

"We got her out of Moscow to Leningrad with the help of Rozovsky connections in Russia. Now we need to get her across the border into neutral Finland. I have assets on the ground. I need two blank U.S. passports from our embassy in Stockholm. I need Secretary Acheson to call our ambassador first thing in the morning Stockholm time. Should this go south, he can always disclaim any knowledge and claim these as forged passports."

"Okay. You are one crazy fucking Russian, Viktor. Call me in the morning and I will confirm if Acheson agreed. You take care and promise to call me once this venture is over."

Neiman again stretched the truth. He did not even know if Natasha Baranovsky arrived safely Leningrad. Nor could he be sure of Zinchenko's further participation in extracting her.

The rest of the night Neiman spent working with Major Ostergard to define the best location for attempting the crossing, and what they needed from Zinchenko.

By early morning, things were falling into place. Inga and Ostergard prepared drafts of the various documents necessary to complete the cover profile once they prepared the U.S. passports. Waiting for Rozovsky to relay Zinchenko's confirmation that Natasha Baranovsky was in Leningrad, Neiman prepared his own message for Rozovsky to send to Zinchenko.

Rozovsky called soon after dawn broke, "Natasha Baranovsky is in Leningrad. Zinchenko is pressing for how long before we take her off his hands."

Neiman replied immediately, "Write this down verbatim, Yuri. I will explain later what this is means."

Circumstances complicated by the unexpected timing to remove the package from Leningrad. Need to contract further services from you for shipment overland to Finnish border. No other option exists. Need transport north to some location close to the border. Require winter trekking gear for three people including snowshoes, a good rifle with a 4X scope, two handguns, ammunition, bolt cutters, and a portable shortwave radio transmitter. Anticipate ready in four days to leave Leningrad with package for final leg of exfiltration. Important to be able to communicate directly with you personally to coordinate. Provide telephone number once arriving in Leningrad. Prepared to compensate you for your prior losses and your additional services. Mr. Jones.

"Are you going into Russia?" Rozovsky asked.

"Yes. Will explain later. Still much preparation. Call me immediately with Zinchenko's response."

Paul Kline called later. "Secretary Acheson was deeply disturbed. Didn't like anything about your ill-advised venture but he reluctantly agreed. Ambassador Butterworth is expecting you this morning."

* * *

Neiman picked up and signed a receipt for two blank U.S. passports at the embassy. Ambassador Butterworth was clearly unhappy about blindly forced to participate in some intelligence operation in his backyard.

Still some work remained in completing the forged documentation to appear authentic and prepare travel arrangements, but Ostergard's staff was working on everything Inga laid out. They set the time to leave for Leningrad in forty-eight hours, contingent on a favorable response from Zinchenko.

Zinchenko responded promptly. Not particularly welcoming, he nonetheless agreed to help.

Mr. Jones. Honoring my responsibilities, I shall assist you as requested. Call the same Leningrad number provided earlier only from a public telephone. Will advise instructions. I trust you to reciprocate with appropriate compensation. BZ.

Recharged and well-rehearsed in their fictionalized legend supporting their new identities as Everett Jones and Anita Smirnova, Neiman and Jansons departed Stockholm airport on a direct flight to Leningrad. The U.S. passports crafted with prior entry stamps to various European countries and suitably worn to appear well used. Their fictitious arrival in Stockholm that morning was consistent with forged tickets showing departure from London that morning.

Landing in Leningrad proved uneventful. Jansons played her part superbly. Neiman responded to Soviet passport control in adequate but accented Russian. Answering the security guard's question how he spoke Russian, he said his maternal grandparents were Russian emigrants to America.

After checking into a hotel, Neiman found a public telephone in the lobby.

Making the call, a woman answered with a curt, "Da?"

Responding in Russian, he said, "This is Mr. Jones. Is Bohdan Zinchenko there?"

The line went silent for several moments before, "Mr. Jones. We must talk. Where are you?"

After giving the name of the hotel, Zinchenko said, "Are you alone?"

"I have a woman colleague with me."

"How can I recognize you?"

"I am wearing a grey overcoat and black fedora. The woman is wearing a white fur hat and black overcoat, carrying a white leather handbag."

"Passports?"

"American."

"In thirty minutes, take a taxi to a restaurant called Romanovs. I shall follow to ensure you are not followed. If clear, I shall approach your table. If I do not show, that means we have a problem. Then call me later at this same number."

The restaurant was a small modest establishment. He and Jansons sat down and ordered glasses of Georgian wine. Shortly thereafter, a tall heavily built man in a cheap suit entered and approached their table. Reaching down without saying a word, he shook Neiman's hand in a strong grip then more delicately took Jansons hand.

Pulling out a chair, Zinchenko sat down and waved for a waiter. Ignoring their glasses of wine, he ordered a bottle of vodka and three glasses.

"Welcome to Leningrad. I prefer its real name Saint Petersburg." Looking at Neiman, "Are you American?"

"Yes. Born in Russia though."

Looking at Jansons. "And you?"

"French. Born in Latvia."

"How is Madame Baranovsky?" Jansons asked.

Zinchenko shrugged. "Grieving over the death of her husband. Terrified by not knowing what comes next. But she seems a strong woman." Returning to business, "Do both of you have experience in this sort of thing?"

Jansons was a little irritated. Did Zinchenko think they were amateurs? "Yes. We both fought Nazis in France. I spent four years undercover in the Resistance. You do not forget what you learned when your life depended on your skills. "

Satisfied, Zinchenko gave a curt acknowledgement with his head and turned to Neiman. "You are planning to attempt crossing the border on foot?"

"Yes. There is no other way."

"Where?"

"According to a topographical map, I am thinking a few miles south of the Finnish city of Nuijamaa. There is a Russian highway leading north out of Vyborg.

"My cover is a salesman for American shipbuilders and marine power plants trying to secure merchant marine contracts with the Soviet Union. Miss Smirnova is my secretary and interpreter since I claim my fluency in Russian is adequate. I am here to look over the ports of Leningrad and Vyborg to determine types of vessels most in demand. Also to evaluate the capabilities of domestic Russian shipbuilding and their requirements for marine engines. Four Russian shipbuilders are in the region. Baltic Shipbuilding, JSC Admiralty, and Almaz Shipbuilding here in Leningrad and Vyborg Shipyard a hundred miles north. The cover is strong. It is known that American shipbuilding firms are seeking to fill excess capacity by looking for new markets."

"What is your plan?"

"We take the train to Vyborg. You transport Madame Baranovsky north with the equipment I specified and suitable winter clothing. At night, you pick us up and drive us as close as possible to the border near the Finnish city of Nuijamaa. From there we head out on foot to a position south of Nuijamaa to cross into Finland. I calculate walking for about four kilometers once you drop us off near the highway. Do you have winter clothing, boots, snowshoes, and the other requested equipment for us?"

"Yes. Surplus Red Army field gear in winter white. However, do you realize Soviet border guards patrol that sector in tracked vehicles? You cannot outrun them in the snow."

Neiman nodded. "I realize that. We shall have help on the Finnish side of the border. People monitoring our progress. Did you secure a portable shortwave radio transmitter?"

"Yes."

"That is to communicate with our support on the Finnish side of the border."

Zinchenko nodded. "And the weapons?"

"I am told the border patrols operate within the one-kilometer wide exclusion zone defined by a chain link fence on the Russian side. Once we cut through the fence, I am relying on the white camouflage to get us close to the actual border before they discover our tracks in the snow. Should that happen, I want the ability to engage the armed guards from a distance before reinforcements arrive. They will not be expecting us to be armed. Did you provide a scoped rifle?"

"I have a WWII Soviet Mosin-Nagant 7.62 with a 4X power scope. The Red Army's standard sniper rifle. Two Tokarev semi-automatics. Ammunition for both weapons."

"That will do nicely."

Zinchenko nodded and took another shot of vodka. "Take the train tomorrow to Vyborg and check into a hotel. When you arrive, call me to give me your location. I will pick you up tomorrow night after dark. I have a large truck loaded with crates of vodka. Behind the crates is an open area. Enough space for both of you and Natasha Baranovsky. You will change into the winter gear on the way. Less than an hour's drive to where I drop you off to make your way to the border."

"We are grateful for your services Bohdan Zinchenko. You are a man of honor. As promised, here is a sum of cash in Swedish krona I believe you will find fair compensation for your additional services and expenses."

Zinchenko responded with a sly grin. "Should I find it insufficient, I will submit a bill through Paris. Enjoy your dinner and get a good night's rest."

After embracing both Neiman and Jansons, Zinchenko left. They remained to have dinner. Once back in their hotel room after shedding their overcoats, Inga put her arms around him. "We are both crazy being here but I could never bear you doing this without me at your side."

Her passionate kisses communicated her desire. "I am too keyed up to go to sleep. Don't want to keep playing the scenario over and over. I want to make love, Viktor."

Her display of affection also aroused him. Did her craving for intimacy under these stressed circumstances come from fear that this might became their last time? Possibly, but making love served to tamp down some of the tension allowing for some rest before facing tomorrow's perilous undertaking.

* * *

A two-hour train ride brought Neiman and Jansons into Vyborg at noon. Choosing a hotel, Jansons checked them in requesting adjacent rooms for two nights. Since their American passports would provoke interest, she volunteered the explanation to the desk clerk that Mr. Jones was in the shipbuilding business. They hoped to interest the Vyborg Shipyard in purchasing American marine engines.

From a public telephone, Neiman called Zinchenko. The same woman answered. After giving the address for the hotel, Zinchenko said, I should arrive at approximately nine o'clock. Do not check out. Leave your luggage in your room. Remain in the lobby. When I arrive, I will step inside, look at my watch, and immediately leave. Follow me to the truck parked close by."

"How is Natasha Baranovsky?"

"She understands the plan. Frightened but prepared."

A long afternoon passed with Neiman and Jansons repeatedly rehearsing the scenario. They worked through possible contingencies so each understood how to react. A great deal of unknowns existed by having no opportunity to reconnoiter. All they knew was the general layout of the one-kilometer wide exclusion zone on the Russian side of the border defined by a chain link fence. Patrolled by Soviet border guards in tracked snow vehicles to ride on top of the deep snow.

Swedish intelligence provided a high-resolution topographical map marked in grid coordinates. This allowed Neiman to communicate their position by shortwave radio at the time of crossing to Sven Norberg imbedded with Finnish border guards. To confuse the Soviet border guards, they would communicate in French once they breached the outer fence of the exclusion zone.

* * *

As planned, Zinchenko arrived at nine o'clock. The bitter cold night held a clear moonlit night sky. Leaving the Vyborg hotel, they followed Zinchenko to a WWII-era military surplus truck with a canvas cover over the cargo area. The engine was running. Stepping up into the bed of the truck, Neiman and Jansons squeezed around wooden crates of vodka stacked high.

Toward the front behind the crates was a roomy area between the crates and the truck cab.

Standing inside the canvas flaps at the rear of the truck, Zinchenko handed them flashlights. "Take these but keep the beam low. Change into the cold weather clothing. Snowshoes, weapons, radio, and a bolt cutter are there. Change into the clothing immediately. You have one hour until disembarking the truck. "

As Zinchenko gave them instructions, the woman looking after Natasha Baranovsky opened the canvas flap to the cargo area and helped her up into the truck.

"This is Natasha Baranovsky," Zinchenko said. "We must leave now. Once I stop, you will get out. I will drive away. We shall not see each other again. Good luck."

Jansons guided Baranovsky toward the front telling her this will be over soon.

Without exchanging words, Neiman shook hands with Zinchenko who then jumped down and secured the rear canvas flaps.

Inside the truck, all three began shedding their coats and shoes. Donning heavy wool sweaters and socks, they pulled on the insulated military white jump suits and insulated boots. Proven Red Army gear used against the Germans on the Eastern Front during WWII. Surprisingly comfortable even with the sub-zero temperature.

All kept their leather gloves on but after leaving the truck, they would put on bulky white insulated mittens over the gloves.

As the truck rumbled north, Neiman checked and loaded the weapons, pocketing extra ammunition. He handed one of the 9mm revolvers to Jansons and hooked the bolt cutters to his waist. Final preparations included a check of the shortwave radio, setting it to the frequency for contacting Norberg. With Jansons' assistance, he secured the transmitter to his back with shoulder straps.

Examining how to fasten the snowshoes was the final preparation. Putting them on must wait until outside the truck and done using only moonlight. During these preparations, Natasha Baranovsky said nothing but followed Jansons instructions.

After fifty minutes, Neiman felt the truck slow then make a slight turn before coming to a stop. Zinchenko had pulled the truck slightly off the highway. Neiman opened the canvas flaps at the rear of the truck and threw out the snowshoes. Climbing down from the truck, he helped the two women down.

Walking up to the truck cab Zinchenko opened the door. Neiman showed him the map. Zinchenko placed his finger identifying their location then pointed indicating their direction across the expanse of snow. "Good luck." Putting the truck in gear, he backed the truck onto the highway turning around to return back to Vyborg.

Neiman hurried the women into the snow to get away from the highway. The area was exceptionally remote. Although they could see no headlights in either direction, they must disappear into the snow quickly. A tough slog through the deep snow until far enough from the highway to take time fastening the snowshoes to their boots. Once ready, Neiman looked at his compass to establish a heading in the direction indicated by Zinchenko.

Once underway, making progress with the snowshoes was still slow going, but with less physical effort. He calculated about three kilometers before they reached the outer fence that created a one- kilometer exclusion zone on the Russian side of the actual border with Finland.

An hour later, they reached the exclusion zone fence. In the distance, Neiman could see a bright light moving south a couple of hundred meters inside the fence. A border patrol tracked snow vehicle Norberg called a *snowcat*, because of the caterpillar-like treads, moved parallel with the border in the distance. Moving at perhaps 20 kilometers per hour, it could quickly overtake them if spotted. They would let it pass before they breached the outer exclusion zone fence.

The moonlight was sufficient to consult the map without the need for a flashlight. Unfortunately, it also increased the risk of detection even with white camouflage. Following a straight heading from the starting point at the highway allowed Neiman to identify their location coordinates.

Time to alert Sven Norberg across the border by shortwave. Speaking in French, "Jones calling Sabreur. Acknowledge."

There came the sound of static for several seconds after switching to receive. Moments later the reply, "Sabreur here. Preparations in place. Advise location."

"Coordinates Alpha three zero. Making entry outer barrier then heading due west."

Keeping the transmission short, Neiman began opening a hole in the fence with the bolt cutters. The short rest afforded the women to catch their breath and prepare for the last kilometer push moving as fast as possible.

As the snowcat in the distance moving south moved past their line of travel toward the border, he said, "Move as quickly as possible."

Ten minutes later Neiman saw another set of lights in the distance. After a few moments, it became clear this was another patrol vehicle moving northward. The Soviets apparently ran snowcats in counter directions to better patrol the width of the exclusion zone. Even without knowing the frequency of the snowcats passing a given point, the Soviets likely considered how long it took to traverse the exclusion zone on foot. The vehicle now approaching from the south would cross their tracks before they could make it to the border.

Norberg might have a diversion arranged but Neiman decided to wait until the Soviets discovered their tracks and began pursuit. The more immediate task was figuring a way to buy time.

To Jansons, Neiman said, "Keep moving as fast you can. That approaching snowcat will spot our tracks before we make it to the border." He pointed to the lights in the distance. "Before that happens I will split off to the left forcing the Soviets to make a choice. If they pursue me, keep heading for the border. Norberg knows our expected point of crossing the border. If they catch up to you, I will engage them with the sniper rifle."

Ten minutes later the snowcat crossed their tracks in the snow and stopped. Turning its strong headlamps, it picked up Jansons and Baranovsky a hundred meters ahead. Neiman was now far enough to their left to be outside the beam of the snowcat lights.

Five minutes later, the snowcat caught up to the women. Taking deep breaths to slow his rapid breathing from the exertion, Neiman knelt down to take up a firing position with the rifle. Removing his mittens, he propped his left elbow on his knee to steady the rifle. He was only seventy meters away with the windscreen of the snowcat in full view through the scope. The glare of its headlamps angled away from him.

A guard emerged from the snowcat holding what Neiman recognized as the classic Red Army submachinegun from WWII. Neiman's riflescope brought the guard's head into sharp detail. Close enough to see the guard speaking to the women.

Neiman debated for a couple of seconds before deciding on the surer target of the upper abdomen rather than the chancier head shot. The shot struck the guard just below his neck dropping him to the snow instantly.

As Neiman swung the scope attempting to pick up the second guard still inside the vehicle, he was too late. The driver was already outside scrambling to get behind the vehicle for cover. Neiman's shot missed.

Neiman could see both women with their arms raised but the guard remained concealed by the snowcat. Moments later the women moved out of sight only to reappear this time shielding the guard standing behind them. The man's head sufficiently visible but far too risky to attempt a shot. Neiman was unsure of his marksmanship abilities with an unfamiliar weapon.

The guard was yelling something difficult to hear over the engine noise of the snowcat. Probably threatening to shot the women unless he surrendered. Soon other border guards would arrive. Surrender was not an option for any of them.

Using the radio, "Jones calling Sabreur. Activate diversion immediately!"

Seconds later large searchlights cast long beams across the border into the Russian exclusion zone from different positions. One light was a couple of hundred meters to the north and another south of their intended crossing location. The Finns attempting to divert Soviet border security to alternative false locations suggesting others trying to attempt crossing into Finland

Neiman knew that would not be enough. He must rescue Inga and Natasha so he began moving forward in a direction to attempt coming around the snowcat from behind.

The moonlight proved a liability as the guard spotted Neiman struggling through the snow to get closer. The guard pushed past the women. Moving toward Neiman, the guard let loose a burst from his submachine gun.

Neiman dropped into the snow to acquire a firing position and borrow into the snow for some concealment expecting another burst from the guard's submachine gun.

Inga removed her mitten and reached into her pocket extracting the semiautomatic. She understood weapons from her days in the Resistance. Thumbing off the safety, she pulled the hammer back and fired a round point blank into the back of the head of the distracted Soviet guard followed by another two rounds into his back.

Neiman heard the shots and saw the man go down. He got to his feet and moved as quickly as possible with the cumbersome snowshoes.

Getting to the idling snowcat, Neiman could see lights moving in the distance coming from the south. Probably the other snowcat that first passed now turned around.

Yelling to Inga, "Get out of the snowshoes then get Natasha into the snowcat quickly."

Neiman removed his snowshoes then pulled off the radio. Handing it to Inga, she placed it on her lap. Getting behind the wheel, Neiman grabbed the radio handset and yelled, "Jones calling. Under fire! Heading to border in stolen Soviet snowcat. Arriving five minutes!"

Norberg and a company of Finnish military quickly helped them cross through a breach in the chain link fence representing the border with Finland. They were inside a Finnish armored personnel carrier when the first of several Soviet patrol vehicles converged on the Russian side of the border.

Natasha Baranovsky began crying as her terror turned to relief. Jansons said to her in Russian, "You are now safe, Natasha. Have you ever been to Paris?"

Baranovsky's eyes brightened. As an assistant professor in classical literature, she was also fluent in French. She shook her head no then responded in accented French. "Nikolai told me though of the beauty of Paris. How the city was full of life."

Gratified to see her brightened frame of mind, Jansons said, "Mr. Jones and I live in Paris. We shall take you there. There are many Russians living in Paris and you already speak French. A fine place to begin your new life."

Turning to Neiman, Jansons said, "And what will we do when we return to Paris, Viktor? I would rather it not be more of this."

Neiman some time ago made up his mind. "No, I am through with intelligence work, Inga. Through with working for the U.S. government. As promised, we are not leaving Paris. Thinking about returning to the art world. I worked in museum acquisitions in the past. No more perfect place than Paris to resume that career."

Chapter 31

Sarov (Arazmas-16), Russia | February 1953

Dimitri Galyorkin felt utterly alone now without Nikolai Baranovsky. The image of his lifeless body haunted him. Murdered by the secret police. With his deepening depression, it was
a supreme effort to resist the urge to just retreat into a shell. Doing so however might invite renewed interest by the MGB. If he
failed to resume contributing to nuclear weapons development,
he becomes expendable. With everything that transpired, the
State would never allow him to leave the program and resume a
normal life. Exile to a Siberian labor camp or something similar
remained a possibility.

Better to turn his thoughts toward revenge. Make the effort
to creating the appearance of normalcy in his personal interactions with his colleagues. Thinking him a gifted scientific contributor with a personality inclined toward introversion, required only forced congeniality and attention to expected social
protocols to get along. Act the part of a good communist until
determining how to retaliate in some dramatic way.

Galyorkin was descending deeper into psychosis. His emotional isolation counterbalanced with increased thoughts about
lashing out at the source of his emotional distress. Suicide an acceptable ending only if accompanied by some meaningful act of
rebellion. Revenge against those imposing a life of servitude that

crushes everything within the human spirit. Taking from him everything that gave meaning to his life. Deprived of using his intellectual talents in doing beneficial work. Imprisoned in this scientific Gulag. Losing Nikolai Baranovsky. Denied his relationship with Talia Zubarev.

Exposing Soviet secrets to the West served as a tangible form of revenge against the Soviet system. That was no longer available. His darkening thoughts becoming more frustrating as even possible acts resulting in giving up his life proved unsatisfying.

The only act sufficiently dramatic seemed creating a nuclear accident. Cause a sufficient quantity of fissile material to reach critical mass triggering a chain reaction releasing massive amounts of radiation. To what purpose? The contamination likely causing only limited disruption to the program and killing those to which he did not wish harm.

Galyorkin's dilemma resolved unexpectedly when Andrei Sakharov excitedly pulled him aside to show him a letter. "Look at this, Dimitri. How would you like to meet Comrade Stalin?"

Galyorkin looked puzzled as he took a copy of a letter from project head Lavrenti Beria to scientific director Igor Kurchatov.

Not waiting for Galyorkin to read the letter, Sakharov said, "It includes the senior theoretical team. Kurchatov, Tamm, you, Ginzburg, Zeldovich, and myself. We fly to Moscow in three weeks for an audience with Stalin at his dacha in Kuntsevo. My guess is Beria wants to show off his nuclear geniuses. Those responsible for the science that gave Stalin the atomic bomb. Soon to deliver the next generation hydrogen super bomb."

Galyorkin smiled at Sakharov, "That is extraordinary news Andrei. It is you most of all of us that should be getting the credit."

Sakharov replied, "I am just one part of the effort. Combining our skills as a team has produced remarkable results. Tonight we shall celebrate."

Galyorkin forced these celebratory comments to his friend Sakharov. The idea of meeting Stalin face to face stirred an entirely different emotion. This might be his singular opportunity.

Being that close, could he find a way to kill the monster? That was an act worthy of sacrificing his life.

That evening participating in the celebration of their recognition by General Secretary Stalin, Galyorkin's thoughts turned instead on how to kill Stalin. Most conventional means of assassination seemed out of reach. He had no access to a firearm. A knife was entirely unreliable. Making and hiding a bomb on his person unrealistic. No means to poison him. Yet perhaps there was.

The thought of poisoning immediately triggered an idea. So obvious and so perfect it made him smile. All he needed was to contrive a means of delivery. He regularly worked with an exceptionally lethal substance in the lab. Invisible, odorless, difficult to detect, and with no antidote or treatment if ingested.

Polonium-210, the rare radioactive isotope was a key atomic bomb component. Acting as a sparkplug, it boosted initiating the chain reaction of the compressed core of fissile material when achieving critical mass at the moment of the detonation. The initiator consisted of a pellet made of a sandwich of polonium-210 and beryllium separated by a layer of gold. Its function served to deliver an intense discharge of neutrons into the fissile core of plutonium-239 or uranium-235 to amplify the start of a chain reaction and prevent a miscarried detonation.

The properties of polonium-210 provided unique delivery options as a poison. Unlike most other radioactive elements that predominately decay through gamma radiation emissions, polonium decays through alpha particles radiation. Gamma radiation is pure energy whereas alpha particles have mass. Gamma radiation emitting material requires impractical specialized shielding for handling. Alpha radiation however cannot penetrate human skin presenting possibilities for an assassin to deliver it to the victim.

Polonium-210 is extremely deadly if ingested or inhaled. One microgram, one millionth of a gram, represents a lethal dosage to a human being. By mass, that is 250,000 times more toxic than hydrogen cyanide. It is also soluble in dilute acids but extremely volatile and subject to rapid evaporation unless remaining contained. Those properties suggested an idea to Galyorkin of how to possibly deliver a lethal dosage to Joseph Stalin. Stalin was a heavy smoker. Everyone knew his favorite brand was *Herzegovina Flor,* widely known as *Stalin's cigarettes.* Cigarettes were the answer.

Galyorkin often worked with polonium in his involvement in conducting laboratory tests for optimizing initiator design. Because of the danger of inhalation, he used a device called a glovebox to handle polonium. A sealed transparent work enclosure accessed by mounted gloves allowed the technician to work from outside the box safely. Dissolving the soft metal in a dilute acid would produce a solution that he could inject into cigarettes. Producing a small sealed glass vial of the solution in the lab would preserve the solution from evaporation. Using a facemask and goggles for protection, he could rig the cigarettes unobserved in his own quarters. All that remained was how to deliver the doctored cigarettes to Stalin.

Security around Stalin was extreme. Stalin had no friends, only those that feared him, which made them synonymous as potential enemies. Ruling by fear and ensuring that no one close to him amassed sufficient power to depose him dictated security bred of reality rather than paranoia. A battalion of special MGB troops guarded the dacha. The officers specifically selected and rotated frequently. His food pretested by tasters.

The solution obviously was the doctored cigarettes to be secondary to something representing a token of appreciation from his nuclear scientists. Therefore, a cigarette case. Yet it must be something with representational significance.

The next day the solution became obvious to Galyorkin. Replicate in miniature the design of the first Soviet thermonuclear bomb that dominated current project efforts. A design incorporating both fission and fusion using lithium-6 deuteride in a layered configuration around a plutonium core. The bomb classified as RDS-6. The weapon scheduled for test later this year.

A design advance not yet tested by the Americans. While not a two-stage fission-fusion weapon of the type tested by the Americans in the South Pacific just months earlier, the Soviet

RDS-6 represented a deployable design. Although the American detonation yielded over 10 megatons, it was a concept test rather than a deployable device. While the RDS-6 design was a *boosted* nuclear weapon employing fusion to increase the energy yield, it represented a major advance as a deployable weapon. A weapon with a projected yield of 400 hundred kilotons of TNT. A Soviet two-stage fission-fusion thermonuclear bomb in the megaton yield range was perhaps only a couple of years away.

The RDS-6 weapon was of major significance. A Soviet propaganda coup of the first order. Stalin recognized that and wished to encourage the scientists. A finely crafted reproduction of the RDS-6 casing would make the perfect gift. A befitting token of appreciation for the recognition bestowed by Stalin on the theoretical physics team.

Galyorkin began immediately to design his lethal cigarette case. The RDS-6 casing making for a distinctively and functional piece to set in a prominent place in Stalin's office. The stabilizing fins for when the actual bomb dropped from an aircraft provided a convenient base for sitting the replica vertical. The hinged, egg-shaped body of the bomb would contain cigarettes standing on end. Made of finely worked polished machined brass.

Sketching out his design, Galyorkin approached an engineer in the machine shop to draft a working blueprint. This he needed for presenting his idea to Tamm and Kurchatov for approval. Making the model bomb milled from a ten-centimeter diameter solid brass bar was comparatively easy for a machine shop producing high-tolerance nuclear bomb components. *Stalin's cigarettes* readily available at the commissary.

***

Showing the blueprint of the model RDS-6 to Igor Tamm his immediate superior as head of the theoretical section evoked a rare enthusiastic response.

"Very creative, Galyorkin. A presentation uniquely suited to the occasion. Come with me. We must show this to Kurchatov."

Igor Kurchatov was equally delighted. "How soon can you produce this?"

Galyorkin replied, "In a few days, Sir. I also discovered someone in the machine shop with the skills to produce a presentation box for the cigarette holder. A fine cherry wood box to match Comrade Stalin's pipes known to be of the same wood. I have seen this fellow's work. Perhaps you could draft some words of dedication. We can affix an engraved brass plaque to the box."

"Yes, of course. I will do so immediately. A wonderful surprise for Comrade Stalin. A celebration of our hard work. You should be proud of your contribution Galyorkin."

"Thank you, Sir."

"I am anxious to see this piece as soon as completed," Kurchatov said.

Later in the day, Andrei Sakharov came up to Galyorkin and slapped him on the back. "I just came from Tamm's office. He told me of your project to create a replica model of RDS-6 to present to Comrade Stalin. A brilliant idea. Good to have the old Dimitri back. It has been a difficult couple of years but we are making remarkable progress."

* * *

He gave the task of supervising the making of the brass model to the engineer that drew up the design. Explaining it to be a gift to Comrade Stalin ensured meticulous workmanship.

Turning his attention to producing the polonium solution, involved some planning. He needed to manufacture an excuse to do work inside the glovebox. The solution proved simpler than imagined. He would actually delegate a skilled technician to produce a vial of polonium in a diluted acid solution. Cleaned of any residual contaminate on the outside of the sealed glass vial after removal from the glovebox allowed for safe handling.

The only danger for him occurred when opening the vial. Evaporation contaminating the air while working to impregnate the twenty cigarettes. He needed to inject each cigarette with more than a fatal dose of polonium-210. Already rumored in declining health, inhalation of the toxin would kill Joseph Stalin with certainty. Nothing could save him. How long that might take, Galyorkin had no idea. Not about to make inquiries, it did not matter.

The inhalation of radioactive alpha particles would immediately begin to disrupt the function of vital organs. What limited medical knowledge existed on the effects of radiation remained secret within the nuclear program. All Galyorkin knew was a range of symptoms that began worsening rapidly depending on exposure dosage. Whatever the duration, doctors would have no way of way of diagnosing the cause. The range of symptoms would likely point to poisoning yet there was no treatment that could save Stalin.

Eventually, the cigarettes provided by Galyorkin would fall under suspicion. Testing might discover polonium. Stalin might offer a cigarette to someone. Once that person fell ill with the same symptoms, then the focus would turn toward Galyorkin.

No question the act of killing Joseph Stain warranted forfeiting his own life. Reconciled to that becoming his fate, it was the thought of suffering death by some horrible means of torture that was frightening. Therefore, he must prepare for death by a means of his choosing.

As much as he feared the agonies that a lethal dose of polonium might represent, it was probably a better death than at the hands of a practiced torturer. He resolved to keep the vial containing the polonium solution close at hand to serve as a suicide pill. Perhaps a massive ingestion might speed death.

* * *

A week before the scheduled audience in Moscow with Stalin, the engineer and two machinists asked Galyorkin to join them in the machine shop office.

The engineer introduced the machinist that produced the brass bomb replica and the other fellow who constructed the wood presentation box. The beauty of the pieces astounded

Galyorkin. The polished brass shape of the bomb stood 14 centimeters with a diameter of 8 centimeters. The stabilizing fins provided a perfect base.

A seam around the mid-point of the body of the bomb was the parting line for tilting back the top. A hinge concealed on the inside allowed the top to tilt back only so far. Inside a lattice made of sheet brass produced holes for individual cigarettes to stand upright. An added touch created by the engineer.

The wood presentation box was equally impressive. The grain of the cherry hardwood polished like a fine piece of furniture. The cover fitted with brass hinges and a brass catch. A small brass plaque inlaid into the front of the box with the inscription drafted by Igor Kurchatov read, 'To Comrade Joseph Vissarionovich Stalin in recognition of his scientific leadership of the Soviet Union. Presented by the scientists and engineers of the Soviet Nuclear Weapons Program.'

Galyorkin said to the three men, "These are magnificent works of art. I must show them immediately to Comrade Kurchatov. Comrade Stalin will know your names as the craftsmen creating these pieces. My thanks for your exceptional work."

Unveiling the cigarette case was a resounding success for Galyorkin. With the senior scientific team gathered in a conference room, Kurchatov, having examined the piece earlier, opened the ornate wood box, and extracted the gleaming brass scale replica of the RDS-6 bomb.

Several of the scientists gasped at the beauty of the piece. All began clapping.

For Galyorkin, the accolades were meaningless. He smiled with humility, but his actual gratification was something quite different. He was confident that Stalin would appreciate the piece and equally confident of his plan to kill the dictator.

The day before departing for Moscow, Galyorkin locked the door to his room. Time to complete the delicate process of loading the cigarettes with polonium. He purchased a pack of Herzegovina Flor cigarettes at the commissary. Made of tobacco from the Balkans. Stalin being a Georgian smoked them for decades. The vial containing the polonium in solution was ready.

Outfitted with a mask, goggles, and latex gloves afforded for protection against inhalation. Once he opened the vial, evaporation by the polonium generating heat would begin contaminating the surrounding air. A small fan would blow air away from him close to an open window. He could only hope that was sufficient.

To inject each cigarette was the dangerous part even with the extra protection. He would use an opened paperclip dipped into the polonium solution that he then inserted well into the cigarette tobacco. It should deposit more than a lethal amount of the toxin into each cigarette. Once he opened the vial, he would close it off periodically with a rubber stopper to restrict further evaporation while he let any contaminated air evacuate. He repeated the process until completely treating each cigarette with a deadly dosage of polonium-210 that should absorb into the tobacco.

The final step was loading each cigarette into the replica bomb. Might evaporation still occur or did the tobacco fully absorb the polonium solution? No way to tell.

The process took less time than expected. He let the fan run for a time to ventilate the room with the window open. Eventually the temperature in the room became unbearably cold. Were his precautions enough? It no longer mattered. Life no longer held meaning.

Nonetheless, he felt a sense of achievement rather than anxiety. Events would now move forward beyond his control.

Chapter 32

Moscow | March 1953

On February 27, Galyorkin and others of the theoretical physics team boarded a WWII Lisunov Li-2 transport plane, essentially a WWII licensed DC-3 design fitted for passengers for the two-hour flight from Arazmas-16 to Moscow. In his lap, Galyorkin carried Stalin's gift and death warrant wrapped as a present.

Arriving in Moscow, several ZIM-12 black sedans pulled up next to the aircraft on the tarmac. Within minutes, they left the airport in a caravan usually reserved for Moscow elites.

Kuntsevo Dacha was located 15 kilometers west of the Kremlin. As their automobiles exited the Mozhaisky highway for the road to the dacha, armed guards manned an outer barrier.

A dense forest of birch surrounded Stalin's estate. Approaching the grounds, the line of vehicles passed through a heavily manned gate then through a double perimeter of high wooden fences. As they approached the main building, they stopped at a third barrier. Fruit trees populated the surrounding open ground of the dacha. Looking closely, anti-aircraft guns draped in camouflage netting were visible.

Exiting the vehicles, Kurchatov brought everyone together. "Once we enter, stay together. No talking. When ushered into the presence of Comrade Stalin, I alone will greet him and make a brief introductory statement. Follow my lead. Do not speak with Comrade Stalin unless he addresses you directly. I have no idea how long we may be here."

Standing outside the front entrance, Galyorkin looked at what Stalin now chose as his principal residence. Appearing only occasionally in the Kremlin this was his preferred work center. Although in the middle of a forest, the dacha did not have the look of a rustic retreat. Painted dark forest green, it perhaps blended in when the trees displayed leaves come spring. Nevertheless, structurally the front of the main building had the appearance of an office building with two floors of tall, closely spaced windows.

A man immerged from the entrance door and announced, "Comrade Kurchatov, if you and your associates will follow me, Comrade Stalin will see you in his personal study.

They entered into a large lobby with two cloakrooms where they deposited their overcoats and hats. When ready, the man opened a door off the left side of the lobby and they filed into the spacious room where Stalin spent most of his day.

Occupying the center of the room was a large desk from the war years set in front of a large window. A radio sat on a matching credenza below the window. A gift from Winston Churchill on his first visit to Moscow in 1942. An avid reader, bookshelves lined with leather bound books occupied one wall. On the other wall, hung a large format oil on canvas painting by Ilya Repin titled *Reply of the Zaporozhian Cossacks* dominating the wall. Beneath the painting was a couch. Stalin often preferred to sleep on the couch instead of the bedroom.

Joseph Stalin set down his pipe in a pipe rack as he stood behind his desk. "Welcome to Kuntsevo, Comrade Kurchatov and Comrade Tamm," Stalin said and came around to shake hands with Kurchatov and Tamm. "I wanted this opportunity to express my appreciation for the remarkable achievements of the entire nuclear program, but especially to those of the theoretical physics team responsible for making that possible."

Kurchatov replied, "Thank you, Comrade Stalin. We also would also like to acknowledge the confidence you inspired by your continued support and providing the necessary resources required to advance our scientific work. As a token of our appreciation and recognition of your leadership, we would like to present you with a gift. Something to commemorate our success moving closer to achieving a nuclear weapon of extraordinary destructive power that will ensure the security of the Soviet Union.

"Let me introduce Dr. Dimitri Galyorkin of our team. A brilliant theoretical physicist. The design of this gift was his idea."

Kurchatov nodded to Galyorkin.

Galyorkin focused his mind as he stood before the person that embodied everything he hated about the Soviet system. In reality, that system was Stalin's creation while ruling the Soviet Union for the last three decades. The person ultimately responsible for the death and suffering of millions.

"Comrade Stalin, may I put this down on your desk as it is heavy?"

Stalin smiled his characteristic expression that revealed nothing of its true meaning.

Galyorkin set the wrapped box on the desk and stood back.

Stalin pulled apart the paper wrapping revealing the finely crafted cherry box. "Ah, now what is this, Comrade Galyorkin?"

"The gift is actually inside, Comrade Stalin."

Stalin opened the lid of the box and pulled out the replica bomb setting it down on the desk.

Kurchatov said, "A gift befitting the occasion, Comrade Stalin. This is a scale replica of the bomb design designated RDS-6. The first Soviet thermonuclear bomb of the next generation of weapons employing the increased energy potential of nuclear fusion."

"When is this scheduled test to take place, Comrade Kurchatov?"

"August this year, Sir."

"The expected yield?" Stalin asked.

"We believe in the area of 400 kilotons. That is close to twenty times the yield of our first test three years ago."

Stalin ran his hand over the brass replica as if caressing it. Discovering it also had a lid, he opened the top revealing the cigarettes. This time his smile was genuine. "Ah, such a beautiful functional piece for my office."

Withdrawing a cigarette Stalin took a match from his pipe rack and lit the cigarette. Turning to Galyorkin, "This is a fine gift and most appropriate, Comrade Galyorkin."

As Stalin shook hands with Galyorkin, he then moved along shaking hands as Kurchatov introduced the other scientists. By the time Stalin finished exchanging comments and asking questions of the team, he finished the cigarette. Returning to his desk, he extracted and lit another cigarette.

Galyorkin understood he was looking at a dead man walking.

The entire time spent at Kuntsevo was less than thirty minutes. An hour later, their aircraft was airborne for the return flight to Arazamas-16.

Galyorkin had no illusions about what was to happen. Once Stalin fell ill, the doctors would be at a loss to diagnose the cause. What little was known about the effects of radiation on the human organism remained restricted only to medical professionals within the nuclear program. The effects of alpha radiation even less understood. However, eventually as the symptoms worsened, those treating Stalin must surely conclude poisoning as the cause. Although, they might never discover the actual source, once Stalin died, chaos would ensue.

Those within Stalin's closest circle would jockey for power. Everyone having the ability to poison Stalin would fall under suspicion. If Stalin offered any of the deadly cigarettes to others, they too would fall ill pointing to the gifted cigarettes as the source of poisoning.

On the plane trip back to Arazmas-16, Galyorkin fingered the vial of the deadly polonium in his pocket.

* * *

That evening after the meeting with the nuclear scientists, Joseph Stalin attended a performance of *Swan Lake* at the Bolshoi Ballet. The next day, a Saturday, he went to the Kremlin to watch a film with his most frequent companions, Nikita Khrushchev, Nikolai Bulganin, Georgy Malenkov, and Lavrenti Beria. Stalin kept unusual hours preferring the nighttime and not starting his day until very late in the morning. Following the viewing of the movie, he invited his companions for a late supper at Kuntsevo. No one ever dared refuse Joseph Stalin.

They began eating a meal around midnight accompanied by much drinking. As typical, the revelry did not end until Stalin chose to retire. That night the gathering broke up at 4:00am in the morning of Sunday March 1. Everyone returned to their homes in their chauffeured limousines to get some rest. Most expected Stalin to call again sometime in the late afternoon. Possibly to see another film. Perhaps to just talk. Often again to eat and drink through the night. Stalin was lonely and becoming increasing erratic. Heavy smoking, poor sleeping habits undoubtedly aggravating his serious arterial sclerosis and hypertension.

On Sunday March 1, the service staff came on duty at 10:00am. Everyone was under orders not to disturb Stalin until someone heard movement in his personal quarters or he called for something. A telephone system linked very room in the dacha, including bathrooms.

Inaction among the staff continued throughout the day of March 1 although household and security staff became increasing uneasy throughout the day. It was not until 10:30pm that night that Pyotr Lozgachev, assistant to the dacha security commander entered Stalin's quarters using the pretext of delivering a documents packet from the Central Committee delivered earlier in the day.

Lozgachev found Stalin lying on the floor of the small dining room dressed in an undershirt with his pajama bottoms soaked in urine. Stalin was unconscious yet appeared to be breathing shallowly.

The dacha staff carried him to the dining room sofa and covered him. Most wanted to call a doctor but Lozgachev insisted they wait for instructions from the party leadership. Eventually they reached Beria by telephone.

Beria and Malenkov were the first to arrive at the dacha. Stalin appeared to be sleeping. Inexplicably, it was not until 7:00am of the following morning that they called the minister of health to send a team of doctors.

Doctors arrived finding Stalin unresponsive with his right arm and leg paralyzed. These symptoms with his blood pressure at an alarming 220/110 indicated he probably suffered a stroke. However, Stalin's recent aggressive actions toward medical professionals made those attending him that night fearful of the consequences in treating Stalin.

Stalin once infamously ordered his personal physician arrested after the doctor cautioned him to work less, get more rest, and quit smoking. Two years earlier, Stalin also began an inexplicable attack on the medical profession. Accusing Jewish doctors of conspiracy to murder Soviet leaders led to an anti-Semitic purge reminiscent of the Great Purge of the late 1930s.

Understandably fearful, instead of moving Stalin to a hospital, the doctors began what amounted to no treatment by ordering continued rest, applying leeches behind his ears to lower his blood pressure, and applying cold compresses on his head.

On March 5, Stalin vomited blood, indicating hemorrhaging in his stomach. Doctors pronounced Joseph Stalin dead at 9:50 pm that night.

The final report submitted to the Central Committee omitted mention of the hemorrhaging. To those aware of the circumstances, this suggested the possibility of poisoning. Possibly the new blood-thinning drug warfarin.

Rumors of this would immerge only later because the most likely suspect pointed to Lavrenti Beria. Recently falling out favor with Stain, he may have possessed motive. With Beria's legendary reputation for ruthlessness, murder to affect a palace coup was not out of the question. He had the means with the late night drinking and eating on the night of February 28 afforded opportunity.

As Minister of the Interior and former head of the NKVD until 1946, Beria still retained vast powers of ordering arrests unofficially even to high-ranking party officials. Given this and the uncertainty of succession with the death of Stalin, no one in the medical profession dared openly to speculate this might be murder by poisoning.

Stalin's body was taken to an undisclosed medial physical facility and an autopsy performed. On March 7, the official Communist Party newspaper *Pravda* reported the official pathology report summary.

Pathologic examination revealed a large hemorrhage, localized to the area of subcortical centers of the left cerebral hemisphere. This hemorrhage destroyed important areas of the brain and resulted in irreversible changes in respiration and circulation. In addition to the brain hemorrhage, there were found significant hypertrophy of the left ventricle of the heart, numerous hemorrhages in the myocardium, in the stomach and intestinal mucosa; atherosclerotic changes in the vessels, more prominent in the cerebral arteries. These are the result of hypertension. The results of the pathologic examination revealed the irreversible character of J.V. Stalin's disease from the moment of brain hemorrhage. Therefore, all treatment attempts could not have led to a favorable outcome and prevent a fatal end.

With Stalin's known medical history of arteriosclerosis and hypertension, the official cause of death made sense. No reference to performing toxicology tests. Finding evidence of poisoning might prove dangerous for the medical staff.

Regardless, the pathologists got it wrong. They misdiagnosed the root cause of the stroke. Medically speaking, Joseph Stalin died of a stroke or series of strokes brought about by radiation-induced vasculopathy. More specifically, the cause was ingestion of alpha particle radiation emitted from the rare isotope polonium-210. The pathologists would have no familiarity with the pathology of this deadly toxin on the human body.

Radiation-induced vasculopathy is a condition whereby radiation causes a narrowing of the blood vessels through creating lesions. With someone suffering acute arteriosclerosis and hypertension, stroke becomes the most likely mode of death brought on by a lethal dose of alpha radiation.

Immediately following Stalin's death, the MGB closed and secured the Kuntsevo dacha. They sealed Stalin's personal living spaces consisting of his study, bedroom, and small dining room with everything left undisturbed. The brass replica atomic bomb remained untouched. No one else within Stalin's circle, any of the staff, or security personnel at Kuntsevo fell ill. No other poisonings to raise suspicions about the cause of Stalin's death.

Eventually the polonium-210 with a half-life of 138 days contained in trace quantities within the contaminated cigarettes decayed to the stable metal lead-206. Unless specifically searching for the residue, practically undetectable in such limited quantities.

Along with his undiscovered espionage, Dimitri Galyorkin pulled off the murder of the century by concealing the true cause of Joseph Stalin's death, officially declared as resulting from natural causes.

Epilogue

The Soviet Union formally protested to Finland about the murder of two Soviet border guards south of Nuijamaa. Finland largely ignored Moscow by blaming the violence on Soviets imprisoning their citizenry trying to seek sanctuary in a free country.

The Rozovsky network collapsed as a source of intelligence on the Soviet Union with the loss of their principal high-level sources. The MGB executed Vladimir Mishnyov after he endured terrible physical torture without revealing information compromising Nikolai Baranovsky or Dimitri Galyorkin. Dasha Mishnyov escaped execution with a sentence of twenty years in a Siberian forced labor camp.

Without explanation, Swedish intelligence informed American intelligence via the U.S. State Department that their walk-in sources went underground fearing discovery following the compromise of a dead drop.

The struggle for power between Lavrenti Beria, Nikita Khrushchev, and Georgy Malenkov intensified following Stalin's death. Khrushchev and Malenkov feared Beria's power as Minister of the Interior. With the death of Stalin, the fear of Beria assuming control of the Ministry of State Security became all too real. Khrushchev understood he could not coexist with Beria.

Khrushchev therefore, enlisted the aid of a new ally, Soviet WWII hero Marshal Georgy Zhukov. Zhukov hated the secret police and the universally hated and feared Beria. With control of the Red Army, Zhukov commanded an even greater physical force than the Ministry of State Security.

Succession for leadership of the Soviet Union resolved within a few months of Stalin's death. Backed by Marshal Zhukov and the weight of the Red Army, Nikita Khrushchev mustered enough support within the Communist Central Committee to denounce the feared Beria publically. Arrested by the military and imprisoned in the Lubyanka, the Central Committee found Beria guilty of crimes against the state and ordered his execution. Like thousands of Beria's victims, a Red Army general executed Lavrenti Beria by a bullet to the base of the skull as he begged for his life.

The domestic terror inflicted on all those living within the Soviet Union eased under the rule of Nikita Khrushchev. However, Soviet aggression directed at the democratic West continued with little change from the Stalin era. East-West Cold War hostilities would continue unchanged for decades.

With the deaths of Mishnyov and Baranovsky, and the death of Stalin, Dimitri Galyorkin escaped further investigation for spying. The strain of the last couple of years followed by the decision to forfeit his life to assassinate Stalin however proved too much. Within months of Stalin's death, he suffered a nervous breakdown. Hospitalized, he left weapons development. After eventual release from a high-security sanitarium, he secured a position in the nuclear energy sector through the efforts of his colleague Andrei Sakharov.

By the later 1950s, Sakharov also began to question the moral and political implications of nuclear weapons development. This later led to his becoming an outspoken activist against nuclear weapons.

With the efforts of Viktor Neiman, Yuri Rozovsky, and her uncle Oleg Leonov, France granted Natasha Baranovsky political asylum. Settled in Paris, she resumed her academic career in classical literature on the faculty of the Sorbonne.

Inga Jansons' career as a recognized photographic artist continued flourishing. Viktor Neiman resigned from the American foreign service immediately after returning to Paris. His involvement with the invented Swedish espionage operation officially disappeared following a new American administration coming into office in January 1953.

Neiman accepted a position as director of acquisitions at the Musée d'Orsay in Paris. With his intelligence experience and background in the arts, combined with fluency in several languages, he gained a reputation for researching the provenance of potential acquisitions. That reputation led to various international Jewish organizations contracting his services for recovering art stolen during the Holocaust and WWII. Following several noteworthy successes, Viktor Neiman created Services Récupération d'Oeuvres d'Art.

www.ingramcontent.com/pod-product-compliance
Lightning Source LLC
Chambersburg PA
CBHW031958060726
47497CB00015B/283